One Good Man Or Two

By Winter K. Anderson

****

To all those who encouraged and helped me
on this journey, I can never thank you enough.
To my dear friends Gayle, Suzi, Matt, and Stephanie for your
countless hours of edits, research and being my sounding boards, you
have my unwavering appreciation and affection. To my co-workers
who made me laugh when I was down, to my Starbucks crew and
friends for my new wonderful addiction and hours of patio
conversations, and to all those who shared their own experiences with
me in the world of writing, you have all made this possible.

Special thanks to:
Shane Connelly for all his work in helping to prepare the final product
of this project. I would have been lost if not for your involvement and
professional advice.

And a BIG
Thank you to the administration at
The Bloom & Quill for their support

Winter K. Anderson

Published by: CreateSpace

The characters and events portrayed in this book are fictitious or are used fictitiously. Any resemblance to real persons, living or dead; is purely coincidental and not intended by the author.

ISBN-13: 978-0615653068
ISBN-10: 0615653065

Cover design by: Shane Connelly
Photograph by: Matt Blum

Chapter 1

It had been eight months since Elizabeth had been dancing, she recalled as she nervously entered the club to meet her best friends Charlotte Lucas and Lacey Wickham. She had always enjoyed a night out dancing with her friends, but once she had started to date Bill Collins, those girls' night out evenings had become few and far between, and never at this particular club.

Elizabeth spotted her friends at a table near the dance floor, and as her eyes roamed the room, they fell upon Lacey's exceedingly handsome brother George and his latest conquest burning up the dance floor. George had been the center of some of Elizabeth's hottest dreams for years now— his abs rock hard, inviting her touch; his biceps so strong, offering safety; and his eyes dark blue, filled with confidence. Elizabeth sighed, He was several years older than she was and, since he never seemed to notice her, she tended to shy away from him knowing she was nowhere near as hot as all his other girlfriends always seemed to be.

Joining the two girls, she ordered herself a double Bailey's over ice to ease her nerves. She had enjoyed her time with Bill; the last nine months had been wonderful, but she knew deep down they would never work out long term. When he had suggested a few weeks ago that she move in with him, she gave it serious thought and decided this was the opportune time to break it off. He was a steady, handsome man in his own way, but more conservative than she. He had never liked this club or her friends. He worked for her father as one of his top executives, and she had known him for some time before they started to date. Mr. Bennet had been thrilled that his favorite daughter was dating Collins. Her father thought highly of him and believed he would make a wonderful husband for her. Even Elizabeth's mother had touted Mr. Collins qualities to her on several occasions over the last several months. They enjoyed many of the same things and had similar friends in the business fields in which they were involved.

When Elizabeth turned down the invitation to move in with Bill, her mother had flown around the house all in a flutter. "Lizzy what will become of you? Bill Collins is the best man you will ever find. You go back right this instant young lady and beg for his forgiveness. What were you thinking?"

Elizabeth was never so happy to have her own place. Once she had been finally able to escape her childhood home, she did not answer the phone for a week when she noticed it was her parents calling. She loved caller ID. She had kept herself holed up for the last week reading romance novels and lurking about the Internet to pass her evenings.

It was Wednesday when Charlotte had come bursting into Elizabeth's office and demanded that she stop such nonsense and plan to come out with her and Lacey for a girls' night out—at the end of the week.

The club was crowded as usual for a Friday night. Elizabeth chatted with her friends and sipped at her drink. She registered the cold smooth taste of the Bailey's flowing effortlessly down her throat as she watched George out of the corner of her eye. How had her life come to this—sitting in a club, lusting after a man who was her best friend's brother and way out of her league?

*****

He observed at a distance from the back corner of the club, his usual spot for watching her over the years. Elizabeth Bennet sat with what he had determined were her best friends drinking her favored Bailey's over ice. She had not been here in sometime. Once she had started to see one of the executives at Bennet Industries, she suddenly stopped going out with her friends and dancing. He had heard from his cousin just this last week, after he had been in a meeting with Mr. Bennet, that Elizabeth had broken things off with Collins, not that he hadn't kept tabs on her since he met her.

Now it was his turn to gain access to her; he had watched and wanted Elizabeth Bennet for three years. She was just out of college when he first ran into her at her father's offices, so eager to get her own place and stretch her wings. He knew what he wanted from her almost immediately, but she was not ready. He watched her though, closely, waiting for the day she would become aware of her own inner desires and needs.

Being the CEO of his own company gave him many advantages, one of which was having his cousin, a man who knew his deepest desires and secrets, as head of the security detail that worked for his family's business. They were like brothers, almost twins. There was a sense of knowing what

the other needed or felt at any given time; even their sexual preferences were identical.

Fitzwilliam Darcy sat quietly alone in the dark corner watching as Elizabeth nursed her drink. She chatted and smiled much like she used to. She wore low-rise jeans and a cream cap-sleeve blouse that fell just a bit off her left shoulder, the neckline low enough to show the tops of her breasts where a large metal medallion drew his eye. Her dark hair cascaded about her shoulders, so rich and shiny he could see it shimmer from his chair. The high heels on her petite feet were the same cream color as her blouse, and they made her legs look long and quite shapely in the hip-hugging denim— altogether a sexy feast for his eyes.

He continued to watch her when George Wickham approached the table. He could see the light blush cross Elizabeth's face as he spoke to her. Darcy observed Elizabeth as the man escorted her to the dance floor and they began to dance. He knew men like Wickham, men who had more confidence than sense when it came to woman. He could see that this man would not be able to pleasure Elizabeth in the way she deserved or needed. He watched in fascination as the couple swayed and danced. He was not threatened by George Wickham one bit. He had known George almost all of his life. They had even attended the same college. George had left a wake of women in his path his entire life. He would date them, impress them with bobbles, and meals, and expensive vacations, and then once he had slept with them a few times, he would move on to his next victim. How many times had Darcy warned ladies away from him?

Finally, George escorted Elizabeth back to the table where her friends waited, and he took his sister to the dance floor for a spin. Lacey was a sweet girl; she and his own sister Georgiana had become close friends while in high school years ago. Though Georgiana had never met or associated with Elizabeth, he felt sure that they, too, would become close friends.

The bulge in Darcy's pants tightened as he spotted Elizabeth moving towards the bar. The sway of her hips, her hair bouncing about her shoulders, made him so hard he could hardly think straight. This was his chance to have a few moments alone with her away from her friends, so he quickly rose and moved in the same direction.

Elizabeth had just ordered herself a drink and a few others for her table, no doubt. He leaned in close behind her, careful to not startle her, his lips close to her ear.

*****

It was Elizabeth's turn to buy a round of drinks, so she approached the bar in a haze. The dance with George had been unexpected. He made her heart beat so incredibly fast that she hardly remembered what happened on that dance floor. She was kicking herself for acting like some teenager who had just been asked out by the captain of the football team. "That's the way to impress him," she shook her head as she muttered the words softly under her breath.

She reached the bar and ordered the drinks she needed. Suddenly she felt someone behind her and, before she could glance over her shoulder, she heard him. He was so close to her ear, his soothing, deep, almost husky voice made her gasp. She could not move, and her heart skipped a beat as her brain listened to what was being said.

"I know you have a thing for that man you were dancing with a moment ago. When you tire of him, and you will, I will be waiting for you. I alone hold the key to all the fantasies you have ever dreamed of—and more."

Still reeling from this man's words, Elizabeth could feel her face flush as her breasts began to tingle at this stranger's suggestive comments. Then he spoke to the bartender.

"Tom, see that whatever she orders is put on my tab."

"Yes, sir," he replied and went about his business.

"Call me when you're ready for a real man, Elizabeth."

She felt the heat of his hand brush up next to hers as a business card was slipped under her palm while a kiss was placed at her neck. She watched as the bartender placed her drink order on the bar before her and handed her back her credit card, stating it was paid for. When she turned to see who was behind her, all she could see was a tall dark haired man, his well-built back catching her notice as he headed to the exit. She took a breath and then looked down at her hand to the card she held.

"William Darcy, is it?" she wrinkled her brows wondering why she knew the name. Her body was alive; she could still feel his breath as it rushed past her ear, the warmth of his hand as it brushed hers, the words he had spoken echoed through her mind. Fantasies, what did he know of her fantasies?

6

She made it back to the table and set the drinks down. She glanced at the dance floor where George was busy with some redhead. She had never felt with George Wickham the sensations she just now experienced from William Darcy. What could it mean, and why did she suddenly look at George in a different manner?

Chapter 2

Elizabeth woke the next morning with the ringing of her phone. "Lizzy, where are you? I expected you here half an hour ago."

"Jane?" Elizabeth's sleepy voice squeaked over the line.

"Who else would it be? Is everything alright?"

"Oh Jane, I went out with Charlotte and Lacey last night and forgot to set the alarm. I am so very sorry. Give me an hour, and I'll be there."

"Don't bother, it gets crowded there after 10. I'll grab some pastries and be at your place in half an hour."

"You're the best Jane, thanks."

"You owe me; you know that, right?"

"Yes I know, I'll give you all the details once you get here. I'll make a fresh pot of coffee, so hurry over."

Elizabeth hung up the phone and sat on the edge of her bed. She had several more drinks after William Darcy left her his business card. Her mind had a hard time forgetting his words. George had returned to the table and, if she was not mistaken, he had kept watching her. Just how weird was it to have him do that, while she was breathless from another mans softly spoken words in her ear— and that kiss, her neck still tingled.

Taking a deep breath, she rose from her bed and headed to the bathroom. She freshened up and put on some ragged jeans and an old t-shirt. She had started the coffee and cut up some fresh fruit when a knock came to her front door.

"I'm coming, Jane," she said in a raised voice.

She opened the door to find a deliveryman with a bouquet of flowers in hand. Surprised, she signed the paper and took the flowers. Just before she could close the door, Jane walked up, "Flowers… so just what were you doing last night, sis?" Her voice exuded both teasing and curiosity.

8

"I have no idea who these are from. Come in; I have the coffee brewing now."

Both sisters walked into the kitchen, Jane placed a bag of pastries on the counter and retrieved two coffee mugs. "So, who are they from?" she prodded, excited to know who would send such a beautiful arrangement that was not your run-of-the-mill carnations or roses.

Elizabeth reached down and pulled the small envelope from its holder. Pulling out the card, she read it, and a smile spread across her face. Instantly, her heart began to beat quicker, and she could feel her hands growing damp.

"Well?" Jane was impatient; she could see the reaction on her sister's face and was dying to know who could invoke such a look.

"I don't really know this person," Elizabeth said in a casual calm voice.

"What do mean? Your smile could not get any bigger. Let me see that card." Jane took the card from between her sister's fingers and read it. Damn if her own heart did not skip a beat. She decided to read it aloud as if she could hardly believe what her eyes had read.

The feel of your silky flesh against my lips has only made my desire for you grow. Elizabeth, when you are ready, I will be here.

"You seriously want me to believe you don't know the person who sent you this. Come on Lizzy, dish. What did you do last night?" Jane was almost breathless with anticipation.

Elizabeth poured herself a cup of coffee, took a scrumptious looking cream cheese Danish over to the couch, and made herself comfortable. Jane followed suit and took the opposite corner. Her eyes were wide, and her brow rose in readiness for the story.

"Well, I had gone out like I said with Lacey and Charlotte. I danced with George, if you can believe that. Then as I was ordering the next round of drinks, a man walked up behind me, and in the sexiest voice you could ever imagine, told me he knew what I needed, and when I was tired of playing with George, a real man would be waiting to take care of me and fulfill my fantasies. Then he slipped his business card under my hand and kissed my neck. When I came to my senses to turn and see just who this man was, he had already walked off, and all I got was a glimpse of his perfect backside."

"You are kidding me, right? Oh my god that has to be the best pickup line ever!"

"I know, right? Jane, his voice still rings in my ears and his lips, so warm and soft as they kissed my neck… I just froze."

"Well who wouldn't. You are one lucky woman, Elizabeth Bennet. What was on his business card?" Jane's eyes were bright and wide.

Elizabeth rose from her perch and went to retrieve her purse. She pulled the card out and handed it to Jane. Jane glanced at the card, and her eyes became even wider.

"Elizabeth is this who sent you the flowers, the same man that kissed your neck and whispered in your ear last night?" Jane's surprise was evident in the curl of her lips.

"Yes, why?"

"Elizabeth, do you not realize that William Darcy is the man who has been doing business with father for years. Before him, it was his father. This man has millions and his own business to boot. Don't you remember meeting him? It was like three years ago, I think right when you returned from college. Father had just asked you to come join us in the family business with your new shiny degree."

"No, I don't. Should I?" Elizabeth could hardly believe what she was hearing. How could she have already met this man, this mysterious, sexy man, and not remember it?

*****

Sitting behind his desk, William reviewed several piles of contracts and business papers that needed to be signed. He had slept restlessly last night. The remembrance of Elizabeth's soft skin against his lips, the smell of roses and her gasp as he had kissed her neck still made his cock twitch and his heart race. He had sent her flowers Saturday morning hoping it would keep her thinking about the encounter.

"Good morning Darcy, and how are you this fine Monday morning?"

Richard Fitzwilliam, William's closest relation and dearest friend, came into his office wearing a big smile. He would know instantly that something was up. They both knew each other that well.

"Good morning, Richard."

Placing himself in the chair in front of the desk, Richard reclined after snatching a Dove chocolate from his cousin's desk. "So where have you been all weekend? I tried to call you twice Saturday and never so much as got a call returned. I don't want to hear that you were busy working either. I know damn well you went out to that club Friday night. SO fess up, it's all over your face. Did you take Elizabeth home?"

Richard was nothing if not direct. Leaning back in his chair, William steepled his two fingers up to his lips, elbows resting on the arms of his large black leather chair, and stared at his cousin. He knew he could not hide what he had done. It was too important a move, and Richard deserved to know. "No, I did not take her home." He said in a mild voice.

"Then what did you do?" Richard's impatience was beginning to get the better of him

"I made a move." Darcy replied his tone deep and matter -of -fact.

Pulling himself forward so that his elbows rested on his knees, Richard's eyes widened and an impassioned gleam sparkled in his eyes. "Oh do tell, what move did you make?"

Making the man wait just a few more minutes would make it so much more fun. William watched his cousin and how he reacted, as he waited without breathing to hear what he had to say. Both men had been taken by Elizabeth Bennet's beauty for the past few years.

"Come now Darcy, don't toy with me, tell me what have you done." Richard was almost ready to drool in anticipation of what William had to say.

"Fine, I gave her my business card."

Throwing himself back into his chair, Richard sighed. "Your business card... seriously, man, we need to work on your wooing skills."

11

"Richard, it is not the card that is important. It is how it was delivered." William smiled; a sinfully dashing grin appeared on his lips while he raised one brow toward his cousin.

*****

"Really Liz, George has been wondering around the house all week in a fog. Throw the man a bone will you. Go out with him Friday. He will drive me crazy if he keeps this up." The voice on the other end of the line implored.

"Lacey, your brother has not noticed me in how many years, and now he wants me to go on a date with him. Then he asks you to set it up. Come on, if he wants to take me out, tell him to call me. I have to run; Jane and I are expected over at our parents' for dinner tonight. Lydia has something important to tell us all, it seems."

"I'll pass your message on. Have fun. Hey, let's go dancing again soon. I had a blast last weekend. Since your single and free to enjoy yourself again, we need to take advantage of the opportunity."

"I'd love to. I'll call Charlotte; how about Saturday night?" Elizabeth was excited to go out with her best friend again so soon.

"Sounds good, say 9ish."

"Done, I'll text you later in the week."

"Okay, bye."

"Bye."

Elizabeth finished her makeup just in time to hear the knock. She grabbed her purse and walked to the door. "OH!" she gasped, startled by the man standing before her.

"Elizabeth, I wanted to know if you would join me for dinner this Friday evening?" The voice was alluring, just like the man standing before her.

"George, I didn't expect to see you. I am just on my way out to meet my family for dinner." Elizabeth looked around George to see if Jane had pulled up yet, but sadly, she had not; so, sighing, she offered for George to come in for a quick visit.

12

"My sister texted me your request. It was stupid of me to have her ask you. I'm sorry. I'm just a bit nervous. I...I've thought a lot about you over the years, and Friday, while we were dancing, I decided that I wanted to ask you out, have a real date. Please come out with me and allow me to make up for being such a bonehead. I should have come straight to you myself to start with." He sounded apologetic and Elizabeth could not stop staring at his eyes. He had great eyes.

Elizabeth knew Jane would arrive any minute, and she wanted George gone before she pulled up. Quickly, she agreed to go out on Friday, if nothing more, she would be able to tell if she felt anything for him. He was very handsome, and he had been the center of her dreams for years now. With a smile, she escorted him back to the door and promised to call him later in the week for more details.

He had just made it to his car when Jane pulled up. Elizabeth grabbed her purse and locked her door. Once in Jane's car, she knew what was coming.

"Elizabeth, was that George Wickham leaving just now?" Jane was very inquisitive and kept looking over her shoulder at the departing red sports car.

Chapter 3

The night had been long. Lydia was her usual high-strung self; since things only ever revolved around her and her life. Naturally, the entire family had been subjected to listening to her ramble on about a new job assignment. She was beside herself with excitement at being sent to Los Angeles. Elizabeth groaned, just picturing the sorts of trouble Lydia would get into so far from the family. Lydia had the opportunity of a lifetime, if she did not blow it.

Elizabeth had fallen into bed almost as soon as she had arrived home. Jane had questioned her about George all the way to their parents' place, and on the way home, Jane discussed Lydia and the many reasons their father should deter her from accepting the LA job. Tired and ready to collapse, Elizabeth had quickly made her way to her bedroom. She lay in the dark, sinking into her bed and finally drifting off to sleep. Her last thoughts were on the flowers that were next to her bed; the slight smell had wafted towards her pillow, leaving the intriguing William Darcy foremost on her mind.

*****

Friday had finally arrived, and Elizabeth dressed carefully for her date with George Wickham. She had dreamt her entire life of going out with this man. He was so handsome with his blond hair, blue eyes and a body built to fantasize over. His arms and abs were to die for. She couldn't count the number of times she had ogled him from behind her sunglasses at the swimming pool over the years. She put on her best tight jeans and a red low cut top that accentuated her best assets. Smiling and a bit nervous, Elizabeth sat on the couch, eager to start the evening. She had spoken with George yesterday to get the plans finalized. He was going to take her out to eat and then for drinks afterwards.

When the knock finally came at her front door, Elizabeth felt all the nerves of a teenager settle into her stomach. She inhaled deeply, and then opened her front door.

"Hi, you look beautiful." George apprised Elizabeth's body with a smile, "I brought these for you." He handed her a small vase filled with an arrangement of carnations, daisies, and assorted greenery. It was a nice gesture, but Elizabeth could not help but compare it to what William had sent her just over a week ago. She thanked him with a smile and set the vase down on her coffee table before heading out.

"Thank you George, what a wonderful surprise. I love fresh flowers." Elizabeth smiled. She felt strange, both excited and nervous at the same time. All these years she had wanted to have the attention of George Wickham, and here he finally was, and Elizabeth was not sure if this is where she wanted to be now. The flowers had brought William to her mind, and somehow she felt a little awkward. Taking a quick cleansing breath to settle her nerves and clear her mind, she decided to let things just happen and see where this date would lead.

They had enjoyed a wonderful dinner at a local restaurant. Conversation had been nice and seemed to flow well, and Elizabeth was actually having a pleasant evening. George was dressed in a pair of khaki slacks and a light blue dress shirt, selected no doubt to enhance the effect of his bronzed body, his ice blue eyes, and golden hair, giving him an amazingly handsome appearance. She became nervous when they arrived at her favorite dance club since she suddenly remember Mr. Darcy having been there, but her unease quickly dissipated when she noticed her dear friends gathered at their normal table.

"Lacey, what are you doing here?" Elizabeth asked. Her questioning brow had George's sister smiling in return.

"George wanted us to meet you guys out here for some fun. I hope you don't mind." Lacey felt a bit uncomfortable for intruding on her brother's date but knew it might be beneficial if she were there for her dear friend.

Elizabeth glanced at George, his expression only showing a quizzical gaze. "I hope this is okay with you, Elizabeth. I figured it would be nice to have a group of us here dancing, and when you're ready, I'll take you home."

Elizabeth thought for just a moment and turned back to her friends. "This is perfect. Thank you George, it was very kind of you to invite everyone."

Immediately the girls took off for the restroom to refresh their makeup and find out how the date was going so far.

*****

From his perch in the corner, Darcy watched as the group enjoyed drinks and dancing. He had heard from the bartender that Elizabeth would be coming later in the evening, so he had decided to come and see what was up. He did not expect to see her arrive with George Wickham. He knew from asking around that Elizabeth had always had a thing for him, but he had hoped that she would be smart enough not to indulge this particular fantasy. George was a playboy, and even though he was one of his closest friends in college, they did not have much in common any longer. George never even seemed remotely interested in Elizabeth. He knew that George's sister Lacey was a dear friend to Elizabeth. The two had been friends since middle school. Why George suddenly had to ask her out he had his suspicions.

Sitting in the shadows of the corner table, Darcy heard a familiar voice come up next to him. "How long have you been here watching her?"

"About an hour or so," he replied in an even tone never taking his eyes off her.

"Have you made any moves?" the soft strong voice replied.

"No, just observing. She came with Wickham. I think they are on some sort of a date. Her friends were here before she arrived. George has danced with her a few times along with several other ladies at the table as well. I have not seen anything that would cause me concern, so I figured I would just let the evening play out. You know George couldn't be interested in her; he has been around her for years and never taken notice. Anyway, what are you doing here?"

"A bird told me you were here, so I figured you were up to your old tricks of just watching. How do you plan on making yourself known to the one woman who has so captured your heart, if you don't get out there and introduce yourself?" the man chastised.

"That is for me to decide. I will do it when I feel the time is right," Darcy replied in a stern but low voice. He took another sip from the tumbler in his hand. He had his eyes glued to Elizabeth. That red top and plunging neckline had his mouth watering to just kiss her neck and anything else his lips could find. His hands itched to caress her and hold her close. He had not even so much as looked at the person standing next to him even though he was conversing with him.

"How about I make it easier for you?" Richard put an empty glass down on the table and walked towards Elizabeth and her party. George was on the dance floor with one of the ladies as Elizabeth sat sipping at her drink. He walked up behind her and softly whispered in her ear. "Excuse me, would the lady care for a dance? I could not help but notice you have not been on the floor much this evening. It would be a shame not to allow the men here this evening the pleasure of watching you move." His smooth velvety voice asked.

As Elizabeth turned her head, she gasped inwardly as she took in the tall, broad shouldered man standing to her side. He was so drop dead handsome she blushed immediately having lost all rational thought. Was this Adonis actually asking her to dance? He offered her his hand, and she slowly placed her hand in his. Their eyes were locked together and Elizabeth could feel heat rising to her cheeks. "Yes the lady would care for a dance, go Lizzy" the voice of Lacey Wickham quickly accepted. Elizabeth broke her gaze and turned to her friend who urged her up.

Suddenly parched Elizabeth finally replied, "Thank you, I would love to dance" her own voice cracking as she swallowed,

As the couple walked towards the dance floor, Richard could hear the ladies giggling before whispers suddenly overtook the table. Once on the dance floor, the music changed to a fast grinding beat. Richard took the opportunity to use his skills and brought Elizabeth close to his body. One arm wrapped around her waist as they started to dance. Elizabeth smelled wonderful. Her body, well toned, melted against his touch. She trembled slightly but he knew she was not scared, he could see it in her eyes, she was timid, a bit cautious, and if he was correct, she was a bit excited as well. He knew why his cousin desired her so much since he did, too. He was hoping Darcy would get the hint and make a move to take control of the current situation and ask this temptress out. That was what he had intended to happen in taking her hand to dance, but if the indication of the hardening bulge in his pants was any signal of what was to come in the future, he couldn't wait another day. If Darcy did not take the initiative and ask her out, he might well ask her himself.

Elizabeth's mind floated as the handsome stranger danced with her on the crowded floor. His touch electrified her; she could feel her breath short and quick as her body moved along his. He was strong and she couldn't tear her eyes from his chest or her hands from around his neck. They moved so well together. They had not even spoken since arriving to the dance floor, which was just fine since she didn't think she could form a coherent word at the moment. So lost in her own thoughts, Elizabeth didn't even notice that another person had come up behind her. Suddenly she felt another's hand on her other hip. She was being sandwiched, and she did not even know who this other person was. She glanced up to the man who had asked her to dance as if to ask for help, but all she could see was desire in his green eyes. It astounded her, and then she heard him, the voice of the man behind her.

"Are you having fun Elizabeth? You look gorgeous." He slowly spoke near her ear. "My cousin Richard here is a very skilled dancer, I must admit, but I am sure you will not find me lacking in that regard either. Perhaps I could persuade you to go out with me some evening and I'll show you. As I have said before, when you are tired of playing with boys like George Wickham, I will be waiting to indulge you in more than just some girlish fantasies." The tone in his voice was strong and confident, the heat of his breathe feathering against her skin as he whispered his words close to her ear. His hand trailed down from her shoulder to her hip making goose bumps spring to life all along her body.

Elizabeth sucked in her breath as she slowly turned her head to behold the most exquisite set of eyes she had ever seen. Their depths were so intense, filled with so many emotions; she could not pull her gaze away. "You're William Darcy aren't you?" she said in a quiet voice. He leaned down slowly and kissed her lips possessively. When he coaxed her mouth open with his tongue, she could not argue and allowed him entry. His hand cradled her jaw tenderly, but his kiss was deep. Elizabeth's hands still hung around the neck of the man before her as they both held her steady.

His sensual investigation of her mouth made her hunger for more of this forbidden stranger. Both men continued to dance with her, swaying to the beat of the music, their hands holding her close and secure. Elizabeth became lost in a haze of sudden passion. Her own desires were beginning to overtake rational thought as they moved together to the fast grinding beat, when the music stopped. The spell was broken then and when she glanced up between her, both men's countenances were filled with hunger and deep need. She could feel the heat rush to her cheeks, the air around them electrified in a sensual haze as they all tried to regain their normal breathing from the fast paced movements. The man who asked her to dance slowly let his hold on her waist go. "Thank you for the dance Elizabeth. Perhaps we can do it again sometime my beauty." His voice was like silk and sent shivers down Elizabeth's spine. Richard released her hands from his neck giving a kiss to each of her knuckles, a smoldering look in his eyes.

"Please allow me to escort you back to your table Elizabeth. I think your date is beginning to glower at us from across the dance floor." The sexy voice from her side sent a sensual chill down to her core as she turned to lock eyes with William Darcy once again.

All Elizabeth could manage was to nod and allow herself to be taken back. Once both men had deposited her with her friends they departed from the table. Elizabeth took her glass and downed the remainder of her drink. She had never in her life felt such an instant attraction to anyone, much less two men at the same time. She must be going mad.

The table was still silent when George returned from the dance floor with a young blond woman in tow. They all chatted for a few moments then the blond left. George asked if Elizabeth was ready to leave, seeing she was apparently not going to forget what he had just witnessed while she was dancing with his old classmate.

George seemed miffed but Elizabeth hardly noticed, she had tried to look around the bar and find the two men she had danced with not 15 minutes ago but they were not to be found, so she bid her friends a soft farewell. Charlotte promised to call her tomorrow, as did Lacey. She knew her friends wanted to know what had just happened out on the dance floor, but she also knew she needed time to compose an answer for them.

Chapter 4

Sitting in a nice warm bath, Elizabeth was still in a haze. George had dropped her off at her place and left quickly after a mostly silent ride home from the dance club. Now stripped and submerged in the warmth of the water around her, Elizabeth closed her eyes and replayed what had happened at the club.

Goosebumps appeared on her skin as she thought of the dashing man who had come to claim a dance with her. Then the intoxicating voice of William Darcy made her stomach pull and constrict as his words repeated in her mind. Both had been so close to her, the warmth of their hands on her waist and back as they had danced, the power they exuded and the confidence they emitted just left her breathless in a sensual haze of remembrance.

Then there was George, gorgeous, tall, blond, exquisite George. He had been her fantasy for so long. She had taken such care to dress to be appealing to him. The evening had gone well; they had enjoyed a lovely dinner, and he had danced holding her close to him. However, he also danced with several other ladies, some who were her friends at the table and others who were not. So, with her brow wrinkled, she pondered how it was that two men she knew nothing about had stolen her senses? Why was she not as taken with George Wickham as she was with William Darcy?

The man seemed pretty freakin' sure of himself. Heaven help her but the man made her weak in the knees, and that was something George had never been able to do. Knowing that Lacey would be calling in the morning, Elizabeth closed her eyes and groaned. "What am I to tell her?" she thought aloud. Elizabeth quickly toweled off and threw herself into bed. Maybe tomorrow she would find the words that eluded her now.

*****

"Richard you could have cost me everything tonight with that little stunt!" William Darcy snapped at his cousin as they walked out of the dance club.

"You needed a little help, I figured. You know damn well you want her, so I just helped you move things along; that's all," he teased in a lighthearted tone.

William walked quickly to his Aston Martin and stopped to face his cousin. "I'll let you know when I need your help. Tonight was not one of those times. I hope that she accepts my apology. If you have ruined my chances with her in any way..." he threatened in a low strangled voice.

"Ya, ya, I know, you'll tie my balls up and hang me up by them from the rafters. Go home and cool off, Romeo. I just lit a small fire for you. It's up to you to make it blaze." He smirked.

"Don't interfere, Richard. If we are going to make this work, it has to be on my terms and when I believe she is ready." He growled once more in a low tone.

Darcy climbed into his car and before he could close the door, Richard yelled out, "You're welcome." He chuckled loudly enough to be heard over the spinning tires of the departing car.

*****

Jane had been the first to call Elizabeth Saturday morning. She invited herself to join the girls later that evening, so Elizabeth figured she would need to steel herself for the onslaught of information she would be expected to dole out. Lacey and Charlotte both sent her texts stating they wanted all the juicy tidbits when they met at the club later.

Elizabeth had just returned from running a few errands when she settled down to lunch. She had just taken a bite of her sandwich when a knock could be heard at her door. Not expecting anyone, she wiped her mouth and strolled to the front door. She was dressed in her torn jeans and a ratty t-shirt. Her hair was pulled up in a sloppy ponytail. She wore no shoes so whoever it was, would just have to deal with her appearance. They should have called before they came unexpectedly knocking on her door. She pulled the door ajar just a bit with the chain in place, and to her utter surprise, before her stood William Darcy.

"Elizabeth, if I might have a moment of your time, I want to speak with you." He looked amazing, and his voice seemed soft, down cast almost.

"Mr. Darcy," her voice cracked in surprise, "just a moment, please." She closed the door, swallowed nervously and looked down at her appearance, breathing a deep sigh. Her heart beat fiercely in her ears as she slowly unlocked the door.

"I am sorry. I did not expect anyone" she tried to apologize, a slight blush to her cheeks.

"No, it is I who should be apologizing to you. I should have called first; I wasn't thinking." He looked truly regretful.

Not knowing how to remedy the situation at hand, Elizabeth stood and waited for a few moments before blinking and stepping aside. "Please, won't you come in?"

"Thank you, I'll only be a moment," he softly replied. He passed her swiftly while Elizabeth allowed his scent to penetrate her senses. Goodness, the man was handsome. She could not believe he was even at her place; why he was here? How did he know where she lived? She could not even begin to fathom at the moment. She was thankful the place had just been cleaned and the only room in disarray was her bedroom, and that, he would not get a glimpse of, at least not today.

Once indoors, Darcy glanced about the room. It was a cozy place, not large but comfortable. He walked towards the center of the living room and stopped. "Miss Bennet, it would appear that my cousin might have taken some liberties last night in asking you to dance. I do hope that you were not offended by his actions or boldness."

Elizabeth froze; she was not expecting such a remark. She didn't really know what to say, but decided to make him squirm just a bit. "No, I was not, though I must say that having you both dance with me in such a manner did make for some interesting looks and questions from my friends who will hold me accountable later this evening. Then there was the issue of my date, who could not whisk me away quickly enough." She gave him a slight smile.

"I am terribly sorry. I would like to make it up to you, however. Your father's annual charity ball is in a few weeks. Would I be too bold, if I were to ask you to accompany me, that is if you're not already being escorted?"

"I don't see a need to be escorted to a ball that I must attend and have helped to put together for several years now. Perhaps, instead, you could have the majority of my dance card." She tilted her head with a raised brow giving him a moment to consider her offer. "That is, with the stipulation that you can dance in a more conservative manner," she teased with a smile.

Darcy watched her exhibition of liveliness and decided not to press her further on his offer of attending as his date. She had every right to be furious with him and Richard for the way they had danced with her the night before. If all she wanted were a few dances at a public event, then she would have them. He would do anything for her.

"I believe I can accommodate you this one time, Miss Bennet. Perhaps we could have some coffee sometime and get to know each other better. I would very much like that opportunity." His eyes grew darker and he gazed directly at her. Elizabeth could feel heat starting to crawl up her neck. His eyes were like an extension of his hands; they roamed up her body and caressed her cheek.

"Please, there is no need to be so formal; call me Elizabeth. Coffee you say... perhaps sometime. Our companies do business together Mr. Darcy, so I'm not so sure it would be the right thing for us to see each other." She turned and sat in an oversized chair wiggling in until she was comfortable.

"Please won't you have a seat? Can I get you something to drink?" she asked finally remembering her manners. Her eyes widened at her own recognition of being so remiss.

"No. I should go; again, I'm sorry for not calling first. I hope the rest of your weekend is enjoyable." He smiled slightly as he stared into her eyes. Wanting nothing more than to pull her close to him and kiss her hard, William restrained himself and walked towards the front door before he embarrassed himself further. She had said she didn't think they should see each other. That did not set well with Darcy and he would have to make her see otherwise.

Elizabeth popped out of her chair and followed him, holding the door as he left. Just as he passed her, he turned back and confidently spoke in a low deep voice, "Elizabeth, my offer still stands. I will be here waiting for you and just because our companies do business together, does not mean we cannot see where a relationship between us might go. We are both adults here, I know you can feel something between us; I wish you wouldn't fight it. I have much to offer you Elizabeth. I'll see you at the Ball. " He turned and left, not giving her the chance to reply.

*****

23

Stunned was not the word for it. The music was drowned out around her as she sat at the high bar table at the club with her friends, staring into her glass of Bailey's. They had held true to their words, and all had tried to pump her for information about the dance with the two handsome men just the night before. Elizabeth answered as best she could. Her mind kept replaying the last words William Darcy had spoken to her as he had left her apartment just a few hours before.

"Elizabeth, did you hear me?" came Jane's quizzical voice.

"No I'm sorry, Jane; what did you say?" Elizabeth had to talk loudly above the music playing out on the dance floor.

"Father wants to go over the final details of the ball Monday morning. Will you be in the office?"

"Yes, I can be there. I will be out most of the week at client sites and finalizing the arrangements for the ball, but Monday works for me."

"Good, are you sure you're okay? You don't seem like yourself tonight. Are you still thinking of William Darcy or that handsome cousin of his?"

"Oh Jane, I'm fine, … really I just don't know what to make of all this. Things I always thought I wanted are suddenly changing. I mean I left Bill three months ago and now George is asking me out finally, after a lifetime of wishing he would. Now these two beautiful men want to dance and take me out. I just " Elizabeth sighed as she stared into her empty glass. She could feel the shift in herself, her mind making room for the forbidden thoughts that William Darcy brought to her.

"Hey there, come on and dance with us, Elizabeth; it's not like you to sit out all night." Lacey Wickham pulled her friends hands and lifted her to her feet, smiling and bouncing to the beat of the current song blaring over the crowd. Elizabeth sighed and went to the floor, but as she danced the song from the night before came on. It had her mind racing with the memories of the two men that had made their way into her head as no others before.

*****

"Bill, I said I will meet you there. I have things to do now. Please, I have to go."

Elizabeth had fielded calls from Bill Collins all week long. Tomorrow was the big annual charity ball, and she was up to her eyeballs in last minute details. Bill wanted to escort her there, and she had turned him down not once but three times. The man just did not know when to give up.

"Elizabeth I understand this is not the best time, but you have not agreed, and I will just keep calling until you accept my offer. You should not go alone; please come with me. "

Elizabeth thought for a few moments. Jane had been right. Bill had been coming around to her office more these last few weeks. Her father had even hinted that Bill wanted to accompany her to the event. Why were so many men determined to have her as their date? Never before had she needed a man to escort her, and this year three were practically begging her. George Wickham had also called and wanted to come to the ball. He had pulled the contributor card on her a few days ago, since his father's business had donated space for advertising in the program, so before she lost her mind completely, she agreed to have Bill pick her up along with Jane and Charles Bingley. If she was going to have to be seen with him, she wanted it to look like a group thing and not a date. If William Darcy found out about it, she would never hear the end of it. It was apparent that he did not think highly of George Wickham after his comment a few weeks ago and Bill Collins probably didn't rate much higher. She wondered if William Darcy even knew she had dated Bill Collins. He seemed to know so much about her. She would have to speak with him on how he came to have her address as well.

No sooner had she hung up the phone with Bill than a knock sounded at her office door. "Yes, enter!" she barked out, louder than she had intended to. Standing behind her desk, she arranged a few files in her hand and plopped them down on her desk as the door opened. Her face showed surprise when her father and Jane came strolling into the office and behind them, a man she only knew by first name.

"Elizabeth, I'm sorry if we have interrupted you," her father said rather coolly with a look of disapproval on his face.

"No, allow me to apologize; I just got off the phone. Please come in and have a seat. Can I get you anything?" she offered, trying to make amends quickly.

"We won't be here long. I wanted to introduce Mr. Richard Fitzwilliam, the liaison between Mr. Darcy's company and ours. He will be providing the security for the event. Jane has given him the list of attendees, and we were just wanting the final names of the performers if you have that." He was firm in his question, and his annoyance was evident to her.

"Yes, it is right here. I could have emailed this to you, Mr. Fitzwilliam, there was no need to come here in person," Elizabeth replied.

His eyes burned into her, his body fit in that suit like it was a second skin, and all she could do was think about how close he had been to her, pressed against her body, his hands holding her close.

"It was no trouble at all, Miss Bennet. I had a meeting with Miss Bennet and your father, and we where about to go to lunch. So you can see there is no need to concern yourself." He was confident and gave her a nod and slight smile. He loved how she looked in her business attire. That blouse hid nothing and her skirt made her hips look so curvy. When Elizabeth spoke, he snapped back to attention.

"Of course. Here you are. It is all there in the file. If you have any questions, I can give you my cell number. I plan on being at the hotel several hours before to make sure all is in order and going smoothly." She couldn't believe she just offered her cell number to the man. He smiled as he accepted the file from her and flipped it open while taking a pen from his coat pocket.

"If you don't mind I will just jot your number down in case I do need to get hold of you." His eyes spoke of more than the need of business matters in acquiring her private number.

She quickly spilled the digits to him and smiled what she hoped was a confident business smile. Her body seemed unable to keep from responding helplessly to his every look, every smile or touch. What was she thinking? "Mr. Bennet, if your daughters are not otherwise occupied, perhaps they would like to join us for lunch?" He suggested with a smug smile. He eyed Elizabeth before turning to speak to her father.

"I don't see why not. Ladies, if you are not otherwise engaged, what do you say? Would you like to come to lunch with a few workaholics and listen to us discuss topics of world dominance?" Her father smiled, easing Elizabeth's distress at their earlier arrival.

Jane watched her sister warily while saying she was free for lunch. "Elizabeth, how about you?" Jane asked.

Elizabeth could not think quickly enough to get out of it. How would she survive without blushing the entire time or thinking of all the ways she wanted that man to touch her.

"Elizabeth, whatever it is, it can wait. You need to eat. Come with us; we won't bite." her father cajoled with half a smile curving his lips.

"Yes, if you could give me just a moment. I need to send out one email and sign a few things that need to go out, and I will meet you in the lobby in say, 15 minutes." She acted assured and confident or so she hoped. They all agreed and departed her office. With a sigh of relief, Elizabeth fell back into her chair, her head in her hands.

"What was I thinking?" she spoke aloud to the empty office. She quickly signed the few items on her desk to pass off to her secretary and sent the email. She used the attached washroom to refresh herself and collect her nerves. Believing she was prepared, she grabbed her purse and headed towards the lobby.

Chapter 5

Elizabeth took her own car; she didn't think she would be able to sit so close to Mr. Fitzwilliam without blushing if she rode with her father. Jane decided to ride with her, so they followed his car to the restaurant just a few blocks away. Conversation was minimal, which Elizabeth was most grateful for, though she could feel her sister's eyes on her for most of the ride.

Once they stepped into the finely decorated foyer of the restaurant, the owner escorted the party towards the private dinning room her father usually reserved for client meetings and such. Elizabeth's eyes grew wide at the sight of Mr. Darcy rising from a chair at their table. The sight of him made her heart thump wildly in her chest. What was he doing here?

The group found their seats, Mr. Darcy holding Elizabeth's chair for her, before he took a seat next to her. Richard Fitzwilliam stealthily sat on her other side wearing a smug grin. Jane took a chair across from them next to her father. The two very handsome men exchanged pleasantries while Elizabeth tried to concentrate on the menu in her hands. They smelled so … male, and she felt small when placed between them. Jane just kept staring at her sister trying to read her thoughts. Their father began the meeting talking about the ball and asked Elizabeth for confirmation of certain details. Before she could respond, another person joined them at the table.

Elizabeth just could not believe her luck today. It was none other than Bill Collins. He was dressed in his best blue suit, his briefcase in hand. Elizabeth stared at her father with questioning eyes.

"Ah Mr. Collins is finally here; now we can enjoy our lunch. Elizabeth, I have asked Mr. Collins to bring the contracts and outstanding paperwork so that we can finalize everything to Mr. Darcy and Mr. Fitzwilliam's satisfaction. I understand you have a room at the hotel for the night and will be on the premises most of the day, preparing and seeing to all the details personally. There should be no reason for you to come back to the office once these contracts are completed. I would like you to take the rest of the day off." Her father spoke matter-of-factly as he waited for the contracts from Bill.

Shocked at what her father just said, Elizabeth looked to Jane. She could not offer any comment on the situation, and Elizabeth could feel the two men next to her watching her every move.

"Thank you father, but I was not quite finished with a few things I will need to return to the office once we have eaten to get those items squared away." she tried to remain calm in her speech but her stomach was churning.

"Elizabeth, I don't want you to run yourself ragged. I see you do it every year. I would prefer you rest. Jane can finish whatever needs to be done." Her father was sterner in his tone, as he flipped through the pages in his hand without looking at her.

"If I may, Miss Bennet, your father is right. I understand you work tirelessly on this event every year. It is to your credit that the funds collected on this one night are so plentiful. Your father is only watching out for your best interests. I am sure my cousin will find everything in order and to his satisfaction. You should take this opportunity for yourself." William politely expressed.

Elizabeth watched as Bill Collins stiffened and shot his eyes towards Mr. Darcy. Slowly Elizabeth turned to him and thanked him for his kind words.

"Thank you, Mr. Darcy, for such a glowing testimonial. Thank you, father, this is very generous of you." Not wanting a battle to ensue in front of either of these men, Elizabeth just decided to take the afternoon off and gather her shredded wits. " Jane, if you have a minute, we could go over what I have left on my desk, while Mr. Collins reviews the contracts with Mr. Fitzwilliam. Gentlemen, if you will excuse us just a moment."

The two ladies removed themselves from the table to head to the ladies' room. She needed to speak to Jane and find out what she thought.

"Jane, why did father ask Bill to come here? It is so awkward to have him stare at Mr. Darcy so."

"Elizabeth. I had no idea he had invited him. Honestly, I can see why he would react as he has. Those men on either side of you look as if they want to just lick you up and eat you." Jane tried to hurry her into the ladies' room, her voice a little higher than normal.

Blushing at her sister's remark, Elizabeth entered the ladies room and noticed her appearance. She was just as flushed as she thought. "Jane?"

"Come on Elizabeth, Mr. Darcy sent you those flowers, he has called you, and he showed up at your apartment. Throw the man a bone. See where this leads you. He is quite handsome, rich, has wonderful manners— what more could you ask for?" Her smile said she had more on her mind than his smile.

"Jane, I have made mistakes in my past, and I do not intend to make another. I am doing fine on my own. Why it was just the other day, when George asked me out, and you know how long I have wanted to date that man. Even Lacey has been trying to help get us together for years."

"George Wickham is nothing like Mr. Darcy. Oh, and do not get me started on his cousin Mr. Fitzwilliam; that man is just pure eye candy." Jane sighed as she spoke, her own features glowing at her thoughts as she added a little blush to her cheeks. "You need to get over George, he is just a womanizer, and he has no idea how to remain in a relationship longer than it takes to pull his pants down, screw a gal, and run out the door. You know it as well as I do," Jane said running a finger over her lips to adjust her lipstick.

Elizabeth listened to her sister and sighed. "Fine, I will give it some thought, but I am taking father's offer and resting tonight. Bill offered to take me to the hotel tomorrow, and I accepted since he would not leave me alone. That man will get on my last nerve if he keeps intruding on my life. We broke up a month ago he needs to move on. You know I turned down both George and Mr. Darcy for the same right and now I think I am regretting just going alone. I'm not so sure that any of this will go over well with any of them should they find out." She smiled and wiped her hands. They discussed what was left on Elizabeth's desk that needed to be tended to and left to return to the meeting.

*****

Once the ladies had left the table, the men waited for Mr. Bennet to read the contracts. Richard and William both glanced over them and signed off on them. Bill Collins had taken a seat next to Richard, and Mr. Bennet and was staring the two men down.

"Mr. Bennet, if I may, Elizabeth should really be given time off after the ball this year. She is always so stressed and tired once it is all over. I would like to request some time off as well, perhaps take her to the lake house." Bill spoke with confidence as he ignored the men at the table.

"Hmm, I think you had better ask my daughter about that plan yourself. I believe she would have a different idea. It is hard enough to get her to take the rest of today off; you know how she is, Bill. "

Richard and William just listened to the two men chat as if they were not even there. Darcy believed that Collins was making sure he staked his claim on Elizabeth, perhaps not knowing William knew of the break up; however, Darcy knew full well Elizabeth had called off the relationship with the man at least a month ago. He could tell as soon as Bill Collins entered the room that he had daggers in his eyes for him and his cousin. Apparently, he threatened this man and Elizabeth's affections for him. All the better, he thought to himself as he continued to listen to Collins speak with Mr. Bennet about Elizabeth's well being.

"Darcy, I do believe Mr. Collins is going to try his hand at being a knight in shining armor. Why don't you find the restroom; I'm sure the ladies are on their way back by now," Richard whispered finding amusement in the way Bill Collins was puffing up his chest at what he believed was a victory.

Nodding, Darcy excused himself and strolled out of the private dining room, headed toward the restrooms. He spied Elizabeth and Jane approaching and made his mind up then as to his next course of action.

Chapter 6

Sitting in the plush leather seat of the Aston Martin, Elizabeth stared out the side window. How had she been talked into leaving the restaurant with William Darcy? Oh, she knew all right— Jane, that's what. She had handed her sister the keys to her car and was practically shoved into his arms, all the while; Jane smiled so sweetly and whispered that she would call her later in the evening.

"You have been very quiet, Miss Bennet, are you well?" he said with some concern in his voice.

Snapping her head toward the handsome man, Elizabeth swallowed slowly. "I am fine, thank you. I just have so much on my mind with the ball tomorrow evening. I thought we agreed you would call me Elizabeth." She smiled faintly at him and turned back to the window.

"So I did. You know I understand completely where you're coming from. When I am in the middle of a business deal, I find it difficult to divide myself between work and personal time, but I do believe your father is right. You have worked very hard on this event every year since I can remember you taking over the duties. It would be in your best interest if you could put it aside, if only for a few hours, and relax a bit," he said in a smooth soft voice filled with actual concern for her, or so she thought.

Turning back to face him, she replied, "Yes, you're right. I should. Jane is perfectly capable of tying up the last few things on my desk, and Mr. Fitzwilliam has the contracts and the line-up for the entertainment; it is just difficult for me to let go." Elizabeth tried to acknowledge his concern.

"Then allow me to help you. What do you enjoy doing when you are not in the midst of large corporate contracts and event planning?" William asked with just a bit of playfulness.

Looking forward, Elizabeth thought a moment, and then stated matter-of-factly, "I don't think I ever gave it much thought, honestly. I usually go out to the club with my friends for a drink if I have some free time. Though you know that, I suspect." She blushed thinking of the last time she was with this sexy man at that very club.

A smile drew up the curves of his lips as he agreed with her statement. "So you have no other life than work and that club. Well, perhaps I can do something about that. Would you allow me to treat you to an afternoon of relaxation followed by a lovely dinner? I promise to have you home early for bed, Miss Bennet, I mean Elizabeth. You do have a big day tomorrow, and I have your word already that I will be on your dance card quite often. I want you to be well rested." He smiled genuinely at her.

Chuckling at his remark, Elizabeth agreed, "Deal, Mr. Darcy. You drive a hard bargain, but I will leave myself in your capable hands for the rest of the day, and I will endeavor to enjoy myself and relax." She turned to face him, her eyes dancing and full of life as a smile spread across her lips.

"Wonderful idea and please call me William, my father is not in the car."

With a nod towards him, Elizabeth sat back and began to relax a bit.

*****

Believing he had just won a contest, and giddy at the prospect of spending the afternoon with this bewitching lady beside him, Darcy quickly picked up his cell phone and placed a call. Elizabeth would be treated to a day of pampering, leaving her relaxed while hopefully capturing just a piece of her heart in the process.

After some few minutes later, William pulled into a parking garage. Once at the valet station, they both got out and headed into an elevator. "Where are we going?" she asked, her anticipation evident in her eyes.

"I am going to spoil you with a large dose of pampering and a little fun along the way. I hope you trust me." His eyes spoke of a little mischief and definitely a touch of control.

"I do; I just like to know what is happening when I have been kidnapped for the afternoon by handsome strangers." She flirted back at him.

"And are you often kidnapped by handsome strangers?" He cocked an eyebrow at her, a gleam in his eye.

"No, you are my first." Elizabeth shrugged back with a brilliant smile.

"Well then, I have my work cut out for me." He said in a promising voice.

"How so?" She tilted her head with a raised brow that intrigued him.

"I want this to be an experience you won't soon forget, Elizabeth." He said with a slight smile.

Darcy reached down and pulled her hand to his lips. His warm mouth made contact with her knuckles sending a spark of current running straight to her nipples. He never released her eyes from his own as he moved ever so slowly down to kiss her hand before lowering it once again just as the doors opened. A smile graced his lips. "I told you before, I know just what you need and desire" his voice very low and whispered across her ear as he lead her out of the elevator.

*****

Oh, my goodness, his hands are the best. Yes..lower…lower, Ooohhh… that's it, right there. Elizabeth lay face down on the massage table as her masseur Carlos ran his strong hands down her spin to her lower back. The man had talent. Elizabeth was sure she had died and gone to heaven as Carlos worked over every inch of her back, shoulders, legs, hands and, lest she forget, her head. She was so relaxed now; she feared she was drooling on the table. William Darcy was definitely a man of his word. She had been pampered for the last three hours at the hands of various people.

When they had arrived at the front desk of the spa earlier, Moira, the receptionist, smiled brightly and ushered them both into a private room. There a team of men and woman came in and began to softly speak with Elizabeth. She had a manicure and pedicure then was whisked into a room for a quick facial before heading over to see Carlos. Now as he finished up, she lay still on the table alone, unable to gather her wits about her to move and put on her robe.

Elizabeth heard a soft knock at the door. "Yes," she replied.

"Elizabeth, may I come in." The deep voice belonged to William, and here she was naked on a table with only a sheet to cover her.

"Oh, William, if you will give me just a moment. I'm not quite ready." She replied a bit panicked at her appearance.

She hurriedly jumped up from the table and tried to gather her clothes.

"Elizabeth, if you could just slip on your robe, I have one last surprise for you." His voice seemed to chuckle slightly at her flustered response. Not to mention the commotion she was making by falling off the table, her feet hitting the floor with the grace of a linebacker.

Elizabeth's eyes widened a bit as she stared at the door. However, she did as requested and hastily pulled on her robe and opened the door.

" I believe you have done enough for today. Really, you have gone above and beyond. I couldn't possibly..."

William placed his finger across her lips gently to hush her ramblings. Smiling down at her, he softly spoke, "I have one last surprise Elizabeth, if you would indulge me just a bit longer. Then we will leave. Now follow me." He took her hand and she followed behind him as they wound their way back to the private room they had initially been in.

"Now Elizabeth, if you will take a seat, Moria will be right in with you." He kissed her knuckles and nodded his head towards her as he retreated.

Sitting in the plush room alone, Elizabeth wondered what he was up to. The door opened shortly, and Moira walked in with four ladies behind her. They were all carrying different styles of clothing and all about Elizabeth's size.

"Miss Bennet, this is for you."

She handed Elizabeth a note. Elizabeth stared at the card a moment then flipped it open.

Elizabeth, if you would do me the honor of choosing one of these four ensembles for yourself, we will be on our way to dinner as soon as you are dressed. You would look lovely in any of them.

"For me? I am to pick one of these outfits?" She questioned Moira.

"Yes madam, all has been taken care of; it is your choice. I will have each one presented to you so that you can make your decision. "

Moira did just that. The first ensemble was a lovely black cocktail dress, form fitted with a knee length hemline, short capped lace sleeves, and a bodice that featured a square neckline. There were black heals and a dainty diamond necklace that accompanied it. It was very lovely and Elizabeth smiled thinking of how she would look in such a garment.

The second was a pair of black slacks, a white silk tank shell with a short-sleeved silver sweater. A set of pearls in a twist of cream and black, and black leather heeled boots completed the collection. Another fine choice and she could see herself wearing that many places.

Her third choice was a wonderful pair of jeans, a brown leather belt with a short sleeve scoop-necked knit shirt in a cream color, a light weight denim jacket with a cream and brown stitch design on the sleeve cuffs and on the back. A pair of fashionable brown leather boots and a large chucky necklace in brown leather with a silver, cream, and brown medallion accompanied the ensemble. She really loved that choice; it was so her.

The fourth was the most comfortable yet. A pair of navy knit crop pants with a pale pink t-shirt and a pair of tennis shoes. Something for hanging out and reading, which was one of Elizabeth's favorite past times. She had visions of herself all curled up in her large chair in her bedroom enjoying a good romance novel.

She thanked Moira and glanced at each outfit again. Now that she was a bit more relaxed, she could see that each outfit was truly something she would wear for any number of occasions. She decided on the jeans. She wanted to be comfortable and yet still look nice, and this particular combination just spoke to her. Smiling, she requested the items from Moira and began to dress. The cloths she was wearing when she arrived were brought in so she could don her undergarments and rifle through her purse for her makeup. Once she was finished, she opened the door to find Mr. Darcy sitting in a chair enjoying a glass of wine while reading a book. He looked up and smiled at her.

"That was my favorite choice as well," he said as he admired her from his seat. He could feel his balls throbbing just from looking at her. She was glowing and it gave him deep satisfaction to know he had placed that shimmer on her face and the light in her beautiful eyes.

"Thank you so much; really it is too much. I loved it, though. You are too kind. I will reimburse you for the clothes…" Elizabeth rambled feeling overwhelmed by his generosity.

"I don't want your money, Elizabeth. All four ensembles are yours and will be delivered to your home. I just wanted you to choose how the rest of our evening would go." He rose from his seat and gave her a quick motion to spin for him. She followed his command wishing to please him as much as she had been pleased with her day.

"The rest of our evening? Really, there is no need; you can just take me home. You have done so much already." Elizabeth blushed at all the attention that was being lavished on her by this man. Though she loved every moment of it, she also felt a bit awkward in accepting so much from him. They weren't dating, though he seemed to want to. Elizabeth found herself gazing at him with a new found fondness. He really did know her and what she liked. Perhaps she should consider what dating William Darcy might be like. Sure there was the sensual mystery that surrounded him, his obvious suave appearance, and he emanated control and that more than anything concerned her. She was very independent. Darcy began to reply to her protest and it brought her back to the present moment.

"First, I will do no such thing and it is no trouble at all Elizabeth." He smiled. "Second, I said I would deliver you home early after I took you out to dinner. So now that you have chosen where we are going, we should be on our way." He offered her his arm and smiled down at her. "Shall we be off?"

"That sounds wonderful". Elizabeth looked up at his face and inhaling his scent, wrapped her hand about his arm enjoying the strength and feel of his muscles as he escorted her out of the spa and down to the garage below. His Aston Martin was waiting for them, and he quickly had her situated, and then they were off.

Sitting on the butter soft leather, Elizabeth could not remember a time in her life when she felt more relaxed or pampered. William had been wonderful to her, just as he had promised. She looked over at him and noticed he was in a pair of black jeans and a different shirt. "William, when did you change your cloths?"

He smiled as he watched the road. "Moira told me your choice and I came prepared. How about a little music while we drive the restaurant will take about 10 minutes or so to get to." He found a great station, and then placed his hand on her left leg while he continued to drive. She glanced down enjoying the warmth of his hand on her thigh when he spoke and she looked back up to him. "Elizabeth, have I told you how beautiful you look tonight. I will be the envy of every man."

As soon as he said it she blushed and he removed his hand from her leg. She instantly missed it and then asked where they were going.

37

Chapter 7

Darcy had stayed busy while waiting in the spa's private dressing room, wrapping up a few things via his laptop while Elizabeth was being pampered. Richard had called as soon as he was back at the office with a few details from the lunch and to ask how things were progressing with Elizabeth. Richard expressed how much he wished he could join them later but had several issues to handle before the gala tomorrow.

Darcy could not have been more pleased when he noticed the ensemble Elizabeth had chosen. He had a feeling she would opt for that one; it looked like it was made for her. He loved to see her dressed in creams and browns. Those colors complemented the coloring of her skin and the chestnut locks that swirled around her shoulders. And what man could resist skin-tight jeans hugging a woman's shapely ass, especially when her chest was also displayed quite nicely for him to enjoy? The scooped neckline of the cream top dipped just low enough to show some enticing views of Elizabeth's silky skin. The jacket and boots, along with the chucky leather necklace, completed the look he had in mind for her.

He hoped she liked steak; he knew just the place to go for excellent food and a good time. He hoped to kick his heels up with her on the dance floor, if for only just one dance, before taking her home. With that in mind, he had changed, too. By the time she was ready to go, he was dressed in his own jeans and boots with the sleeves of his dress shirt turned up at the cuff.

They arrived at his favorite steak place in town Longbourn's. It was casual fun with a relaxed atmosphere. He figured a little kickin' back was in order, and Elizabeth would be at ease in no time.

"William, if I forget to tell you later, thank you so much; this has been the most wonderful day I have ever had. I can't remember the last time that I pampered myself and just enjoyed the day. Thank you," she said sincerely.

"Elizabeth, your father was the one who offered the day off; I merely took the opportunity to enjoy it with you and make sure that you relaxed. Tomorrow will, no doubt, be a long and tiring day for you. Now, let's get something to eat; I am starved." He turned to exit the car noticing as Elizabeth's radiant smile.

He came around, opened the door, and extended his hand to help her from the vehicle. "I am a bit hungry myself." She stated. "I love a good steak. Do you come here often?" she queried.

"Not as much as I would like, but if I'm in the mood for a great steak and a relaxed atmosphere, this is the place. Richard and I come here from time to time, and I bring my little sister occasionally."

"You have a sister?" Elizabeth asked as she looked towards Darcy, her eyes wide in surprise at the news.

"Yes, Georgie, or rather Georgiana, she loves to come here and two-step. She can't get enough country music, cowboys, and charred flesh." He chuckled.

"Really? That surprises me."

"How so?" Darcy replied in a nonchalant tone.

"I figured the Darcy family, with all its wealth, would frequent the more upscale chop houses in this fair town. I don't quite picture you as the cowboy two-stepping type." She smiled as she slid her eyes towards him with a raised brow.

Chuckling at her assumptions, Darcy addressed her notion. "Well, I can say we do frequent more of the so-called higher end eating establishments about town; I rarely get out to just relax and enjoy myself. I have so many dinner invitations to charity balls, business dinners, political events, and corporate fundraisers that I am, more often than not, found in a suit or tuxedo. Georgiana however, is not one to dress up as often. She works in her own studio as a fashion designer of women and men's western wear. She owns a small studio here in town but has a larger place on our family estate outside of town with an art studio there to work from. We own many horses, and Georgiana spends most of her weekends tending to them and helping in the corrals. Ever since I can remember, she has loved horses," he fondly recalled.

Elizabeth smiled as she listened to Darcy talk so lovingly about his sister. She had never given thought to this man and what family he may have. She knitted her brows together in thought when Darcy stopped walking and turned to face her. "Did I say something wrong?"

Caught off guard, Elizabeth looked up to see the concern on his face. "No, I'm sorry; I was lost in thought. I'm embarrassed to say that I never gave thought to …I mean I never imagined you had…. I'm not saying this well, am I?"

Darcy grinned and decided to help her out. He took her hand and continued to walk "You didn't think a man of my position and wealth, with my prowess in business dealings, could have a family. Is that what you are trying to say?" The corners of his mouth lifted upward into a smile as he teased Elizabeth.

"Well… yes, sort of… I have only seen you in the office or at the affairs you spoke of and just lately at the club dancing, well not even dancing… you just sort of appeared then disappeared. " Blushing and stumbling over her words, Elizabeth turned her face downward, a feeling of discomfort creeping up her spine.

"Well, I am only human, and I hope I can show you just how human I can be. I have no crown or court jesters, mind you. Come on, my stomach is rumbling so loud I might very well pass out from hunger." Elizabeth chuckled as she heard his rumbling stomach on queue, so they picked up the pace.

He took her hand and with his fingers entwined with hers, he pulled her gently alongside of him into the restaurant. The smell of beer, peanuts, and char grilled meat assaulted their senses while the rowdy sounds of the live band on stage filled the room. Darcy whispered into the ear of the hostess, and they were immediately escorted to a corner booth at the back of the main area. It was not very crowded, and a few patrons were on the dance floor, while others enjoyed their meals and companions. "If you don't mind, I would like to order for us both. The chef is a dear friend of the family and prepares something off menu when we come."

"Sure that sounds great. I'm game to try something new. I like my meat medium rare if that matters."

Smiling at Elizabeth, Darcy whispered into the waiter's ear. The man nodded and set a few beers on their table along with a bowl of warmed shelled peanuts before he left to place their order.

"Now, that is service." Elizabeth grinned.

"Like I said, this is a great place. Now, drink up; I intend to have my first dance with you on that floor over there before we leave tonight."

Choking down her first swallow of beer, Elizabeth wiped her mouth and stared wide-eyed at Darcy. "Dance here, as in two-step?"

"Yes, is there a problem?" He said between sips of beer as he watched her reaction.

"I have never danced a two-step; I think I would be a poor partner. You should dance with someone else—I really don't mind." She hastily replied with a bit of nervousness in her voice.

Reaching across the table for her hand, Darcy kissed her knuckles and gave her a smoldering look. "I don't have a problem holding you close and teaching you Elizabeth. Just enjoy your drink for now; I want to eat first. We will dance later."

Darcy went about eating nuts and drinking his beer. Elizabeth enjoyed the band, relaxing as time passed. The music was fun and toe tapping. She got a tingle in the pit of her stomach remembering Darcy's words about holding her close. *Close* described how she was sandwiched between both him and his cousin Richard Fitzwilliam not so long ago. Her nipples perked up, and her lower regions became damp at the mere thought. Heaven help her but she was looking forward to that dance.

*****

Elizabeth could not remember when she had enjoyed a meal more. The food was excellent and the service outstanding. The beers kept coming, and by the time they had chatted about family, business, hobbies and anything else that came to mind, Elizabeth was so relaxed that she felt she had known William for sometime. He was so not what she had thought he was.

William rose and excused himself for a moment while Elizabeth finished her dessert. She savoured every mouthful of the homemade apple crisp with vanilla ice cream. It had hit the spot. She was surveying the couples on the dance floor knowing she would soon be asked to attempt a two-step. She watched the feet of a few couples, trying to imitate the rhythm and timing with her own feet safely hidden under the table.

From across the room, William watched Elizabeth; she had her eye on a young couple dancing close in a two-step. The closer he got, the better his view, and what he saw brought a smile to his face. He could see her feet moving under the table. She was trying to learn the dance. His heart skipped a beat at how wonderful Elizabeth Bennet made him feel. It had been so long since a woman brought him such joy. She was always on his mind—not a day would go by that he didn't think about her in some way; even his dreams were invaded by this lovely creature. That she wanted to please him, made him very happy.

When he reached the table, he stretched out his hand and smiled "Are you ready to two-step now? I see you have been practicing," he toyed with her.

Elizabeth's cheeks flushed at having been caught, but she took his hand, eager to dance with him. They walked to the floor, and Darcy pulled her in front of him, holding her tight to his tall frame. He slid one arm around her waist, and the other held her hand up. "Elizabeth I want you to relax and just let me lead you. This isn't hard, and I do believe a nice slow song is about to start."

"How do you know?"

"I have my ways." He winked at her playfully. The band announced ladies choice and began a slow ballad. Darcy moved smoothly across the floor, his eyes never leaving Elizabeth's. She could feel his body guiding her around the floor. She was so close to his chest, she could see his pulse beat in his neck. His eyes were so clear, so filled with warmth. As they made there way around the floor, she began to pick up the steps and style. It was like floating on a cloud.

William could feel her tension slipping away as they continued across the floor. Her body felt so good next to his. The hand wrapped around her waist felt every breath she took; his chest felt her breasts pressed against him. If he was not mistaken she was aroused for her nipples were tight against him. He slowly lowered his hand down to her backside. Feeling the firm rounded arch of her back and butt cheeks in those tight form hugging jeans. His own body reacted to her and he could feel his balls tightening with need for this woman in his arms.

When the music ended, Darcy leaned in and kissed her cheek gently with his warm lips, then whispered in her ear, "Thank you for trusting me. You did very well for your first attempt at a two-step, you should be proud of yourself."

Elizabeth glanced down for a moment; embarrassed at the praise he bestowed on her, and then smiled up to his awaiting gaze. "I had a patient teacher. Thank you, I have really enjoyed myself today. You have made me feel so comfortable being with you. I can't imagine how much trouble you have gone to for me today."

"It was all my pleasure Elizabeth. I have said it before, I have many things to offer you when you're ready to take the chance." They looked at each other in silence for a split second before he continued. "Well, I think it is time I take you home, Miss Bennet. You have a big day tomorrow, and your father expects you to be well-rested after giving you some much needed time off."

"That he does," she agreed as she gave him a big toothy grin. He wrapped his arm about her shoulder and held her to him as they walked off the dance floor and into the parking lot. They chatted and laughed enjoying each other's company.

*****

Once back at her apartment, Elizabeth let her eyes linger on her home out the car window. Darcy placed his hand on her knee again and she smiled to herself. She loved when he did that. She turned to smile back at him "Thank you again William for everything, the spa, the cloths, the meal, all of it. It has been a day I won't soon forget."

"I was more than happy to Elizabeth. I only wish there had been time for more. How about if I escort you to your door? Just give me a minute." He turned and exited the car walking across the front to her side. She enjoyed watching him move. He opened her door and offered his hand to help her out. She gladly took it and as she stood he pulled her into his arms. "I couldn't let this day end without a proper kiss." He leaned in and took possession of her lips. He was gentle and she melted right into his embrace. When he released her she could feel his body responding to the closeness and it made her head light. What if he wanted to come in?

"Could I interest you in a night cap perhaps?" She asked.

"If I came in Elizabeth, I would not want a night cap. It's best if I let you go in alone tonight. You have a big day tomorrow. Come on, I'll walk you to the door. " He announced. He was being such a gentlemen she thought. Her

43

body began to hum inside as they walked hand in hand in silence; the sexual tension growing between them. She was conflicted as to what she wanted. On one hand he was right, she needed the sleep, but on the other hand her body reacted so well to his every touch, every word. Once at the door he took her key from her and unlocked the door. He stepped in and turned on a light for her.

"Good night Elizabeth. I look forward to dancing with you tomorrow." He kissed her cheek again lingering for a few moments to inhale her scent and then turned to leave. Holding the door, Elizabeth leaned on it as she watched him walk away. She sighed and slowly closed it behind him. Leaning against the slab, she looked around her apartment, which suddenly felt very lonely. What a day it had been. After she took a few breaths she wondered into the kitchen and noticed the number of messages on her answering machine.

Chapter 8

Beep… "Elizabeth I wanted to talk about tomorrow night; please pick up," the familiar male voice sounded stern and demanding.

Elizabeth shook her head. That was the third call from Bill she had so far. She hit the delete button and waited for the next voice message to come across the line.

"Hi, Elizabeth, this is George, and I was wondering when you planned to meet me tomorrow. I received the invitation to the ball you mailed to me, but your note said that you would just see me there. When you get a moment, give me a call. I also wanted to see if you might be interested in perhaps having brunch on Sunday. I hear from Lacey that you have been busting your tail on this ball for some time. I'd like to take you out for a meal once it's all over. Can't wait to hear from you."

Sigh. Who else could possibly call her? This machine had never had so many messages on it before.

Beep,,, "Lizzy, it's Jane, I got what you needed finished, and since I have your car, I take it we're still on for the ride together tomorrow night. I want details, and you know what I mean. Call me."

Beep… "Elizabeth, I will be there to pick you up tomorrow around 3. How could you have left with that man? I swear— if he did anything to make you feel uncomfortable, you let me know. William Darcy is not a man you want to have around. There are things you need to know about him." Bill's voice was strained. She had heard that tone many times in the nine months they were together. As handsome as Bill was, he still had issues with jealousy and letting go.

Bill had taken her in hand at the office shortly after she returned from college, helped her fit in, helped her to see the world in a more adult way by taking her to the opera, the best restaurants, the theater—he even lavished expensive gifts on her. They had started to date a few months after her return. He was always a gentleman, but he knew how to manipulate her; he knew what her weaknesses were. After a while, he became more demanding. She couldn't give him what he wanted' she couldn't move in with him. Sex was good, but something was missing, and no matter how handsome he was, how talented a businessman, Elizabeth needed to break things off and find her way to something she didn't even know how to describe. She cleared all but the last message and waited to hear its contents.

Beep..."Elizabeth I just wanted to tell you how much I enjoyed our afternoon together. It was my pleasure to ensure that you were completely pampered and relaxed and able to enjoy yourself. I hope that you're able to get plenty of sleep tonight, and I look forward to sharing many dances tomorrow evening." The sultry soft voice was warm and wrapped around her body like a blanket. She melted against the counter with a sigh, as she replayed the message a few more times. William Darcy, now that was a man who was confident, sexy as hell and so eager to please her. But did she dare lose herself to a man who might make her forget who she was—an independent woman with a career, a place of her own, and responsibilities. She thought for a moment, remembering the soft gentle kiss he had bestowed upon her at her door, then a sudden shock hit her square in the head and she gasped.

Quickly, she picked up the phone and dialed the familiar digits. "Bill, hi, yes, I'm fine, and no, nothing bad happened. I had a nice relaxing day at the spa. Please, Bill, I don't want to hear it right now; I'm tired and ready to go to sleep. Listen; about tomorrow... since I took off this afternoon, I'm going to take myself to the hotel. I have so much to do, and I will need to spend most of the afternoon setting up. No, I don't need your help. I will be fine. Thank you, but I will drive myself. I will see you there, okay? Good night, Bill." She hung up the phone, her exhaustion from the day rapidly overtaking her body. Talking with Bill Collins had zapped the last of her will to stand upright.

Elizabeth peeled herself out of her jeans, smiling as she looked down at them and remembering how she came to own them and what that day had entailed. Pulling on a comfortable soft short pale pink gown with spaghetti straps, Elizabeth slid under her sheets and shut off the lights. Staring at the dark ceiling, she remembered how it felt to dance next to William... was it only an hour ago? How his body held her securely, guiding her around the dance floor. She was eager to repeat that tomorrow night at the ball, many times over she thought with a smile, perhaps he would kiss her again to She was starting to really enjoy how William Darcy took such care of her.

*****

"Jane, thanks for meeting me here. I'm so sorry if I caused you any trouble. Charles wasn't terribly upset, was he?"

"No, he understands. He is going to meet me here later for a light dinner before we have to start getting dressed. He really is the best of men, Lizzy. Now, I haven't heard anything about yesterday. You know that once I returned to the table alone, Bill almost came unglued?"

"Oh, I can just imagine. He left me five messages at home." Elizabeth said with a roll of her eyes.

"No, he didn't?" Jane almost dropped her jaw as he spoke.

"Jane, he is having a hard time with 'no' and a harder time letting go, if you haven't figured that out. Bill Collins is a beautiful man to look at, but once you get past that suit and find the man deep down inside, he just isn't the man for me."

"Lizzy, just be careful. Father thinks very highly of him. I think Bill wanted to take you to the lake house next week, but father said it was your call to make." Jane's worried looked caused her to grow angry with Bill for making her sister worry.

"What! I will not go to the lake house with him. He just wants to persuade me to get back together with him and move in, perhaps marry me. He knows my weakness is being up there in that house. I just love it there so much Jane. You don't think ill of me for turning him down and breaking things off do you? "

"Lizzy you have your reasons. I can't tell you how to live your life, anymore than I can tell you what to wear. Now how about we get busy so we have time to eat and make you look drop dead gorgeous for tonight. I understand your dance card is filling up fast." Jane turned up her lips with a raised brow, lightly tapping Elizabeth in the ribs with her elbow, letting Elizabeth know just how popular she apparently was becoming.

Elizabeth smiled and agreed. She loved her sister so much. She was hoping that Charles Bingley would pop the question soon. They had been together for almost a year, and tonight it was rumored that Charles would be bringing his sister to the ball. No one had met her yet, but Elizabeth was hopeful that she would make a great sister-in-law for her beloved sibling. Charles was so easygoing and down to earth. She was so happy that they had found each other.

*****

"Lizzy…" the word slipped out as a gasp on a whisper as Jane gazed upon her younger sister.

"Jane, is it okay? Did I rip something? I don't know if I could fit anything else into this dress." Elizabeth tried to not get any more frazzled than she already was. She had spent the entire day working with security and the hotel staff. Her back ached, and her feet were already a bit swollen from the day's hectic schedule. A little over two hours ago, she and Jane had quickly enjoyed a light meal in a small café in the hotel with Charles Bingley, before heading up to prepare for the big night. Elizabeth hoped she had chosen the right dress. It was a deep blood-red color; the neckline plunged down past her breasts but only showed a moderate amount of cleavage. The top of the dress wrapped around her neck like a halter, and it was backless down to just above her lower back. The fabric fell in a shimmer to the floor where it flowed into a short train at the back, just enough to lend elegance when she walked. It had clean lines, and she felt like a million dollars in it.

"Lizzy, you are simply breath taking. I have never seen you look lovelier. If you had a space on your dance card, it would be filled the minute you make an appearance in that dress."

"Jane, please, look at you? Your golden hair and those soft blue eyes, how can I compete with that body-hugging royal blue scrap of cloth you call a dress? You have always been the beauty of the family," Elizabeth pronounced with an air of awe in her wording.

"Not tonight Lizzy, I mean it; turn around and look." Jane walked up behind her sister, and they both just stared into the mirror.

"OH! Jane, look at us." Her voice catching as she softly spoke.

"I know. I hope that Mr. Darcy is the one for you, Lizzy. He seems so taken with you."

"Jane, I have such mixed feelings. I love the mystery. I love how he showers me with attention, but he is older and worldlier than I am. What if I can't live up to his expectations? I'm…. not bold and have always had a problem voicing my wants and needs. What if I loose myself if I were to take a chance with him."

"Elizabeth Bennet, don't you short change yourself. You walked away from Bill Collins when you knew how much father and mother approved of him. You have craved George Wickham since I can't remember when, and as handsome as that man is, I don't think that he is what you need, either. Deep down, I think you know what you want. You need a man Lizzy, a real man. You have such a spirit about you. You live to love life. You have accomplished so many things. It is I who is not as brave as you," Jane said in a firm but loving tone. She turned to her sister and took hold of her hands and looked her in the eyes, "Go out there tonight and enjoy what you have worked so hard to create. Be the princess of the ball, Lizzy. Let your prince sweep you off your feet. you know I love you no matter what you decide. He is a good man; I just know it. Give him a chance to show you how good he can be."

Elizabeth felt her eyes welling with tears at the unexpected praise from her sister. She released Jane's hands so she could give her a tight squeeze. Both sisters giggled nervously before they looked once more into the big mirrored vanity. "Ok, then let's do this!" she said with determination. Jane nodded her agreement and off they went.

*****

Bill Collins was pacing the foyer near the elevators. He would make damn sure he escorted Elizabeth into that ball so that no one got the idea she was available. He would help Elizabeth see that he was the man for her. He wanted to marry her, and he wanted her family business for himself. No Darcy would take what was his, what he had worked so hard for over the last twelve years. He was Mr. Bennet's right hand man, a man to be trusted, a man who knew this business inside and out; and he wanted the hand of the prettiest daughter on his arm. She was beautiful, had a smart head on her shoulders, and she seemed to be submissive enough to do just as she was told. He still couldn't believe she broke things off with him after the nine months he had invested in her. He all but proposed to her. He would make her see that he was the best man, and that William Darcy was just a sick animal. He had dirt on him and that cousin of his, and if he had to, he would use it.

The elevator tone chimed, signaling its arrival, and the doors opened to reveal both Elizabeth and her sister Jane. "Ladies, I waited so that I might escort you both into the ball. Some of the guests have started to arrive already," he said coolly with a smile on his face.

"Bill, that is very nice of you, but I have to meet someone. Jane, I'll catch up with you later." Elizabeth turned quickly and started to stroll down to the main lobby.

"Elizabeth, wait I'll come with you," he called after her, leaving Jane as she rolled her eyes and moved towards the ballroom doors.

"Bill, really, I don't need you to follow me. I have someone to meet; I'll be in shortly. Just go on without me."

"No, a lady dressed as you are tonight should not be left unattended. You never know who might be lurking around. I don't mind."

Elizabeth stopped short and turned to face Bill. He did look handsome; his best black tuxedo fitted his frame very nicely. She could smell his cologne, a familiar and masculine scent she always found appealing. He had dark hair trimmed close to his head and chocolate brown eyes. There were moments when she still thought of him and what they shared. She had believed in the beginning that he was what she wanted in a man. However, the possessiveness he had demonstrated had made a relationship impossible. He needed to quit treating her as if she were still involved with him.

"Bill, we are no longer together. I need for you to stop following me, calling me, and just let me be. I am moving on, and so should you. Please, I don't want to offend you, but I don't need you following me. I am meeting someone. I don't owe you any explanations, nor do I need you to babysit me. Do you understand?" She looked into his eyes trying to will him to comprehend that their relationship was over.

"Liz, let me just warn you again. Stay away from Will Darcy. He is not what you want. He has a dark side you could not even begin to imagine. I would strongly urge you to check into his personal life before you do something rash." His voice was low and heated. He stared back at Elizabeth with great intent in his eyes before he turned and stalked off.

Blowing out a deep breath, Elizabeth shook her head and tried to put what he had just said out of her mind. What did he mean *William Darcy had a dark side*? Why did things always have to get in the way of her happiness? If it was not one thing, it was another. Caught in her own thoughts, she started when a hand touched her shoulder.

"Elizabeth," came the masculine voice behind her.

*****

Darcy knew that tonight was important. He would have most of the dances with Elizabeth, but that left a few available to other men in attendance. It would be wrong of him to expect too much from her; this was after all, a business function. She had a job to perform. William had called Richard earlier in the day to make arrangements for them to ride over together in his limo. Now that they were en route to Richards's apartment, Darcy tried to formulate a plan. He needed Elizabeth to be just as comfortable with Richard as she seemed to be with him. Convincing Richard that he needed to tone down his charm would be a task.

He and his cousin had found many years ago that they had an appreciation for the same type of woman. Richard figured on being a bachelor all his life now that he had been burned. He loved women, many women. Darcy could not fault the man's taste. They had shared on a few occasions. There had even been one woman who came close to capturing Richards's heart a little more than two years ago. Darcy was unsure if he wished his best friend to find that one love to last a lifetime. Richard was a free spirit. He loved that about him. Richard was almost the opposite of himself. He needed Richard to give him those pushes, to help him bridge the gap between his business and personal life. On that same note, Richard needed the stability Darcy offered him—the control, the business end of things, the ability to see that life needed some structure, some boundaries. Richard needed someone to remind him to take it slow when he was recklessly headed into something before he had thought it over well enough. They were great for each other, and there was no one he trusted more in life.

The limo pulled up to Matlock Manor, and the driver opened the door to Richard.

"Good evening, Cousin," Richard happily announced. "Are you ready for this wonderful night to get started?"

"Yes, I think I am. Can I get you a drink? You seem quit chipper this evening, Richard. I suppose all your business dealings are well in hand so that you can enjoy the benefit tonight."

"Indeed, they are. So tell me Darcy, are you really ready for this evening?"

Darcy smiled his dashing grin, and the two started to plan. It was going to be an evening for Elizabeth to remember if he had anything to do with it.

51

Chapter 9

"Father, how good to see you." Elizabeth breathed a sigh of relief. Bill had finally left. Her father had arrived just in time, and she turned to give him a big squeeze.

"Is everything okay, child? What is Bill so angry about? Is there anything I can do to help?"

"No, I'm fine. There is nothing to worry about. Bill is going on ahead. Are you ready to be introduced? Mary is manning the stage tonight; Lydia is at the front door with name badges to greet everyone; and Catherine is handling the kitchen to make sure all goes well. Jane as always is on the floor mingling with our clients. I believe mother is off tending to the bar." Elizabeth chuckled at her last statement.

"Well, that is where she normally finds herself, now isn't it? Come, let me see all your wonderful work." They started towards the big ballroom doors with arms linked. "I am pleased that you took my offer to relax yesterday afternoon. I understand from Jane that Mr. Darcy escorted you from the restaurant." He looked with a raised brow at his favorite daughter.

"Father, not now." Elizabeth gave him a warning glance.

"Well, then let me just say before we are besieged by patrons of this lovely affair, Mr. Darcy is from a fine family. His father and I go way back. He has a good head for business; he is honest and trustworthy; and if you care what this old man thinks, then I would heartily give you my blessing if anything were to come of this, whatever it may be. I may be old, but I have ears and eyes, daughter."

Elizabeth stopped and turned to her father. She studied him for a moment, and then placed a kiss on his cheek. "Thank you, father, but there is nothing going on. Now, if you don't mind, we have money to raise."

*****

"Oh really, then Catherine, what should we do? This was your one responsibility; why must I see to everything?" Elizabeth was enraged. Not only was Lydia off flirting and dancing with all the eligible men, Mary had somehow lost the keys to unlock the stage cage where the microphones were encased for the night's entertainment. Now it appeared, that the kitchen was short by about six servers and the wine was running low. This was not the way Elizabeth had envisioned her evening going. Luckily, Jane was keeping things running smoothly for the guests. If just one more thing went wrong, Elizabeth was going to scream.

She flew out of the kitchen and right smack into William Darcy. "Oh, my gosh! I'm so *so* sorry! Mr. Darcy, please let me help you."

Elizabeth began to wipe the spilled Champaign from his lapel when he caught her hand in his. "I'm fine, really; there is no need in that. You appear to be a bit out of sorts. Let me help you, Elizabeth; take a deep breath and look at me." His voice was smooth and calm, nothing akin to how Elizabeth currently felt.

She stopped and looked up into his eyes. They were warm and welcoming, and she inhaled slowly so that she could settle her mind and take in all he had to say. "There now, that's better, isn't it?" He gave her a small smile.

Elizabeth nodded. "I really am sorry, I should have been more careful," she explained in a softer voice.

"Come, let me get you a drink, and then perhaps I could have one of my *many* promised dances, and you can forget whatever crisis you're faced with for just a moment. You did promise me *most* of your dance card remember." He flashed her a dashing smile and placed his hand to her lower back to guide her towards the bar. In the distance, Elizabeth could see her mother. She cringed at what might come out of her mouth if she saw Mr. Darcy escorting her.

"Perhaps we could just go dance," she tried to persuade him.

"I think you need the drink first, Elizabeth. Have I told you how absolutely stunning you look in that dress? Red is so becoming on you." His eyes glittered, and his smile melted her tension.

Blushing at his words, Elizabeth looked down and thanked him. "Lizzy, there you are! Did Catherine tell you we are running out of wine? Really, you would think that this place would know that when the Bennet's host a gala, they need to be prepared. It's so unlike you Lizzy, to let something like this happen."

53

"Mother, if I may, I would like to introduce you to Mr. William Darcy." Elizabeth tried to quickly cover for her mother's outburst.

"Ah, Mr. Darcy, so good to meet you. I have had the pleasure of meeting your father. Very nice man. He was always such a great dancer. You must take my Lizzy out for a spin. She is single, you know."

Embarrassed beyond belief, Elizabeth tried to escape with some dignity intact. She was afraid to look in Darcy's direction for fear of what would be in his expression. "Thank you, Mrs. Bennet. My father has long been known for being light on his feet. I was just coming to get Miss Bennet a drink before I escorted her out to the floor. What would you suggest, madam? I am sure your taste is exceptional." He quickly covered for Elizabeth's apparent affront from her mother.

Elizabeth was floored by the way William Darcy was handling her mother. He must be the most tolerant man in the world. She watched in fascination as her mother became flustered and ordered two glasses of champagne. Darcy thanked her and quickly led Elizabeth away from the offending parent.

"Mr. Darcy, I must apologies for my mother. She means well; it just never seems to come out as such."

"There is no need to apologies to me. She loves you dearly, I am sure. I am however more concerned about you and want to make this evening better for you in any way that I can. Come, let's go over there, and we can enjoy our drinks in relative peace. I would love to hear all about your day and why you came barreling out of the kitchen. Don't get me wrong — a man loves to be bowled over by a gorgeous woman." He winked down at her up turned face and quickly had her nestled into a quiet corner off to the side of the stage.

They enjoyed a few sips of their drinks while Elizabeth retold some of her evening so far. The next thing she knew, Richard Fitzwilliam had come up to speak with them. "Good Evening Miss Bennet. I wanted to tell you how much I appreciate all the hard work you have done in putting together yet another Gala. My man in charge tonight has had nothing but the most flattering things to say about you and your company. The preparations have been marvelous, and I see nothing that would interfere with the success of tonight's festivities." He smiled, having paid her the best compliment of the night so far. He was relaxed and looked like a million bucks. He had a glass in his hand and offered up a toast to Elizabeth. All three clinked their glasses and each took a sip of the sparkling French wine.. They chatted about the crowd and the expected donations that would benefit each company. Before long, the band found their microphones and began to play. Elizabeth was starting to relax and enjoy herself when Richard asked her to dance.

"Miss Bennet, if I might have the honor of a dance. I'm sure Mr. Darcy wouldn't mind." Richard took her glass and gave it to Darcy. He took her hand in his and turned her towards the floor. Elizabeth glanced over her shoulder to say with her eyes how sorry she was. Darcy smiled and nodded his approval to her. He loved how she swayed in that blood red dress as she walked away. He could hardly wait to dance with her next.

*****

Near the stage, Bill Collins watched as Darcy escorted Elizabeth to the bar and then the far corner. She seemed to relax instantly when she was around him. She actually seemed to enjoy his company, and that angered Bill. Elizabeth was his, and he would see that she remained so.

"Mr. Collins, how good to see you this evening."

Turning to see his boss standing next to him, Bill spoke, "Mr. Bennet, I believe Elizabeth has created yet another successful event for our company. I only hope that she is not spending too much time with Mr. Darcy. She has a roll to play and needs to mingle with our guests."

"Bill, I don't want you to worry about Elizabeth. She is old enough to handle herself, and after putting such an event together almost singled handedly, if she wanted to dance the night way and have a few drinks, I would be more than happy to see her do so. She has worked very hard over these last few months." There was a slight pause before he continued to speak as he watched his lovely daughter dance. "I hate to say it, but perhaps her leaving you was the best thing for her."

Shocked at what he had heard, Bill turned to voice his uncertainty at the remark, "Do you? I was hoping that she would rethink my offer and move in with me. I love your daughter, sir; I have never given you or her a reason to believe otherwise. I am as dedicated to her as I am to the success of this company. She just needs a little more time to reconsider the offer. I fully intend to have her as my wife."

Mr. Bennet listened to his most trusted man; a man he knew could lead his company if he were to marry one of his daughters. But they, not him, would inherit the family business. From all he had heard from Jane and from what he himself had witnessed, Elizabeth was not going to return to the arms of Bill Collins. Before things turned ugly, Mr. Bennet thought to give Bill a little advice.

"Bill, as Elizabeth's father, I would have you consider my daughter's feelings before you make any rash moves. She seems very happy and content in her present situation. If you badger her or push her, she will put up her walls. You, of all people, should know how her mind works. If I were you, I would let her go. I hear you when you say you love her. But sometimes, when we love someone, we have to let them go and be happy with what they choose. That is the most selfless thing to do for those we love." With that, Mr. Bennet squeezed Bill's shoulder and walked away.

*****

Darcy stood in the corner for a few more moments watching Richard and Elizabeth dance. Richard was on his best behavior and being his charming self. Darcy trusted him implicitly; they were much alike in many ways. Darcy knew it was important for Elizabeth to have a connection with Richard. He knew Richard found Elizabeth to be beautiful and smart; he appreciated her business sense and how she handled herself. But both men knew that just under all her control was a woman screaming to be released. A woman who had not yet identified her inner strength and desires. A woman they both wanted to show the world.

He began to drift amongst the crowd speaking with clients, friends and acquaintances he knew. He had just finished speaking to an old family friend when a woman's voice caught his attention.

"William Darcy, you are a sight for sore eyes. How long has it been?" The silky soft voice was one he knew well. He and Richard had been pulled into this woman's spell a few years ago. The relationship had lasted close to a year, but all had parted on friendly terms. He turned to find this woman just as sexy as the day she left for Paris.

"Caroline Stanton... It's been a long time." He smiled at her but didn't make a move otherwise.

"It's back to Bingley; my divorce was final a few months back. I see you're still the bell of the ball. Do you ever *not* attend a Gala, Will?"

56

"Rarely happens, as you are well aware. I am sorry to hear about your divorce. How are you? How is your career? I have not kept up with the tabloids, magazine, or internet fodder, I'm sorry to say."

She smiled but questioned him in return, "I wouldn't have expected you to. Now tell me who is that beauty that is dancing with that charming cousin of yours. She is rather fetching."

Darcy turned to see Richard and Elizabeth smiling at each other. His heart leaped at the fact that they were getting along so well. He turned back to Caroline, a grin spread across his lips. "That is Elizabeth Bennet. She is the lady who has put all of this together. She is also the daughter of the owner who is a close family friend to my father and a business associate of mine."

"And I would have to say by the looks of that smile, you are either seeing the lovely Miss Bennet or soon will be."

"I will be. What brings you to town?" Darcy tried to turn the tables and get some information from Caroline.

"My brother is going to ask a lady to marry him. He wanted me here, and I figured it was time for a visit. I had hoped to find you without any attachments for old time's sake, but I see that is not a possibility considering that smile on your face or how your eyes hardly leave that girl. So instead, would you give an old friend a spin out on the dance floor?"

Darcy nodded and took her hand. He wanted to get this over with so that he could dance with Elizabeth. He had waited long enough.

Chapter 10

Richard and Elizabeth were leaving the dance floor when she noticed Darcy dancing with another woman. She was the most striking woman she had ever seen. She was tall, thin, and had the perfect body. Her radiant auburn hair fell in long flowing curls down her back. The backless silk dress she had on was a dark hunter green. It fell to just below her hips. Elizabeth thought Darcy held her a little too close as they danced. The woman was obviously comfortable with him as she smiled and flirted. Even from this distance, it made Elizabeth a bit jealous not to be the one at his side.

"Richard, who is that woman that William is dancing with? I have never seen her around." She tried to keep a check on her voice, but there was a slight tremble in it.

Richard scanned the dance floor, and then he saw her. His heart stopped for a moment, as he knew exactly who that was. It had been a year or more since he had said goodbye to her. She looked wonderful. He glanced down to see Elizabeth intently staring at the pair. He knew Darcy would not wish for her to concern herself with Caroline Bingley so he placed his hand on her back and whispered into her ear. "That is Caroline, and we both know her. She must be in town visiting. She moved to Paris over two years ago, I believe. She married shortly after from what I understand. There is nothing to concern yourself with, I promise." His voice was velvet soft, and he pressed his hand to her lower back to comfort her as best he could under the current circumstances.

Not sure he had convinced her since her eyes were still leveled at the two on the floor, he decided to act, and began to move back to the floor with Elizabeth at his side. His hand gently caressed her lower back to give her some security, as he guided her towards the pair. He could feel her tension, and he wanted nothing more than to reassure her that she was whom they wanted not Caroline. "Well, aren't you a sight for sore eyes! Caroline, it has been too long." He spoke in a clear cheerful voice so that the couple could hear him.

They stopped dancing and turned to greet Richard. "Richard, how good to see you. It has been a long time." She reached her arms out and pulled him close to her for a welcoming hug. Elizabeth watched in silence, feeling awkward. Even up close, the woman was gorgeous, with no visible flaws.

Her eyes were just as green as her dress; her skin so creamy and smooth, Why did she ever go to Paris if she had dated either one of these men? Darcy noticed Elizabeth's discomfort and thought to see if he could get any clues from Richard as to what was bothering her, but Richard began to speak before he was able to get a word in.

"I know my cousin is the best dancer in town, but I wonder if I could possibly step in to finish this dance? I wouldn't want to miss an opportunity, especially before the rest of the men here decide to see what they have before them." He was charming, and Elizabeth began to understand what he was doing. "Elizabeth, you don't mind if I take an old friend out for a spin, do you?"

"No, not at all," she replied.

"Then if you will excuse me..." He smiled down at her and squeezed her hand as he took Caroline into his arms and began to dance.

Darcy bridged the gap between Elizabeth and him swiftly. She looked down at the floor, her hands clasped in front of her. With a rush of civility Elizabeth didn't think she had at that moment, she glanced up to William and in a small voice said, "She is a beautiful woman. Richard told me you both knew her, and that she has been in Paris for some time."

With a commanding face and soulful eyes that bore into her, William tried to convey his deep and true feelings without overstepping his bounds. His voice low and even, he began slowly, "Yes, I know her, and yes, she has been in Paris; it was her choice to move and pursue a career. I have had no contact over these last few years with her, I was surprised to see her here myself. She asked me to dance with her for old time's sake since she knew instantly that I would not be interested in her in any way other than as a friend." He would not lie to her; he respected her too much. He wanted Elizabeth to understand that she need not be jealous of any other woman of his acquaintance. He could see by the rise in her brows that she began to understand what his reply just implied. "Elizabeth, I have not yet had my first dance with you. You did promise me the majority of your dance card. Would you care to join me? I believe this song is about over." He took her hand in his, using his thumb to caress her knuckles, and waited for her answer. His smile was heartfelt.

Though the woman he had been dancing with made Elizabeth feel self-conscious and a bit jealous, she had been looking forward all day long to dancing with William tonight.

Staring at their hands and how they fit together, she glimpsed up to his waiting eyes and nodded with a small smile. He ushered her further out onto the floor, making his way to the center. As the current song ended and couples began to leave the floor, he whispered into her ear, "Elizabeth, I have to tell you something; one, I only have eyes for you, and two, do you know the Argentine Tango?"

The warmth of his breath across her ear made her body come to attention. His hands ran down the sides of her arms to take both hands in his. He pulled back slightly to see her reaction to his declaration, and the blush on her face so sweet, he just wanted to hug her to him and kiss her deeply.

When the next song started, all Elizabeth could think of in that instant was that William Darcy wanted to dance with her. She placed one hand in his, feeling the large palm settle up next to hers, his warm fingers wrapping around her own as he held her tightly to him with his free arm. William's strength radiated through her while her other hand lay softly on his muscular shoulder. Quickly she tuned into the beat, the music reached into her soul and began to make her blood simmer slowly as Darcy started to move. She was never more thankful for all those ballroom dance lessons her mother had insisted she and her sisters take while they were growing up.

The beat was fast, sensual, and with his eyes locking onto hers, William whispered, "Feel the music Elizabeth; let go and let me lead you. Let me show you what it is to be with the one person who knows what you need." The words came off his lips like fine melted chocolate, smooth and warm. Elizabeth closed her eyes for just a moment, soaking in the rhythm. Then he moved forward, taking her backwards across the floor with power and determination, while at the same time being thoughtful and encouraging her to trust in him.

"Elizabeth, open your eyes; let me see your thoughts reflecting in them," he crooned. With his body pressed close to hers, he quickly began to lead her, and the sensual battle began to take shape. They moved fluidly, feet and arms in time with the music. "Yes Elizabeth, show me; show me what you have inside of you. Let your body speak where no words can."

Elizabeth felt as if she were in a movie, the way he looked at her, gave her strength and confidence as they danced across the floor. It was as if no one else were there, it was just the two of them, the song, the dance, the exchanging of looks and a promise of what was to come — if she were brave enough to accept it.

Darcy continued his sensual seduction across the dance floor. He lifted Elizabeth in a circular motion then he dipped her. She ran her hands down his chest and arched back for his eyes to behold her breasts offered up to him; he licked his lips and ran a hand down between them as the song continued. When she eased up, both of her hands were on his chest, and the flare in his eyes was not lost upon her. On they danced, moving around the center of the dance floor while couples stood back in awe, watching them.

From the corner Bill observed them, his teeth grinding in anger. That was going to be his wife, and he would find a way to make that man pay for putting her on display at a gala with others watching. He would expose Darcy's depraved desires and tastes; he would see to it that Elizabeth knew it all. No man would take from him what he had worked so hard to earn.

Watching from the bar, George Wickham could not but help notice the scene unfolding in the center of the dance floor; he could feel his own groin pulsing as he gazed upon Elizabeth. How was it that he had never noticed her before? William used to be a friend of his, and now all he could think of was to posses what his friend wanted. Darcy always got everything, while he was left with nothing. Even once his own father had hired him into the family business, George was not the man his father had hoped he would be. He was well off for sure, but Darcy — Darcy was beyond prosperous. George would beat him at something. Elizabeth would be the one way he could beat Darcy. She had always wanted him, Lacey made sure to tell him weekly what a fool he was to let a girl like her get away. Having grown up with Elizabeth in his house, he knew her as an awkward teenager; he wanted nothing to do with his sister's best friend until he noticed Darcy watching her. Now, he would have to up the ante and make sure he claimed Elizabeth as his.

Richard enjoyed the short dance with Caroline, but from the corner of his eye, he could see William and Elizabeth in the center of the dance floor. They were wonderful together. He loved how they moved and enjoyed watching them become the music, the dance. He wanted to take her in his arms and do the same. He wanted to have Elizabeth melt against him, to trust him as she trusted his cousin. He turned to see Collins across the room with heat radiating from his face. He was livid; he could tell that from this distance. Not wanting him to cause a scene, Richard strode across the room after excusing himself from Caroline.

*****

Mr. Bennet watched all the men in his daughters' lives. He knew with five daughters to marry, he would be very careful in the blessings he gave out to those who would become his daughter's husbands. There was, after all, a family fortune and business to consider. He was a fair man and a good father. He hardly ever denied his daughters what they wanted. With Lydia moving to LA soon, he would have to hire someone to trail her. Of all his daughters, Lydia worried him the most. She was so vivacious, so fast to trust and fall in love, he worried she would be harmed.

Catherine was a sweet girl, always happy to help the family and content to fill supportive roles when called upon at the office. Mary was his accounting whiz. She had been working with the CFO for many years, and upon the man's retiring, she would be prepared to take over the position. Then there was Jane. Jane was a vision, her lovely features and kind heart made it very easy for all of those around her to love her. Jane worked on the marketing aspects of the company. She was great at what she did; he knew that one day, she would leave however. Jane wanted a family, and if her current beau had anything to say, she would be walking down the aisle soon. He had kept an eye on Charles Bingley for some time. They had been dating for quite a while and with the arrival of the man's sister from Paris, it meant that a proposal must be forthcoming.

His last daughter Elizabeth was his pride and joy. They had so much in common. He loved how they could easily enjoy long walks together on a warm spring day, play chess for hours, read some of the same books and talk about them over coffee on Sunday afternoons. He would miss his Lizzy most of all. He had been pleased when, after returning from college to work for him, Bill had shown an immediate interest in her and taken her under his wing. It had led to a personal relationship for her that he was happy with. Bill Collins was his Chief of Operations, and someone he felt was very loyal and trustworthy. Since he knew it would be Elizabeth who would ultimately take his place as the CEO when he retired, he liked the fact that she would have a man well placed to be her confidante within the company. However, Elizabeth felt otherwise after dating Bill for most of a year. He was saddened at the split, but understood her need to go out and be alone and find what she was missing in life. Now with the appearance of William Darcy who was seemingly trying to woo his second daughter into dating him, he was very much encouraged.

Yes, there had always been talk of what William and his cousin Richard enjoyed in their private lives. He was best friends with William's father

George Darcy for most of his life. They often talked about their children. He never would have thought that a man of William's taste and worldly experiences would want Elizabeth as a potential mate, but upon closer thought, she would be perfect for him. They would have so much to share and learn from each other.

Taking a sip of his wine, Mr. Bennet smiled as he watched his daughter tango across the floor. He thought she had never looked more beautiful than at this moment. It was as if her heart had found its mate, and his own chest burst with joy for her. He glanced around the room and noticed the others watching them. He was so proud of her. When he came to Bill Collin, his face registered a frown. Bill was very agitated and, by the looks of it, Richard Fitzwilliam was about to take matters into his own hands. He prayed nothing would go wrong; the night had been such a success so far.

*****

"Oh Lizzy, can you believe it, I'm engaged!" The pure joy in Jane's face made Elizabeth squeeze her sister in a tight hug.

"Oh Jane, I knew he could not be so wonderful for nothing. Where is Charles? William, did you see, my sister is engaged!" she exclaimed with bright shiny eyes.

"Congratulations, Miss Bennet. I'm sure you will have many years of wedded bliss. Let me go and grab a few glasses of champagne, and we will have a toast."

"Thank you, William, that would be wonderful." Elizabeth beamed.

Once Darcy had left, the sisters squealed in delight. "Oh Lizzy, I'm so happy; I want you to be as happy as I am."

"Jane, no one could ever be as happy as you. Father will be overjoyed, I just know it."

"Lizzy, when I came into the ballroom, I saw you with Mr. Darcy on the dance floor. I can't believe your cloths have not melted off from the scorchingly hot way you two were pressed up against each other. The Tango is such a sensual dance. Are you just buzzing with excitement of your own?" Jane was expectant, and with her two eyes begging for details, Lizzy had to share just a bit of her feeling.

"Jane, William is so.... he is so amazing. That was the most intoxicating dance I have ever had. The man is so commanding, so masculine, so..." she sighed as she thought, "perfect," her eyes taking on a dreamy look.

"Lizzy, I'm so happy for you. He is a good man. Father has known his family for so long. He will be so pleased."

"I don't know, Jane. I don't know if I should date a man with such an alpha persona. I mean, I'm very independent, and I don't think he wants an independent woman."

"Excuse me ladies, I have your drinks. A toast to happiness, to love, to the new experiences life has to offer."

Both sisters raised their glasses. "CHEERS!" they cried as they all smiled and clinked their glasses, sipping at the bubbly refreshment.

Charles found his love, and they chatted happily for a few moments before Charles whisked her away to meet his sister.

"Elizabeth, I wanted to say that I overheard your concerns about dating me. I hope that you will allow me the opportunity to talk with you about them. Tonight isn't that time but soon. I want you to just relax and enjoy all that you have accomplished here tonight. I have it on good authority that the funds being raised have almost exceeded last year's. I am very pleased, and I believe your father will be as well."

"Thank you." Elizabeth looked around at all that was going on. So many of the faces were people that she knew, and everyone seemed to be having a wonderful time. She had not heard from any of her sisters, so whatever horrors had been going on must have been handled. She turned back to Darcy and smiled. "William, thank you. This night has been very special for me and, thanks to you, I have been able to smile through it all."

William leaned down next to her ear so that she could hear him clearly. "Elizabeth, the night is not nearly over. I have many more dances, and after that, I would like the opportunity to escort you home." She could feel her heart speed up at his breathy remarks. He was so close; she wanted to turn her head just ever so slightly so he would kiss her. She wanted to be kissed. She wanted to run her hands down his chest. she wanted very much for him to take her home.

With lowered lashes and a blush to her cheeks, Elizabeth inhaled sharply. "William, I believe this next dance belongs to you."

Chapter 11

Richard had just seen to the removal of Bill Collins when Mr. Bennet came around the corner. "I take it that Mr. Collins had too much to drink tonight, Mr. Fitzwilliam. Surprising too … he is always so conservative with his liquor at these events. I wish to thank you for tending to him. It would have been a shame to have had Elizabeth's hard work ruined by someone who was less than at his best."

"Yes, I heartily agree with you, Mr. Bennet. I think that Mr. Collins will sleep it off. I had a couple of my men escort him home so that he would not find himself in any unfortunate incidences on his way there. I would like to congratulate you on your daughter's fine work here. It seems that the donations have increased quite a bit from last year. As always, it is a pleasure to team up with you for such a worthy cause. If you will excuse me, I should get back inside."

"Yes, please don't let me hold you up. Give my regards to Mr. Darcy and tell my daughter I expect her to call me in the morning." With a nod of his head, Mr. Bennet turned and re-entered the ballroom. Richard smiled to himself and left to find the charming Elizabeth Bennet and hopefully to have one last dance with her. He had missed so much of the evening dealing with Bill Collins. He was sure Darcy would wish to hear what he had to say on the matter, but that could wait until tomorrow.

*****

Richard entered the ballroom and noticed that George Wickham was dancing with Elizabeth. He found Darcy huddled in a corner drinking a glass of wine, his eyes glued to Elizabeth. "Darcy, why is Wickham with her on the dance floor?"

"You know as well as I do that she is here to work. His father's company is a contributor, and they have provided marketing materials. I am sure it is nothing," he said, his voice laced with grit.

"If it were nothing, you would not be staring so hard at his back as if you were throwing daggers. He is holding her rather close, is he not? Would you like me to go cut in? I would be more than happy to. I have not had but the one dance with her tonight."

"Where have you been? Caroline was looking for you earlier; did she find you?"

"No, she didn't find me, which is just fine, and I was with Collins. I had to have a little chat with him, and then he had to be escorted out. But that is news that can wait for another time. Our girl is on the dance floor with that lowlife. Come Darcy, I cannot stand by and watch it another minute. Look at his hands all over her." Richard's voice was rising higher with each remark. He was not about to watch a woman he cared for mauled by a man of George Wickham's ilk. He snorted and took off across the dance floor.

Tapping George on the shoulder, he said in as nice a way as he possibly could under the circumstances, "Pardon me, but might I cut in? I have only had one dance with the lady, and the band is about to close out for the night."

"Well, I think the lady is fine with her current partner. I have not had the pleasure of dancing with her much myself," he replied in a passive tone.

"Gentlemen, if I could interject. I think I will say good night to you both. I really should check on how the evening is wrapping up. You don't mind, do you, George?" Elizabeth did not wish to have them fight in front of her. She smiled sweetly at George and dropped her arms away from him.

"Of course, I understand. Are we still on for brunch tomorrow?" George asked for Richard's benefit, expecting an easy confirmation.

"I don't think so; I'm sorry. Jane just got engaged tonight; I believe I will be with my family tomorrow celebrating. But thank you for the invitation. If you gentlemen will excuse me…" Elizabeth quickly made her escape. She had an unpleasant awkward feeling while dancing with George just now. It was not like their date; he was different somehow. She quickly made her way to the stage area and found Mary clearing up items back stage.

"Mary, have you seen Lydia?"

"No, she was with a couple of guys earlier in the hall. Perhaps you should text her. She may have left already. It would be so like her not to stay and help clean up," Mary grumbled.

"Let's hope not. I needed to talk with her."

Elizabeth left to find her youngest sister and almost immediately spotted her. George had her off to the side of the dance floor, kissing her. What the hell was that all about? She just left him not fifteen minutes ago. She stormed down the steps to find Lydia coming around the corner. "Lydia, did I just see you kissing George Wickham?"

"Lizzy, you can't have all the men to yourself. I have seen how you danced with Will Darcy and Richard Fitzwilliam. You can't have George as well. He asked me to brunch tomorrow, and I said yes. If you have a problem with that, take it up with him. Now, I am going to help Mary backstage." Lydia raised her nose in the air and stomped past her still furious sister.

"Why, that little ….oh, I will just..."

Her thoughts were interrupted by the soothing voice of William Darcy. "Elizabeth, would you like any help. I can see you have a few things to tie up. I would be more than happy to help out. I would only be waiting around since I am taking you home."

Swallowing slowly, she inhaled through her nose to calm her nerves, then turned and replied, "Thank you, Mr. Darcy, but it has been a rather long evening. I have a room here at the hotel, and I think I will just stay here this evening. I'm so sorry to have kept you waiting; that was very inconsiderate of me." She looked down, not sure how he would react and not wanting to see either disappointment or anger on his face.

"Elizabeth, since you don't have anything for me to do in here, please give me your room key. I will make sure that you are all packed, and I will meet you in the lobby in an hour. How about that? You won't have to worry about anything. I will take care of it all while you finish, and then I will drive you home. Nothing is better after a long night than falling into your own bed." He placed his fingers on her chin and lifted her face so that her eyes met his. How could she deny him? He looked so expectant of her compliance, and his eyes just stroked her face with such tender regard.

"Fine, you win. I'm too tired to argue right now." She pulled her key from her small purse and handed it to him. He simply kissed her cheek and smiled.

"You won't be sorry Elizabeth. Now go and finish up. I will meet you in an hour, and if it is longer, I will come find you myself," he playfully said as he winked at her and left.

Elizabeth sighed as she admired his well-chiseled figure as he walked away. Before she could lose herself in her daydream, her mother's voice caught her attention from the kitchen.

*****

"Darcy, tell me again why are we packing her things?" Richard asked yet again. "Why not just bring her back up here? It's late, and she is tired." He was concerned for her; she obviously was a little distressed once she had left George and him on the dance floor.

"Richard, you know as well as I do that Collins is up to something. George? Well he is up to something as well, I think. NO, tonight is the night. I think she will be so tired that she will be happy to just rest in my arms in the limo. You can rub her feet, and we will do what we do best. We will take her home and see to her needs. She needs us; you know it as well as I do."

"I don't know, cousin."

"Just come on. I told her an hour, and I mean to hold her to it. She needs rest, and I mean to make it the best rest of her life."

"I know you care deeply for her. I care just as much; you know that. But take it slow; don't mess this up, Will. Remember I understand how it feels to be left behind when the one you love leaves you." Richard's concern was rising. He wanted to see that Elizabeth got the rest she needed and deserved, but he wasn't sure he had spent enough time with her to make her comfortable with him yet.

Darcy stopped for a moment and looked at his cousin. He could see the concern on his face. He was tired himself and perhaps not thinking as clearly as he ought to, but he loved Elizabeth, and something told him that if he didn't take her home tonight, things would go wrong, terribly wrong. He just couldn't shake the thought, and it had been bothering him for most of the night. He would ask Richard about Collins later. Something about that man was not setting well with him.

"Richard, what has you so worried? It's not like you to turn away a beautiful woman, especially one you care about. Elizabeth trusts me; she is ready."

"I haven't spent the time with Elizabeth that I believe I needed to establish a relationship with her. She may not be comfortable with me around tonight. Perhaps it would be best if I caught a cab."

Darcy thought for a moment, and though he hated not to have Richard with him and Elizabeth, he understood his concern; perhaps, he was right. "Then how about this— you ride with us to her place and see that we get in, then you can take the limo home. Send the driver back for me in the morning. I don't want her to be alone, and if that means I sleep on the couch tonight, then so be it. I think Collins is up to something, and I don't trust the man. I want to keep a closer watch on her, and I can do that best from inside her place."

"I understand. How about we take her things down to the car, and I will tell you what happened earlier. I think you need to know that before you take her home. He is not a man to be trusted; I will give you that."

*****

"I will make those men regret everything they have ever done." Bill Collins had given his shadows the shake after he was dropped off at his own place. He had used his time there to search on his computer, making sure to print the best of the images he had hidden there from a few years ago. Then he had gathered together a couple of things he needed, changed his clothes, and left out the back way. Now he was at Elizabeth's apartment, taping up pictures of Darcy and Richard in the bathroom, mainly around the mirror. He scattered a few others on the top of her bed. She would be made to see just what that man was, what they both were. Then he would be the man to give her comfort, when she was appalled by the revolting sexual preferences of William Darcy in full view and in living color. Yes, this was the only way to ensure that Elizabeth would come back to him. He would have her back at his place, and she would become his wife.

Finished, he glanced at the clock. It was already one o'clock in the morning. She would be home soon he figured and if like in years past, she stayed at the hotel, then she would come home in the morning to find this. He would make sure to call first thing tomorrow afternoon and check on her. With an evil glint in his eyes and a sneer on his lips, he stalked out of Elizabeth's apartment and drove home.

*****

"Elizabeth..." Darcy whispered. They had been in the limo not ten minutes when she had fallen asleep on his shoulder. With his arm wrapped protectively around her, Darcy lowered her to his lap and stroked her long hair. He loved just to look at her. She was so beautiful, even in her sleep.

"She is an angel, Darcy. I will grant you, she is the loveliest woman I have laid my eyes on in some time. How do you propose we tell her about us? I don't want to see her hurt. I couldn't live with seeing those soft brown eyes filled with pain." Richard had been watching her breathe as she rested in his cousin's lap. He wanted to reach out and trace a finger along her cheek. To feel her soft breaths caress his hand. She was so charming, so lively, so perfect in every way. He needed time to get to know her better, and he hated the fact that tonight hadn't gone as he or Darcy had planned.

"Richard, are you sure you don't want to stay? We can both sleep in the living room, and when she wakes tomorrow, we can fix her breakfast and pamper her and give her time to get to know you, to know us." Darcy spoke softly so not to wake Elizabeth. He knew this was an important night, and he and Richard had planned to ease Elizabeth into their lifestyle.

"No, you stay; you take care of her for us. I will go back home, and we can meet up later for lunch perhaps, if she is feeling up to it. I mean it Darcy; she is someone we both care about. If we rush her or make a wrong move, we could lose her. Neither one of us wants that to happen. We have waited too long."

"I'll call you then once we are up." Richard nodded as he glanced back at the sleeping woman in his cousin's lap.

They pulled up to Elizabeth's apartment. Darcy got her key from her purse. As he slowly removed her from his lap so as not to wake her, Richard held her close. She was soft and warm. She reminded him of a kitten all curled up and purring. He hated that he was not going to be staying. He hated that Collins had done this, had ruined this important night for both of them, all three of them.

"Okay, help me get her out, and then you can grab her bag," Darcy told him.

Darcy pulled Elizabeth up and out of the car into his arms and carried her into the apartment. Richard was on his heels with her bag. Once in the house, he turned on a lamp in the living room and then carried her down to her bedroom. When he flipped on a light, he noticed the bed was covered in pictures. Thinking it was odd; he drew closer only to see that they were pictures of Richard and him with a redhead. He knew who that was; it was Caroline, and if Elizabeth saw these, she would be very upset. He quickly removed her from the room and laid her gently on the couch.

Motioning to Richard to follow him, they went into the room and stared at the pictures on the bed. "Where the hell did these come from?" Richard growled.

"I have no idea. Come on, let's get them off of here and dispose of them before she wakes up." It took but a moment, and they were gone. Richard walked into the bathroom to find a trash can when he gasped.

"Richard, what it is?"

"You had better get in here," Richard said with dread in his voice.

Once both men were in the room, they stared at the scene before them. Pictures had been taped up all over the bathroom mirror. "Who would do such a thing?" William ground out, his temper rising at the shock Elizabeth would have faced had he not been here.

"I think I know who. Collins. He was so angry; you should have seen his face while you were dancing the tango with Elizabeth earlier. How he got these pictures, I have no idea. But he needs to pay for this. If Elizabeth had seen these, we would not have been able to..."

"Don't say it. My stomach is churning with the possibilities. This is not how I would want her to find out. Shock and awe is not us, and this is not fun and games. The person who did this is a person out for revenge. These pictures take something very personal and very intimate and make it look cheap." Darcy started to rip the pictures from the glass, his face twisted in anger with each one. "WHO thinks they have the right to do something like this? When I find out who took these pictures and gave them to Collins, I will have my lawyers on them so fast. Collins needs to be dealt with immediately if he is the one who placed these in Elizabeth's apartment."

"I agree. You need to take Elizabeth away from here. If Collins got in here once, he can do it again. I don't want her left alone, Darcy. One of us should be around her at all times. I will call in my best agents and have Collins watched. I will also have someone shadow Elizabeth," Richard suggested. The fear in his head matched the tremors in his voice as he spoke.

"Yes, you do that, and I'll grab some of her things and pack another bag for her. She will stay with me until Collins is no longer a threat."

The men quickly took the remaining pictures and stored them in an envelope they found so they could have them finger printed. Darcy quickly packed a few things for Elizabeth. He found her new outfits that he had sent over and retrieved a few other necessities for her. What ever else she needed, he would get for her. Richard took the bags back down to the limo and waited for Darcy to join him.

Darcy reached down to scoop up Elizabeth when she stirred. With her eyes fluttering, Darcy pulled her up quickly but gently and started for the door. "William, am I home?" she asked as if in a fog.

"You will be very soon. Go back to sleep, Elizabeth. I am here, and you are safe with me," he said softly to her, his grip secure around her body.

She snuggled into his chest and seemed content to let him take care of her. His heart melted just a bit with her trust. He made his way to the limo, and then they headed out.

*****

"Richard, just stay; it's so late, and tomorrow we are going to have to explain to her what has happened. She will want to go home. Her family will be asking for her."

"Yes, her father expects her to call. You know, he all but gave me his blessing earlier tonight. He came across me as I returned from taking care of Collins. We spoke briefly, but he knew that we would both be with Elizabeth tonight." Richard spoke softly from Darcy's bedroom door. They were both looking at her snuggled up in William's bed. Neither wanted to leave her but knew she needed the sleep, and they needed to talk.

"I know my father and hers spoke often, and there were many times they would dine together and go out after hours. It would not surprise me if my father had confided in Mr. Bennet at some point when the family discovered our sexual preference to share important women in our lives."

"Darcy, do you know what it would mean to have his blessing, that he would trust us with one of his daughters? I think I will take you up on the offer to stay. It's so late, and I'm wiped out. I can't think straight any longer."

"I'm glad you decided to remain with us. If you're finished making calls, then I suggest we get some sleep ourselves. Elizabeth will have many questions in the morning."

Both men walked back into the bedroom and stripped down to their shorts. Each slipped quietly between the soft satin sheets of the super king size bed Darcy owned, one on either side of Elizabeth. Each took a turn to kiss her cheek or shoulder and wish her a good night, and then they all were fast asleep.

Chapter 12

The early morning sun peaked in through the window. Richard turned to see Elizabeth's back next to him. Darcy was curled up around her, looking quite content. Richard remembered feeling just like him a few years ago. He couldn't believe Caroline had come back to town. How long had it been since he had seen or talked with her, over a year? He wasn't sure how to feel about Caroline after what she had done to them both, but he did know that he cared about the lady right next to him in this bed. He carefully turned and let his fingers stroke Elizabeth's silky hair; on they traveled to her soft creamy skin. He didn't want to wake her yet; she seemed so peaceful as his fingers gently trailed down her arm. . He rose slowly and quietly slipped out of bed. He figured he would dress and make breakfast for all of them. There would be lots of explaining to do today when Elizabeth woke, and he needed large amounts of caffeine in preparation.

*****

Elizabeth woke to the feel of a muscular arm across her waist and a long leg draped over hers. When she opened her eyes, she saw William. She studied his face for a moment, looking at the stubble on his chin, his ruffled hair, and decided he looked quite handsome in this state. She glanced around the room and guessed that she must be at his place. She tried to peer under the covers and noticed that she was dressed only in her lacy panties and wondered why she didn't remember him taking her clothes off. She didn't recall being drunk; that would have been preferable to the actual end of her evening. Her family had a way of getting under her skin like no others could.

Just as she was about to try and wiggle free, William moved. "Good morning, Elizabeth, are you sure you wouldn't like to sleep a bit longer?" His scratchy morning voice gave her shivers as he pulled her closer.

"I don't think that I can. I'm sorry to have awakened you. If I could just slip out and use your restroom, I can dress and call a cab and be on my way. You can sleep longer," she quietly tried to explain.

Darcy opened one eye. "You are not leaving. Richard is here; we have a few things we need to discuss with you. I, however, was hoping to sleep a little longer; it was a very long night. Come snuggle up with me and see if you can't close your eyes for a bit longer— you had such a long day yesterday."

She giggled at his attempts to pull her to him. "William, I really do need to go to the restroom." She wiggled free from his arms and legs and quickly shot out of bed before he could capture her. Realizing she had nothing on but her panties, she grabbed a shirt from the floor next to her and pulled it on. "I'll only be a moment." She dashed away, leaving him alone in bed.

Richard chose that moment to amble in. "Ah, good morning Darcy, so you're alone in bed, are you? Doesn't say much for your prowess, now does it?" He poked fun at his cousin's sour expression.

"She needed to use the restroom. Why are you so perky this morning, Richard?" Darcy groused.

"I have been busy. I made a splendid meal for us to enjoy along with a very large, very black, pot of coffee. What have I missed?" He walked over to his side of the bed and sat down in the empty space. He noticed his shirt was missing from the floor and scanned around the room for it.

"Elizabeth has your shirt on, and you have missed nothing. I said you were here, but I'm not sure if she heard me or not."

Just as the men were about to say something, Elizabeth came back with a spunky, "Here I am, as promised— OH! I'm sorry. I didn't realize you were in here." Elizabeth's voice fell a few octaves when she noticed Richard in the room, and she pulled to a stop at the door.

"Good morning, beautiful" Richard smiled. "I rather like you in my shirt. Come here and sit with us. We wanted to talk with you." His smile was devastating to her senses. Her heart beat swiftly as she watched Richard pat the side of the bed next to him. He was so handsome, dressed in a pair of loose jeans and a tight black t-shirt that exposed his ripped body. She looked away from him to see William's upper body exposed while he rose up on his elbow to watch her. He had hair scattered across his chest, and he looked so striking. Both of them were watching her, and she started to feel a bit self-conscious at her appearance. She played at smoothing out the shirt, and her toes were fidgeting against each other. She could feel the butterflies in her stomach as she gazed back and forth between the two men. She knew William wanted her, but Richard, did he desire her as well? She had never given thought to two men, much less at the same time, in the same room.

With her heart rate beginning to increase, she tried to swallow, while continuing to fidget.

"Elizabeth, nothing will happen you don't wish to happen. But we really do need to talk with you. Please. When we are done with what we need to say, Richard has made breakfast for us." Darcy's voice was calm and reassuring to Elizabeth. She trusted him to keep his word. She gingerly walked towards the bed and sat in the vacated spot she had made in the middle of the bed. Using the headboard as a chair, she pulled her legs up criss-cross and draped the sheet around her lap.

"May I ask something first before you gentlemen have this talk with me?" she asked, looking back and forth to each man.

"Of course, you may. What would you like to know?" Darcy replied. His hand moved under the covers to her foot to make contact with her in a non-threatening way.

"I don't remember coming here last night. The last thing I remember is all three of us in the limo, and me falling asleep on your shoulder." She glanced down at William as she spoke. "How did I come to be here? Whose bed is this? And who removed my clothing?"

Darcy started the explanation, "I carried you up here from the limo, Elizabeth; you were very tired. This is my place; Richard comes often when we have work related things to discuss or just to hang out. We are extremely close, like best friends or brothers would be. We hide nothing from each other. As for your clothing, that would fall to me as well, though I kept my eyes closed for the most part." He winked at her. "But I promise, nothing happened. I tucked you in, then Richard and I discussed some important business in the living room. He decided to stay since it was already early morning and we just fell into this very large bed and went to sleep. Does this satisfy you?" he asked.

"Yes, that pretty much sums it all up," she agreed. Her butterflies were growing by the minute, and she thought for sure her hard nipples had to be poking at the shirt she had on. Why these two men affected her so much she wasn't sure, but she really liked it.

"I helped to pack your bags at the hotel, then again at your place, and then I watched as Darcy undressed you. I, however, did not close my eyes. You're very beautiful, you know." Richard smiled and placed a hand on Elizabeth's knee.

77

She looked over at Richard's hand, not sure what to think. Her stomach was still filled with butterflies. Richard's wickedly dashing smile and smoldering eyes, as he spoke to her, made her feel very desirable. She did not feel threatened by him since he was being very gentle and soothing. He was terribly handsome, and that t-shirt was making her hands itch to touch him. She stopped herself from thinking such thoughts and glanced up to his awaiting eyes.

"You said you made breakfast. Would there, by chance, be any coffee, also? I think I might need some fortification before you boys start to explain whatever it is that is on your minds." She glanced back to Darcy. "Could we eat first; I'm starved?" And on cue, her stomach rumbled quite loudly.

Chuckling at her embarrassment, Richard glanced at Darcy. "I think we best feed her first. I don't want her passing out from hunger on us. Come on, Elizabeth, I'll be happy to serve you while Darcy gets dressed." He held out his hand as he rose from the bed and smiled down at her.

Elizabeth drew up her lips in a quick smile, her eyes sparkling in delight. She placed her hand in his and felt the warmth and support he gave to her as she pulled herself to the edge of the large bed. Chuckling at herself, she hopped back down and allowed Richard to lead the way.

"Hurry up, Darcy, if you want to have any. I know how you like to lie in bed all day," Richard flippantly said as he walked away with Elizabeth in tow. Elizabeth looked over her shoulder and smiled at the dour face Darcy wore. He looked like he just lost his favorite plaything.

*****

Darcy walked into the kitchen a few minutes later to find Elizabeth giggling as Richard told her stories of their childhood. He watched them interact for just a bit. Elizabeth seemed relaxed and able to enjoy his company. It made him feel good to know that they both got along so well. Both of them were very important to him, and he wanted them to get along well and form their own bond. He cleared his throat and entered to smiles from both of them. "What did I miss?" he asked with a grin.

"Oh, you know me, I was just telling Elizabeth about your finer points." Richard winked. While he talked he walked behind Elizabeth and kissed the top of her head. "Come on and take a seat. I'm serving up now."

Once they had all eaten their fill, Richard cleared away the dishes.

"Thank you, Richard, I never expected you to cook so well; that was wonderful," Elizabeth complimented him.

"You're welcome. I enjoy cooking as often as I can." He relished the praise she bestowed and smiled as he worked.

"You're very good at it. Now what has you both so worried. I can see it in your eyes. Out with it," she demanded.

Both men stopped and looked at each other. Then Darcy inhaled deeply and began, "How well do you really know Bill Collins, Elizabeth?" Darcy started off in a somber voice.

"I know enough. We are no longer dating if that is what concerns you."

"We know you are no longer seeing each other, but what I meant to say is, has he expressed to you anything that would give you cause to think he could harm you or perhaps shown a tendency to be jealous of other men you speak to or hang around with?" Richard watched her carefully as she listened to his question.

Elizabeth looked back and forth between the two handsome men. She certainly didn't want to discuss Bill Collins. She had just awakened in a man's bed, mostly naked, and not one, but two, handsome men had said that nothing would happen she didn't want to happen. What if she wanted them to kiss her, to make her feel all quivery like jell-o? Now they wanted to know if Bill was the jealous type.

"Elizabeth, did you hear Richard? Do you?" Darcy could see she was lost in thought. With her cheeks turning a soft pink and her breath having quickened, he could well imagine what she might be thinking. He wanted nothing more than to take her in his arms and carry her back to his bed and make love to her for hours. Richard was in the same boat from the looks of his jeans. They needed to talk, though, and getting side-tracked with the best sex ever was not the best way to ease her into anything.

"Sorry, um…he did leave me several messages the other night while we were out, and then last night he was angry that I wouldn't allow him to escort me into the gala. He also made a remark about you having a dark side, William. Would you know what he means by that?" she asked trying to focus on the conversation at hand.

"I think I know what he wanted to warn you about, but what I am looking for is something different. We will address that so called 'dark side' soon enough. I don't want to worry you Elizabeth, but I am going to have to ask that you trust me on this. Richard and I have placed several calls since last night, and what we are about to tell you might be a bit disturbing."

Elizabeth started to get anxious. What did Bill do that was so bad that both of these men were acting in such a way? Feeling a bit unnerved, she stared down at the table and tried to sort out what they were saying, or not saying.

"Elizabeth, listen to me." This time it was Richard who spoke. He pulled a chair closer to her and placed his hand on top of hers. "Last night, we did go to your place." With that statement, Elizabeth moved her eyes to meet his. His face was somber, but in those eyes, she could see something else. She saw concern, protectiveness, and strength. Darcy had moved behind her and placed his hands on both her shoulders. "We intended to put you to bed since you were sound asleep, but when we entered your bedroom, there were pictures scattered all over your bed and then more taped up in the bathroom. Darcy placed you on the couch while we cleaned up the mess, and we placed the photos into an envelope to take to the office so I could have them finger printed."

Elizabeth's eyes grew wide, and she started to move her head as if to say no. "Elizabeth, you're safe here. The pictures were of Richard and me. Someone wanted you to be scared of us. They were pictures of a personal nature— something that my lawyers will be looking into," Darcy softly said from behind her. He lightly squeezed her shoulders, allowing her to know he was there for her.

"Pictures of you both? But why? Who would do something to make me scared of either of you? I don't know anyone who would do such a thing." Her voice was low and shaky, and she could feel the men holding her tighter. She was trying hard to understand what they were saying, but the thought of an intruder in her apartment placing what must have been horrible pictures of these two men frightened her.

"We have discussed it, and there were events that happened last night at the Gala you are not aware of. These events have to do with Bill Collins. I don't think it would do any good to give you all the details, but several men in my security detail escorted him out of the gala. Your father is aware of what I did and knows you came home with us. We just want you to know the reasons why you are here and what we are about to ask of you," Richard calmly explained.

"Ask of me? My father knows I'm here? Does he know of these pictures?"

Darcy moved down next to Elizabeth and placed one hand on her thigh, bringing the other up to cup her face. "Elizabeth please, I know this is all hard to hear and understand, and we will help make it clearer to you. But Bill Collins is a threat to you, and what I would like is for you to stay here until we can make sure it is safe for you to go back to your apartment. I don't like the idea of you being there alone and Collins getting in without your knowledge. I don't trust him after what we believe was his doing."

"Why would Bill do this? I know he has issues with me breaking off our relationship but why bring you both into it? What were those pictures of?" She looked back and forth between the two men on either side of her. They knew something they were not telling her, and she was starting to wonder if she was right to trust these men.

She tried to pull her hands from under Richard's, and he seemed hurt that she would. He removed his hand and moved back a bit. Darcy noticed the change in her and stood up and reclaimed his chair across the table. "I want to see the pictures," she said in a voice that let them know she expected them to comply.

"I don't think that is a good idea until we discuss something else with you first," Darcy said.

"What else do you need to say? I want to call my father. Where is my purse?" She was starting to become just a bit more hesitant than either of the men liked, and they knew if they didn't let her call, she would become too emotionally upset to continue to talk about all that needed to be said.

"I'll get it," Richard said. He moved to the bedroom and retrieved her bag. Elizabeth pulled out her phone and rose from her chair. She moved towards the living room so she could talk with some degree of privacy.

"I don't think this is going well," Richard said in a hushed tone as he watched Elizabeth pace the living room floor.

"No, but she will be fine once her father confirms a few things for her. Let's just take this slowly," Darcy answered in a posture similar to Richard's as he watched Elizabeth.

Richard's phone rang, and he pulled it from his pocket to see it was from the office. "I have to take this," he told Darcy. He removed himself from the kitchen and stepped out onto a balcony, closing the door behind him.

*****

Elizabeth returned a little more solemn than Darcy would have liked. He rose and walked to meet her half way. Placing his hands on her shoulders, he slid his palms down her arms and pulled her gently to him for a hug. He kissed her crown, inhaling the scent of her hair. "Do you feel a little better now that you have spoken with your father?" he asked.

"He was aware that Bill had been removed from the ball. He also said he had spoken to him earlier in the evening. It seems that you are right in thinking he is jealous. My father would like for me check in with him after a while. He also said I could trust both of you implicitly and that what ever you thought best, I should take into consideration."

With that, Darcy raised his eyes to the sky and said a silent thank you. He was relieved that her father had said enough to give her peace of mind to stay with him. He squeezed her a bit harder and kissed her head again. "Elizabeth, I'm so very sorry this is happening. I promise I won't let anything happen to you. I care so much about you, as does Richard." His feelings came through in his voice, and Elizabeth could not help but notice. She leaned into him, resting her cheek on his chest so she could listen to his heartbeat.

Elizabeth could feel the tension in Darcy's body release just a bit at her revelation. She was glad her father approved of William; she did feel safe with him and trusted him. Richard was also very protective of her, and that too, made her feel good. Two strong men watching over her at a time like this gave her great comfort.

"Where is Richard?" she finally asked.

"He received a phone call and took it outside on the balcony."

Elizabeth pulled away so she could see William's face better. "What do those pictures show that's bad enough that Bill thinks it will scare me away from you both?"

Caressing her face, Darcy peered into her questioning eyes and leaned down to kiss her. The feelings he had for her ran deep. He was not ashamed of his life choices or his sexual preferences, but when it came to this woman, he was unsettled. He wanted so much for her to accept him, to be a part of his life forever. He could feel Elizabeth kissing him back. He knew if he could only show her how much he adored and loved her that she would not be as shocked when she was told about the pictures. Just last night she was so unsure of herself around Caroline. Those pictures were sensually graphic in the way they were taken. Richard's heart had been left broken and empty when Caroline left. The time they had all shared together was wonderful, and the attachment Richard had formed was great. Darcy had cared about them both, but when she had left, he hurt for his cousin, and therefore, Caroline had hurt him too. Now Elizabeth would not only have to deal with what Bill was attempting to do to win her back by discrediting him, but also the reality that Caroline had meant something to both Richard and him. He wasn't sure if the relationship formed during their short time together would be able to withstand such revelations yet.

*****

Richard cleared his throat and waited until Elizabeth pulled away from Darcy's embrace. "I think it's time we had that chat now. I have confirmed that Bill was at your apartment last night." Elizabeth's shocked face felt like a man punching him in the gut. "I had my men dust for prints after we left last night so we could figure out who we needed to watch out for. I have ordered the locks changed, Elizabeth. I figure that is the best way to ensure that you don't have any unexpected visitors. I will need to leave soon and take the pictures in to be tested as well. See if we can figure out who took them. We need to know who would deal with Collins or have something to gain by discrediting either of us or you." Richard was looking at Darcy as he quietly relayed the information. Once he had finished, he turned to Elizabeth.

"I know this is a lot to take in. For the time being, either Darcy or I will be with you at all times when you're not at work. I'll have someone shadow you and watch your apartment. If Collins or anyone else makes another move towards you, we will know and will stop them as best we can. Do you think you might be able to take some time off from work or perhaps work from here on a laptop?" Richard asked. He was trying anything he could think of to keep her safe. Elizabeth picked up on this and thought for a moment.

"I need to get some things from my apartment. I would also like to go into the office Monday and grab some files. My sister got engaged last night. I really would like to go see her. Father says my family is gathering tonight for dinner with her fiancé. Perhaps you would both like to come?" she asked shyly, unsure what would be best for her to do or not do in the current situation.

"I think we could run by your apartment on the way to your parents. I see no reason not to celebrate with your family, Elizabeth. Richard, what about you? Do you think you can come as well?"

"I need to leave now for the office. I'll run some things there and set up the shadows. I'll also check in to see what Collins is up to. I'll try to make it back in time to go with you both. If I'm held up, I'll give you a call." Richard walked over to Elizabeth and leaned down to kiss her cheek. "Be safe, beautiful. Darcy will take good care of you. I'll see you later tonight if I don't make it to dinner."

His whispered words in her ear gave her shivers, and his heartfelt expressions made her heart flutter. "Stay safe yourself." She smiled up to him as he once again kissed her head and started towards the door.

"Keep in contact Richard," Darcy said in a strong voice. "Watch your back."

"Always do cousin." His voice was reassuring as he closed the door behind him.

*****

With adrenaline making her a little jittery, Elizabeth moved toward the couch.

"Can I get you anything, Elizabeth?" Darcy asked. He wanted to wrap her up in his arms and make all this just go away. He would do anything for her. Anything she asked of him, he would willingly give.

"Can you just come sit with me for awhile?" she answered, sinking into the plush couch.

Darcy joined her, placing his arm around her shoulders and pulling her to him. "Does this help?" he said softly to her.

She sat quiet for a few moments, enjoying the feel of his strong arm wrapped around her and then decided her course. She needed to be brave; she wanted to be bold; and she needed him. "Kiss me William," she whispered as her amber orbs turned up to meet his gaze.

He looked into her eyes, seeing the need, feeling the desire within her and knew he would not turn her away. He slowly lowered his head to take her lips with his. They started off slow, gentle, then increased, as they both grew bolder. Elizabeth drew her left arm up to his chest placing her palm next to his heart. He reached around to hold her head to him. They continued to feast, kissing each other deeper; using their tongues to explore each other, to taste, to feel and to relish a newfound passion.

"Elizabeth," he moaned as his hand began to travel down her back, over her hip, and he pulled her legs over into his lap. She didn't argue; she came willingly. His heart leapt at the feelings rushing through him. He wanted all of her, to explore everything that made her gorgeous in his eyes. He moved from her lips to her neck, slowly nibbling her earlobe, down her jaw, under her chin while she slowly moved her head backward to grant him access. Her small groans of approval surged through his blood. He began to run his palm back up her leg and under Richards's shirt to caress her hips.

Elizabeth was in heaven. William's skillful lips skittered across her skin softly. The effects of his caresses on her body were not lost to her— the goose bumps down her back, her pearled nipples, and the ache growing between her legs— all a testament to how much she wanted this man.

William drew Elizabeth securely in his arms and then lifted both of them from the confines of the couch. He released his lips from her flesh to look into her amber eyes. "I want to make love to you, Elizabeth," he whispered in a husky tone. His eyes were filled with need, a need she knew too well. "If this is not what you want, you need to tell me now," he said as a side note as he started to walk towards the bedroom. Elizabeth didn't utter a word; she just started to kiss his jaw, taking small bites and licking the marked places.

William placed her on the bed and leaned down to kiss her passionately. Holding himself over her allowed Elizabeth the freedom to let her hands explore. She them under his shirt to inch it up as she pressed her palms next to his flesh. He was warm, so muscular, and she loved how the hairs on his chest felt as she roamed about, her fingernails gently raking against his body.

The little vixen had him so hard, he thought he would explode. He pulled away from their kiss to quickly remove his shirt. Then, staring down at her in Richards white shirt, her hard nipples poking tightly against the fabric, almost drove him over the edge. He reached down and started to unbutton each button, exposing her flesh like a present. He hungered for her, to feel her bare flesh next to his. He worked faster as she slowly arched up towards him, purring like a cat. Her eyes fixed on his. Once the last button came loose, he parted the halves to expose her to his appreciative eyes. She was perfect. Her round full breasts were flawless, with their tight pink nipples that lead down to hips made to be held on to. She was trim but not overly thin. She worked out— he could tell from the tone of her body. Taking his finger, he blazed a path down between her cleavage, circling her navel and then coming to rest on her lacy red panties. "I loved you in that red dress Elizabeth. I can't tell you how much I wanted to peel you out of it as soon as I saw you. It was my pleasure to help you out of it last night, but now, these panties are no longer needed." He used both hands and ripped them from her body.

Elizabeth gasped at his animalistic display. It turned her on to know he wanted her so much. She let her eyes roam over his sculpted body as he felt his way around hers. Stopping at his jeans, she reached up and began to unbutton them. "Let me take care of these," she said and they were off faster than he could blink. "Elizabeth, are you on birth control?" he asked in a matter of fact tone.

She stopped for a moment and nodded her head yes. "I want to feel you bare, Elizabeth, but I have never done so with another woman in my life. I have been tested, and I'm clean, but I understand if you wish me to protect you." If she didn't hurry and answer him, he might well come before they even started. His head was engorged, and he needed to gain some control. He took several deep breaths of air, his nostrils flaring, trying to calm himself while he waited for her to answer.

"I trust you, William," she cooed as she stretched her arms towards him. Every muscle in his body tensed at her words. Staring at her on his bed, a temptress with long brown hair flowing around her shoulders, her body displayed for him to pleasure over and over again was more than any man should have to bear, but he would. He wanted Elizabeth Bennet to scream his name today.

He got down on his knees situating himself between Elizabeth's dangling legs. He took one leg in his hands and started to kiss the top of her foot. Elizabeth rose up on her elbows watching in fascination. His touch was perfect, firm but not overly rough, his lips warm, as they seemed to meld to her skin. She continued to gaze at him, looking at his face, his shoulders, the way he moved. Working up her leg to her knee, he lifted his eyes to hers and requested, "Lie down Elizabeth. I want you to close your eyes and trust me. Let me pleasure you as you have never been pleasured before. I want to make your deepest fantasies come true," he softly spoke as he stroked her legs slowly, up and down.

She did as he asked, smiling at her good fortune, Giddy, she found herself ready to finally experience what William had offered her several times. How could a man not want anything in return? He expected her to lie back and do nothing. Closing her eyes, she opened up her senses to what he was doing, allowing her body to take in every move of his lips, each stroke of his fingers, and his warm body pressed against hers. She could feel her breath coming in shorter inhalations, her mind looking deep into its recesses to visually see in her head what he was doing, just like so many romance novels she had read. Her heart beat wildly in her chest, as he grew closer to her hips. What would he do? She anticipated each connection from his lips or fingers; she began to yearn for more than just his touch. She could feel the dampness growing between her thighs. Would he think her wonton? Would he only tease her? As he approached that special juncture, he used his tongue to swirl and kiss each hip, moving slowly across her lower belly to tease her more.

Darcy watched her chest rise and fall as he licked and nibbled across her tummy. Her flesh danced below him as he moved. He inhaled her womanly scent, wanting to taste her more and more. He held off on what he wanted for now. Elizabeth was wet, but he wanted her needy; he wanted her to have no inhibitions when he moved in for the greatest pleasure he could give her. She tried to move her hips, indicating her yearning, but he only smiled to himself. He began to kiss his way up each of her sides and across her midsection.

He kissed around each breast skimming his fingers gently across the overly sensitive pink buds. He could hear her gentle gasps as she arched up to offer them to him. Again he ignored his own fiery need to please her. He loved her and wanted her to gain so much more from this first experience than just a quick lovemaking session. He wanted it to involve her mind, her emotions, her entire body. He wanted her to crave him with everything in her being just like he did her.

*****

For years, he had watched and waited, letting her live her life, spread her wings, become the woman she was at this moment. Their fathers knew each other very well, having been friends since college. Darcy had always known since he was a teenager that Mr. Bennet favored his second daughter. Her spirit and life force, from what he had been told, so matched his own, that as he grew into a man and entered college he only had eyes for Elizabeth. He didn't however, dare ask her out as a teenager, but as time passed, he knew it was only a matter of time. Now he had her, he had a few dances with her, bought her a few drinks, and had taken her out on a date. He even had the pleasure of taking care of her now at a time when she could be in danger from a man whose mental status was in question.

He started up her neck, gingerly moving up to her ear, and then took a slow breath. She shivered visibly, and a small moan escaped her mouth. "Are you enjoying this, Elizabeth?" he asked in a deep husky whisper. "Do you like it when I run my hands down your body?" He demonstrated his meaning by taking his fingers and gliding them along her neck, down between her breasts to her navel, before teasing the short hairs at her mound.

Elizabeth felt herself grabbing more of the covers in her hands. God, he was good. This man was making her wild with desire. Her breasts tingled with need, her heart raced with anticipation of what else he could possibly do, and if she got any wetter down below, she was afraid his bed would become a waterbed. She licked her lips and nodded yes to his questions. Afraid to speak, she released the covers in one hand and opened her eyes.

When Elizabeth's eyes fluttered opened, Darcy could only see how dark those brown orbs had become. Her hand cupped his cheek while she stared straight into his soul. He could feel the power of her touch and thoughts. He leaned down and pressed a kiss to her parted lips. Soon they became ravenous, both wanting more. Their tongues tangoed around each other's mouths, exploring and tasting one another. Darcy moved his hand to her hip before he moved one leg up to hook over his own hip.

*****

Elizabeth had barely touched William. She wanted to see all of him, to feel his skin beneath her own fingers and lips. Taking a deep breath, she pulled herself up as he rolled to his back. Still kissing passionately she straddled his midsection. Her hands were wrapped about his neck holding him close while his hands roamed down her back and cupped her butt, squeezing the flesh and pulling her down closer to his rock hard form.

Needing some air, Elizabeth broke the kiss. She pulled up to stare down at his face, for just a moment, before she placed her palms on his chest. Using her fingernails, she roamed through the dark chest hair, relishing the soft feel against her skin. Her gaze took her from shoulder to shoulder, then downward to his midsection. She inched farther down his body before removing herself from him. Once she passed his lean torso, she found want she really wanted. He was definitely larger than Bill, and to her surprise, the head of his rod was dark and leaking. He looked succulent, and her mouth watered in anticipation of what she planned to do to him. She carefully traced her fingers down his lower abdomen then made a circle around the base of his manhood. Darcy had his hand on her back and was running it up and down patiently, giving her time to take her fill of what she was seeing.

Elizabeth turned her head to see that William's eyes were a dark chocolate and staring right at her. "Do I please you, Elizabeth?" he asked in a low tone.

"Very much. Would you mind if I pleasured you for a bit? I was a good girl for you while you teased me." Her raised brows and the hint of playfulness in her tone made William's blood pump faster. He inhaled deeply, flaring his nostrils again at the thought of what she might do to him. He was so close to the edge now that it took all his control to not throw her down and ride her until he exploded deep into her over and over again.

Using her fingers, Elizabeth ran one hand down his upper thigh and back up the inside of it until they met with his sack. She again asked if he would indulge her, all the while she lightly drew circles around him until the flesh hardened in her hand. Smiling that he failed to deny her, she sank down onto her feet and began to caress him.

Darcy gritted his teeth as Elizabeth began to stroke him. Her warm breath so close, and then suddenly he felt the wet hot confines of her mouth envelope his member. He reached up and began to move his palms around her backside. It seemed the more he caressed her and petted her, the bolder she became. He loved a woman who could give a good blowjob, and though he didn't think her experienced at all, that she attempted to please him and was doing a fine job of it, made his heart soar. With a few more licks from her delightful tongue, he had had enough.

"Elizabeth, please," he croaked. He pulled himself up to sitting and took Elizabeth's face in both his hands and kissed her hard. He couldn't wait any longer, and though this first time was not at all what he had hoped it would be, he knew he would have more opportunities. He laid her back against the pillows and used one hand to slowly move down her body. He began to kiss her neck and worked his way down again to her breasts. This time he pulled one tight nub into his mouth and suckled, licking and teasing her as she arched into him. "You're so very beautiful, Elizabeth," he complimented her as he moved to the other side. Again he kissed and suckled the creamy pink flesh, listening to each small gasp and groan that came from her lips. Finished with his feast, he moved lower, his fingers finding her wet outer lips and rubbing along them, encouraging her to part her legs wider for him.

Elizabeth's world was spinning in colors. William definitely knew how to please a woman. How long had it been since she had felt like this? Never, really. Bill had been good but never like this. He didn't take the time to know her every curve or touch every ounce of flesh on her body. He didn't even make sure she was ready; he mostly took without giving. Putting Bill out of her mind, Elizabeth focused on William. She placed her hands in his hair and pulled lightly as she arched into his fingers. Those fingers should be outlawed. They ran circles around her clit and then dove into her wet hot depths tempting her more. "Oh William please, no more; I can't take any more," she breathlessly whimpered. Her head moved from side to side as she felt her own body tightening like a string on a bow. She needed release, and she wanted it now.

"Not yet, I want you to enjoy even more, Elizabeth. Can you do that for me?" With his words floating over her skin like warm chocolate, she suddenly jumped when his mouth made contact with her mound. He overwhelmed her senses as he played with her clit, his tongue plunging into her core. He felt so good. She felt her orgasm ripple slowly until she could hear herself gasping loudly. "Good let me hear you, Elizabeth."

Darcy rose up as he felt her orgasm hit. Her hips rocked up and down, and he took the opportunity to plunge into her in one smooth movement. His own mind exploded when, for the first time, he felt her hot liquid fire surround his bare cock. Elizabeth lifted her hips and let out a harsh groan, her hand immediately going to his arms to hold on tight. He pulled out slowly and dove back in. Her body clenched around him like a vice. William could feel his own orgasm building and started to move faster within her tight confines. Elizabeth met his pace, and together they both soared into a final orgasm.

William couldn't remember when he had felt anything more satisfying. Carefully he withdrew, feeling the cold immediately once he left her warm body. He pulled her close to him and covered them both with the sheet. He kissed the top of her head and stroked his hand up and down her damp back. "Elizabeth, are you okay? I'm sorry; I just couldn't wait any longer to have you. I will make it up to you; I promise."

Elizabeth heard the breathy words from William and rose to place her chin on his chest. "You don't have anything to be sorry for. That was the best experience of my life. I may not be the most knowledgeable person at sexual pursuits, but I am very impressed, and if you allow me to just catch my breath a moment, I'm sure you could persuade me to give you another opportunity to impress me with your manly ways."

Her smile and playfulness did him in. He could already feel his lower region springing back to life. "You are going to kill me, aren't you, Elizabeth Bennet?" He grinned in return before he pulled her on top of him for another kiss, her squeals of delight enchanting him as they leisurely started another round of lovemaking.

Chapter 13

Mrs. Bennet was busy in the kitchen humming away, when Elizabeth arrived at the Bennet's with William in tow. Kitty and Mary were in the living room watching *Emma* for the thousandth time, Lydia was up in her room on the phone, and her father was in his study, sitting in his favorite chair. Elizabeth opened the door to see him look up from a book he had been reading. "Lizzy my dear, do come in. Ah, Mr. Darcy, so glad you could join us."

"Please, since we are not in the office, if you would, call me William. I always think my father is with me when I hear 'Mr. Darcy,'" he replied in a playful tone.

"As you wish. Now, what has Bill Collins done to involve you and my daughter along with your company's security detail? I have it from Elizabeth's apartment manager that the locks were changed earlier today." Mr. Bennet's voice was firm but low key. He placed his book down on his desk to give his full attention to William.

"Father, this is not an inquisition. I'm sure there is a reasonable explanation for all of this. You know Bill has issues with letting things go. It is what makes him a good business man." She really didn't want either of these men to get bogged down in this discussion. She wanted to enjoy her time with Jane. She had thoroughly enjoyed her morning with William and most of the afternoon and didn't want it ruined with talk of Bill. The smile that lit her face at that happy thought had her looking down at her lap to hide her blush. William had promised to take her to her place on the way home since time seemed to have gotten away from them. Richard had called shortly after they showered to inform them he would see them later and how sorry he was to be missing dinner. William had seemed disheartened by that announcement, and Elizabeth figured he just felt bad for his cousin missing out on some social down time. She snapped back to the current conversation when her father answered her.

"Yes Lizzy, it does; but this time, it seems he is focused on not giving you up. I don't like finding out any of my daughters are being harassed by anyone, much less a much-trusted employee. Now William, I would like to hear from you what is going on and what is being done."

"I would gladly give you the information you seek, Mr. Bennet. . Perhaps Elizabeth would like to speak with her sister while we talk. I know she has looked forward to seeing her all day."

Elizabeth heard Darcy, and though she didn't like the fact they would not drop the subject, she was in too much of a good mood to sit and listen to them. She wanted to talk with Jane very much. She had so much to tell her. So she didn't complain when her father said, "Yes, I think that would be best. Elizabeth, why don't you go find Jane. Charles is here and so is his sister Caroline. I believe they were going to walk out back in the rose garden."

Darcy's eyes widened as he heard that Caroline was here in the house. He prayed that nothing would be said to upset Elizabeth while he was busy explaining the situation to Mr. Bennet. He would rather not have Elizabeth here for this conversation but was nervous to have her go, knowing she would be in Caroline's company.

"Please do not stay in here all night, father. I wish for William to enjoy himself, not be badgered." With that she rose from her seat and kissed William on the cheek. "Don't let him keep you too long; I would hate to fall asleep in my old room alone tonight," she whispered with a sexy growl. She nodded to her father with that look in her eyes he knew so well and pivoted around to leave. Both men watched her go, each with differing thoughts.

*****

"Oh, Lizzy, there you are. Come, I could use your help. Where have you been? You know your sister is engaged now, and Lydia, well she is leaving in a few weeks for LA, and that handsome George Wickham has offered to escort her there. Is he not your best friend Lacey's brother? How is it you have never dated him? He is so rich and good-looking, but then again those things have never really caught your eye, unlike Lydia. Now come along, I need you to help me set the table. We have extra guests today you know."

While her mother fluttered about, Elizabeth digested what she just heard. George was going to escort Lydia to LA. How did that happen? How could she have ever seen anything in that man? She would speak with Lydia once dinner was done. She needed to be warned about him. Something was just not right there. He seemed to really want her attention, but then he kisses her baby sister, apparently went to brunch with her today, and now suddenly, he is escorting her to LA. As she set the dishes on the table she

93

could hear the men coming out of the study. She was glad that it didn't take as long as she had feared it might.

Darcy saw Elizabeth bent over the table, her shapely form begging to be touched, to be possessed in all sorts of manners. What he wouldn't give to take her right there. It seemed that even though he had spent the better part of the day making love to her, he still hungered for her.

"I can read your thoughts William. Not in my house, if you please. I do draw the line at my own daughters being ravaged under my own roof," Mr. Bennet teased. He was very impressed with what William had divulged to him. He understood the danger Bill presented and would talk with him Monday morning himself. It didn't matter if he was the best mind in the world of business; he was no longer going to be employed come Monday. Nobody would threaten his family. "Now if you will excuse me, I'll go see to my eldest daughter. I'm sure our guests could use some refreshments after walking in the gardens."

Once Mr. Bennet had slipped away Darcy moved closer to Elizabeth. Looking around him, he gently placed his hands around Elizabeth's waist. "Now this is a site I could get use to," he said playfully.

"Is it now? I did notice that you have a very large wooden dining table at your place. Do you hold many dinner parties there or is that just another room for deviant sexual behavior?" She turned in his arms and flashed him a raised brow with her sly smile. Oh, how she enchanted him!

"I am sure it could accommodate both functions quite well," he teased back as he winked at her.

They leaned into each other and kissed, Darcy placing one hand on Elizabeth's cheek and the other around her waist. They heard a throat clear and broke the kiss with blushes on their faces, turning to see Mr. Bennet smiling at them. "If you two have finished setting the table, why don't you come and join us in the living room."

"We were just on our way father," Elizabeth quickly replied, prying William's hand off her waist.

Darcy relented and followed them both. This evening was going to be very long; he could see already.

*****

"Lizzy, you have not stopped smiling all night. I see how you watch Mr. Darcy." Jane said quietly as she smiled at her sister.

"Jane, please. I have not watched him all night." Elizabeth blushed and turned her attention back to a bridal magazine spread across her lap.

"Oh, yes you have. You have it bad, Elizabeth Marie Bennet," Jane chided with a smile and chuckle.

"What do I have bad, Jane? I'm just enjoying myself. I have not enjoyed myself in – I don't know how long. William is so wonderful, so considerate, and so easy on the eyes. He is…." She sighed as she thought about how awesome he was in bed but didn't dare tell her sister that.

"He is in love with you and I think you are falling in love with him. Remember that card he sent you with the flowers? God, what I wouldn't give to have a man say those words to me. Then there was the dance at the Gala last night, everyone in that room saw you both. It was spellbinding to watch, like a movie. You are the luckiest girl I know, Elizabeth. Do me a favor and don't let this man go." Jane placed her hand on her sister's arm to gain her attention.

Elizabeth smiled at her sister's hearty approval. "Jane, it is too soon. We have only really gotten to know each other over the last few weeks, mostly over the last several days. Honestly, how could all this last? He is simply too good to be true. There has to be something wrong with him. Why is he not dating, or better yet, not married?"

"I'm sure there is a good explanation. I like to think he waited for you since you were dating Bill almost as soon as you returned from college," she smiled sincerely.

"You are such a romantic, Jane. Now enough about me; what about you? You're engaged; have you set a date yet? What about his sister Caroline; have you spoken to her much?" Elizabeth was eager to find out more about Caroline Bingley. If either Richard or Darcy had dated her, what happened? She was such a beautiful woman. She was friendly and seemed like a well-educated lady. She was apparently a model, and from the conversations she had heard, that career had led her to Paris. Though recently divorced from her manager, she didn't seem like the type of person who would be hard to live with. She actually seemed like someone she might be able to be friends with.

"I don't really know much about her. She arrived just a few days ago and will only be in town for a few more weeks. She promised to return for our wedding once we set a date. She seems to be really kind. I might even get along with her once given the opportunity to get to know her better. It's too bad that she ended up divorced. From what Charles has told me, she moved to Paris on the advice of her manager. After a few months there, he asked her to marry him. It was a short marriage I think, just over a year. Charles didn't go into details, but I got the impression that her husband was cheating on her with some of the other models."

Elizabeth thought that was the worst thing she had ever heard. To move away from your family, marry a man you trusted and cared about, only to have your heart trounced upon. The sisters chatted for a bit longer about wedding details before being called to dinner.

Elizabeth found herself seated with Lydia on her left and William on her right. Next to him was Caroline, and of course, her father had the head of the table, her mother the opposite next to Lydia. During most of the meal, Elizabeth had to listen to Lydia and Kitty ramble on about Lydia's upcoming trip to LA. Her mother seemed so happy that an older rich man, who was so handsome, would take the time to escort Lydia. Apparently he claimed to have business in the area and didn't mind at all. She tried to interject some reason why it wasn't appropriate to allow George to escort her, but Lydia would just roll her eyes.

"You are only jealous of me Lizzy. George and I enjoyed a wonderful brunch today. He is coming over tomorrow to speak with father about the details. Why can't you just be happy for me? You never know Lizzy; we may just be perfect for each other." Lydia whined. It was of no use to try to talk some sense into her; perhaps their father would be able to listen to reason.

William spoke with Caroline and Charles at his end of the table. Rarely did Elizabeth even catch what was being said. Caroline seemed so easygoing and likable. Her father was enthralled, she thought, since he continued to speak with her at some length.. It wasn't that she was jealous of Caroline; it was obvious that Darcy was only being sociable with her, especially when his hand kept stroking Elizabeth's knee from time to time or when he would lean back and drape his arm around the back of her chair. She wanted the night to hurry and end so that they could go back to his place.

Finally, dinner was done, and the evening came to an end. Elizabeth wished Jane well, and they made plans to get together soon to go over more wedding details. Caroline said her good byes and hugged Elizabeth, and as she did, she also had a few words of whispered wisdom to pass along. "Elizabeth I know we have just met, but I have known William for some time. He is a wonderful man. You may find him a bit out of the ordinary, but that is what makes him so special, so extraordinary. Don't let him get away. I was foolish enough to let someone I truly cared for get away from me, and I don't recommend it." With those words she smiled and left with her brother.

*****

Driving to Elizabeth's place so she could pick up a few more things, grab some of her work, and her laptop, William gently stroked her knuckles as their joined hands rested on Elizabeth's thigh. "Thank you for coming with me today William. I know my family can be a bit overwhelming at times," she shyly admitted.

"It was my pleasure. Your family is not so different from my own. We all have relatives we wish we could hide away. Sometime, I will have to take you to my family's country estate. I would love to introduce you to my sister Georgiana. My parents will adore you as well. Then there is Aunt Catherine; she is the one you need to watch out for. She may be 85 and use a cane, but she is as sharp as a tack and very straightforward. She has lived with my family for the past several years. I promise you, she is a handful," he explained.

"She can't be all that bad at her age, William."

"Oh, yes, she can," he snickered. "You have already met my cousin Richard, his brother Alex is the complete opposite. He is really into technology, and I suspect he lives under a rock. You will hardly see him since he is usually glued to a computer. My uncle Henry Fitzwilliam, whom I was named after, is a character but a very generous and kind man. His wife, my aunt Madeline, well, you have to, let's just say, *experience* her." He chuckled again slightly at his last statement, making Elizabeth wish she could see them all someday soon.

"William your family sounds nothing like mine from what you said the other night. Character in a family is endearing, don't you think? I would love a chance to meet them someday." She sincerely meant that and hoped she conveyed that to him.

Darcy squeezed her hand a little tighter and smiled as his heart felt lighter from her admission. If everything went the way he hoped with Elizabeth, then perhaps all three of them could go for a visit in the near future. It had been a while since he or Richard had gone to visit with the family, though his mother called him every Sunday to invite them to dinner.

"You seem to have a very good relationship with Caroline Bingley," Elizabeth said softly. "How long have you known her?"

Darcy knew Caroline would come up at some point. He didn't really want to get into this discussion now, but perhaps it would be best if they discussed her before they got back to his place. "I have known Caroline for several years. It was actually Richard who met her first. They became close after several months of dating, and then he introduced her to me."

"She seems like such a nice person. Why did it not work out with Richard and her... if you even know? I don't mean to pry."

"I don't mind. Like I said Richard was the one who met Caroline and started to date her. Once they got a little more serious, he introduced me to her. We were all very close for some time. She even met our families. She left suddenly for Paris with her manager. He had a new job for her, but she needed to leave within a week. It was all very sudden. She was excited about the prospect, and her manager seemed like a really great guy. She had worked with him for several years. However, I think that Richard really was falling in love with her. He was very shaken and heartbroken once she left, something I don't wish for him to experience again. It was hard on us both. We found out about six months later that she had married him. At the time, she claimed to love him and Paris. She was in several tabloids. We both lost contact with her after that." Taking a deeper breath, Darcy thought now was the time to breech the news he had to share with Elizabeth. Since they were on the way to her apartment, they could talk about it there in better detail. "Elizabeth there is something else I need to talk with you about. It has to do with both Richard and myself. "

Elizabeth turned to look at William. He seemed to be seriously thinking about something. She reached over and touched his leg. "You look troubled about what you need to tell me. I'm a big girl and can handle whatever it is you feel you need to say."

*****

Darcy followed Elizabeth as she made her way toward her apartment. She fumbled inside her purse to find her new door key. Darcy immediately took it from her and helped to open the new locks. Once inside, Darcy scanned the apartment before he let Elizabeth collect what she needed. "Elizabeth can I help you with anything?" he asked.

"No, I'll only be a moment, and then we can talk." Elizabeth walked to her room, and though it had only been a few days, she felt odd as she entered it. Knowing that Bill had been there without her permission was very eerie. She packed enough to last her a week, making sure to take some better choices in night wear and panties for William to see her in. She then grabbed a few files from her nightstand that she would need for work. Her laptop was in the living room, so she would snatch it on the way out the door. When she returned to the living room, she found Darcy holding two glasses of wine. She smiled and sat next to him.

"I'm all yours. Now what would you like to discuss? It can't be all that bad. I hope it's not Bill. Did Richard contact you?"

Chapter 14

Elizabeth sat on her couch and listened as William told her more about the man he was. He expressed how long he had held an interest in her from afar and that after learning about her break up with Bill Collins; he had decided to try to make himself known to her. He continued by telling her that he had dated several women in his life but did not considered himself to be promiscuous. Elizabeth listened and grew fonder of him with each sentence he uttered. This man, this gorgeous hunk of a man, had wanted for over three years to date her. She asked why he had not introduced himself to her earlier.

Darcy swallowed what was left in his wine glass and stared into Elizabeth's eyes. She could see he was torn. He wanted to say something but was holding back. "William, let me say this before you continue. I am very flattered by all that you have said, that you trust me enough to share so much of your past and what has been in your heart for some years now in regards to me. I have to claim ignorance in ever knowing you felt like that. I know you have done business with my family for years. I remember seeing you a few times in the office when I was a teenager helping my dad in the afternoons, then later when I started to work full time, and you attended meetings in our offices. I can also remember as a young girl how our fathers spent evenings together on occasion. They are quite old and dear friends and have stayed in touch for so many years it seems. Sometimes, my father shared a few stories of his and your father's college days with me when we were alone in his study. I envied him a friend like that at times. I think that's why I've never considered you as a potential partner prior to these last few weeks; I thought you had to be so much worldlier than me. You are 32 years old, and as you have mentioned, you have dated several women. I am a college graduate and only 26. I have only dated a little, and Bill was my most serious relationship up to this point." As Elizabeth explained, Darcy listened quietly, gauging her mood and watching her reactions to all she was saying.

"I didn't think that you would be interested in a girl like me, I suppose. I find you so incredibly handsome and was intimidated by those good looks and my own perceptions of who I thought you were. When you and Richard danced with me at the club, I cannot begin to tell you what that did for me. You have made me feel sexier, more beautiful and more desirable than anyone else I have ever dated. You made me feel more like a woman, and I can't thank you enough for that." She smiled.

"I am glad you feel like that. You are a very beautiful woman. Both Richard and I agree on that." He winked.

"This morning when I woke up in your bed, I was not shocked or worried, perhaps a little confused as to where I was at first, once I knew Richard was there. Over the last several weeks, you have shown me that you're a good man, a man I can trust. Even my father thinks highly of you and your family. Having Richard there was a bit intimidating to me since I was dressed only in a man's shirt, but I didn't feel uncomfortable around either of you. I actually, and don't think ill of me please, find you both very attractive, and I will have to admit to having some very ..." she paused, her cheeks blooming in pink as she thought how best to say what was on her mind. She figured truth was a good thing at this point, and he seemed to want to say something, so perhaps if she were more forthcoming, he would be as well.

"Did you find yourself wanting us both?" William asked softly as he watched Elizabeth's reaction to his comment.

She blushed a bit more and took a sip of her wine. Her heart began to beat wildly in her chest, but she would be brave and tell him how she felt. She nodded her head in affirmation. Darcy could tell she was timid about sharing her thoughts; possibly thinking it would stun him. He felt it was the right time to ease her mind.

"Elizabeth, let me just say that I don't find anything wrong with what you have said. That you are able to confide in me your deepest desires just heightens my feelings for you. Never be ashamed to voice what you want or hide your needs. I'm pleased that you trust me and are comfortable enough around me to share such things. It also pleases me that you are comfortable around Richard. Let me ask you this. What would you have thought if I had kissed you in front of him while sitting on the bed?" He asked an innocent enough question, he figured, to get the ball rolling.

"I don't expect it would have bothered me," she said without hesitation.

"Then what if I had laid you down and kissed you harder, running my hands along your body? What if Richard wanted to kiss you to after watching us, or touch you in some manner?" He asked. She didn't seem to be rattled, just blushing and coming to terms in her head with what she wanted and what she thought she should say in reply.

William scooted closer to Elizabeth and took her empty glass from her hands. "Am I making you uncomfortable talking about this?" he asked very calmly, mindful of her reactions.

"It's not that I am uncomfortable, but I have these thoughts in my head, and I'm just not sure what you will think of me if I tell you. I am a hopeless romantic, William. I have read more romance novels than I really should have read. Some have even been fairly racy you could say. I am not experienced, and I don't want to give you the impression that I know anything, or expect anything…"

William placed his finger up to her lips gently to quiet her reply. He gazed into her eyes and smiled a slow knowing smile. "Elizabeth, would it surprise you to hear that I have the same thoughts that I think you are having? I would like to tell you something rather important about me. When either Richard or I have met and gotten to know someone we believe is very special to us, we share her in the most intimate ways. I don't mean just sexually, but by being a part of each other's lives, by showing that special person complete honesty, trust, compassion, and devotion. We enrich each other's lives in ways that bond all of us together. "

Elizabeth just stared into William's eyes. He was being so open, so completely honest. He was not trying to distress her or persuade her; he was trying to explain something that ran very deep in his heart. It was an amazing thing to see, that moment when a person really lets you into his life and who he is at his most vulnerable. It humbled her that he was actually sharing something so personal with her. Yes, she had thought that having the best sex of her life with two hot men would be the most exciting thing in her entire life — ever, but this was more. This man was informing her that what he had to offer was not just a fling, not just great sex, not just a passing moment in time where two guys could have their jollies. She sensed that he was offering her so much more.

Elizabeth took his finger away slowly and held on to his hand. "May I ask you something then?" she softly requested, her eyes glued to his.

"Of course, I want no secrets between us. I want you to be honest with me. Nothing good can come from jealousy, anger, or confusion," he said in a respectful manner. He hoped she was not freaked out; he so wanted this relationship with her to work out.

"Do you both enjoy being with each other? Are you bisexual?" she asked with her brows scrunched together in wonderment, hoping he would not be offended.

"No, we have dated more on our own, and only those very few women who we believed would perhaps become more than just a date have we brought into this special relationship. There has never been a time when we both were dating a woman we thought of so highly, so there has never been an instance of two women at once. When one of us found someone, the other became part of the relationship until it ended. Just like anyone else, we would both feel the hurt that comes from ending a relationship. We discovered we both enjoyed the same type of woman during our college years. We didn't want to fight again over the same girl since that did happen once. We discussed it rationally and decided since we shared so much of our lives, talked about our dates and family and all that goes on with a best friend or close relative, that we also wanted to try to share our similar joys. Bonding in this intimate way took some time, and we would discuss our level of comfort in each situation. We feel that making someone feel so special and loved helped us to gain a better understanding of each other and helped to make us better men. We had someone to help in awkward moments, when life issues could not be helped; one of us was always there for our girlfriend. It takes a special woman to have two men at her beck and call, to be cared for and pampered, to know she is secure in all aspects of this unique type of relationship. "

"What would happen if one of you were to marry, or wanted to marry the same person from one of these relationships?" Elizabeth asked.

"We have discussed that, but it has never really happened. Most of the women had fun for a time or were turned off almost immediately. There has only been a handful between us both over the years since we decided on this life style. As you can see, neither of us is married yet."

"Caroline was one of those women, wasn't she?" Elizabeth knew the answer; she just wanted to hear it from William.

"Yes, Richard was very much falling in love with her. I cared for her; anything she needed we would attend to. We doted on her, and we loved her each in our own way. He was the lead, and it would have been he who would have married her if it had come to that. I was very drawn to her, but was not as emotionally involved as Richard was. Should the relationship have worked out between them, I would have stepped aside for them to marry. I did not feel that she was the woman ultimately for me. I enjoyed our time together and the relationship just like anyone else I would have dated. I really got to know her; she is a great person. Both Richard and I hurt for a long time once she moved away. I haven't dated anyone since her actually and neither has Richard. That was over a year ago. Instead, I focused more on the woman I believed would be the one for me." He gave her a simple smile filled with affection and thoughtfulness.

"Does Richard know how much you care for me?" she asked with a quizzical gaze.

"Yes, he is fully aware of my feelings for you. It was he who wanted to help me along in introducing myself to you. He has favored you for some time as well. He would have asked you out himself if he didn't know how strong my feelings run for you. It is not offensive to me that he finds you attractive or wants to spend time with you. We usually meet the same ladies at functions or in business. One of us is usually drawn more to a person, though. The one fight we had in college that almost tore us apart is what also made us stronger. We vowed to never let a woman come between us again. There is always one of us more drawn to a woman than the other once an introduction is made. When the relationship gets to the point that we involve each other, it is to make sure we can all get along and that there is no animosity, no jealousy, no doubts about who the woman would choose since we will always be around each others homes, lives and business functions on a daily basis. He understands I am the lead where you are concerned. If you have other desires, however, we are open to them. We have no set rules, and each person who we feel is brought into this life style will have different needs."

"What were those pictures of in my apartment? Will you tell me?"

"I don't want to upset you. It is in the past, and I would rather you not take it personally or offend you in any way."

"Is it Caroline? Were the pictures of the three of you together?" she asked flat out.

Darcy stopped and looked at her. After a moment, he nodded yes to her questions. She rose from the couch and walked to the kitchen with both the empty wine glasses. She was not appalled by what he had confessed to. That Richard was the person he would want her to bond with was not so bad; she was very attracted to him. He was a fun guy; he had a quick wit and was very protective of her, and he seemed genuinely to care for her, too.

His actions earlier this morning in regards to her safety, the way he made breakfast — he was wonderful to her, and that made her feel comfortable around him. William was there, and the lack of jealousy between the two made it easier to feel relaxed around them both at the same time. If this relationship went anywhere, she knew William, not Richard, was the man for her. But what if her heart became attached to both in the process? She set the glasses down on the counter and turned around. William was standing in the doorway watching her. He seemed a little lost, more anxious of what she might say or do. She had more questions about what expectations and boundaries there where, if any; however, the big question on her mind was why would Bill think that by shocking her or making her turn on William, he would regain her affections.

William stared at her and softly spoke, "Elizabeth, I have given you a lot to digest tonight. I would still like to spend time with you to get to know you better, and you to understand me more. As much as I care for my cousin and would hope a bond could be made for the both of you, I would abide by your wishes if this arrangement were something you could never accept or are not yet comfortable with. It is a lot to ask of a person, to understand what Richard and I have come to desire out of our lovers."

"Thank you. I'm not sure how to feel and not for the reasons you might think. I'm very drawn to you, and my feelings for you grow stronger the more I get to know you." She paused, holding on to the counter behind her for support. She didn't want to mess up what he had spent so much time explaining to her, always being respectful of her needs and sensibilities as she thought it all through. She was thinking of how to word her next statement when he spoke her thoughts out loud.

"But you are attracted to Richard as well, aren't you?" he said with a tilt of his head.

"Yes, but in a different way. It's hard for me to explain." She looked to the floor trying to sort out what she felt for Richard and how best to word it. Darcy advanced towards her and pulled Elizabeth to his chest, his hands framing her face. Elizabeth's eyes widened at his sudden move. When his lips pressed firmly onto hers, she welcomed him by gently biting his lower lip. William was warm and comforting, passionate and exciting. He moved his lips across her lower jaw to her earlobe. Slipping the soft skin into his mouth, he quickly laved it before whispering, " I want to take you to my place and show you a pleasure beyond your wildest dreams, Elizabeth." He slowly inched down her neck nipping and licking at her flesh, his hands moving down along her sides, coming to rest on her hips. He drew her closer to his body, enjoying the feel of her up next to him.

Working his way up the opposite side of her neck he could hear her small noises and grinned with satisfaction at how he affected her. She wanted him to push her whether she would admit it or not, and tonight he would. She was a very sensual woman; one he knew could always fulfill his desires for the rest of his life. Coming back to her other ear, he once again whispered softly, "I want to give you a gift. One filled with exquisite pleasure and all for your enjoyment." This time his hands moved up under her shirt as he spoke to her, tantalizing her flesh with his fingertips. Reaching her lace-covered breasts, he cupped each one, caressing them until her peaks grew hard.

Elizabeth's hands rested at William's waist. Between what his fingers and lips where doing to her body, his words only added fuel to her rising desire. His voice could melt her faster than the sun. Its deep husky tone shot into her mind like a narcotic, making her weak in the knees. Each whispered word that blew past her ear, sent sparks of fire down her spine, igniting her deepest darkest cravings.

William kissed Elizabeth once more, wrapping his arms completely around her back. She arched into him, her hands easing slowly up his back. Forcing himself to pull away, Darcy peered down to watch Elizabeth open her eyes. Her sexually dazed appearance gave him great satisfaction. "If you have what you need from here, let's go."

*****

Richard had finished filing paper work with the local police department for a restraining order against Bill Collins. He had a good working relationship with a few of the investigators on the force and that allowed him certain privileges pertaining to his security job with the Darcy & Fitzwilliam firm. He was tired after such a long and tedious day. He wanted nothing more at the moment than a long hot shower and some food. He had missed spending the day with Elizabeth and William. After the morning had started off so well at breakfast, he had thought relaxing with them tonight would be just perfect.

He had texted back and forth with Darcy some so they could keep each other informed about the day's events. He quickly glanced down at his watch after entering William's apartment and figured he had just enough time to eat and take a quick shower before they arrived home. With a little spring in his step, Richard fixed himself a light dinner and then made his way to the bathroom.

*****

Bill had sat in his car, parked outside of Elizabeth's apartment complex, most of the afternoon. She had not called by lunch, so he figured she must have slept in and was just taking her time to come home. He hadn't slept much last night, his mind consumed with thoughts of Elizabeth and Darcy dancing the tango across the ballroom floor. If that man so much as laid a hand on his future wife, he would be sorry.

Bill had dated a woman several years ago who, come to find out, knew Darcy and Richard. She had enjoyed a fling with both men, but knew the arrangement would go nowhere. Once Bill started to date her, he found out just what their depraved kinky minds were into. Then he met Caroline Bingley a year later at a charity event. They talked some before Richard Fitzwilliam had come to claim his girlfriend's hand for a dance. Caroline had left her camera on the table, Bill looked around, and with no one looking swiped it. When he developed the pictures a week later, he knew he had something to hold over the heads of both businessmen should he ever need it. He decided to keep the damning photographs in his safe at home. If he ever needed leverage on a business deal, he would not hesitate to use them. He always liked to have the upper hand in all negotiations. Since Mr. Bennet believed these men to be trusted business associates, he figured it would do no harm to keep them. He never guessed they would become so vital to his plans for his future happiness.

While he sat mulling over what could be taking Elizabeth so long to return, since it was now evening, he noticed a car pull up. When William Darcy got out and helped Elizabeth from his car, Bill growled and slammed his hand into the steering wheel. The two entered into her apartment, closing the door behind them. He sat gripping the wheel for what seemed like forever. All the while, his anger only grew. He wanted to know what was happening inside of that apartment.

After half an hour, both Elizabeth and William stepped out from her apartment. She wasn't upset but instead was smiling, of all things. Darcy held her hand and walked her to his car, placing a suitcase into his trunk.

"NO! NO! NO!" he burst out, his face red from rage and disgust. "How could she be leaving with him?" Bill decided to follow them.

*****

The short ride back to William's apartment had only made Elizabeth's anticipation of the evening ahead grow. William's low sultry voice had continued to caress her mind all the way there. He had enticed her senses by running his fingertips across her thighs and between her legs. Though they mostly made small talk, Elizabeth felt he actually listened to her. When they stopped at red lights, he would kiss her knuckles or look into her eyes as they spoke, giving his thoughts on what the conversation involved. She felt important to him.

Darcy opened the door and placed Elizabeth's luggage against the wall. "Why don't you go and take a nice hot bath. I'll make us a snack and grab a bottle of wine," he offered.

"That sounds like heaven. Would you like to join me?" she smiled, fluttering her lashes at him just a bit.

"How about if I scrub your back" he responded with a gentle glide of his finger down her cheek, down her neck and between her breasts, before looking into her eyes.

"I would love that," she boldly replied. Her heart began to beat faster, and she could feel her body start to respond to his sensual touch.

"I'll be there shortly then. You will find everything you need in the tall cabinet next to the shower." He kissed her softly, his lips filled with promise, before he headed towards the kitchen.

Chapter 15

Bill drove through the streets following Darcy's car. His jaw ached from grinding his teeth together. The drive seemed slow, but when Darcy turned into a posh apartment complex, only twenty minutes had passed. Bill knew the area well, as his own home was only ten minutes down the road. He knew he had more to offer Elizabeth than Fitzwilliam Darcy ever could. At the age of 37, he owned his own home, he held a prestigious position with Elizabeth's family's company that he had enjoyed for over thirteen years, and he could offer Elizabeth the dignity of a monogamous marriage where he treated her with respect. After all, he had been good to her while they dated. He was not a vain man but knew he was good looking by today's standards — he worked out, he ate right, and he cared for his appearance. He was the man, the only man Elizabeth would ever need.

Bill didn't care what old man Bennet thought he should do. He wanted Elizabeth as his wife. Come Monday morning when she went into work, he would make sure she knew what sexually twisted things Darcy was into. He would not let her throw away their relationship for some fantasy sex playtime. He also would not let her behavior bring down the business he believed he would run some day. He would give her an ultimatum she couldn't refuse.

Figuring the night was a loss, he reluctantly pulled away from the curb to retreat to his own place for some much needed rest and plotting. Tomorrow, he would take back what was rightfully his.

*****

George Wickham sat in his apartment with his eyes closed. He had music on in the background as he relived his visions of Darcy and Elizabeth on the dance floor just the night before. His sister was right. He was a fool for blowing his chance to date Elizabeth when she had been interested. With the curves that red dressed displayed and the sparkle in her eyes as she looked at Darcy, he could easily imagine many enjoyable nights with her wrapped around his body.

When Richard Fitzwilliam had tried to insinuate himself into the last dance of the evening with Elizabeth and him, he was not thrilled, to say the least. Elizabeth had pulled away quickly from him. Then to further agitate him, she had declined brunch the following day and then walked off. She had desired him at one time. There had to be a way to make her want to be with him again.

Elizabeth was a woman he couldn't quite understand. He was handsome, had his own money and business to inherit just like Darcy did, he just couldn't understand her brush off. Her little sister Lydia, however, had flirted with him on and off all night. She had a figure similar to Elizabeth's and definitely used it to her advantage. That tight black dress that showed off her assets had really made him eager to spend more time with her. He had danced with her a few times during the course of the evening. That girl was just a spitfire, and he knew just what to do with a girl like that. Perhaps he could make Elizabeth jealous if he dated her little sister. To test that theory, he had kissed her good and hard before he left the ball. He knew Elizabeth would see him, and he would have paid good money to see her face. Then he asked Lydia out to brunch the next day, Elizabeth's brunch. He hoped that would make her a little more jealous. While eating breakfast, Lydia had flirted and talked about her upcoming trip to LA. He had business there himself to attend to, so he offered to escort her there, hopefully making Elizabeth wish she were the one in his arms instead of her little sister.

*****

Caroline arrived back at Charles's home and quietly bid him a good night with a warm smile. She had enjoyed her evening immensely at the Bennet's. Jane was a sweet girl, and Caroline could not be happier for her younger brother. A self-made man of means, he had always done things the right way and by the book. After dating Jane Bennet for near a year, he had finally called to tell her the good news. She would not have missed this special occasion and was honored he would include her. She never expected that she would confront both William Darcy and Richard Fitzwilliam on her first public outing in town. Surprised, as she was, she was also glad to have the opportunity to see both men. She had thought long and hard about all she had missed over the last year and a half. What they had shared was special to her and always would be. She was not the kiss and tell type, and though they had chosen a different path than most, both men were very trustworthy, respectful, loyal, affectionate men. When she had stopped to reflect on all they had shared, she realized that she had never been treated better, than when she had been with the two of them.

Plopping down on the bed in the guestroom, Caroline removed her shoes and looked up at her reflection in the mirror. How had her life gotten so complicated? She had loved living in Paris. When the man who was then her manager had taken her there, she was thrilled and excited. She frequently made the tabloids — the new girl on the party scene. She had always enjoyed a good party and immersing herself in the Paris nightlife was exhilarating for her. She soon found herself caught up in the limelight with her manager at her side. They began to see each other socially in addition to their business association. He had proposed about three months after their arriving in France. She had accepted since he was a good man and she had known him for three years, trusting his judgment with her well being and career all that time. The wedding had been arranged quickly to coincide with fashion week in Paris as all the A-list people would be in town and able to attend. It was good for her growing career, and she really loved her work. It had been a fairytale wedding to be sure. It was six months later that she realized he didn't really love her. She had caught him cheating not once but twice. Angry and hurt, she filed for divorce.

Now thinking back, she wondered where her brain had been. She left someone who meant a great deal to her for no reason other than her own selfish advancement. She had been so caught up in the moment, and it had turned into the worst mistake of her life. She was not even a vain woman, and after a while the crowds and parties had worn thin on her nerves. Richard had been so very good to her. William was better than her closest friend ever could be. Those two men would have traveled across the world for her if she had only given them the chance. Feeling a bit guilty over what had happened and what a mess she had made of things, Caroline went to the bathroom to change for bed. Maybe she should call Richard and see if he wanted to have coffee. Perhaps they could catch up, and she could apologize.

Slipping into the covers she turned off the light on her nightstand and curled up against her pillow. If there was any affection left for her, perhaps she could find a way to make amends and start over with Richard. William would be lost to her now; Elizabeth was a very beautiful woman, and she could tell by just watching them that he was captivated and in love with her. It made her happy to see him find that kind of love. Though they had shared some intimate times together and were very close friends, she felt they would always have that bond between them. Richard was a different story.

*****

Elizabeth could hear the shower running when she entered the bedroom. William didn't mention that Richard would be there; she wondered if he was aware that he was. He did tell her to go run a bath after all. Butterflies

111

started to build in her stomach; she hadn't counted on figure that Richard being here tonight, but she wasn't opposed to it either.

William's actions over the last hour and a half had her body humming with possibilities, and adding Richard to the mix only intensified her body's reaction. With a slight tremble of excitement, Elizabeth slowly turned the doorknob and slipped silently into the bathroom. Off to the side, she could make out the outline of a man's body. Elizabeth watched in fascination as he rinsed his hair and held himself under the warm spray. He looked just as good as she had imagined he would.

Elizabeth had found earlier in the day just how built William was. He was more than she had ever expected. His hard body was so strong and muscular, but he had held her with the most tender of care. His warm body, soft to the touch, the ease and finesse of his every move meshed so well with her own needs and responses. She had begun to feel, over the several hours they had been together, that they were made for each other. Now there stood another male, a man who sexually aroused her; his compassion for her struck a nerve, a soft spot in her heart. She was drawn to Richard in a different way than William. He had shown her his fun, confident, easy manner on several occasions. Having danced with him a couple of times, her body and mind wanted to discover more about him. She gathered from their conversations this morning that he obviously held her in some affection, however she wondered if he still harbored a broken heart over Caroline and it made her want to show him he could be loved again.

*****

Richard leaned back into the hot spray enjoying the quiet, finally able to release some of the day's tension. Thoughts of Elizabeth in his white button up shirt this morning flashed before his closed eyes as he inhaled deeply. She had looked so peaceful sleeping. He knew Darcy was in love with her; he respected that and had for several years now. He had always tried to encourage Darcy to date, but with his heart captured by the brunette beauty, most of his attempts to see other women had failed.

When Richard had met Caroline several years ago, she was charming and full of life. Her tall slender build and her vibrant auburn hair had turned his eyes in her direction during a corporate function he and William were attending. He had enjoyed a few dances and some charming conversation that evening with the model. He asked her out for coffee the following evening before they parted ways. Their relationship evolved swiftly after only a few short months. Both had been so drawn to each other, there was an instant connection, he had thought. They decided to date exclusively, and not long after that, he had introduced Caroline to Darcy.

Darcy had found her just as charming as he had. Though she was educated and quite the beauty, there was a timeless aura about her that appealed to William. She enchanted him, and they had found closeness through a shared love of the arts. They would attend operas, live theater, museums and the many fundraisers that benefited such events. Often times, all three would spend the entire week together. They had been on a few short vacations and even introduced her to their families who had opened their arms to her.

Richard's love began to grow stronger with Caroline's acceptance of their special relationship. They had shared her several times sexually, but it was the relaxed evenings watching TV, meals shared and just the everyday moments when all of them were together or even when it was just the two of them, that he found himself at his happiest. Caroline had moved in with him just a few months before her surprise announcement that she was moving to Paris.

She had been so excited about her future prospects in an upcoming fashion show at a large reputable Paris fashion house. Her career was taking off, and she was caught up in a storm of fashion houses asking for her to model their new lines. She would have to spend no less than two or three months there. Her manager of several years had claimed it an amazing stroke of luck to have so much interest from abroad. He had worked very hard to get her noticed and was taking pride in the fact he had won her such prestige. Richard had thought the man might harbor some feelings for Caroline in the beginning of his courtship with her. Though she denied any such thing, she and her manager did spend a great deal of time together. When he had asked her to marry him after such a short time, for a brief moment, Richard had wondered if he was after her newly found earning capability. But once they were married, and Caroline had assured him of her joy at the event and her love of Paris, he had let it go and resigned himself to the fact that he had lost her.

*****

Sensing something was wrong with Richard, Elizabeth did something extraordinary. She slipped out of her clothes, leaving them pooled on the floor at her feet. Suddenly feeling very vulnerable, she stood frozen in place. She wanted to reach out to him, to comfort him, but this bold move on her part had her questioning herself and her appearance to him. She knew he held some affection for her but was not sure if he even desired her in such a way at this moment. She continued to watch him as the water fell across his broad shoulders, now seemingly slumped in resignation. He seemed so strong on the outside, yet almost weak at the same time. He bowed his head down to stare at the floor, the water dripping from his face.

*****

William walked into the kitchen and noticed Richard's satchel on the barstool. Smiling to himself, he quickly put together a snack tray and grabbed three wine glasses. His night was about to improve immensely. He set the items down on the nightstand and moved towards the bathroom. Slowly he opened the door to find Elizabeth on the other side, naked and staring towards the shower where Richard stood. He took in the scene before him and quietly approached Elizabeth. Trying not to startle her, he barely placed his hand on her lower back and lowered his head to whisper into her ear, "Elizabeth, are you okay? Would you like to get in the shower with him?" He was a little puzzled at her facial expression. Her eyes were not filled with desire like when they arrived but seemed to reflect her concern.

She nodded and replied, "He seems almost sad, doesn't he? I wanted to go to him, to comfort him in some way."

"Then why don't you?"

"How do I know it is the right thing? I've never gone to a man like this; what if I'm not what he wants?" She turned her eyes to William, her face filled with doubt.

He could see her conflicted feelings "He will not reject you. Richard cares for you more than you give him credit for. Elizabeth, if you would prefer, I can run that bath for you. He will be out shortly, and you can relax, and I'll wash your back — just as I promised." He moved his free hand to cup her face, then slowly moved his head towards her for a gentle reassuring kiss.

Elizabeth responded to William instantly — his warm hands on her cheek, his ability to see that she wanted to comfort Richard, even as they themselves were becoming closer to each other; yet, there was no jealousy, no fighting. His confidence and faith in her gave her the courage to show him that she was willing to try. She wanted to do it. She wanted to do it for him.

*****

Richard heard the glass doors release and shut, he opened his eyes to a sight he was not expecting. Before him stood Elizabeth, watching him closely, but not making a move towards him. She seemed to be waiting for his acceptance or approval. Her beautiful brown eyes were filled with concern; a concern he felt was for him. His eyes traveled down her body. She was perfection — her skin was creamy and flawless, her breasts were exquisite to his eyes, her shapely hips called to him, and her long luscious legs just begged to be caressed. She was everything he had ever imagined she would be, and she stood there uncertain of herself, of her place in this out-of-the-ordinary relationship. He slowly extended his hand towards her, inviting her to come to him. She glanced at his offering and placed her hand gently into his. She turned up her gaze to meet his. No words were exchanged between them as she moved towards him. He could not believe what a treasure she was. She was offering herself to him of her own free will; she wanted to console him, and right now it sounded damn good.

He pulled her slowly into his embrace, wrapping his arms completely around her, hugging her to him. She placed her cheek on his chest where his heart beat strong and loud; her arms draped around his waist. Resting his chin on her head, they stood there in silence, the warm water falling against them the only sounds to be heard. It felt good to have her in his arms. He had not had the opportunity to just hold her and experience the blooming affection between them. It was fragile and new, neither of them wanting to break the spell of this new acceptance between them. He knew Darcy had to have spoken with her, that he was in the apartment and that he wanted them to have this time together.

*****

Elizabeth entered the shower, Richards's eyes opening to look upon her. She was self-conscious of her naked body, but he did not show any disgust or rejection, only something akin to what she felt was thankfulness on his part for her coming to him. He offered her his hand, and she took it. He guided her into his embrace, and she hugged him as his chin rested on her head. She felt content in his arms, safe. This man with whom she had danced several times with great enjoyment, with whom she had eaten breakfast that he had taken the time to prepare for her; this man who had massaged her sore feet while escorting her home in the limo; this man she had felt an attraction to all this time, though not as strong as the one for William, it was there. The more they had been together; the closer she was feeling to him. She felt oddly aware that her need to comfort him was not born out of some duty she felt she would have to perform, but rather from her heart, her own emotions taking a step towards a relationship that was so out of the ordinary, so different than any she had ever thought possible.

She was greatly relieved that she could show this man, this funny, gentle, witty, handsome-as-hell man that she felt something more than just friendship for him, without feeling guilty for her evolving emotions. She would see Richard often should she and William continue to date. There would be no need to hide the natural desire she had for him. She could be free to enjoy a relationship with two men who held different parts of her heart without jealously, secrets, and guilt. It was freeing to her, and as she stood there holding on to him, her heart and head started to merge into a new idea of what this relationship might hold.

*****

Richard began to run his hands down the length of Elizabeth's back. She felt so soft against him. He could not help that his body physically reacted almost immediately when she came up against him. But he would not apologize for it either. He wanted this time with Elizabeth. He didn't want her hurt or confused. He knew that if this relationship were to work, it would take an investment of time by all three of them. He and William only had a few steadfast rules; William was the lead with Elizabeth, and he would respect that; however, it could go in any way they wished it to go according to what they all discovered as the relationship moved forward. Right now, he wanted to show Elizabeth how much he cared for her and adored her.

"Elizabeth," he quietly spoke. She lifted her head from him to look in his eyes. "Are you okay with being in here with me? I don't want you to do anything you are uncomfortable with. We haven't had the opportunities I would have liked to build a better understanding of each other, and I want to thank you for what you are doing. It shows a great effort on your part to accept what William and I are offering you."

"I came in here to run a bath. I saw you in the shower; you seemed upset, almost sad. I wanted to reach out to you, and William told me you would not turn me away. If I'm doing something wrong, you will have to tell me. This is not something I have ever done or heard of others doing, and I find I have so many questions. But for now, I want to be here, just the two of us; that is my choice. If you have no problem with my being in here, I would like to stay for just a little while," she said, her dark eyes looking deeply into his.

Richard leaned down and placed his lips on hers. She didn't automatically respond to him, so he knew that she needed time to accept him. Instead of deepening the kiss, he eased his lips from hers and softly kissed her jaw up towards her ear. "You are an amazing woman, Elizabeth Bennet. I adore you," he whispered into her ear. He nuzzled into her hair and moved his hands to hold her a little tighter in a hug.

Elizabeth swallowed and licked her lips. Richard was going to undo her. His gentle touch upon her skin left her back tingling. Even though she didn't kiss him in return, he had moved on, not pressing her to do anything she didn't want. His low tone in her ear made her butterflies worse, and without thinking, her hands began to rub slowly up and down his back. He felt wonderful to her, and his appreciation and affection towards her began to ease her trepidation for coming to him.

"Elizabeth, may I wash you?" Richard finally asked. William was the only man who had ever washed her before, and that had only taken place this afternoon after hours of making love. She had found it very erotic when William had washed her; it had lead to them making love yet again. This time she wondered how it would feel to have a man she didn't know as well do the same. She pulled back a little to look into his eyes. She didn't reply vocally but nodded her acceptance. He reached around her for the soap and began to make a rich lather. Her eyes watched, glued to the frothy bubbles.

*****

He wouldn't make love to her now. She needed to understand that this was not a relationship that was based purely on sex; it went beyond that. Yes, he thought she was very beautiful and wanted to enjoy all she had to offer in that respect, but for right now, this is what he wanted to give her. Trust. If this was going to work, she needed to trust him. William had already earned her trust and devotion, and that was how it should be. He hoped at some point down the road, Darcy and Elizabeth would marry. He had expectations that he would marry the woman of his dreams, too. He wanted that for Darcy. If he could be there to support and encourage them both in that direction, he would.

He gazed into Elizabeth's eyes for just a moment, and then bent down on his knee. He took one foot and placed it on his raised knee and began to wash her toes, up her calf and her thigh, careful not to get to close to her intersection. Then he removed it and took up the other to repeat the process. He made sure to massage her feet to help her to relax. Once he had

117

completed her legs, he rose from the floor. "Would you turn for me, please? I would like to do your back."

She did as requested and faced into the warm water. His hands removed her hair from her back and placed it over her shoulder. He started at her lower back and eased his way up. Massaging fingers caressed her skin in soft stroking circles. Elizabeth closed her eyes and enjoyed the pleasurable touch of Richard's hands against her skin. He continued to move up until he reached her shoulders. He lathered his palms up again and started at the base of her neck. She leaned forward, granting him access to move better. With her hands splayed against the wall of the shower it made his mind ache to hold her and make love her. He worked up to her neck, and then taking the shampoo, he started on her hair. She rose and leaned her head back a little so he could lather her tresses. Using his hands he also gave her scalp a gentle massage. Soon her groans of approval had him smiling. She was definitely more at ease now.

Giving her all his attention, his own mood began to shift. No longer was he thinking of his own hurtful past or the tension from the day. Elizabeth had given him a gift of peace and contentment. Making her happy was making him happy in return. Finished, he spun her around and washed the soap from her hair. "Now does that feel better?" he asked her in little more than a whisper.

"That was marvelous. You have very good hands." She smiled up at him.

"Thank you. Now how about you get out and dry off. I'll be out right behind you."

*****

Elizabeth opened the door to find William waiting with an oversized towel spread open in his hands. "Come, I'll dry you off." She was enfolded in a lovely soft warm towel. William carefully and diligently dried every inch of her body. Once he made it to her face, he kissed her soundly on the lips. "You smell wonderful. Perhaps I can have a rain check on that bath and back scrub for another time," he said playfully with a wink.

They walked out of the bathroom and into the bedroom where William had placed her pajamas. He had also warmed them, and as he slipped them on her she felt so cared for. "Thank you so much, how wonderful of you to warm up the towel and my pj's. You know if you keep this up, you will spoil me." She chuckled softly.

118

"Oh, I intend to spoil you if you allow me the opportunity. Why don't we go sit in the living room and enjoy those snacks and a glass of wine? Since Richard is here, I'm sure he would enjoy hearing about the evening."

"That sounds fantastic."

The two made their way to the couch, Darcy taking the far left and Elizabeth the middle. She had just reached down to snag a slice of cheese and a cracker when Richard joined them. He sat next to Elizabeth, and with a casual smile, said, "I think I'll just have a glass of wine,. I've just eaten, so I'm not hungry at the moment. Care to share how dinner was tonight?" All three were feeling very comfortable and started to share the events of the day.

Elizabeth marveled at how they all chatted in comfort. The food and wine were soon gone as they enjoyed each other's company. Elizabeth had her feet in Richard's lap and her head against William's shoulder. Richard massaged her feet as the guys talked about work and what needed to be accomplished in the week ahead. Elizabeth chimed in about needing to go to her office at some point. They decided Richard would go with her. Darcy had meetings scheduled all day so could not personally accompany her. As the evening turned late, the threesome grew tired. They all decided to turn in for the night. Richard rose first and offered his hand to Elizabeth. "Come Elizabeth, I'll tuck you in while Darcy straightens up."

"I'll be in shortly. Save my spot," William requested with a smile.

It had been a wonderful, relaxing evening, and Elizabeth felt right at home. Her body and mind were very aware of the men and where they where and what they did or said, and she did not feel threatened in any way. She actually was a little disappointed that nothing had happened. Her body was humming with sexual desire. All of this pampering had her ready to experience what the two men could do to pleasure her. Perhaps she needed to make the first move.

Chapter 16

Richard was unconsciously rubbing his finger over Elizabeth's knuckles as they walked hand in hand to the bedroom. It didn't escape Elizabeth's notice that Richard was the first one to offer his services to tuck her in. She thought that perhaps after having lounged around the couch together, he had determined that what was started in the shower might have been unfinished. She certainly thought so. Having sat for the last two hours between two extremely gorgeous men, who had petted and stroked her body as they all drank wine and chatted, did nothing to soothe her rising hormonal state.

Elizabeth had enjoyed an amazing day filled with new experiences and feelings. William had been simply wonderful to her all morning, loving her into the early afternoon. Then earlier in the evening, when he had explained what he and Richard had to offer her if she were willing to accept them, had caught her a little off guard. William had quickly assured her that he still wanted to see her — even if she chose not to accept them both. She was curious about Richard; his fun loving side and easy manner had definitely given her pause these last few weeks to consider a relationship with him. She hadn't given William any clues as to what she was thinking, only asking a couple of questions before his attentions had started to turn her mind to mush. The scene in the shower just a few hours ago gave her logical mind just what it had wanted, a full body image of that man's physique. He was a god, a tanned, blond-haired, blue-eyed god with arms, abs, and, if she was not mistaken, equipment that matched, and possibly exceeded William's.

He had been all that a gentleman should be. He didn't pressure her into anything she didn't want, and she had to admit, she had been very timid and cautious of Richard when she entered the shower. She was naked, after all, and had not really gotten to know him much. It was so unlike her to do something so bold. She had felt safe around him to be sure, and she could tell from his actions along with William's disclosure that Richard felt something for her, so she had taken the plunge and gone to him. She supposed she wanted to prove to herself that she was not scared of the offered relationship or of her own sexual desires. Mostly what she had wanted was to be near Richard, to see if there was a connection between them. She also wanted to comfort him; he really seemed to need it. She considered after meeting Caroline tonight and receiving her whispered advice as she departed from her parents' house, that it was possible Richard still harbored strong feelings for the auburn-haired beauty. She also

120

suspected that Caroline might hold the same for him as well. She didn't know either well enough at this point to act on those suspicions, and right now her body was sending her unmistakable signals that she badly wanted Richard Fitzwilliam.

They reached the bed, and Richard drew the covers back from his side for her to slip in. Elizabeth paused; she remained standing, trying to decide if she would act on her impulses. "Elizabeth, are you ready to go to sleep?" Richard asked, his wrinkled brow questioning her hesitation.

"I'm not sleepy," she slyly explained, looking up at him from lowered lashes. With her eyes focused on his ice blue ones, Elizabeth used her hand to run up the front of his thigh and under his fitted t-shirt, stopping over his heart. "I think we should get to know each other a little better. Perhaps you could help me with this gown. I sleep so much better when I have nothing next to my skin but the soft feel of silk sheets." Her voice was laced with sensuality as she dared him to make a move.

Richard could read between the lines. He was no fool in the bedroom or ignorant of a woman's advances. Elizabeth wanted him to make the first move. The shower scene flashed before his eyes as he remembered the feel of her soft skin under his touch. How easily he had glided along her supple flesh leaving a trail of bubbles. She never flinched, and she didn't shy away as he had washed her; she actually enjoyed what he offered her. He had thought she was not ready to accept him; perhaps he was wrong, or perhaps the wine and cuddle time had helped to ease any doubts she may have harbored earlier. He would test her to see if what she claimed to desire was truly what she wanted.

Richard's gaze transformed to one of consideration as he moved closer to her, capturing her lips with his. His right hand carefully wrapped around her neck, easing her to his face. He was firm, demanding, and took what he wanted. Elizabeth didn't hesitate this time. She complied and responded with equal measure. Richard knew she was not holding back, and so broke the kiss to stare back into her brown eyes. "I would be more than happy to oblige you," he seductively replied. His eyes bore into her while his hands ran down her sides to her hips. He scrunch the material up in his hands to pull her gown up and over her body, tossing the fabric onto a chair in the corner without looking, his eyes holding her captive. "Is that better?" he dared in return.

"Much, you do have such good hands. Seems rather a waste to have such a talent; perhaps you should reconsider your current occupation," she teased with a tilt of her head.

"And what would you suggest I do?" He took one finger and ran it from the dip in her throat down in a straight line between her breasts until he found her navel. He stopped and splayed his fingers out, using his palm to finish his travels against her warm skin. He moved tenderly around her waist and down the small of her back to cup her rear in his hand. Still holding her in an eye lock, he waited for her to respond.

*****

Elizabeth licked her lips slowly, considering her options. She really wanted the opportunity to see where this would go with Richard. He was so suave, so male, so freakin' hot she would be stupid to stop. In the back of her mind, she knew William was still around. Would he be shocked if he walked in on her behaving like this with Richard? Would he sit and watch her? Would he want to join in with them? She didn't know the rules and wasn't sure how this would all work. She was going to have to rely on them to help her along the way. She wasn't nervous, she was turned on, and she wanted one of them to ease her raging desires. If Richard didn't want to be that man, she knew William would not disappoint her.

"I think you should consider opening your own day spa — with hands like these you could make a fortune." She reached down and took hold of his dangling arm. Raising it, she moved her eyes from his to look at the strong hand before her. Taking her smaller one, she pressed the two together looking at how they fit; then she intertwined them, bringing her gaze back to his.

"I rather like my position with the family firm. It affords me many opportunities I might not otherwise have. I do, however, enjoy using my talents on occasion should a worthy patient come into my path." His sensual voice sparked her already heightened need for him to take her.

Richard started to caress Elizabeth's exquisitely silky flesh in his hand while he inched her closer, bringing his mouth down to hers. Keeping her hand in his, he kissed her deeply. This time his tongue pressed its way between her parted lips so he could taste and explore her. She was as sweet as he thought she would be, and that only lead him to believe that the rest of her would be the same, if not better. With his own burning desire to posses her rising, Richard knew this was the night he and William would share

Elizabeth. She wanted to know, wanted answers, and the best way to give her what she wanted was to show her.

Richard opened his eyes to see William standing in the doorway watching the pair before him. It only took one look in William's direction for them both to know this was it.

*****

William walked towards his nightstand and clicked his light off. He undressed quickly and slid into his side of the bed. He could tell Elizabeth was entranced with Richard's kisses; her skin had begun to glisten as her body started to flush with her building arousal. It made William's heart beat wildly in his chest to witness Elizabeth's pleasure. He knew what she felt like, and his fingers itched to touch her, to taste her, to make love to her. From this vantage point, he was able to see how she responded and what she liked. It was a benefit of sharing that gave him great satisfaction. Taking the time to see how a woman he cared so much about reacted to sexual situations only enhanced his ability to bring her to greater pleasure. He knew Richard would treat her well; he cared for Elizabeth, wanted to bond with her, wanted to know the real woman inside. Darcy wanted his dearest relation to always have a piece of her heart; theirs would be a bond that over time would not be broken. By sharing, each one knew where they stood; there was no wondering as to what it would have been like with the other. The intimate and daily aspects of what they would share would only make them closer, able to share everything for the rest of their lives. He lay in bed, resting his head on his hand as he stared at Elizabeth's back, her long hair falling in curls along the creamy flesh. The way her hips gently sloped out creating an amazing silhouette. How he wanted to reach out and caress her. The small groans she made as Richard kissed her were driving him mad. He would wait and when the time was right, he would join the twosome and give Elizabeth more pleasure than she had ever dreamed possible.

*****

Richard eased Elizabeth around, lowing her to the bed. He never broke his kiss till she was seated; then using his lips, he moved across her cheek to her ear, sucking in the tempting flesh of her earlobe. He savored her soft sounds of pleasure before whispering in her ear, "You're so incredibly beautiful. Tell me what you want; what do you desire?"

Swallowing the sudden lump in her throat, Elizabeth moved her hands to his shirt and began to lift it up. "I want to feel you, all of you."

Richard quickly rid his body of every stitch of clothing while Elizabeth silently watched. He could see the fire in her eyes and was eager to do his best to please her. He knew Darcy was behind her and doubted that Elizabeth was aware that he was there. It had been so long since he had been with a woman that Richard hoped he didn't disappoint either Elizabeth or himself. The one thing he had learned from the relationships he and Darcy had shared, was that no matter what, the woman would be the focus of the attentions of both men. Darcy would see to her pleasure if he were to fail in some way. Right now, she felt so warm and soft, her eyes pulling him into her web of desire. He was finding it difficult to take his time with her when his body screamed to just take her over the edge and make her lose herself in ecstasy.

Taking a deep breath, Richard made his way to stand between Elizabeth's legs. He asked her to spread her knees from her sitting position. With his body up close and personal, he looked down and tilted her head up to meet his gaze. "Is this what you want?"

Elizabeth could only stare into those blue eyes. God, he was magnificent, so strong and virile. He bent down on his knees, keeping contact with her eyes. He brushed his thumb gently across her lower lip before trailing it down her chin and throat. She could feel the goose bumps explode along her arms while her nipples tingled with anticipation. Her legs touched his hips, the warmth of his skin next to hers called to her so she gripped the edge of the bed harder, not sure what she should do.

"Relax Elizabeth, there is nothing to be anxious about," Richard explained in a low tone. Then, as she watched him, he moved in and took hold of her breast bringing his mouth over it and licking her tight peak.

Her sudden gasps had William's rod pulsing with anticipation. He closed his eyes, momentarily reliving his earlier time with Elizabeth, remembering how he had relished that sound as he himself had suckled at her breasts.

Richard blew gently across the wet flesh creating more fire in Elizabeth's already flushed body. She arched sweetly back, showing him she wanted more. He gladly took her offering and sucked the second tip into his mouth. This time he swirled the pink bud with his tongue while his other hand flicked the soft wet tissue of the other. Using his free hand, Richard palmed his way down her torso to her thigh. Slowly he moved along her leg to her knee and up again. Releasing her breast, he cupped both in his hands, rolling the tight nubs between his fingers. "Open your eyes Elizabeth; I want to see your eyes."

Slowly, she did as he requested. With a slow inhalation, she gazed at Richard, locking her sight with his. He increased the pressure on her nipples making her eyes grow wide and intense. She was getting very wet between her legs, and she wanted relief in the worst way, but she had yet to move an inch.

Richard could see that she was getting so very close. Taking pity on her, he thought to give her a little relief. He removed his hands from her breasts and placed them on her knees. He moved his eyes down to her lap and began to slowly glide his palms up her thighs. "You have the softest body Elizabeth. I don't think I will ever tire of feeling you beneath my fingers." As his hands approached her hips, Elizabeth began to hold her breath. What would he do?

*****

Richard griped either side of Elizabeth's hips, lifted his chin and sealed his lips with Elizabeth's, the intensity of his actions so strong it almost took her breath away. She broke the hold she had on the edge of the bed and wrapped her arms around Richard's neck. She immersed herself in the tide of passion flowing through her veins. With their lips pressed firmly together, Elizabeth's hands began to wonder across each of his shoulders, down the front of his body and up again. Sighing in contentment, the ache between her legs started to grow more insistent.

Pulling one leg from the floor, Elizabeth rubbed her inner thigh against Richard until she wrapped it around his hip. Wanting to experience more of her, Richard moved his palms along Elizabeth's back pulling her closer to his body. They were so close, pressed together, flesh next to flesh. Elizabeth felt the unmistakable bulge of Richard's long hard length firmly touching her belly. She craved to feel his manhood beneath her fingertips. She longed to be able to caress this virile man's body, and without any more thought, she did just that.

Richard's elation at Elizabeth's bold move would earn her a reward from him. Moving from Elizabeth's lips, down her neck and across her shoulders, he kissed a trail along her fragrant skin then whispered, "I want you to lay back, Elizabeth."

She stopped stroking his shaft and complied. No sooner had her head hit the mattress, than she caught sight of William hovering above her face. His eyes were intense and dark. She could see the desire in his flushed appearance and knew hers had to be no different. He moved down to meet her lips, kissing her deeply and possessively. Instantly, Elizabeth's palm cupped William's face, the familiar scent and comfort of his touch igniting Elizabeth's heart.

*****

Able to allow his eyes to roam freely over Elizabeth's naked body, Richard ran his hands along her thighs up to her belly and down again. His appreciation of her form only increased when he could see the influence of his heated desire on her body. Elizabeth's flesh was glowing with arousal and between her legs; the glistening dew dampened her inner lips. Gently, Richard started to kiss her knee, slowly licking and nibbling his way up the slender limb. His palm traced a similar pattern along her other leg until it met in the middle. Using his fingers Richard parted the skin before him to inhale and taste Elizabeth. Swirling his tongue along her most sensitive area, he could feel her react and bow into him. He sucked in the tight little bulb and stroked it with his tongue. Feeling her hips rise slightly, he slipped a few fingers into her core, glancing up to watch her response. She grabbed Darcy harder, their kiss becoming a mixture of hunger and desire. She was so hot. He stroked Elizabeth a little longer, driving her closer to the edge, before he slipped out from her warm confines to find a condom.

*****

William wanted to crawl under Elizabeth's skin. She was so consumed with need that she feasted at his lips like a starved animal. He moved from her lips downward to her breasts, sucking into his mouth the rigid pink peak, which he began to nurse vigorously. She simpered, lifting her breasts closer to his mouth. How he loved when she became consumed by her own fiery needs!

Elizabeth's hands moved all over William's back and through his hair, grabbing the ends and tugging him closer to her body. Her sweet surrender to both he and Richard had his balls throbbing in near pain. Needing to do more than kiss her, William looked quickly to the end of the bed. Richard had placed a condom on and was ready to move forward. Rising up William asked Elizabeth, "I want you to take me into your hot mouth. Can you do that for me, Elizabeth?"

She agreed and watched as William moved to sit against the headboard with pillows against his back. He helped to situate her between his legs. Up on her knees, Elizabeth was more than eager to have him in her mouth. She had tasted him earlier in the day and was anxious to do so again. She quickly took hold of his enlarged shaft, smiling in satisfaction at its magnificent hardened state. She stuck her tongue out, watching his face as she licked tenderly at the nearly blue tip. He tasted earthy and his hiss of pleasure made her only want to drive him more to the same edge she was on. She was so close to her own orgasm that her body hummed wildly; she wanted to feel him inside her, needed to be touched in the worst way. She could hardly control the urge not to do it herself with her own free hand. William held her hair back to watch as Elizabeth wrapped her lips around his shaft. Her mouth so warm and eager to feast on him drove him insane. How he loved watching her enjoy his body.

The bed dipped as she licked at William. Richard was there, but she was not concerned with what he had in mind; her sole focus was on William and her need to make him hunger for her more. Greedily, she took him all the way to the back of her throat and eased out. She repeated herself, lingering the second time to swirl her tongue along his length, sucking at the tip as he had her breasts.

"Elizabeth, please I can't take much more," William gritted between his teeth. He was so close; one more move like that, and he would explode. Before she had the opportunity to see how far she could push him, she felt two hands run up the back of her thighs, across the globes of her ass and grab onto her hips.

Without a word, Richard pressed his rigid length between Elizabeth's legs. Her audible sound took both men by surprise. She was so hot, so wet; Richard's cock slipped in with ease. He pulled back only to dive in again swiftly. Elizabeth tried to lean back into him, she wanted more, and she wanted it harder, deeper. She was no longer focused on what William had to offer her, but what Richard was doing. Richard picked a pace and started to move in a rhythmic pattern. With each penetration, both he and Elizabeth moved in concert building to a desperate crescendo of need. William sat watching Elizabeth's face, awash with pleasure. Her eyes closed as she arched up, dipping her breasts closer to the bed. She was so beautiful — he couldn't look away from her. "Elizabeth, look at me; open your eyes and look at me," he huskily ordered. When she did, he saw the flare of fire behind her brown orbs. She intently bore her eyes into his, her body totally consumed in a firestorm of arousal.

William moved in under her and began to work at her breasts. "OH GOD" she moaned. Richard ramped up to a frenzied pace as both he and Elizabeth started to fall over the edge of control. William continued to tweak and suck at Elizabeth's breasts listening to the noises of extreme pleasure coming from both of them. His view of her torso was magnificent and his palms took great care in caressing her flesh and her tight pink nipples. The sounds of skin slapping against skin gave his mind vivid images of himself earlier in the day as he had taken Elizabeth in the same position. He found he had to hold on to his shaft to control his own release.

Not able to hold back any longer, Richard shot everything he had, releasing a year of pent up control loose into his lover. Sated, he could feel Elizabeth starting to grip him tighter; she was going to orgasm, and he wanted William to savor this moment. He withdrew at Elizabeth's protest only to fall back as William pulled her over his own body.

Screaming out into the night as William drilled into her, Elizabeth could only see flashes of light as her orgasm rocked her body for what seemed like an eternity. William had her straddling his lap as he powered into her repeatedly gripping her hips and soothing the ache that had built to an amazing climax within her. She arched back holding on to the top of his thighs, her hair trailing behind her as she bounced into ecstasy. Never in her life had she had so much pleasure bestowed upon her at one time. There was not an area on her that had not been touched or caressed and she reveled in the sensations these two men had generously given her. It was the most erotic and sensual experience of her life. Collapsing upon Williams's chest, Elizabeth could feel her heart begin to calm. William's comforting arms were wrapped around her, holding her close, while he extolled his delight in her over and over again. When she glanced around for Richard, she didn't see him. Then the sound of the shower was heard in the bathroom. Relaxing back into William, he slowly stroked her head and back. "Are you alright, Elizabeth?"

"I'm perfect," she purred as she let her eyes close.

*****

It seemed like they had just gone to bed when the alarm went off. Richard rolled to the edge of the bed claiming his need for coffee at such an early hour to start his morning. Chuckling, William stroked his hand down Elizabeth's body, "Good morning, I hope you slept well?"

Elizabeth smiled and curled into William's embrace, "I did thank you."

Richard returned passing the two in bed as he headed for the bathroom, "I suggest you both get a move on it. Darcy your meeting this morning is at 9 and Elizabeth I have an appointment with your father." He closed the door behind him while Elizabeth and William looked at each other. "Hmmm…He does have a point sorry to say. I suppose we should dress." Elizabeth agreed.

Everyone got ready for work in record time to Elizabeth's surprise. When it was time to head out, William kissed Elizabeth goodbye with a promise to call her at lunch. The ride into Elizabeth's office had been nice. She and Richard had enjoyed a second cup of coffee from Starbucks since they had made good time. They chatted about the money raised from the gala. Then Elizabeth explained what she hoped to accomplish in the coming months with a few other benefits that were already lined up. Richard had listened intently as they sat on the patio enjoying the morning air. He offered some encouragement to Elizabeth on her new ventures and hoped they would work out well for her. Continuing on to the office, they enjoyed genial conversation. It had been a pleasant ride, altogether Elizabeth decided.

*****

The elevator doors opened, and the pair stepped off and headed down the familiar hall. "Elizabeth, I am going to speak with your father for just a bit. Should I just meet you in your office?"

"That would be great. I need to check my email, sign a few things for my secretary and grab my work folders. I'll see you later."

He smiled at her and headed down the hall to where her father's office was located.

Elizabeth greeted a few of her colleagues and knocked on Jane's door. "Good morning, Jane. How is everything today? Have you heard from Mr. Moreland?"

"Elizabeth, there you are. You didn't answer your phone this morning. I wanted to tell you that George Wickham is here."

"Here in the office? Whatever for?"

"He is here to speak with father about escorting Lydia to LA next week. Honestly, I think Lydia could use an escort but not that man. Lydia spoke with him all evening long after you left the house yesterday. He even came by mom and dad's to pick her up and bring her into the office this morning. Can you believe it?"

"Yes, I think I can. I will speak with father once I grab a few things from my office. Richard brought me in this morning. I will be working from William's apartment while we settle some things with Bill. Honestly, it kind of creeps me out that he got into my place without my permission. Richard had the locks changed, but I don't know, there is something different about Bill, something dark. I don't know how to handle him anymore."

"You need to be careful," Jane warned.

"Don't worry, Jane, both William and Richard are watching me like a hawk. I can't make a move that they are not with me. I have to admit though, I am very much liking the attention." Elizabeth smiled.

Jane looked at her sister and smiled in return. "I just bet you are."

The sisters made plans to have lunch tomorrow to talk about more wedding plans before Elizabeth headed off to her office. So far, it was turning out to be a great day.

*****

Richard took a seat outside of Mr. Bennet's office. The secretary informed him that there was someone meeting with him at the moment. Richard sat paging through his blackberry when the door opened. George Wickham walked out with a dour expression on his face. Behind him, Mr. Bennet followed, stopping at his entryway. "Thank you again for your offer, Mr. Wickham. I will explain everything to Lydia. Ah... Mr. Fitzwilliam... won't you come into my office? I have been expecting you."

Richard and George made eye contact briefly. Once he passed, Richard rose from his chair and entered into the office with a firm handshake and a nod. This wouldn't take too long, and then he would be off to meet with Elizabeth. He looked forward to spending most of the day with her. He had even thought of taking her out to lunch at one of his favorite cafes.

*****

Elizabeth was humming when she opened the door to her office. She had quickly sat at her desk and turned on the computer when a man's voice was heard. "Good morning, Elizabeth, I'm glad to see you came to work today."

She froze and slowly turned to see Bill Collins sitting on her couch. He was not happy, judging by the look on his face. "What are you doing in here, Bill?" she asked with a slight lump in her throat.

"I left you several messages at your apartment after the gala. Didn't you get them? I would have thought you could have taken the time to let me know you were home and safe," he said in an even, dark tone.

"Bill, like I have said before, we are no longer dating, and I do not owe you anything, much less an explanation of what I do and with whom I do it," Elizabeth replied with more courage than she felt. It was starting to really anger her that Bill was being so possessive of her.

"You were with William Darcy, weren't you? I saw how you danced with him at the Gala. You should be ashamed of yourself. There were clients there watching you parade around like a common whore, Elizabeth. I thought you had more respect for yourself and this company." His condescending tone brought a chill down her spine.

"You have no right to say such things to me, Bill. I want you out of my office." Elizabeth stood and pointed toward the door.

"When I'm ready to go, I will. If you're going to act like a child and throw away all that we have been to each other for some sexual games with that man and his cousin, then don't think you can just come back to me as used goods. You know that I want you to live with me, to marry me. You are sorely mistaken if you think I'm going to let those men paw you and play games with you. I want you to move in with me, Elizabeth, and I don't want to hear anymore on the subject. I have some very damaging photos that I could put out in the media that would destroy both of those men; then where would you be? Your father trusts me with this business, and I'm sure if I told him all about that man and his kinky ways, he would have no problem telling you exactly the same thing."

"STOP, I won't listen to anymore of your vile words. GET OUT! What I do and with whom I do it is my business. What ever you think you know about William Darcy or Richard Fitzwilliam is all a figment of your imagination. I will speak with my father myself, and if you think you will be praised for your behavior, then you are mistaken. I also want you to give me back my key. You are not welcome to come to my home, to call me, or conduct any conversations with me outside of business, and I would prefer that to be by email. Do you understand me?" Elizabeth's voice became more demanding and angry with every minute that she was forced to listened to Bill Collins. She had taken enough, and she was going to take a stand.

Bill pulled his key ring out of his pocket and tossed the key on Elizabeth's desk. "You have turned into someone I don't even recognize anymore. How much would it take for me to fuck you? What types of games do you like to play, Elizabeth? I'm sure I can accommodate you. I treated you right, showed you the finer things a man with honor has to offer. You have sold yourself to the lowest bidder, Elizabeth. But hear me now — this is not over. You will be mine."

"Over my dead body! Now get out of here before I call security!"

Just as Bill turned to leave, Richard walked in. His face reflected his steely rage, focused and ready to pounce. "Collins, what are you doing in here? I believe you have been served papers in the way of a restraining order. Should I find you near her again, I will not even bother calling the cops. I will take care of you myself," he gritted out.

"Bill, I want to see you in my office — now, if you please," Mr. Bennet smoothly said from behind Richard. Bill had pushed the limit of his tolerance. He could see Elizabeth was shaken, and this would go no farther. Bill Collins had just sealed his own fate.

Bill pushed past Richard as he walked ahead of Mr. Bennet. Richard immediately went to Elizabeth and enfolded her in his arms. "Are you okay? What did he say? I could have killed him just now. I heard some of the conversation out in the hall as I was coming to meet you. I'm so sorry I was not here with you."

Taking in a deep shaky breath, Elizabeth took the offered comfort from Richard. "I'll be fine. He really has lost his mind. He thinks I will still marry him and move in with him. I don't understand what has happened to him." Her voice was now shaking, and Richard could hear the uncertainty in her words. He hated that she had to endure such a conversation. He would take care of Bill Collins later.

"Don't you worry about him. Have you gotten everything you need?"

"No, I haven't even had the opportunity to get into my computer; he was here waiting on me when I sat down."

"Ok, then I will stay with you while you do what you need to, and then we can get out of here. I spoke with your father, and he is aware of everything that concerns the police and the restraining order. William explained the locks at your apartment and the pictures already, so he is up to date on everything that's going on. He also knows you are staying with William for a few days, should he need to reach you."

"Thank you. You both have been really great. I don't know what I would have done if I had walked into my apartment and seen it littered with pictures. I never would have guessed it was Bill to start with. That is just what he wanted from me, to go running back to him so he could have me back. Just thinking that someone got into my place and did something like that is really upsetting."

Richard kissed Elizabeth on the head and gave her one last squeeze before he released her to go sit on the couch. He pulled out his blackberry and began to work on it. Elizabeth felt better knowing he was with her. She sat at her desk and began to gather all the things she needed for the next few days. Even if she didn't stay with William, she was not ready to be alone at her place. She decided she would speak with Jane tomorrow when they met for lunch and see if she could stay with her a few days. With Bill acting so strange and possessive, she wasn't sure she was safe alone anywhere right now.

*****

"Bill, take a seat," Mr. Bennet darkly ordered.

"You have no idea whom you are leaving your daughter in the care of. Richard Fitzwilliam and William Darcy are not what you think," Bill began in a defensive tone.

"I know exactly who they are. What I don't understand Bill, is this sudden obsession with my daughter. I told you last night to let it go. She is no longer interested in you. You have gone beyond all rational thought. Did you think I wouldn't find out about what you have done?" he snapped at Bill.

"I have done nothing that didn't need to be done for Elizabeth. If you know so much, then why are you leaving her in the hands of those, those animals?

They will only use her for sex and games. It's what they do to women. If you can't see that with your own eyes, then I will just have to do what you should have done a long time ago," Bill angrily retorted.

"And what is that, Bill? I have worked with you for over thirteen years and I have never seen this side of you. Bill are the best in the business when it comes to working the best deals but when it comes to my daughter, you have failed miserably. I won't tolerate this kind of behavior."

"My behavior! That's rich! So allowing your daughter to sleep with two men who do who knows what to her is more acceptable to you than my defending her and wanting to marry her. I thought you had more sense than that. More respect and love for Elizabeth than that. But I can see now that I was wrong."

"Bill, I'm sorry you see it that way. Elizabeth is old enough to make her own decisions. I will not interfere with her private life unless I feel she is in danger."

"She is in danger."

"Yes, I agree she is, but not from them, from you. I want you to clear out your desk, Bill. You are fired. Security has been alerted, and you will be escorted out in the next hour. If I so much as hear that you have gone near my daughter or my family, I will have you arrested on the spot. I am fully aware that there is a restraining order placed on you; so, if I were you, I would go home, cool off and start working on my resume."

"You are a damn fool if you think I will go quietly. I have negotiated the best deals and made you more money than anyone else in this office. You have no reason to fire me, and I will have my lawyers contacting you. This is shit, and you know it, Bennet. Who the hell do you think you are? This company will be mine and so will Elizabeth."

Bill turned and stormed out of the office, slamming the door behind him. Mr. Bennet picked up his phone and called security to immediately cover both Bill's office and Elizabeth's. He knew Bill had gotten out of hand with his need to possess Elizabeth over the last few weeks, but now he was out of control. Reaching into his desk, Mr. Bennet withdrew a handgun he kept there for emergencies and put it in his jacket pocket. He would walk down to Jane's office, which was just across the hall from Bill's, to make sure she was safe first. He knew Richard was with Elizabeth, and he felt secure in his ability to protect her.

Chapter 17

Bill was on his way to Elizabeth's office, prepared to drag her out, when security arrived and swiftly escorted him out of the building. They did not allow him any time to pack his office, a fact that angered him greatly. He had many important papers and files that belonged to him, not to mention a lifetime of references in his Rolodex. He cursed Bennett and his company but vowed it was not over yet.

Mr. Bennet had gone directly to Jane's office, and without causing her to panic, explained that Bill had been fired. Jane, not surprised by the news, called over to Elizabeth's office to speak with her briefly. Her father paced near her desk while she dialed the extension, adding to Jane's already frazzled nerves about the entire Bill ordeal.

"Elizabeth, you need to be extremely careful. Father is really on edge right now, and he told me he is carrying his handgun again," Jane said worriedly.

"You can't be serious! I swear, what has gotten into that man's head? Bill has lost his mind. I will be very careful Jane. Thank you."

"Elizabeth, maybe you should come home. Though I think William and Richard are doing a fine job of protecting you, father would be a lot more at ease if he knew you were close and safe."

"Jane, please don't concern yourself with me. I want you to stay safe. Can Charles come and get you later? I don't want you to go home alone. Dad can see to Mary and Catherine since they still live at home. Richard is here with me now, and William will be home later this evening. Richard has his security team watching my every move— and Bill's. I feel very safe with them both around. If you need anything or something happens, please call me. I still want to do lunch tomorrow; are you up for that?"

Jane could see there was no talking her sister into returning home with her father so she gave up the effort. "Sure, do you mind if I bring Caroline? She is leaving on Sunday, and I don't think she has much to do till then. Charles and I are having dinner with her later tonight."

"I don't mind at all. She should have some say in this since it is her brother's wedding, too. I need to go now— Richard wants to get me away from here. I'll call you later, okay?"

"Okay. Elizabeth, please be careful."

"I will Jane. Goodbye"

*****

Bill sat across the street from the parking garage watching for Elizabeth and Richard to emerge from the building. He was not done with any of them. He had already placed a call to his lawyer whom he would be meeting first thing in the morning. William Darcy would not get away with brainwashing *his* future wife with his tasteless sex games, nor would his depraved cousin lay another hand on her. This was not how things were to turn out. He had not spent all those hours of hard work helping to build this company, to be summarily dismissed like some high school clerk. As for Elizabeth, he would teach her a lesson she would not soon forget. You don't just go off whoring yourself to men when you are in charge of a company like she would run some day. Scandals had ruined many a career and business over the years, and his would not be one of them. Bill cared for this business and considered it his own. Once old man Bennet died, he knew he would have great influence and power as the husband of the new owner. If he needed to, he would call in favors to help pave the way for a take over.

He noticed movement near an exit and watched as a couple stepped out onto the sidewalk. Bingo! It was finally them. He observed Elizabeth and Richard as they walked through the side parking lot, watching to see which car they were going to get into. Richard stopped in front of a black SUV and opened the door for Elizabeth. She smiled sweetly up at him as she slipped into the interior, which only added to Bill's hatred of the man. He followed them down a short ways to a small café about ten minutes from the office. Angry at the turn of events, he pulled into a metered spot and sat waiting for them to reappear. He wanted to know where Richard lived, and if it took a few hours of trailing them, so be it. He had nothing better to do.

*****

Richard felt much better now that he had Elizabeth away from the office. Bill was too much of an unknown. He had a tail on him, so hopefully he would have a report later tonight to review. Then he could make some adjustments to the security detail for Elizabeth if he needed to. He was happy that Elizabeth could relax a little and enjoy a nice lunch. His favorite café was definitely the place to do that. They had a wonderful outdoor courtyard in the middle of the restaurant, and he had called ahead earlier in the morning to have a table reserved.

"Richard, this is amazing! I just love it here. I could spend hours sitting here eating and drinking." She smiled happily.

"I'm glad you like it; it is one of my favorite places. I love to come here on Saturday mornings and enjoy brunch. They have the best spread around. Maybe we can come this weekend. Darcy isn't opposed to eating here; we just have to convince him to get up before noon, dress and get out the door." He chuckled.

"So, he likes to sleep in, does he? Well I am an early bird. I always have been. My father and I have often enjoyed early morning talks on the patio while drinking coffee, chatting about what ever came to mind," she happily replied.

Richard marveled at Elizabeth's sincerity and joyful attitude. She was just a naturally bubbly person, full of life. She was so easy to talk to; it never seemed forced or fake. He asked her if she would mind if he ordered for them. She was more than happy to let him make a selection since he regularly dined there. Soon after he placed their order, their drinks arrived, and they sat soaking up the afternoon sun and conversing on a great many things.

"Elizabeth, would you mind if I ran by my place? I need to pick up a few things before we head back to Darcy's apartment. It won't take long."

"Not at all. I would love to see where you live." She beamed at him. The twinkle in her eyes did funny things to his stomach, and he couldn't help but reach over and take her hand, kissing her knuckles.

"I have to tell you, I'm not as impeccable as Darcy in how I keep my house. I own a condo with two bedrooms, a small study, nothing terribly big, but it suits me just fine. My older brother comes to stay with me from time to time, so the second bedroom is his."

"I would love to hear more about your family at some point. William told me a little about his. He mentioned that your brother was a bit of a computer guy."

"He is at that. Alex is not one to step away from his computer too often or for too long. He makes a good living at it, though, so who am I to judge? He still lives at home with my parents. Both Darcy's family and mine live out in the country on land right next to each other. My dad's sister is Darcy's mother. So we are what you call a close knit family," he said with a grin and raised brow.

"I see. I think it sounds wonderful. I'm not as close to my family, but Jane and I are sort of like you and William. We share everything." At that, Elizabeth blushed a deep red and gasped at her words.

Chuckling at her sudden embarrassment, Richard squeezed Elizabeth's hand. "It's okay. I know what you mean — and what you don't."

"I mean, we talk about everything..." she tried to cover for her slip of the tongue, "well, almost everything," she added, her eyes huge circles and her face beet red.

Richard chuckled at her muddled state. "Have I told you how adorable you are when you get all flustered, Elizabeth"? He stared at her with honest eyes, smiling at the woman before him. Once Elizabeth settled down, the couple finished their meals and headed to Richard's.

*****

Caroline Bingley set out to think, with the car radio blasting as it played her much loved I-pod tunes. It was a beautiful day, and with the windows rolled down, she found herself in deep thought. It was Monday, and she would be leaving town for Paris on Sunday. She drove past spots that brought happier memories to her mind — the little café where she and Richard had enjoyed brunch on many Saturday mornings, and the city park where she would walk everyday after she had moved in with Richard. Soon she found herself outside of the one place she couldn't forget. Richard's condo complex was right next to her when she pulled to a stop at a red light. Sighing, she stared over at the one that belonged to him, hoping he might actually walk out or in while she sat there. How silly of her to even think such a thing, she chastised herself. He had moved on, and why wouldn't he? She knew Darcy and Richard would share someone as special as Elizabeth; she seemed like a great girl. If she was anything like her sister, she knew they could be good friends one day, and that made her happy

The light changed to green, and she shook her head and continued her drive. She would need to return to her brother's place soon. She had promised Jane she would go to dinner with them tonight. She wanted to shower and change before they left. She continued her way around town enjoying the sun and good weather. Then she had a thought. She really wanted to call Richard, just have a cup of coffee with him, and give him an apology for her behavior then to thank him for all they had shared. She never really got closure, and she felt now was the time. Perhaps they both needed it in some small way to move on.

She withdrew her cell phone once she pulled into the driveway at Charles's house. Dialing the familiar digits she had never forgotten, Caroline listened to Richard's voice come over the line instructing the caller to leave him a message. Inhaling deeply, she listened for the familiar beep, and in her most cheerful voice, left the message she hoped would lead to a date for later this week.

*****

"Well, you've been saved; this is my place." They pulled into a complex right off the road. The grounds were beautiful. Lots of trees and flowers were scattered about the walkways and open spaces between buildings. Richard pulled past the gate and down a few buildings to park. "So, are you ready to go in?" he asked, glancing at her with a hint of playfulness.

"Yes, I am. Perhaps you could even offer me a glass of wine; I think I may need one," she said, her blush barely visible as she shook her head and opened the car door. They had been sharing each other's most embarrassing moments in childhood, and Elizabeth was just about to confess one of her many.

Richard chuckled to himself as he watched her close the door and walk to the front of the car. He hadn't had anyone over of the female persuasion since Caroline. He wondered what Elizabeth would think of the place. He was actually glad to have an opportunity to bring her over. He walked up to meet her and placed his hand at the small of her back to escort her to the front door. He opened it up and allowed her to go in first.

*****

Once the door was opened and Elizabeth stepped through, she was instantly impressed. There was nothing boyish about his place. The woods were all in a dark walnut or cherry finish. He had great hardwood floors in a rich

139

brown. There was a fireplace in the living room with two couches and two recliners. She touched the leather couch, and then dragged her fingertips along the fabric of one of the chairs. "You have a wonderful place. Do you mind if I look around some more? I know I'm nosey." She smiled.

"You can do what ever you wish. Please feel free to look around. I'm going to go down the hall to my study and check a few things on the computer and grab what I need. Why don't we go to the kitchen first, and I will get you that glass of wine."

"I would love that," she said eagerly.

They walked into an amazing sunlit kitchen with rich cherry wood cabinets and granite counters in a gold and rust tone. There was a great 6-burner stove, double ovens, a large farmhouse sink — everything a serious cook would enjoy. "You really love to cook, don't you?" she asked, marveling at the beauty of everything.

"I do. This was the first room I had remodeled when I moved in here about three years ago. I must admit, if I hadn't gone into the family business, I would have become a chef, I think. I have had a love for cooking since I was a child. My fondest memories of my mother and grandmother are moments we spent in the kitchen; some even include my crazy Aunt Catherine, back in the day." He smiled as his mind wandered back to those days.

"I think it's wonderful that you enjoy cooking. So many men don't cook or have a clue as to how to go about it. It's refreshing to find a man who enjoys it so much. Maybe you and I could fix something together tonight for William. He has had to work all day. I can see from your kitchen, his doesn't compare. Maybe we could have him over here for dinner. Is that something we can do?" she asked unsure of what the expectations were for such things.

Richard walked up to her and placed his hands around her hips. "I think that is a fantastic idea. We can make a run to the grocery store, grab a few things, and come here to whip up dinner. It will be our surprise for him," he happily agreed.

Elizabeth beamed with excitement at the thought of doing something nice for William while enjoying this wonderful kitchen and the company that Richard would provide for the afternoon. "Elizabeth, there are no set rules. If there is something you want, all you need to do is ask. William will not have an issue with us making him dinner I can assure you. That man couldn't cook if his life depended on it. If you haven't noticed, you have either eaten out or had something along the lines of cheese, crackers and fruit since you have been at his place... well, besides the breakfast I made you." He winked and placed a kiss on her lips. The gentle brush was kind and simple, and Elizabeth smiled up at him in delight.

"Well, you do make a valid point. If I'm going to be coming over often, I'll have to make sure he keeps some better items stocked in his kitchen. I do like to cook, and I suppose that will fall to me when you are not around, or when it's my turn," she quickly added.

"That sounds like a fine plan. Tomorrow we can hit the store near his place if he goes to the office. Well, I'm going to leave you to peek in all my closets and under my bed while I go get a few things taken care of. If you need me, please feel free to just come get me."

"Okay, thanks."

They parted ways, and Elizabeth sipped at her wine as she went from room to room. Richard had a great place. It was very homey; she knew she could spend many happy hours curled up on one of the couches, warmed by the fire. The last room she entered had to be Richard's. It had a bed just like William's did, an extra large California king. The room was large and had two chairs and a small table between them that resided near a large window overlooking a treed area below. Elizabeth moved over to the window to look around. It was just gorgeous. She opened the window to let the fresh air in and turned to face the room. She decided to check out the bathroom while she was there.

Just like she expected, there was a shower large enough to accommodate three or more. Two rain heads and a wall of body sprays gave her an itch to shower. She liked William's shower just fine but this looked to be one awesome system, and she would have to try it out some time. Her eyes glazed over as she remembered the first time she had showered with William. They had made love for several hours when they finally got out of bed to get ready to eat at her parents. He had taken such care in seeing to all her needs that day. She could still feel his hands as they gently glided along her body, placing sudsy bubbles along her flesh. Oh how she had enjoyed every caress, every touch of his hands against her body. How his lips felt as they traveled along her neck, her shoulders, and her entire body. When they were together it was like magic each time. Their minds seemed to be in sync, always knowing what the other needed.

Elizabeth could remember each contour of William's body, each inhalation he took as she pressed her hands against his skin. Just the feel of his long body against hers as she held him against her breasts, their chests becoming one as they kissed beneath the warm water... The way William's strong arms encircled her until they could fight their rising desires no more and made love again on the tiled floor underneath the spray... It seemed they couldn't keep their hands off each other, and that thought made Elizabeth smile even more. She missed William today. As much fun as she was having with Richard, she could tell there was a special connection with William. When Bill said all those hateful words to her earlier, it was William she thought of first. How she had wanted to be in his arms. Tonight she would make him a wonderful feast, and if she was extra lucky, she might be able to talk her two favorite men into going out dancing later.

Moving back to the bedroom, she finished her wine and set her glass down on the nightstand. She crawled up on the bed to see how the mattress felt. Full from lunch and the three glasses of wine she had enjoyed during the afternoon, she found herself a bit sleepy. She reasoned that if Richard had some work to do, then she could just lie down and take a quick catnap. Then when she woke refreshed, they could head to the grocery store for the dinner items.

*****

Having just hit the send button on the last of the emails he had to get out, Richard looked at the time at the bottom of the computer screen. It had been nearly an hour since he had logged on. He stopped and listened — nothing. Wondering what Elizabeth could be up to, he decided to seek her out. He didn't see her in the living room or the kitchen so walked down the short hall past his brother's room to his own. When he got to the door, he found her sprawled out on his bed. She looked so sweet, so lovely. He hated to wake her, but if they were going to go to the store and have time to cook, they needed to go. Darcy was going to be there in about three hours, hungry and ready to sit down to dinner. He was not one bit happy with what had transpired at Elizabeth's office with Bill and would want all the details and to see for himself that Elizabeth was fine. He couldn't blame him either.

They might even stay the night if everyone agreed. Then again, Darcy and Elizabeth might leave since her work was still at William's place along with her clothes. He realized that he would need to make her a bit of space for anything she might like to keep at his place in case there was ever a need. He smiled and walked over to one of the chairs. He noticed the opened window and sat down before it, enjoying the slight breeze that wafted though. He picked up his book off the small table, figuring another fifteen minute delay wouldn't hurt. He sat and watched Elizabeth as she slept. He wanted to go curl up next to her and rest himself, but he wouldn't. There wasn't time now; maybe later he would have an opportunity to be with her. They had enjoyed such a lovely lunch, and dinner promised to be even better if they were going to work together in the kitchen. He always did love a woman who enjoyed cooking as much as he did.

*****

Bill noted where Richard lived. He knew he was the better man for Elizabeth; he just had to find a way to make her see it. He decided to call it a day and go home. After he met with the lawyer in the morning, he could make up his mind what direction he would take.

*****

"How many times did I tell you, George — hundreds, thousands? Elizabeth liked you for so long and you, you finally ask her out and do what? Then to make matters worse, you kiss Lydia at the Gala. Have you lost your mind? I can't believe I have to call you my brother. What a jerk you are." Lacey fumed as she berated her brother. He was sitting on the couch, looking at her with no change in expression. She picked up a small pillow from a chair beside her and tossed it at him. "You couldn't leave town fast enough for me. Perhaps Dad can have you stay there permanently. It serves you right that Elizabeth has moved on. I can't believe I tried to hook you two up all these years. She is my best friend, George. You have no respect for women. You make me sick." Lacey turned and stormed out of the room. She had just finished the last email from Elizabeth and couldn't believe her own eyes at what she read. Well, it was over now. Elizabeth had moved on to those hunky men, and Lacey was glad of it.

George sat pondering what to do next. He pulled his cell phone from his pocket and dialed the now familiar digits. "Hi, it's me. Can you get away and meet me for a drink?"

*****

Richard's pocket vibrated, alerting him to a new voice mail. He glanced at the caller and scrunched his brows together at the name. It was Caroline. What could she be calling for? He hadn't spoken with her in so long, and now in the span of three days, he had seen her, danced with her, and chatted as if nothing had ever happened. The only thing it had gotten him was a mind full of memories he had tried to forget.

"What is the matter? You look upset," the soft voice of Elizabeth reached his ears. He glanced up, placing his cell phone down on the table.

"Nothing to concern yourself with." She looked up at him with a slight smile. He rose from the chair, placing the book there, and strolled to the bed. He sat on the edge, stroking Elizabeth's cheek with his finger. "Did you sleep well?" he softly asked.

"I did. Those three glasses of wine and the wonderful meal you fed me must have made me a little sleepy. Were you able to get your work done?"

"Yes thank you. I'm sorry I left you for so long. So, what do you think of the place? How many dust bunnies did you find?" he asked with a wink.

Elizabeth smiled and swung her legs over the edge. "Well Mr. Fitzwilliam, I am sorry to say I did find one thing wrong with your place." She tried to act so serious. Richard found it quite endearing.

"Oh, you did, and what would that be?" he played along.

"That I have yet to be able to take advantage of your shower. I think that has got to be the best set up I have ever seen," she said, her words of praise bringing a smile to his face.

Laughing at her enthusiasm, Richard replied, "Well, by all means, I don't mean to deny you any pleasure you might have in enjoying it. It's one of my favorite things, also. Perhaps we should have William go by the apartment and pack you an overnight bag. That way you would have something to put on when you're finished soaking in it." He smiled.

Elizabeth's eyes lit up. "Oh, do you think he would mind? Your place, by the way, is wonderful. I really like what you have done with it," she complimented him.

Richard placed a text to William. Then the two set out for the grocery store after checking out the kitchen contents and making a list.

Chapter 18

William sat behind his desk, fingers tapping next to his computer mouse; he couldn't concentrate. The latest text message he had received from Richard stated that he and Elizabeth were at lunch at the café near Richard's place. Darcy was never so happy to have insisted on Richard's staying with Elizabeth. Still Bill Collins was a real danger to her. He wished Mr. Bennet had informed him the other night that he intended to fire Bill. He would have had time to rearrange his own schedule to be with Elizabeth himself.

After the initial text from Richard earlier in the morning about the argument he had overheard between Bill and Elizabeth, William had done nothing but worry about her. If it weren't for an extremely important meeting he had to attend in a few minutes, he would have left hours ago to be with her. Suddenly a thought came to his mind. Darcy picked up the phone and placed a call to the one person he knew who could possibly be the most help to him right now.

Finished with his call, Darcy had his secretary prepare a few things. He heard the beep of his phone and glanced down at the screen to see the new text. His attitude instantly changed into a smile when he read the contents.

(Meet us at my place once you're able to get away. Perhaps go by your apartment and grab an overnight bag for you and E. All is well.)

This was perfect, just what he needed. With a new outlook on his afternoon, Darcy headed off to his meeting in a much better mood.

*****

Their arms laden with plastic white bags, Richard and Elizabeth finally reached the kitchen. Their trip to the grocery store had been a great success. Elizabeth unpacked the bags while Richard put everything away. It had been a long time since Richard had shopped with anyone, and he had enjoyed himself immensely. Elizabeth had found so many things she wanted to prepare for both William and him, it made him smile just thinking about her face all lit up with excitement. She had chatted about each dish while filling the cart. She walked and talked so fast, it fascinated Richard just watching her. He was caught off guard when he heard Elizabeth clapping her hands while saying, "Well that's it, nothing left but to cook it all now." She smiled up at him.

"I may have met my match. I've never seen a woman who enjoyed a trip to the local market more than you. All that shopping must have left you parched. Can I get you something? A glass of wine perhaps?"

"I'll save the wine for later. How about a glass of ice water?" she sweetly replied.

"Coming right up. We can go relax in the living room," Richard offered, "or if you prefer, we can walk over to the pool and put our feet up."

"Oh, I would love to see more of your complex," she enthusiastically answered. "Let's go to the pool."

"Let me grab some plastic tumblers, and we can be on our way then."

The two set off, with Elizabeth admiring Richard's development as they walked. The grass was a dark luscious green, with tall shade trees and flowerbeds scattered about. A few benches dotted the walkway for residents to sit and enjoy the beauty of the outdoors. There was a wonderful breeze that kept the heat of the afternoon at bay quite nicely. They arrived at the pool and quickly found a couple of lounge chairs to kick back in. They spent the next few minutes in happy conversation, laughing and learning more about each other.

Elizabeth's cell phone went off in her pocket. "Oh, this is Jane; I really have to take this. Will you excuse me for a moment?"

"Sure, go right ahead; I understand completely." Richard nodded as he sipped his drink. He watched Elizabeth walk off to a grassy area not too far away. He took the opportunity to pull his own phone out and glance at his last call. It was from Caroline, and there was a message. He looked back up at Elizabeth who continued to chat with her sister as she paced back and forth on the grass, so he decided to quickly check his message.

(Hi Richard, it's Caroline. I'm only in town for a few more days and wondered if we could have coffee sometime. It was so good to see you Saturday night. I'm staying with my brother Charles, so you can reach me at 606-555-9721 or on my cell. Hope to talk with you soon. Bye.)

Richard saved the message and sat pondering what to do. Since seeing Caroline at the Gala, he had been thinking of her quite a bit. Some of those memories were good ones; others just brought painful recollections of a time he just didn't wish to revisit. There was also the small issue of the pictures that Bill Collins had put in Elizabeth's apartment. He knew they were hers, but how Bill had gained access to them was a mystery. He really needed to speak with her about that since it was important to the case he was building against Collins.

But seeing her, no matter if it was for personal or business reasons would be difficult. He had really started to fall in love with Caroline back when they were dating, but now, he didn't know what to think. He again glanced up at Elizabeth. She was so beautiful, so much fun to be around, and after the last several days he was really starting to form a stronger attachment with her. They had enjoyed such a fantastic day together. He truly was starting to get to know her and didn't want to spoil what he had begun to build with her. She was like a breath of life into the stale existence he had endured since Caroline had left. He could see that both ladies might well hold a piece of him in their hands; he knew that, but Elizabeth was here now, warm and loving.

He decided to speak with William about this new revelation. They had always confided in each other about topics big or small. This was one of those times he really needed his best friend. It was, after all, just coffee and he really needed the information, but if he saw her and the old feelings came back, where could that lead? Was he willing to give up what he had now with Elizabeth for something he had once before and lost? Taking a deep breath as he stared off at the pool, he didn't hear Elizabeth come back.

"You seem miles away. Anything I can do to help?" The soft voice floated over his senses as Elizabeth placed her hand on his leg while taking a seat at the end of his lounger.

"No, not at all." He tried to cover by turning the conversation, "How is your sister?"

While Elizabeth sat stroking his leg, she sensed that he definitely seemed to have something on his mind, but she let it slide since he didn't seem willing to share. "She is safely at home. Charles picked her up at the office. They were having dinner with his sister Caroline tonight anyway, so it was no problem." She witnessed Richard's eyes widen ever so slightly at the name she mentioned. Quickly, she rose from the chair and took his hand in hers.

"Why don't we head back to your place? I'm sure we should start working on dinner; it's getting late, and William will be arriving soon, I'm sure?"

A slight smile lifted his lips at her offer. "As you wish. We have plenty of time; Darcy is never one to leave the office on time. Though if he thinks of you as often as I do, he might." Richard flashed his brilliant eyes and dashing smile at Elizabeth as he grabbed her hand. Elizabeth felt a ripple of electricity travel up her arm at his words and his touch.

*****

Standing in the kitchen, Elizabeth watched Richard pull out all the items they needed to start cooking. It wasn't going to be a fancy meal, but there was lots of chopping to be done. They had decided who would do what and started their tasks. Richard was at the stove working on one dish while Elizabeth prepped some vegetables. She started to hum softly to herself. Richard caught the faint sound and turned to see Elizabeth's back. She still had on her clothes from the office, nothing terribly dressy, but still nice. Her long brown curls fell along the back of her emerald blouse drawing his eyes farther down to her hips that curved so nicely in her khaki slacks. He vividly remembered how those hips looked as he had held on to them just last night. The rounded curve of her butt, the creamy skin beneath his grasp as he made love to her from behind made him yearn to do it all over again.

He forced himself to snap out of his daydream. Turning back to the stove he tried to concentrate on his task, but he really had enjoyed their time together today. He had gotten to hear so many stories of her childhood, her family, and her work. He paused a moment, then realized they hadn't really talked much about what was happening with Bill, let alone with William and himself. So much had transpired in the last three days, it had to have had some impact on her.

He lowered the fire on the burner to a simmer and walked over to the island. He leaned back against it and stared at Elizabeth's back. She finished rinsing the last of the vegetables and turned to take the bowl to the chopping block. She was startled just a bit as she turned. He smiled at her response and watched as she placed the bowl down and picked up her knife. "Are you finished already? I'm sure a kitchen as well stocked as this has another sharp knife around; you can join me." She smiled sweetly.

"Sure, I'll get one." He moved from his spot and opened the draw next to him, removing another blade. "Elizabeth, do you mind if I ask you a few things about the last few days?" His voice was lower and inquisitive. She stopped for a moment and looked up at him. He was reaching for a carrot but looking up so Elizabeth could see the expression of his face.

"You can ask me anything. You seem somewhat somber, however. Is this a serious talk?"

"I just want to make sure you're okay. I have had a great day with you. Honestly, it has been wonderful getting to know you. But, over the last three days there have been some real changes in your life. I want to know what you think about them. You can't bury your feelings or just believe they will fade away if you don't think about them."

Elizabeth put her knife down and placed both hands on the counter. She wrinkled her brow just a bit and thought for a moment. It was true, many things had happened since Saturday; she hadn't really taken the time to stop and think or rather dwell on all that had transpired. "You want to know about my feelings over Bill or are you speaking more to what we have shared between us and William?" she replied in a gentle tone.

"All of it. We can start with Bill. You were with him for many months. It can't be easy for you to see this side of him."

"I was with Bill for a long time. He introduced me to many people, and we had a good run. When he asked me to move in with him however, I knew that it had to end. Bill was always good to me, but there was something lacking in our relationship. I couldn't see *forever* in our future. He thinks I need space, that I will come crawling back to him when I haven't found whatever it is I'm supposedly looking for, but he's wrong. I don't want to be with him and even more so now. He has done some really stupid things lately. I'm not scared of him, just mad as hell at him for scaring my family and causing so much trouble. You and William have had to use your own company's security detail to watch him; you had to get a restraining order, not to mention he upset my father enough for him to carry that damn handgun of his again."

At that Richard stopped all he was doing. "Your father owns a handgun?"

"He has for years, but he has never carried it. He keeps it in his desk draw at the office, but Jane told me earlier today that when Bill left his office after being fired, that father was so worried that he took it from his desk and walked to Jane's office. Her office is across from Bill's, and my father was afraid Bill might do something rash since he was so angry. She asked me to go to my parents' house tonight so he could relax, knowing I was safe within his sites."

"Do you wish to return to your family Elizabeth?" Richard asked softly but firmly. He didn't want her to go, but if she needed to be with her family, he would understand.

"No, not at all. I feel very safe with you and William. I just can't believe this has all happened. He was so angry this morning when he was in my office. He …He said some awful things to me." Elizabeth took a deep breath, the memories of their earlier confrontation coming back to her. "He was so cold in how he spoke to me, then he became outraged. When you walked in, I thought for just a split second that he would try to hurt you," she confessed with dread in her eyes.

Richard could see the turmoil in Elizabeth's face and moved closer to her. He took her hand in his and placed the other under her chin to look into her eyes as he spoke. "As long as it is within my power, I would never let that man touch you or harm you in any way. You are safe here or at William's. We live in gated communities for a reason. He can't get in." He leaned in and kissed her lips softly.

Elizabeth could see the conviction in his eyes. His voice was strong but soft as he spoke to her. With her hand in his, she believed everything he said came right from his heart. She did feel safe with both of her men. It had only been a few days, and Richard was working his way into her life rather quickly, she thought. When he leaned in for a kiss, she could feel his affection for her, and she returned it. What they were sharing was new to them both and having opened up to each other all day made this moment more special to her. When he pulled her into his arms for a deeper kiss, she willingly surrendered. He stroked her back, her hair, all the way down to her hips. She pressed herself closer to him using her own hands to wrap about his waist to hold him tight. Before they could come up for air, a noise at the stove alerted them.

Quickly they broke the kiss and turned their heads towards the stove. A small fire was about to start as the saucepan bubbled over the edges. Richard broke his hold and quickly reached for some baking soda in the cabinet beside the pan. After he dealt with it, he turned with a smile and said, "Well, I can protect you from Bill, but I'm not so sure if I can keep you from harm in this kitchen."

They both chuckled and went back to their assignment, the magic of the moment temporarily lost. They continued to talk about the relationship in a lighter tone, both speaking frankly about each other and what they felt was happening. Richard briefly talked about a few of the other relationships he and William had been involved in and why they had broken up. He was just about to reveal their history with Caroline when they heard the front door open.

*****

William had finally been able to leave the office. There hadn't been any more information from the security detail on Collins since earlier in the afternoon. He had followed Richard to the café and then drove past his condo complex. It made Darcy nervous that he knew where both men lived. But they also both lived in gated communities. The security detail was on duty at Collin's house should he make a move tonight. William was hopeful that they could enjoy another nice evening all together without giving thought to that man.

He had missed Elizabeth so much today. Last night had been wonderful and a break through in the relationship for all three of them. When they had awakened this morning late, he had wanted nothing more than to wrap his body around Elizabeth and make love to her all day again. He settled for a quick shower with her, and though nothing happened, just being able to wash her from head to toe and help wash her hair, lifted his spirits for the day. He had always admired her from afar, had known she was special, but the more he learned about her, the more deeply he fell in love with her.

He quickly made his way home to change into something a little more comfortable than his business suit and packed several things for both Elizabeth and himself. He made several stops along the way to Richard's. He wanted a few bottles of wine and some flowers to surprise Elizabeth with. There wasn't anything he wouldn't do for her. He had something special planned for her this weekend. He had made sure his schedule was cleared, canceling every meeting that he couldn't do with a conference call. With all of Elizabeth's work at his place, there was no reason he couldn't work at home with her for a couple of days.

He pulled into Richard's gated community and parked. Walking toward the door, he could already smell a faint scent wafting from the condo. He smiled wondering what those two had been up to. He opened the door to an aroma that made his mouth water. He shut the door and before he could take a few steps in, Elizabeth was smiling at him from across the room, her beautiful brown eyes all lit up.

"Surprise! Richard and I have been hard at work making you a wonderful meal. I hope you're hungry."

Smiling at her excited state, William strolled over to her and handed her the flowers. Richard came up behind Elizabeth and welcomed his cousin, "Nice of you to join us. Elizabeth has found a new past time I believe." He chuckled as Elizabeth gave him a sideways glace and a little elbow to the ribs.

"Has she now?" William handed Richard the two wine bottles before he bent over and tilted Elizabeth's chin up to meet his lips for a welcoming kiss. Elizabeth was delighted to see him. She kissed him happily as she wrapped her arms around his neck to pull him closer for a strong hard hug. She had missed him and was so happy to finally have him home.

"With a welcome like that I should meet you for dinner every night with flowers and wine," he teased.

"I won't argue with that; I love flowers, and you always buy such lovely ones." She closed her eyes and inhaled the lovely scent from the bouquet in her hands, then turned to Richard and asked, "Do you have a vase I might put these in? I'll put them on the dinner table for all of us to enjoy."

Richard scrounged around and found just what she wanted. The men watched her happily go about cutting and arranging the assortment. "How has she been?" William whispered close to Richard so she couldn't hear them.

"She seems to be fine. I took a few minutes to ask her about Bill. She informed me that she was just mad at him for the trouble he has caused her family and us. She stressed that she feels safe with both of us, and admitted that she has no wish to go to her father's house at this time. I'd say she is a strong woman. Bill had some very harsh words for her earlier. We need to talk. Maybe we can let her finish up here while we go to my study. I have something important to discuss with you." Richard's voice was low and direct. William knew something was bothering him, and it had to be important if he wanted to talk right this minute.

"OK, let me just tell Elizabeth, and I'll meet you there."

"Sure." Richard turned and walked away to give Darcy a private moment. He knew that William needed to reassure himself that she was okay after what had happened earlier. This would give him a chance to check the computer for any new information on Bill.

*****

William walked up behind Elizabeth and placed his hands around her waist. She leaned back into him and continued to cut and arrange the flowers. "I missed you today, Elizabeth. I'm so sorry I wasn't with you at the office." He placed his chin on her crown, just enjoying holding her in his arms.

"I missed you, too. I know Richard was with me, but when Bill said all those awful things..." she tensed up just a bit as she spoke. It made William feel even worse that he hadn't been there for her. He turned off the water and turned her in his arms.

Looking directly into her eyes, he apologized, "Elizabeth, I am so, so sorry that he said those things to you. Richard told me a little of what he heard. Do you want to tell me about it?"

"No, it's over now. I'm just happy you're home." She leaned into his chest to listen to his heart. He wrapped his arms tightly around her body, holding her close, then placed a kiss on the top of her head before she looked up at him with glistening eyes. Those bewitching orbs that called to him even in his sleep. With her lips turned up to him, he couldn't refuse the need to kiss her passionately. He was thankful she was strong enough to withstand what Bill had said. That she missed him and wanted him to care for her even though Richard had been there, spoke volumes as to how they felt about each other.

When William pulled back, he took hold of Elizabeth's shoulders. "Richard wants to talk with me for a few minutes. Will you be okay finishing up here? We won't be long."

"Yes, I'm fine." Darcy started to turn away when she called to him, "William, I have noticed several times today that Richard seemed distant... you know... distracted. He has something on his mind, and it is bothering him. He hasn't told me anything, but I can tell. I hope you can help with whatever it is. I hate to see him like that."

153

"I will do the best I can." He turned and walked through the living room to the study. She cared enough to be concerned for Richard's well being. That was a positive sign that things were moving along with them. He hoped that whatever Richard needed to discuss would be brief and not as bad as his gut thought it might be.

*****

"Is she okay?" Richard asked. He could hear Darcy walking into the room and closing the door behind him.

"Yes, she is concerned for you, it would seem."

"For me?" Richard asked as he turned to face Darcy. He couldn't believe that after the morning Elizabeth had endured, she would be concerned for his well-being over her own.

Darcy took a seat on the couch near Richard's desk. "It would appear so. Now tell me what has you so upset. It's not like you to forgo a meal with a beautiful woman."

Richard glanced down at his lap thinking how best to approach the topic. William had been almost as deeply affected by Caroline as he was. He didn't want to put a damper on the evening since he knew Elizabeth was having such a nice day, but this was important. "I got a call from Caroline today," he said somberly.

Darcy took a moment to process what Richard said, and then repeated it to him. "Caroline called you? What did she have to say?"

"I didn't talk with her; she left a message. She wants to get together for coffee sometime this week before she returns to Paris. I know we need to ask her some questions about those photos. So much has happened over the last three days. I mean, seeing her at the gala; I danced with her, for Christ sake, to keep Elizabeth from being jealous of her. She was just so lost when she saw you dancing with Caroline that night. I thought it was the best thing to do, but I don't know. It has brought back some painful memories."

Darcy sat there listening to his cousin. He could hear the anguish in his voice. "Have you returned her call yet?"

"No."

"Good, we need to think this through. We know those pictures came from her camera. We need to know if she gave them to Bill. Do you think that she is trying to blackmail either of us or is in some way still working with Bill?" he suddenly asked as he leaned forward. He hated to take this approach but letting Richard dwell on the love he lost was not what he wanted, he wanted him to think of this as pure business, Elizabeth's safety needed to be addressed first.

"Honestly, I haven't given that option a thought. I don't think she would do that. She was happy with our relationship. I can't imagine that she would do something like that. It could harm her career as much as our own. No, I don't think she has anything to do with either. But if I have coffee with her, we might be able to figure out how he got them."

"Perhaps. I have made arrangements to work from home the next few days. You can meet with her Tuesday or Wednesday. I'll head back to the office before the weekend. I'm taking Friday off, and so are you. We are going on a short trip with Elizabeth."

"And where might that be?" he asked with a questioning furrow of his brow.

"I called my mother today. We haven't been to see our family in a long time. It's far enough away that Bill won't find her. It will give us all a chance to be together for several days straight and see how things work for us. I'm sure Elizabeth will wish to return to her own apartment by next week."

"Well, I suppose I should expect a call from my parents soon." Richard joked. "It will be nice to get away. I'm glad you can stay home; I need to go to the office myself. I have a few things to settle and some paper work to file. I'll make arrangements to see Caroline and go in Tuesday and Wednesday if you're sure you can work from home."

"I'm good. Mrs. Brody knows where to reach me if I'm needed."

Richard nodded his head that he understood. He turned back to his computer and quickly glanced through the entries. It seemed Bill was behaving tonight; the last report had him still at his place. He opened a new email and typed up a short letter to his mother. He was glad Darcy had made arrangements to go home this weekend. It had been too long. He prayed Aunt Catherine would behave herself; the old lady had away of embarrassing him from time to time.

*****

Elizabeth went about plating the meal and lighting some candles. She was thrilled that she had been able to cook for William and Richard. Not that he didn't facilitate it all, but she did feel more useful in helping with the shopping and cooking. The place smelled wonderful, and the flowers and the candles were the finishing touches for a meal that promised to be superb. She served up each plate and placed them at each setting, then uncorked both bottles of wine. Before she could turn, she felt hands run down her shoulders to her elbows. "Elizabeth, this looks amazing."

She felt the goose bumps run down her back as William's voice caressed her ears. Her lips curved into a smile as she turned in his hands. "Thank you very much. Are you boys ready to eat?"

"I think I need to sample some of my dessert before I start my meal." He leaned down quickly and kissed her neck all the way down and across to the other side and up again.

"William..." she whispered, "the food will get cold."

"Let it..." he paused to say before taking her earlobe into his mouth. The erotic sounds he made provoked an immediate response from her body. She leaned her head to the side and gave in to the moment. With her eyes closed, she didn't see or hear Richard come in.

Richard eyed the table filled with the food they had prepared, the lit candles, and the opened wine bottles. He snagged a bottle and filled a glass for Elizabeth. When William released her to face the table and take a seat, he handed it to her. "Elizabeth, this looks spectacular. I can't remember when I enjoyed a day more. Thank you."

Elizabeth blushed slightly and accepted the glass. She took a quick sip and replied, "I had fun, too. We will definitely have to do it again." Her beaming smile and bright eyes made him all the more pleased that he had brought her to his place today.

All three took their seats and began their meal. It was scrumptious. They sat for some time talking of their day's activities and savoring each mouthful. When the meal was over, Richard gathered the dishes to place in the sink. "Oh, I can help you with that!" Elizabeth blurted out.

"No, you won't; you did quite enough today. Just sit and relax. We can continue talking while I clear this away. William has something he wants to tell you."

Elizabeth glanced towards the handsome man on her right, "Do you? What news do you have for me?"

"I have made arrangements to work from home for the next two days. I thought we could both work from my place. Richard has a few things he needs to take care of at the office. I have also made arrangements to take a short trip this weekend, if you are available."

"A trip? Where are we going?"

"I thought I would take you to my family's estate in the country. It's been some time since Richard or I have been there. Would you like to go?"

Nodding as a huge smile spread across her lips, she answered, "Oh, yes, I would love to go. When do we leave?"

"Friday morning. We will return Monday evening, if that is okay with you."

"I will call my father in the morning and let him know I'll be unavailable Friday and Monday. It shouldn't be an issue. The work I have to do can be done from your place, and what I can't do from there, I'll have Jane handle. Oh, I almost forgot, I promised Jane we would have lunch together tomorrow. Will that be okay? I can take myself if you're busy."

"I don't mind at all. I will just drop you wherever you need to go. I can work from anywhere with my laptop. I would feel more comfortable staying near you."

"Okay, thank you I appreciate it. I know this can't last much longer. Bill is just over reacting; he will calm down in a few days. It's unlike him to be like this. I just don't understand what's gotten into him lately."

*****

They finished their wine and moved into the living room to relax a bit. Richard excused himself to go make his phone call. He was dreading it already. But he would only dwell on it more and ruin the rest of the evening if he didn't do it now. He walked back to his study and closed the door. He

157

pulled out his cell and hit the send button. With his heart rapidly beating he heard the phone ring. After two rings, she answered.

*****

Once Richard left, Elizabeth spoke with William. "I'm really sorry this has caused you both so much trouble."

"Don't be silly. And if you are worried about intruding on either of us, you're not. We have loved having you around. I hope you know you're very welcome in my home, and I'm sure I speak for Richard when I say he has enjoyed your presence here, as well. There is no rush on our part to have you leave."

"Thank you, I have enjoyed being with you both. But I do have my own place. Maybe I could just stay until we return Monday. I have work to do, and I'm quite certain all this nonsense will be over by then."

Chapter 19

With the dawn just breaking, Elizabeth woke early, ready to start her day. She glanced to each side of her and smiled at the gorgeous men that lay sleeping there. She had been able to talk the guys into going dancing later in the evening last night. Richard had seemed a little distant after having been in his study, and William claimed to be tired, but both men had been won over by the time they entered the club. They had taken her to a new place. The music was fresh with a great dance beat, the lights just low enough to give the place an intimate feel. The bar sat in the middle on a raised platform, making it the center of all activity.

They had settled on barstools instead of at a table so Elizabeth could get a better look around. Both William and Richard knew many of the people that frequented their favorite bar, and they proudly introduced her to their friends. Each took turns with her on the dance floor. Richard was one great dancer. His mood had improved drastically by the third dance. When they were both finally out of breath, he had escorted her back to the bar where William had their drinks waiting. They chatted a while, and then William took her out for a whirl. She had so much fun. When the club really got crowded, all three had gone out to the floor for the last few dances of the night. She loved when they danced all together. The guys were excellent partners and definitely knew how to turn the heat up.

Taking one last glance at her men, she quietly slipped out from under the covers and made her way to the kitchen. Everyone had things to do today, so she thought she would make the coffee for a change. Elizabeth had noticed that Richard always had to start his day off with a strong cup or two. She gladly went in search of what she needed around the kitchen. While the coffee started brewing, she took out some eggs and decided to make omelets from last night's leftover veggies. As she started to chop, she began thinking back on how her night had ended.

She was wiped out when they had returned to Richard's place, but found herself still on a high from all the great dance music. Feeling dehydrated, they had gone to the kitchen to grab some water before turning in. When Richard had finished, he excused himself while William continued to stand behind her at the counter massaging her shoulders, talking about the evening. Both the guys had been incredible to her all night, buying her drinks and dancing the night away. She even liked the new club, and they had offered to take her again whenever she wanted. Finished with their water, William had taken her by the hand and walked her to the bedroom. She remembered hearing the shower running when they had entered. William immediately turned off the lights in the bedroom, and then began to undress her in a way she wouldn't soon forget.

Just standing at the kitchen counter chopping veggies, Elizabeth could feel herself blushing all over at the remembrance. William had a way of ramping up her body into a heated pile of goo instantaneously it seemed. Smiling broadly to herself, she continued to work on breakfast. She placed the food into a frying pan and let it sauté down a bit. Then her mind took over once again.

William had pulled her closer, kissing her deeply. His hands worked across her back in gentle caresses before slinking down to the hem of her blouse and slowly removing it. With her flesh bared to him, she could sense his heightened arousal even in the darkness. Without warning, he had scooped her up and walked her into the bathroom. The lights were dimmed down low, and she could see Richard was waiting for her. He had all the showerheads flowing while the wall jets were blasting away at his back. Silently William had stepped into the enclosure and stood under a rain head with her in his arms. The warm water flowed over them both. It felt so decadent. The gentle cascade compared to nothing she had ever experienced. It was so soothing and the sound was mesmerizing. He had set her down and begun to wash her hair. She recalled how magnificent his fingers felt as he stroked each across her scalp. She just sighed and relaxed back into him more, his warm naked form fitting against her flesh, igniting her passions further.

Meanwhile, Richard had apparently found soap and while her eyes were closed, started to wash her from the front. His hands glided across her skin from head to toe not missing an inch. Between the two men she thought she would melt right on the tile floor before them. She felt so pampered and cared for. No one spoke; they just went about their tasks. Elizabeth could still hear William's words as he whispered in her ear, "There is nothing we wouldn't do for you Elizabeth. You are so very beautiful, such a great person to be around. We have enjoyed our evening with you tremendously and wanted to thank you for dinner and the great suggestion to go dancing. I hope you know that we appreciate you very much."

It had been the sweetest thing anyone had said to her in a long time. That they wanted to show their thanks to her in such a remarkable way only made her want to please them more. Once they were all cleaned and rinsed off, Richard had led her out of the shower and tenderly dried her off before accompanying her to the bedroom. He asked if she would wear one of his shirts to sleep in again, and she had agreed. He really seemed to like that she wore them. The look in his eyes as he had helped to dress her made her more secure in the connection they were building. He was so gentle and sweet to her, but his eyes spoke of a desire deep within. His palms caressed her body as his lips traced around each of her breasts. The last thing she had heard was his low timbre as he whispered her name breathlessly.

Blinking with a quick shake of her head, she stopped her thoughts. She looked into the pan where the vegetables sat rendered; she grabbed the egg mixture and was pouring it into the pan, when she caught a sound that startled her.

*****

Richard woke shortly after Elizabeth left the bed. He had tossed and turned most of the night. He hoped he hadn't awakened either of them.   He couldn't shake the feeling that something was going to happen to either Elizabeth or Caroline. The talk he had had with Caroline replayed in his mind as he lay there. She had sounded fine, but there was something underlying in her voice that he couldn't quite place. They had agreed to meet on Wednesday morning for coffee before he went into work. With his arms behind his head, he stared up at the ceiling. Caroline had been such an important part of his life at one time; their relationship had lasted just over a year. He thought she was the one. All three had gotten along so well. When he offered for Caroline to move in, it was with the intent that he would propose to her within the next six months. He just wanted to make sure Caroline was ready for the next step. He had told only Darcy of his intentions, which made it that much harder when she left. If he had only asked her sooner, perhaps she wouldn't have moved to Paris. It had been well over a year ago that she relocated, and then the news of her marriage to her manager after such a short period together had left him speechless. He couldn't even bring himself to go to the wedding. Now she was back and wanting to talk.

He could smell the coffee in the kitchen. It brought him back to the present and the woman who had prepared it. Elizabeth was just what he needed in his life. He had missed having someone around to care for. Elizabeth had been someone he and Darcy had wanted to ask out for several years. Though meeting Caroline had changed him at the time. He had really fallen for her. They had even discussed it many times before Caroline came into the picture and figured she wouldn't be ready for the relationship that they wanted to offer her. She was still too young then, and Darcy didn't want to chance losing her. Now, after her break-up with Bill Collins, he was never happier that he had forced Darcy's hand in asking her out. With Caroline seemingly out of the picture, each day was a new experience with Elizabeth, and as they grew to understand and get to know each other, it only made him appreciate and care for her more.

He quietly left the bedroom and softly walked to the entrance of the kitchen. Leaning up against the doorjamb, he watched Elizabeth. She had to have been in deep thought. Her complexion was rosy and flushed from what he could see. He noticed the coffee was ready and waiting with three mugs set out on the counter. She had also diced up some vegetables and looked to be busy making eggs. His stomach rumbled at the aromas wafting past his nose. He smiled to himself watching her work away in his shirt. Her bare toes resting on the hardwood floor, those shapely legs of hers disappearing under his shirttails, and her hair tousled down her back, made an all-too-appetizing picture for him.

With his mouth watering at both the woman and the food, he decided to approach her. He had barely taken three steps when a floorboard creaked beneath his feet. Elizabeth turned around to find him enclosing her in his arms. "Good morning beautiful, you have been busy, I see."

Elizabeth smiled, "I wanted to make us all something to eat before we go our separate ways. I know how much you enjoy a strong cup of coffee to start your day." She flirted back at him as he stared into her eyes, loving what he saw there.

She was incredible. Richard leaned down and kissed her soundly. "So I do," he said once he pulled back, then kissed her again.

*****

Elizabeth buttoned up the top four buttons to her shirt and ran her fingers through her hair to straighten her appearance before she smiled and hugged Richard. The man had talent. Who sweeps a woman off her feet while she cooks? He does. It was fast, passionate, and oh, so good. The only coherent thought Elizabeth could muster at the moment was plating food for the man who had just ravaged her, curling her toes and making her smile like a silly teenager. The man himself was seated at the table eating his omelet when William appeared around the corner. "Good morning," he groused. He was definitely not a morning person.

162

"Good morning, yourself, sleepy head. Can I get you a cup of coffee?" Elizabeth offered. She walked up to him and gave him a quick kiss on the cheek. She was still flushed from her morning quickie on the counter; it all seemed sort of surreal to her actually. Darcy eyed her for a moment, and then nodded his head and wandered over to the table. Cheerfully, Elizabeth took him a plate of eggs and a cup of coffee. He thanked her and took a long sip of the hot beverage.

"So, Mr. Charming, I am going to head to the office in a bit. Is there anything I need to check on for you?" Richard asked while he scarffed down the last few bites of his eggs.

"No I'm good, thanks. I have to take Elizabeth to lunch with her sister a little later; she has already asked to go to the market on the way to my place. She wants to stock it. I can only imagine what the two of you talked about yesterday.

Chuckling at Darcy's defeated look, Richard only added, "Well if it's any help to you, I think I may have met my match for kitchen fondness. Let her get what she wants. I will help cook. She wants to do it. She was so charming yesterday going on about dishes she wanted to prepare for us."

"I'm going to gain 20 pounds by the weekend, aren't I?" Darcy sighed.

"I wouldn't give up that gym membership just yet." Richard got up from the table and took his plate and cup to the sink where Elizabeth was washing the breakfast dishes. "Thank you Elizabeth, that was wonderful," he said aloud. Then he leaned closer and whispered near her ear, "But I found my appetite was sated way before the eggs ever hit my lips. If I failed to tell you, you look so hot in my shirt and nothing else..." He kissed her cheek and turned to head to the bedroom to get dressed.

Elizabeth felt all warm and fuzzy at his whispered words. She finished washing the last few items then went to sit with William and enjoy her coffee. They chatted for a bit and made plans for the day. Richard returned shortly dressed for work. He kissed Elizabeth on the forehead and nodded to Darcy before heading out.

*****

They arrived at a small diner where she and William greeted Jane. Darcy quickly said farewell and headed across the street to Starbuck's to work while they ate. The girls got right to work on wedding details. They placed their order and had started to discuss bridesmaid dresses when Caroline approached their table.

"Caroline, hi, I'm so glad you decided to join us," Jane proclaimed.

Caroline pulled out a chair and sat down with the two ladies. The waiter quickly appeared and took her drink order while handing her a menu. Elizabeth wasn't sure what to say. Jane did the talking for a few moments before she reintroduced Caroline to her.

"Hi, it's great to meet you again." Caroline smiled towards Elizabeth. She seemed just as friendly as she did the other night at her parents.

Elizabeth thought she was just beautiful. Her hair was swept up in a simple ponytail, and she was wearing a brown sundress and the cutest sandals she had ever seen. You could tell she caught the eyes of several men in the vicinity of their table. The waiter quickly reappeared and handed over her drink order and asked what she wanted to eat. She seemed so poised, casual and confident. Elizabeth wished she knew why Caroline had broken up with the boys. On some level, she could tell Richard was still hung up on her.

"We were just discussing bridesmaids' dresses. What is your opinion, since you will be one as well?" Jane asked. She handed over a few selections from the magazines she had brought with her. Caroline picked a few she thought were nice and asked about the colors Jane intended to use.

"Elizabeth, which one did you like? I'm not the only one to consider such things. As the maid of honor, I'm sure your opinion should override mine," Caroline explained. She handed Elizabeth the periodicals and watched her. Elizabeth picked the one she thought would be most flattering on her. If she had to stand next to Caroline, she at least wanted to look her best.

The ladies all agreed on the dress and colors to be used. It was a very productive lunch. They all got along very well. Caroline even told them stories of life in Paris and the runway shows she had loved working on. Elizabeth thought she sounded a little melancholy considering she was talking about such an exciting place. She wondered what might be bothering her.

They finished up lunch, and all hugged as they said their farewells. Jane wanted to get together Saturday night for dinner before Caroline had to return to Paris.

"I'm sorry, I won't be able to make it, Jane," Elizabeth expressed her disappointment.

"Why not?" Jane wondered.

"I'm going out of town for the weekend. Now don't tell father; I plan on emailing him as soon as I leave here."

"Out of town? Where are you going and with whom?" Jane questioned, her tone a little panicked.

Elizabeth eyed her sister, not wanting to discuss it in front of Caroline. "I'll tell you later when I get the details all worked out." She hoped Jane would drop the subject with that answer.

"Fine, but with Bill Collins running around like a mad man, I want to know where and with whom, please. I'll just keep calling you until you tell me, Lizzy." She was imposing her "big sister" look on Elizabeth, and her tone was starting to sound frighteningly like their mother's.

"I'm sorry to interfere; I don't mean to be nosey, but did you say Bill Collins? As in William David Collins?" Caroline asked with surprising interest that had both sisters turning to stare blankly at her.

*****

Bill stormed out of his lawyer's office. He couldn't believe that after all the years of loyal service to that man and to the company, he would have no recourse to being fired. His own lawyer advised him to leave well enough alone and to stay away from the business and the daughter. With a restraining order against him, it would really complicate things for him when finding another job.

Bill got into his car and sat. He contemplated what his next move would be. He knew he had shadows on him. He hadn't yet thought of how best to lose them. Sitting in the parking garage, he knew they would be at the exit waiting for him. He needed to find Elizabeth. If she could just be made to see he was the better man for her, then he would have the girl and the business. Mindlessly strumming his fingers on the steering wheel, a thought came to him. He pulled out his cell phone and thumbed through his contacts. A wicked smile came over his lips when he found what he was searching for.

165

*****

Darcy had been able to accomplish very little work all day. He had just settled himself on the outdoor patio at Starbuck's when he caught sight of Caroline walking into the restaurant. He sat on pins and needles wondering what could be happening. Close to two hours had passed before Elizabeth had finally walked across the street to meet him. They had gone to the market and were just about finished filling all his cabinets, when he couldn't resist the urge any longer.

"Elizabeth, I know you said you had a productive lunch and the wedding plans are moving right along, and I don't mean to pry, but what was Caroline doing there?"

"So you saw her did you? Well, she is going to be Jane's sister-in-law, and as such she is going to be a part of the wedding. Well before she returns to Paris, Jane asked her to come eat with us and help with some of the planning. I think it went very well. We all got along quite nicely. Is that going to present a problem for either you or Richard? She is going to become family you know."

Darcy stopped for a minute, his expression turning blank. He turned and quietly walked out of the kitchen. He had not even registered the fact from the Gala when she said her sister was engaged to Charles Bingley. Damn, if this wasn't the worst thing to have happen. Richard would always be reminded of Caroline. He would see her from time to time — it was going to be unavoidable if any of them were to have a relationship in the future. Darcy sighed heavily and slumped into his couch. He didn't know what to think.

He pulled out his phone and texted Richard. He wanted him to be as prepared as possible for what might lie ahead. He also explained that he would understand if he didn't want to come over after work. Angry with himself, William could not believe he hadn't thought of this before now.

*****

Elizabeth knew that something had been bothering William most of the day. He was so quiet. He seemed to be studying her so much of the afternoon. When he finally decided to ask her about lunch, she immediately figured what must have been on his mind. When he paled slightly at the mention of Caroline and then turned to leave the kitchen, she was not sure how to handle the situation. On the one hand, he had told her several times in the past how much he cared for her, how deep his feelings ran for her. But on the other hand, how should a woman take the reaction she had just witnessed? Did he still harbor feelings for Caroline himself? Was it so bad that she found Caroline to be a great person, that she could see herself becoming friends with her? If the relationship between Caroline and him was truly over, then what was his problem?

Suddenly unsure of her place in this arrangement or relationship or what ever they wanted to call it, she walked into the living room. She saw William text someone on his phone and figured it was Richard. She suddenly felt like she had just been punched. Poor Richard, maybe it was not William who was upset as much as it was Richard who would be affected by the news. Elizabeth went to the bedroom and took a deep settling breath. Why hadn't it clicked for her? Richard was the one who would be most affected. William would want to protect his dearest relation from more heartache. Of course he was stunned at the revelation. But how were they to get past it? Caroline was a great person, and Elizabeth had genuinely enjoyed her company at lunch. All three had laughed and talked just like old friends.

She sat on the edge of the bed trying to think of a solution to this dilemma. She should just go home. The locks were new, and there had been no activity at her place since the photos were left. Bill had a restraining order placed on him to stay away from her. She would be safe for the night, and then in the morning, she would go to the office and get back to her life — her normal average life, free from all the unrealistic dreams and fantasies she had been indulging in for the past several days. She really did have strong feelings for William, and if he decided that he wanted to continue to see her, he knew where she lived.

It would be best for all of them, especially Richard, if she separated herself from them now. She was developing some fairly strong feelings for Richard and would not on her life wish to cause him any pain or heartache. He seemed to have dealt with enough of that already. She noticed her suitcase in the corner and retrieved it. If she were gone before Richard returned, then the guys would have time to discuss what ever they needed without her in their space.

*****

Richard looked at the text from William and knew immediately what he wanted. He typed his response and went back to work. He would deal with

Caroline tomorrow. For now, he had work to do, and he wanted it finished faster so he could return to Darcy's. He wanted to see Elizabeth, now more than ever.

*****

Darcy could hear something going on in the bedroom so decided to check it out. He had sat on that couch staring and thinking for the better part of ten minutes. When he reached the room, he caught Elizabeth zipping up her suitcase. "What are you doing?" he asked softly, disbelief in his voice.

"I think it is best if I go home. My place is safe; you have had new locks installed, I have security following me, and there is a restraining order against Bill. That is plenty to keep me out of harm's way. There is no reason for me to continue to stay here even though I have enjoyed my time tremendously. I want to thank you. You have opened my eyes up to a world I would have never thought possible," she said with conviction in her voice.

"You don't have to go," he said quietly as he slowly approached Elizabeth.

"Yes, I do. Richard will be here soon, and I think that you both have some things to discuss with each other. It is obvious that he still harbors feelings for Caroline, and I think that you might also. I don't want to cause either of you any more pain. Should this situation work out for the long term that would mean you would both see her. I couldn't live with the fact that Richard's heart would be broken piece by piece each time he saw her. How unfair would that be to him? We haven't been together that long; the break should be clean enough at this point." She tried to convince William. However, Elizabeth was not so sure that what she was saying would hold true for her. She really liked being with the guys. She felt so at home with them, so comfortable. Of all the relationships she had ever had, this one seemed the most rewarding, comforting, fun, passionate — just everything she had ever wanted. It sort of made her sad that she was losing something so new and precious so fast.

Darcy stood right in front of her. He didn't touch her; he just gazed into her eyes. Once she was looking right at him, he spoke softly. "Please, Elizabeth, don't leave me. It is not what you think, I swear. Just wait until Richard comes home; we will all talk. I couldn't bear it if you left now."

She could see him pleading with her through his eyes, and his words were honest and heartfelt, she knew. It pained her to see him so affected by her choice. "It won't hurt for me to go home for a few days while you both talk

168

and think things through without me hovering. If this relationship is going to go anywhere with either you or me, or all three of us, we all need to be in it together. If you can come to an understanding between the both of you as to where Caroline stands in your hearts and lives, you know where I live."

"Elizabeth, I don't want you to go home. I certainly know my own mind where you are concerned. I want you to stay. I also don't trust Bill Collins; please just wait until Richard returns. He has already let me know he wants to be here tonight instead of at his place. Just a few more hours; we can talk and then you can determine if you need to leave."

"I think it's best that I go now. I am too attracted to the both of you. If you teamed up on me, I would lose all rational thought. I believe it's best this way." She placed her palm against William's cheek and continued to stare into his eyes. She reached up on her tiptoes and kissed him, lingering against his lips with a gentle loving kiss.

*****

William took the opportunity to wrap his arms tightly around Elizabeth. He didn't want her to leave but knew her mind seemed to be made up. "I will drive you home if that is what you want."

"I'll be fine, really. Call me later if you like and let me know how things went with Richard. I'm going to go into the office tomorrow, so if you are still working from home, maybe we could have lunch together," she softly replied. Her hand was still resting on his face, so he turned into it to kiss her palm.

William placed his forehead against hers hoping against hope she would change her mind if he held her just a little longer. How could he let her go? He cared so much about her; he wasn't prepared for her to go, not yet, not when he had just gotten her into his life.

Elizabeth pulled back and grabbed the handle to her bag. They walked in silence to his door where he stood as she walked through it. She turned back, "I really have enjoyed my time with you. This is not the end, but perhaps just the beginning. I hope you and Richard can really search your feelings and determine what is best for you both. Tell Richard thank you. He is a wonderful man. I just think his thoughts are with someone else, no matter how much he tries to hide it."

"If you don't mind, call me when you get home. I want to make sure you're safe," Darcy asked in an unsteady voice.

Elizabeth nodded. "I will. Goodbye, William." Then she was gone.

*****

Elizabeth arrived home. It was strange to be in her place. She had always liked her apartment, but between Darcy's digs and Richard's condo, hers paled in comparison. She walked to the kitchen and noticed several messages sat blinking on her machine. She didn't really know what to do first. The day had started off so wonderfully. She closed her eyes and thought back to breakfast and what she had shared with Richard. Forcing herself not to relive the passion, she took her bag into her room to unload it.

Finished, she grabbed a glass of wine and sat on her couch with a book. First, she thought to call William and let him know she was fine. Her phone rang just as she was about to pick it up. "Jane, I was going to call you. I know, Jane, time got away from me. Let me explain, Jane, listen."

"No, you listen, Elizabeth Bennet. Father is worried sick about you. He had a call from Bill's lawyer today. Seems Bill wants to sue the family business and father personally. To top it off, Lydia has decided to leave a week early and is now planning to go to LA on Saturday evening. Caroline is returning to Paris Sunday, and you have decided to go on some weekend getaway with Mr. Wonderful. Really, do you not see that my life has become so much more difficult in the last week?" Jane sounded exasperated by the long laundry list of things going on in her life. Elizabeth felt terrible for contributing to her sister's frantic mood.

"Jane, I'm so sorry. I just got back to my apartment about half an hour ago. I plan to be in the office tomorrow, and I will sit down with father and speak with him."

"You're at home? Why are you home alone Elizabeth? Why did William let you leave?" her concern came through clearly. She was tired and run down and Elizabeth felt just awful.

"I have lived on my own for many years now, and I am perfectly capable of taking care of myself. Thank you for your support." She sarcastically responded.

"I am worried for you. Bill is not himself. Please don't open the door to anyone, and if you need me, call me. Lizzy, I'm at the end of my rope with wedding details, work, Lydia and mother's reaction to her leaving, father, and now you. Please, I beg you, for my own sanity, keep safe." Jane's soft voice seemed to falter just a bit at the end.

"I will. I'll see you at work tomorrow. I promise to help you deal with it all. Try to relax and get that fiancé of yours to take you out to dinner. I love you, Jane, you know that."

"I know. Bye, Lizzy."

Elizabeth made a quick call to William who questioned her about the apartment and made her promise to call if anything was strange or anyone attempted to get in. She was touched at his kind words and concern for her. She hoped that once he and Richard had a chance to talk, everything would be fine, and they could go back to seeing each other. She really wanted to make this new relationship work. She spent the rest of the evening relaxing before she turned in.

*****

"She did what!" Richard exclaimed as he set his briefcase on the table. "Why did you let her go?" he almost barked.

"She was determined to do it. She wants us to talk about Caroline and how we feel about her. I have spoken with her, and she is safe. I have had the security team check in every half hour; she hasn't left her apartment."

Richard fell back in a chair and ran his hand over his face. How had things gone so wrong since this morning? "I can't believe she left," he softly spoke, more to himself than to Darcy.

"Let's use this time she has given us and work out a few details. I know you were distracted with Elizabeth yesterday, and she could feel that. I also know you are building a closer bond with her. You have to decide if you want more. You loved Caroline, and you wanted to marry her. I know how much she hurt you when she left and then married someone else. Now she is back, and you are meeting with her tomorrow. Perhaps you need this meeting between the two of you to put things in perspective and figure out how you feel about her now."

"Maybe... I don't know. I did love Caroline, and yes, seeing her at the Gala, dancing with her, hearing her voice when she called — it has stirred up some confusing emotions for me. I did want to marry her at one time, but I don't know now. I don't know that I can give her back what she broke. Elizabeth is wonderful, and you know that. We have wanted to date her for years. Even before I met Caroline. Is it fair to put off a woman we both consider the most positive, loving, beautiful, and caring person we have ever met, when we have barely started to form a bond with her, for someone who has suddenly reappeared in our lives after over a year with no explanation, no communication?"

"I have always known Elizabeth was the woman for me. You have dated far more than I have. The few relationships we shared were good and made me rethink what I might want out of my life, but those women have not compared to Elizabeth, especially now that she has lived here. I did care for Caroline. But I was not going to commit my life to her. I would have been there for you always and you know that. We made that pact a long time ago, to have our families live close, be there for each other in every way. We knew that we wanted the women we chose to get along and be friends, that they needed a special understanding of what we have experienced and the journey we have undertaken. If we were lucky enough to find the one woman who could love us both, we were going to commit to a life-long union, to love her in return, even against what society deemed normal. I don't have the answers for you, Richard; it is a choice you have to make. Tomorrow, perhaps you will get a clearer understanding of what path you need to take. Elizabeth did say that she found Caroline very warm and caring, that she could see herself becoming great friends with her. She is going to be family, after all. That would seem to work to your advantage, no matter which direction your heart takes."

Richard heard what his cousin had to say, and it made his head and heart hurt. What if he couldn't choose? What if Caroline was always going to be the specter in the back of his mind as the love he could never have? It would ruin his future with Elizabeth, and that was unfair to her. Richard rose from his seat and grabbed his briefcase. "I think I am going out for a drive. I'll stay at my place tonight. I'll let you know how the meeting goes tomorrow."

Darcy could hear the weariness in Richard's voice. He walked his cousin to the door. "It will all work out, I swear it. If you need me, don't hesitate to call. I'm here for you. If you decide you want me to come with you in the morning, just ring. I have a clear morning since I thought Elizabeth was going to be here. I told her I would have lunch with her tomorrow. Good luck." Darcy patted Richard on the shoulder as he closed the door behind him.

*****

Bill Collins waited outside of his car in the parking garage. It had been just over an hour since he had made his call. A car pulled up next to him and rolled down the window. "Brother, what can I do for you? What's so important that you have called me away from my spa treatments to meet you in a parking garage? This had better be important," the female snapped in irritation.

With a gleam in his eye and a leer on his lips, Bill replied, "Oh, it is. Now let's get down to business. I need you to take me to Elizabeth's house now."

"What do I look like, a taxi?" the woman sneered.

"You look like a woman who enjoys the money I give her to live in a lifestyle she has become accustomed to. I am not asking for a favor, Whitney; I'm telling you." Bill got into the car and closed the door with force.

"Where are the items I asked you to bring?" he barked in an irritated tone.

"Behind the seat. I don't know what you have in mind, dear brother, but it better not interfere with my evening. I have an important date tonight. There is a rich gentleman who is very close to asking me to marry him."

"Don't you concern yourself with that, my dear. I have plans myself." Bill quickly put on a blond wig and wide-brimmed hat with a pair of sunglasses. His twin sister was quite the high maintenance woman. He had supported her for years since her husband had died. A death he himself had plenty to do with. Now it was time to collect on some of that generosity. Whitney was not the nicest of women to live with; she had strange tastes in both her sexual preferences and men. She had lots of men, always had since she was a teenager. His own sexual appetite had been kept quite a secret, as it should have been, all his life. He only partook in occasional parties when he traveled or when his sister threw one. When Whitney's rich husband decided to come home early from a business trip and found one of her little parties going on, he wanted to divorce her immediately. A high profile divorce would not do. Bill had plans of his own to run a well respected company, and bad press would not be looked upon favorably in the family. He had helped to rid his sister of the man whose morals were so high that he

173

could not turn a blind eye to his wife's way of meeting her needs. Bill had killed him the night he had thrown her out. Whitney's right to the estate of her dear dead husband was found to be non-existent. His older children from a previous marriage were the only ones named in the will. She blamed her brother for her misfortune and had blackmailed him into supporting her ever since.

Chapter 20

Wednesday morning came too soon for Richard. He was not looking forward to this day one bit. He had slept horribly and missed Elizabeth. Her side of the bed still smelled of her perfume, and when he walked into the kitchen, memories of both dinner and breakfast there came to him. How was he to get through this day? The first order of business is extra strong coffee and a long hot shower. If he could just get through the meeting with Caroline, then he could talk with Darcy and perhaps have lunch with both of them.

*****

Bill woke his sister. He was in a surly mood. He had his sister drive past Elizabeth's apartment yesterday only to find more of the Fitzwilliam agents there. He needed a plan, so insisted his sister stay with him overnight. He had, however, allowed her to go on her date; he did, after all, want her off his payroll.

"Whitney, get up," he ordered as he shook her shoulder. "Elizabeth will be at work soon, and I want you to be ready to leave in an hour. I want to go over the plan again before we leave."

"I'm moving already. You just need to calm down. You push me, and I will walk right out that door Bill."

"No, you won't. Come on, get up," he impatiently snapped.

"Fine, I'm up!" She finally gave in, dragging herself out of bed.

The duo started to review the plan that had been discussed last night. Whitney would get Elizabeth out of the office building while Bill waited in the car to take them away. He reasoned that since no one really knew he had a twin sister, he would go to Whitney's house. It was a larger house on the outskirts of town. There were acres of land around the place and a security system that he could use to keep tabs on any unwanted visitors should they suddenly appear.

*****

Elizabeth arrived at work and went straight into Jane's office. "Good morning, I brought you something," she crooned in a soft kind voice while placing the hot pastries on Jane's desk as a peace offering to her sister who was stressed by the mounting pressure of the wedding. She loved Jane and knew that their mother was no help in such matters.

"Elizabeth, I'm so glad to see you," she said as she made her way around the desk to hug her beloved sister. She had missed Elizabeth. The last few weeks seemed like a blur of activity both personally and professionally for Jane. She had never been good at handling too much pressure at one time. She had always counted on Elizabeth to handle the more difficult demands.

"Let's have a seat and enjoy these pastries while you tell me what has been happening at home and here at the office. Yesterday, you seemed so calm at lunch."

"Oh Lizzy, once we finished cleaning up after the Gala ended, you know that Lydia went out with Wickham. Well, then I found out Sunday that he was taking her to LA, but I was relieved that father was going to speak with him about it before granting his blessing. Mother was fluttering about the house, thrilled that she had such a fine older man looking out for her favored daughter. Then, of course, she couldn't deny me my due with a wedding to plan. She wears me out, Lizzy. Father, of course, kept himself locked in his study and was no help whatsoever once you left."

"Oh, Jane."

"Well, yesterday my day started off wonderfully. The lunch was great. I had such a good time with both you and Caroline. I am so fortunate she is amiable. Charles talks about her often. I believe he would love to see his sister move back to the states. He doesn't see her often, now that she lives in Paris. Anyhow, once you both left, my day only got crazier. Mother hated what we had all settled on, so she took me on a shopping trip to show me all the things she thought a proper wedding should have."

"She didn't. OH Jane, how awful for you. Why didn't you call me?"

"What would you have been able to do? I just listened to her go on and on for five hours while dragging me all over town. When we finally got home, Lydia announced she was leaving to go to LA a week early. I had planned to have a nice dinner at my place with the family this weekend as a sort of farewell for Caroline. I hate that I am burdening you with all this news. It is just so much; I'm feeling very overwhelmed," Jane announced with a heavy heart and a deep sigh.

Elizabeth gave her sister a huge hug. "Well, let me start by saying I'm here for you, and you need to let me run some interference for you where our mother is concerned. It is, after all, your wedding and you should have what you want. I'm just at a loss as to what to think about Lydia. What made her change her mind?"

"I don't know. From what I understand, she went out the other night, and then the next day she announced her change in plans. Father was not happy. He refused to allow her to go so early. It would cost extra money to exchange the plan tickets and a hotel room for a week would be so expensive. Not that we don't have the money, but it is the principle. She doesn't need to go so soon; her job doesn't start for two weeks yet. Of course, mother and father got into a spat over the entire thing and had me on speakerphone for half an hour going back and fourth about it. Lydia was being stubborn and wouldn't even talk about sticking to the original departure date."

"I swear I don't know what has gotten into that girl." Elizabeth's tsk-tsk could be heard as she shook her head back and forth.

The girls continued to chat for a little longer before Elizabeth excused herself to walk down to her father's office.

*****

William woke up early for once. He hadn't slept well. He had tossed and turned in his big bed, worrying about Elizabeth all night long, even getting up a few times to check for messages from the security detail to make sure all was quiet. He walked into the kitchen and opened his fridge. It was full of all sorts of fresh vegetables, eggs, bacon, yogurts, milk, and juice. He didn't think he had seen that much food in his fridge – ever. He knew it was all due to Elizabeth, his Elizabeth, who wanted to cook and care for him. He closed the door and leaned his forehead against the stainless tower. Taking a deep breath, he walked to the coffee maker to start a fresh pot. He had several hours before he needed to get ready for lunch. He decided to contact Elizabeth at her office in half an hour to make sure she had arrived okay.

He sat at the bar and began thinking of his cousin. Reaching for the phone, he punched in the number, hoping to catch him before he left to meet with Caroline. He felt he ought to check on him since he was so troubled last night.

"Hello," came the obviously tired voice.

"How are you this morning?" Darcy inquired, his early morning voice scratchy.

"Good morning my ass. I haven't slept a wink," came the sound of a frustrated and irritable man.

"Are you sure you don't want me to accompany you to meet Caroline? I know this is a difficult meeting for you."

"I'll be fine. I just need to get it over with. I missed Elizabeth last night. How about you?"

"Yeah, I slept horribly. Checked with security several times during the night and now my fridge is full of groceries. I can't believe she didn't stay till you came home last night. Something about being too attracted to us and losing her focus," he grumbled.

"Really? Well I have to hand it to her – she is probably right about that. Maybe after I meet with Caroline, I could join you both for lunch. Where are you planning to go?"

"Not sure yet; I'll text you once I wake up a bit more and figure it out. Give me a call when you're finished with Caroline. Good luck. I'm a phone call away if you need me, alright?"

"I know, and . . . hey Darcy . . . thanks," Richard responded in a contemplative tone.

"Anytime, I'm here for you. Take it easy, Richard. I'll talk with you soon."

Darcy hung up the phone and filled his coffee mug. What a day this was going to be. He felt bad for Richard. The poor guy had been through enough with Caroline. He hoped she didn't want to get back together with him. He hated the thought that Richard might actually take her back and risk the chance of her hurting him again. He liked Caroline enough. She was a great woman – beautiful, carefree, and fun. She laughed at all of Richard's jokes. She was slim, tall, had legs that went on forever, but he couldn't forget the pain she had caused his best friend. Fame and the thrill of celebrity had tainted Caroline as far as Darcy was concerned. If she did it once, she could do it again. Having lost his good opinion, he was reluctant to think the same of her as he once had.

He sat pondering how the meeting would go for a while longer as he finished up his coffee. It was going to be a long morning. He figured he could get some work in the event he could convince Elizabeth to come back home with him or at least, go out tonight. He also wanted to make sure they were still on for the weekend. He really did want her to meet his family. Georgiana, in particular, wanted to see *"the woman who had so captured her brother's heart"* he remembered her saying just last week.

*****

Sighing heavily, Elizabeth plopped down in her desk chair. Between Jane and her father, it had been a long morning. Leaning her head back, she closed her eyes for a moment to gather herself, when she heard her cell phone beeping. Glancing around her desk, she spotted it. She smiled when she noticed that a message from William awaited her.

"Good morning, beautiful. Looking forward to having lunch together. Missed you last night. When do you want to meet? May I pick you up out front?"

Thrilled to hear from him, Elizabeth typed out her response with a grin spread across her lips.

"HUGS! Missed you too. Just got to my desk. How about noon? Would love to ride together. Meet you out front. Enjoy the rest of your morning."

Ready now to start her day, Elizabeth turned to her computer and checked the list of pending files. Perhaps her day was looking up after all, she thought, as she got down to business.

*****

Whitney Danielle Ashford had never led a normal life. Since she was a young teenager, she had known she was different. Her parents had divorced when she was in middle school, leaving her and her twin brother to the sole care of their mother. They had watched their wealthy father from afar as he remarried and groomed his newest son to be the heir both to his fortune and business, a fact that William David, her twin brother, had never forgotten.

Their mother had a modest income after the divorce, and she never received any type of support from her ex-husband. She never fully explained the reason for this to her children, but Whitney knew. As a child, she had seen the company her mother had over while her father was away. It had drawn her in; even Bill had watched on those nights she had her so-called "friends" over. They would hide and listen to things that went on in the living room. It had changed who she was and how she felt about herself, and from then on, the same dark things their mother enjoyed became what she and her brother would come to enjoy as well. Both indulged in their particular fetishes at different levels through out the years. Whitney was far more ravenous in her needs than Bill had ever been. But he still fell outside of the norm and had kept those parts of his life well hidden.

She knew her brother desired Elizabeth for her wholesome appearance and her family's business. To have a supportive wife that was beautiful, charming and well connected would help to keep his secret sexual activities just that, a secret. Then there was that little problem of murdering her former husband...

It was no wonder Bill was in such a foul mood. He was losing his marital cover and her business. Bill was a very driven man. Watching their father all these years and growing more resentful as time passed of their half-brother Drew's being handed everything on a silver platter had made Bill bitter. His hatred of the old man only increased with his refusal to acknowledging either him or his sister since the divorce. Work consumed Bill; he was determined to become a powerful man and show the old man he couldn't just toss them aside.

Whitney and Bill had both had their last names changed to their mother's maiden name while they were young children. It was a stipulation of the divorce. His father made it clear to them all; he would never acknowledge any of them or the 12-year marriage. The lawyers made damn sure of that.

Whitney dressed the part of a rich businesswoman well. It was something she was accustomed to on a daily basis. Though she and Bill were twins, she had a different look about her. Bill was tall with dark hair shaved close to his head, a goatee, and dark brown eyes. She was average height with long sandy blond locks and light brown eyes. She knew it would be easy to get into Elizabeth's office. The harder part would be getting her to leave.

180

Bill had slipped her a small handgun so she could use it to persuade Elizabeth to follow her out should she balk at the idea.

Once they had Elizabeth, the plan was to bring her back to her place. No one lived there but her, so there wouldn't be anyone there to see Elizabeth arrive. What Bill hoped to accomplish by all this eluded her. It was not widely known that Bill had a sister, much less a twin. She didn't think that getting that bit of information out would be beneficial. Whitney had moved abroad years ago, living in Europe for a long time. At 37, she had only returned stateside after the death of her husband. She had stayed nearly a year in her former home until all the paper work had been dealt with and the will settled. Once the public's interest in her husband's death had abated, Bill paid to have her moved back to the states since he was now paying her living expenses. He had purchased her a large house on the outskirts of town so she could keep a low profile with her parties and lifestyle in mind.

A year had passed, and now Elizabeth would be in on part of their little secret. Whitney didn't have any hang-ups about her lifestyle, but Bill wanted her married or well cared for at least. He had demanded she make herself presentable in social circles and find a husband. He wanted to accumulate his extra income for a higher purpose. He wanted to take away their father's wealth and prestige, and then he wanted his father's current family to suffer like his former family had done for years.

"Are you ready to go Whitney?" she could hear her brother bark from down the hall.

*****

Richard arrived at his favorite café. He was sitting outside in the courtyard trying to remain calm and enjoy the beautiful morning. However, the knots in his stomach didn't believe calm was the order of the day. He was ordering his coffee when Caroline walked up.

"Hey, stranger," she shyly said.

"Caroline," he acknowledged her. He glanced at a chair across from him for her to sit and the waiter took her order before departing.

"Thank you for agreeing to see me. I know it has been such a long time. The other night at the Gala was a little awkward for us both, I'm sure."

"In some ways, but it was good to see you, none the less."

181

They glanced at each other, and then looked away. Caroline looked at the table fumbling with her napkin roll before placing it in her lap. "This place hasn't changed at all." She smiled a bit, taking in her surroundings.

"Yeah, I still enjoy coming here, and the food isn't bad either"

Caroline chuckled at his statement. He was still the ever-charming Richard she remembered. "So what have you been up to? I figured from the turn out at the Gala that you and William had to have made out like bandits," she teased. "Fundraising always did go well when Bennet Industries got involved."

Richard nodded his agreement to her statement. The waiter returned with their drinks and a basket of assorted mini muffins. Both took a moment to fix their coffee and choose a pastry.

"So you said you are returning to Paris this weekend. Short trip, it would seem, for such a distance."

"Yeah, I know, but Charles really wanted me to meet Jane and be here when he asked her to marry him. I honestly didn't realize I would see you or William while I was in town. I wanted to apologize if I caused you any problems."

"It's fine. Are you still working the runway shows?"

"Yeah."

There was a bit of awkward silence while they each munched on their muffins. Richard knew he needed to ask some questions, but he also could see she was just as uncomfortable as he was. He could sense the tension in the air between them. He took a moment and put his cup down, then just looked at her. She was still just as beautiful as he remembered her. Her auburn locks swirled around her shoulders, her creamy skin so clear and perfect. She wore a lovely sundress in a rust tone with creams and browns sprinkled in. Her eyes still clear emeralds atop rosy cheeks. His heart still felt twinges of love for her as she sat there before him, but there was no way this would work out. She loved her job, she lived in Paris, and he was falling for Elizabeth. What good would come from trying to reconcile, when he had a life here full of family and friends?

Inhaling deeply, he glanced down to his cup and then took the plunge. "Caroline, I have a few things I need to talk to you about. They are of a private nature, and I understand that it will be uncomfortable to talk about; I know it is for me. But I need some answers, if you can help me." He spoke softly so no one around them could hear. He had moved in towards the table and looked her in the eyes as he spoke.

"Is this about Elizabeth?" she quietly replied.

He wasn't surprised that she brought her name up. It had to have been obvious at the gala when he and William had danced with her where his interests lay. "Sort of, but it has more to do with you, William and me."

"I see; then I'll try to do my best to help you," she agreed with a small tilt of her lips.

"Thanks," he said. "I need you to remember back to that one night when we where using your new camera to take some shots. The next night –"

"That camera was stolen, you know that."

"Yes, I remember. Do you recall seeing or speaking to a man that next night at the fundraiser? He would have been tall with dark hair, trimmed real short or shaved, goatee, fit build, brown eyes – goes by the name of Bill Collins?"

Caroline put her coffee mug down and stared at Richard. Her eyes squinted some in concentration as she studied him. "You know, this is the second time that man's name has come up. Yesterday, I heard Jane talking to Elizabeth about him."

"In what way?" Richard suddenly felt charged. Caroline knew something; he could feel it, see it in the way she reacted to the name.

"Jane was talking about Elizabeth's being alone at her place and begged her to be careful with, as she put it, that mad man loose."

"Anything else?" he asked in his professional voice. Caroline could see she had struck a nerve with Richard. He needed information on this man. Something about him was all wrong, and perhaps she should share some of her own information. She did, after all, feel guilty about how things had ended between them. Maybe helping him with this Collins man would be the best thing to do now. He was obviously interested in Elizabeth, and this man was in some way not to be trusted she figured.

183

"No, it seemed like Elizabeth might have plans this weekend to go away. Her sister wanted information about some trip but nothing was discussed."

Richard leaned back in his chair and steepled his fingers up next to his mouth. He wanted to think a few things through before he continued to tell Caroline what he knew he must. "Caroline, there are things you should know about that man. Bill Collins used to date Elizabeth. He is an executive at Bennet Industries, or rather, was. Elizabeth broke up with him a few months back. William asked her out about two or three weeks ago. Bill is determined to have Elizabeth back however, and I have had a restraining order placed against him."

"Why a restraining order? Seems a bit much even for William".

"I asked you about the camera because Bill used the photos from that night to try to persuade Elizabeth to go back to him."

"He did WHAT!" Caroline sat up straight in her chair, alarm written across her face.

"The night of the Gala, William and I were taking Elizabeth home. She fell asleep in the limo. When we got to her place, William was going to put her to bed when he noticed something atop the comforter. They were the pictures of us – the three of us. He had them all over the bed and taped up all over the bathroom. He was trying to warn Elizabeth away from us. We had not yet told her about the relationship we wanted to have with her."

"Oh, my gosh! I can't imagine what Elizabeth would have...that those photos were.... how could he...why would he?" Caroline was just unable to fathom why this man whom she didn't even know, would do something so horrible, to violate her privacy in such a way.

Richard could see Caroline's face, and he watched all the emotions reflected in her eyes. He was unsure how to help but got up and moved to the chair next to Caroline and placed his hand on top of hers. "We removed them all before she saw them. I did have a few of them analyzed by the police. This led to the restraining order and prompted William to have Elizabeth stay with him until things could be sorted out. It just so happened that Mr. Bennet fired Collins on Monday, adding to a situation that was already volatile."

"Why would he do such a thing?" she almost pleaded as she turned her face to Richard's. He could feel her slight tremble. "Those pictures could ruin my career. It could ruin you and William, the family business. I am so so sorry. I should never have even suggested taking the photos. I never believed something like this could happen."

Caroline took her hand from under Richard's to cover her eyes for just a moment. Richard felt she needed to be reassured. He placed his arm around her shoulders and pulled her over to his side. "We thought that this was all being done to regain Elizabeth's affections as his girlfriend. It is our belief that he wanted to marry Elizabeth. He said some very hateful things on Monday in her office. I heard some of the conversation when I went in to collect her. I didn't know he was there."

"Is she okay? I mean, I like Elizabeth, and I wouldn't want to see her hurt by any of this. What else can be done about him?" Caroline was asking questions with her head resting on Richard's shoulder. He felt a little awkward holding her so close while speaking of Elizabeth. But he could tell that Caroline was not to blame for any of this and knew he had been right about her.

"Elizabeth is fine. We had the locks changed on her apartment and have a security detail on her 24/7. William has been even more concerned since she left his place yesterday to return to her own. That trip that Elizabeth was speaking of is to the country estate. William wanted her to meet the family. Caroline, I'm so sorry you had to hear all of this."

Caroline broke away from Richard and looked up into his eyes. "Are you going as well? Do you care for Elizabeth?"

He studied her face and just nodded yes to her. He could see the hurt in her eyes, but she didn't say anything. She pulled herself upright in her chair and picked up her coffee mug. After taking a sip, she took a deep breath. "Well, then I should tell you the reason I wanted to speak with you today. I thought that I should come and apologize to you personally for how I handled my move. It was a decision that I regret now. At the time, my manager insisted that we had to leave immediately for Paris. The producers were not going to hold my spot for long, and the show was only days away. I packed a few things and left without any warning. I'm sorry for that. I loved our time together and thought that I would do the show and return home. I never imagined it would have taken on a life of its own. One show led to another; then there were the parties, the interviews – it seemed to snowball."

Richard listened quietly to her as she spoke. Her voice was solemn and reflective. She didn't look at him, but only stared at the table as she spoke. Her eyes were glazed over it seemed, remembering the past as she saw it.

"After a few months of shows and the spotlight, Michael proposed. I had been with him for three years, I trusted him, he had always done the best for me, and I guess I thought since you were not calling or coming to see me, that I had no reason not to take a chance on love. We were close and he was so supportive of me. Anyway I married him only to find out he cheated on me. LOTS! Which reminds me, did you know that Bill Collins has a twin sister? Her name is Whitney Ashford."

*****

Elizabeth was working in her office when her secretary opened the door. It was already 11:30, and she was closing up business for the morning to have lunch with William. "Yes, Sandy, what can I do for you?"

"Miss Bennet there is a woman here who wishes to speak to you about a sponsorship for the fundraiser next week. Should I show her in?"

Knowing it might only take a few minutes to speak with the lady, Elizabeth allowed Sandy to show her in. The woman came in and shook her hand. "Welcome, please have a seat. Now what type of sponsorship did you have in mind? We are always looking for ways to enhance our fundraising objectives at every opportunity," Elizabeth happily explained.

"Yes, well, my company would like to offer Bennet Industries a way to capture the maximum contributions at its next affair. It is, after all, what a fundraiser is for, is it not? I would, however, like to take the opportunity if I may to show you in person. I have something set up for you just outside of the office. I didn't mean to interfere with your day, and I'm terribly sorry I did not make an appointment to begin with. But it will only take a few moments of your time."

Elizabeth listened to the blond haired businesswoman and saw no reason not to go with her. She was leaving anyway to meet with William. She could go downstairs and see what this woman had to show her and then head to lunch. "I would love to see what you have. If you will just give me a few moments, I will meet you in the lobby."

"Of course, I shall wait for you there. Thank you for giving me some of your time today."

"It is no problem at all. Thank you for sharing your vision with us."
Elizabeth walked the woman to her office door before she returned to her
desk and wrapped up a few loose ends and shut off her computer. She left
Sandy a few letters to be mailed and told her secretary she would return in a
few hours after a lunch meeting.

*****

"Whitney Ashford? Are you sure she is Bill Collin's twin sister?" Richard's
alarm could not be contained at the revelation.

"Yes, I had met Bill or William David Collins as he introduced himself to
me, here at a few fundraisers. The last one was the night after we used my
camera to take those pictures. I was speaking with him for several minutes
when you walked up and asked me to dance," Caroline explained, then she
continued, giving Richard more enlightening information. "While I was in
Paris there had been a very high profile death, Whitney Ashford's husband.
She was average height, sandy blond hair, and brown eyes. They were a
very well to do family. I spotted Bill and Whitney at an art show one night.
He introduced me to her and, actually now that I think about it; he
congratulated me on my success in Paris. He had an odd look in his eyes as
he whispered something to his sister. She seemed a little surprised at what
ever he had mentioned. I didn't pay much attention really. It was a week or
so later that I had an invitation from Whitney to a party – a private function
at her home. I wasn't able to go since my own marriage fell apart during
that time."

"Caroline . . ." Richard hugged her tightly and kissed her cheek.

"What was that for?" she said in quiet surprise.

"You have just given me the best lead in this case. I can't thank you
enough." He quickly pulled out his wallet and handed her twenty dollars.
"Here, let me pay for your coffee. Are you alright?"

Stunned at how fast Richard was moving, she could only give a quick, "Yes,
I'm alright."

"Call me later; I want to make sure you are okay. I have to go. I need to
call Darcy. Thank you again."

187

Richard dashed away, quickly finding his way out of the restaurant and onto the sidewalk. He hurriedly keyed Darcy's number on his cell phone. He needed to tell him this newest information and fast.

*****

William pulled up to the office building just as he noticed Elizabeth and a woman walking out. He smiled to himself at the sight of her. He was just about to pull up to the curb when Elizabeth turned her head and caught sight of him. She pointed one finger up in the air at him and turned back to the woman.

*****

Whitney knew time was of great importance. She met Elizabeth in the lobby and as they walked out, she saw Bill parked next to the entrance. She continued to speak with Elizabeth about the phony sponsorship when she noticed her turn and wave at a car that had just pulled up. This was the worst timing. She had to move quickly if she was going to get Elizabeth away from the building without an incident taking place.

"Miss Bennet, if I could have you get into the car, our demonstration is just down the street. We have another client who is hosting a fundraising event and figured you could see first hand what to expect for your gala," Whitney cheerfully explained.

"I'm sorry, but I really don't have the time to go with you. My next appointment is waiting for me. Would I be able to drop by in a few hours? I would really be interested in what you have to offer Bennet Industries."

Knowing she had to do this now – she could see Bill itching to get out of the car – she pulled the small hand gun from her purse and placed it at Elizabeth's ribs. "I'm sorry, Miss Bennet, but I really think you need to come now. If you would please get into the car, we will be on our way."

Elizabeth looked down at the gun and back to the woman's face. "What are you doing? Who are you?"

The car door opened and a male voice could be heard. "Elizabeth, you need to get in the car this instant if you know what's good for you. My sister knows how to use that gun, and she will," Bill coldly announced.

Elizabeth was shocked to see Bill in the car and panicked. She glanced over to William's car for a split second before Whitney forced her into the car.

*****

Richard had run to his own car and was pulling away as Darcy answered. "Hey, how did it go?"

"Darcy, you will never believe this, but Collins has a twin sister."

"What!"

"Yeah, and Caroline knows what she looks like. Blond hair, average height, brown eyes."

As Richard continued to talk, William glanced up to see Elizabeth's pale face flash at him before the woman she was with forcefully helped her into the car. "SHIT, it's her. Damn it, Richard, call the police. That woman just put Elizabeth into a car, and I'm going to follow them."

"Where are you?"

"At Bennet Industries. I think Bill is driving; they are speeding away!"

"Okay, I'm on it. Be careful! I'll call you right back."

Richard hung up and William moved into traffic to follow the car, trying to stay close to his Elizabeth.

189

Chapter 21

"Bill what are you doing?" Elizabeth demanded.

"I'm taking you to my sister's house to talk some sense into you," he snidely responded.

"Your sister?" She glanced to the woman sitting next to her. "You're his sister? I didn't know he had a sister," Elizabeth said in a stunned voice.

"Don't feel bad, most people don't know. I'm a very well kept secret, you could say. But that doesn't mean I don't know about you. Seems my brother is quiet fond of you. He's a good man; you should listen to what he has to say." Whitney's voice was edged in sarcasm. She wasn't acting like the same woman who had come to her office half an hour ago. A terrible thought started to work its way into Elizabeth's head.

"Shit! That infuriating man is following me," Bill snapped. Whitney turned to look out the back window.

"Who?" she asked, glancing at the cars behind them.

"Darcy," he growled out.

Elizabeth tried to turn and look behind her. She was hopeful that William had seen her face and knew she needed help. At that moment, her cell phone started to ring.

"Don't even think about it, sugar." Whitney placed her arm on Elizabeth's. "My brother wants this to be a one-on-one conversation. Sorry, no threesomes… yet." She wickedly smiled while giving Elizabeth the once over from head to toe.

Shocked at the tone of Whitney's voice, her words, and the leer on her lips, Elizabeth suddenly felt very vulnerable.

*****

William couldn't stop the vision of Elizabeth's face as she glanced at him before being forced into the car from popping into his mind. She needed him! How had he let this happen? A twin sister… William had a very bad feeling. At the next red light he was stopped behind another car while Bill continued moving. He reached over to his glove box and pulled out his handgun. He quickly checked it for bullets and placed it in the console next to him. When the light turned green, he maneuvered around several cars until he caught up to Bill. He had tried to call Elizabeth's cell, but she hadn't answered, which didn't surprise him.

His own cell phone rang and he swiftly grabbed it. "Yeah," his strained voice answered.

"The police are en route. Where are you?" Richard questioned in a determined tone.

"I'm going down Main, about to pass the last light and hit the service road next to the highway. Where are you?"

"I'm on the service road about to come up on Main in two blocks. What's Bill driving?" Richard inquired briskly.

"He's in a silver Infinity FX35, license plate SAM669."

"I'll call it in," Richard replied.

"No wait, the security team is behind me; they are taking care of it," Darcy informed his cousin.

"Fine. There, I see him!" Richard hastily blurted out and disconnected the line.

William watched as Bill passed through the intersection ahead of him through the underpass. Before he could blink, Richard's black SUV came into sight, barreling through the red light from the left making a hard left turn into traffic, clipping the bumper of Bill's silver Infinity.

"Damn it, Richard!" Darcy blurted out in a panic.

He watched helplessly as Bill's car fishtailed and crossed into the on-coming traffic. Two cars swerved to miss them, narrowly avoiding a collision. The cars in front of Darcy had stopped immediately, so he had to weave between a few of them to keep up.

In front of him, Richard took the left turn lane at full speed, tires screeching as he did. Darcy followed closely behind him barely missing an on-coming truck.

William knew Elizabeth had to be scared. If anything happened to her, he would never forgive himself. Having entered onto the highway, both men wasted no time; they quickly maneuvered to flank each side of Bill's vehicle. Bill jerked his car into Richard's SUV to cut him off. Quickly turning his head to check on his cousin's fate at such a high speed, William noticed Richard readjust and give chase again. Focusing back on his own lane, Darcy whipped a quick right to avoid hitting the slower car in front of him.

Richard had always been a far more aggressive driver than he had. Richard came right back up to the side of the Infinity, tapping it with a swift jerk of his SUV to the right. While watching Richard and Bill quickly moving farther ahead of him, Darcy didn't notice the on-ramp ahead of him, where two squad cars came racing up, sirens blaring. William hit the breaks to avoid a collision; the sudden squeal of tires drew his attention to his review mirror. There he saw the security detail swerve left and crash into a gas tankard, the fiery explosion creating an enormous mushroom cloud of smoke and debris.

Darcy's natural instinct was to duck somewhat at the noise that was created by the blast. "Shit!" he let out as he turned his focus back on the cars before him.

The police cruisers took up spots right on the tails of Bill and Richard's cars. Darcy happened to glance farther up the highway and noticed that there were state troopers and more police creating a blockade. They were diverting traffic off the main road. Fire trucks were parked just beyond; indicating some sort of accident must have taken place. With his eyes focusing back to Bill and Richard, Darcy wondered if either had noticed the situation ahead. Elizabeth was in danger, and he was worried for her safety.

He watched as Bill again swerved left to swipe Richard's car. As both continued to battle, the roadblock was quickly approaching. "Stop! Richard, stop! Don't chase him in there!" Darcy said aloud. His concern for Elizabeth's well being was rising as events continued to unfold before his eyes. He felt so helpless. How was he to save her? His mind started to churn as he tried to focus on the cars in front of him.

*****

"Whitney, use that damn gun and shoot his tires out!" Bill barked. He was aggravated that he couldn't shake Richard. The roadblock ahead would be difficult to navigate on his own, let alone if he had Richard right on his tail.

"Don't move!" Whitney ordered while she crawled over Elizabeth's lap to the window. She rolled down the glass and pulled the gun up. Elizabeth tried her best to push her off her lap to stop the gun from going off. "You little bitch!" Whitney growled as she slapped Elizabeth hard across her cheek.

Elizabeth yelped out in pain, grabbing her face instantly. "Do that again, Miss Thing, and I'll give you something to yell about!" Whitney quickly regained her focus as Richard hit the car once again. Taking aim for his tires, several shots rang out. Elizabeth screamed in terror. Whitney watched as Richard's SUV squealed while he lost control of his vehicle, before it slammed into the concrete barrier next to him.

*****

Darcy watched the horrific crash of his cousin's SUV. The two squad cars behind him split away, one barely missing Richard before it flipped over, the other careening into the line of cars exiting the highway. It was like a scene straight out of the movies. The events seemed to slow perceptibly. Darcy braked instantly behind the flipped squad car and quickly went to offer aide. As he ran, he glanced up to see Bill's car escape through the maze of rescue vehicles. His heart sank as a lump welled up in his throat. He thought he was going to be ill when he focused back on the men who needed help.

"Richard, Richard!" he yelled before he ever made it to the mangled mess of metal along the cement wall. He had to maneuver around the flipped squad car, where the officer could be seen crawling out from the back shattered window. He made it to the passenger side of Richard's SUV and looked in the window. "Thank God! Can you move?" he asked Richard, his relief tangible at the sight of Richard awake and moving to unbuckle his seatbelt.

"I'm fine, but my leg is pinned. Get some help," he bit out.

Darcy ran towards the nearby fire trucks. Two rescue workers were already fast approaching to help with what they had just witnessed. Darcy glanced up to the sky and noticed two news choppers hovering above them. He pulled out his cell phone. He called both stations and requested that the choppers follow the silver Infinity that had caused the accident. He gave them the numbers to his office including the direct line to the director of security. With any luck he would know where Bill was headed soon.

*****

Jane sat in her office eating lunch when a traffic alert came over the radio. From the description, the situation sounded pretty bad. Since it was the route she took home, she decided to pull it up on her desktop and take a look. The reporter on the ground was talking about a severe multi-car pile up that had been expanded by a police chase gone badly. It would seem one accident had taken place, and then another added to it. Jane watched as they replayed the aerial footage from the police chase and crash. As she watched closely, she had a sudden feeling of dread come over her.

She remembered that Elizabeth had come by her office on her way to lunch to say goodbye and to tell her that some files that she might need were left on her desk. Jane had gone to retrieve them from Elizabeth's office and just happened to look out the window down at the street. She saw Elizabeth talking to a well-dressed woman; then she saw Elizabeth get into the silver car with her. That same car had pulled away hastily with what she thought was Mr. Darcy's Aston Martin following.

Jane looked back at the computer screen at the replay of the crash. A silver Infinity was reported to have driven through the existing wreckage while a black SUV had smashed into the cement barrier. A car resembling Mr. Darcy's had stopped just a few feet back. "Oh NO!" Jane gasped. Her hands flew to cover her mouth. "It can't be..." She blankly stared at the screen.

"Jane, what's the matter?" Mr. Bennet's concerned voice came from Jane's doorway.

"I – I –" she stuttered still in some shock. "I think something might be wrong with Elizabeth. I'm not sure, but I have a horrible feeling," she replied, still in a daze of confusion.

"What do you mean, Jane?" Mr. Bennet walked towards his daughter's desk. "What do you think has happened?" His voice rose in question and concern.

"The news is reporting on a serious car pile up on the highway. There was also a police chase. I think Lizzy is in one of those cars. OH, Father, What if…" Jane's eyes started to well up as she turned to look at her father.

Mr. Bennet pulled out his blackberry and dialed Darcy's number. It rang several times before the voice mail system clicked on. "Darcy, this is Bennet. I'm calling to see if you have any information on Elizabeth's whereabouts. Jane believes she might be in some trouble." He hung up and quickly dialed Elizabeth's cell only to receive her voice mail as well.

"Lizzy is supposed to be having lunch with William, father. But I saw her get into a silver car with my own eyes," Jane explained.

"Jane there is no need to jump to conclusions. It could be just a coincidence. Why don't you pack up for the day? You have been under a great deal of stress this last week. Go home and rest."

"I have so much to do," she said in some disbelief.

"Nothing that can't wait until tomorrow or Thursday. Now as your boss and father, I'm not asking, I'm telling you. I'll let you know when I hear from Elizabeth."

Jane looked around her desk and sighed. "Okay, I'll go. Please call me as soon as you hear from Lizzy."

"Of course I will. Now, you go home and relax." He gave his eldest daughter a hug and a kiss on her forehead before turning and walking away.

Mr. Bennet left Jane's office and walked down the hall to speak with Elizabeth's secretary. Hearing that a woman with no appointment had shown up to meet with Elizabeth and she had agreed to meet her outside, didn't set well with him. He returned to his office and began to make several phone calls.

*****

"Detective Lucus, you have to listen," Darcy implored. He had been trying to get the detective to send out squad cars to search for Elizabeth.

"No, I don't. This has become an official police matter, and I don't want either of you or your security team in the way. Two men have already died today. Lieutenants Denny and Saunders will be helping me, and if there are

195

any developments, one of us will be in touch with you. I want you to go home; you both look like hell. Go get yourselves cleaned up. There is nothing for you to do here." The detective took his files and left Richard and Darcy sitting in the conference room.

"Damn it! That pig-headed man. Elizabeth can't wait around for them to get their butts in gear. You can't possibly agree with this?" Richard ranted, visibly upset with the turn of events. He looked haggard and in need of rest.

"I think we need to get you back to your place. He is right; we look like hell. But, I have an idea."

"What do you have in mind?"

"Not here; let's go."

Both men left the police station. Darcy drove Richard back to his condo. He had some nasty cuts on his arm and the leg that had been pinned, but he was going to be okay. While Richard stared out the window of the car, Darcy made one phone call. "I need to see you. Can you meet me at the condo? Give me half an hour."

*****

Darcy had showered first while Richard tended to his wounds. He had just put some clothes on and fixed himself a drink when there was a knock at the door. With Richard still in the shower, he answered it.

"Hi. Thanks for coming." He stepped aside to welcome the visitor in. "I really need to ask you some questions. Things have taken a turn for the worst with Elizabeth. What we feared and tried to stop has actually happened, and the police will not listen to reason."

They walked into the living room and took seats. "Can I get you something to drink?" he asked his guest before sitting.

"No, thank you, I'm fine. You don't look well. Are things that bad?"

Picking up his drink and taking a sip, Darcy stared at the glass a few moments as the ice swirled around. He inhaled deeply and replied, "You could say that. It's been one hell of a day so far." The weight of the mounting stress could be seen on his face and in the depths of his eyes. He was concerned for Elizabeth and what might be happening to her. He was

196

also still worried about Richard. Though he was checked out, Darcy would have liked him to go to the hospital. But Richard was stubborn and refused.

"I'm sorry."

"Nothing for you to be sorry about. If anything, you may be the one person who holds the answers I need," he said, glancing at the person on the couch before taking another sip of the amber fluid in his glass.

"You know I'll help in any way I can."

Before the next person could utter a word, Richard walked into the room. He had put on a clean pair of jeans, but he had no shirt on, and his feet were bare. He held a towel in his hand as he dried his hair. He stopped at the entrance of the living room, frozen in place. "Caroline..." he uttered, stunned to find her on his couch.

*****

Caroline swallowed the lump in her throat. Her eyes scanned over Richard's body, taking in his appearance. He wore skintight jeans that conformed to his muscular thighs, enhancing his trim waist. She followed her line of sight up to his exposed navel, traveling up the scattered trail of blond hair that lead up to his broad chest. His shoulders and arms gave her pause, as they had always been a favorite of hers. With muscles like that, she could tell he still worked out. He wrapped the white towel around the back of his neck and held on with his hands at either end. He could still light a fire in her nether region quicker than any other man ever could.

"William called me," she quietly replied. She caught herself staring at his fine form and turned away for fear of giving her heart away.

"Did he?" Richard asked. He glanced towards Darcy with his brow furrowed.

"I did. We need her to tell us more about Whitney. I've already put a call into the office. I'm having security check for possible housing records on her, run credit checks – find out all we can on her. It might lead us to where they took Elizabeth.

Caroline turned her attention fully on William. "Took her?" she asked, concern shadowing her face.

"Just a few hours ago. Whitney was the one who got her out of the office, I believe, and into a car Bill had waiting right outside Bennet Industries.

Richard returned with a t-shirt on, and for just a moment, Caroline couldn't decide if she liked him better with bare flesh or the look of his hot body in that tight tee.

"I'm surprised you didn't see the entire thing on TV or hear about it on the radio," Darcy enlightened her.

Caroline couldn't help but watch as Richard took a seat next to her on the couch. It was hard to concentrate with all his maleness that close to her. She did notice that he rubbed at his shin. His forearm also held several scratches and one big band aide. She hadn't noticed those a few moments ago or earlier this morning. "What happened?" she asked looking right at his arm. How did you get those scratches? They weren't there this morning."

"I'm fine; they're nothing," Richard said, blowing off the nagging pain that reminded him of his failure to stop Bill and save Elizabeth. He was edgy and tired. Caroline could tell something was very wrong.

"Don't let him fool you. He has some nasty marks from the crash earlier," William said, sitting back in the chair and sipping at his drink some more. Richard shot him a menacing look.

"CRASH!" Caroline said dumbfounded, looking between the men. She was about to demand an explanation of what was going on when Darcy's cell phone rang.

*****

"Excuse me, I have to take this," he interrupted as he rose from this chair and walked into the kitchen.

"Hello," he answered.

"About damn time! You had better tell me what's happening with my daughter. Don't sugar coat it either," came the steely hard voice of a father in distress.

"I take it you have seen the news," Darcy replied.

198

"No, but Jane did. I had to send her home. She was distraught to say the least with what she thinks she saw. I told her not to jump to conclusions. I left you a voice mail a few hours ago. Now, you will tell me what is going on," Bennet's stoic low voice hovered on the edge of threatening. Darcy knew he had to explain everything that had gone on today. But he wanted to do it face-to-face, not over the phone.

"We have been at the police station. Just got in not half an hour ago. Can you come to Richard's place? We are waiting on some Intel from the office, and then we will formulate a plan. I'll give you all the information we have so far."

Darcy gave Mr. Bennet directions to the condo. With that done, he went ahead and called out for some Chinese food. It was going to be a long night, and neither he nor Richard had eaten in hours. If there were to be any attempts at finding Elizabeth tonight, they would need all their strength. He only hoped and prayed that Bill wouldn't hurt Elizabeth. He was still in disbelief over the entire thing. If only she had stayed with him, he would have been with her at the office; he would have never let her leave with that woman. He took a moment to collect his thoughts. His chest ached with grief and his head was throbbing. If anything happened to Elizabeth, how could he ever live with himself? She was all he had ever wanted and now she was missing.

*****

Bill pulled up to the security gate of his sister's house. He typed in the familiar code and drove up the long winding driveway. Elizabeth sat still, her arms crossed at her chest. Her face still burned from the slap she had received earlier.

Stopping in front of the large estate, Bill and Whitney got out. Elizabeth sat still; she glanced out the window at the place where they had brought her. Never in her life would she have thought Bill capable of the things he had done or said today. Her mind wondered to Richard. She prayed he was okay after the shots Whitney had taken at his car. Thinking back to the sounds of gunshots mixed with the squeal of Richard's tires and her own screams made her skin crawl. Then there was William, her family, and so many people who would be worrying about her. Shaken by all the action of the day Elizabeth was startled when Bill suddenly opened her door.

"Come on, let's go. We need to have a talk it seems. You just couldn't come back to me, could you? Well, now you will be made to see the light." He snarled.

She had never feared him in all of the months they had dated. Even after the last few weeks of his constant badgering, she hadn't thought of him as a danger to her, but now he seemed different. "Now, Elizabeth, let's go!" he barked. Not sure what he might do, she did as she was told.

All three entered the house together. It was a beautiful home Elizabeth thought, as she tried to look around and get her bearings. It was a large estate on several acres. It appeared that as they drove through the neighborhood, there were only a few homes, all on large lots. They were all expensive homes, she could tell; this particular one was a two-story Mediterranean style mansion. "Whitney, take her to the living room. I'll be there in a few minutes," Bill ordered.

"Sure," she agreed.

Elizabeth followed Whitney down a short hall with terracotta floor tiles to what she assumed was the living room. "Might as well make yourself comfortable. Who knows how long you'll be here," she flippantly admitted. It was a warm welcoming room. The walls were a light golden yellow with lots of aged wood beams along the ceiling. At the back of the room were French doors that opened up to what looked like a covered patio and pool area.

Elizabeth watched Whitney take a seat in a large over sized chair and kick off her shoes. She reclined and put her feet up on the ottoman. Thinking that sitting in a chair would keep Bill from sitting next to her, Elizabeth took the chair opposite of Whitney's. She sat down slowly, not knowing what to expect. She didn't lean all the way back but sat at the edge, her arms still crossed at her chest.

"So tell me, Elizabeth, did my brother not do anything for you?"

"Excuse me?"

"You know, satisfy you. If he had, you wouldn't have turned him down when he asked you to move in with him, now would you? I find most women don't leave men who keep them satisfied." She casually commented.

"I don't think that is any of your business. Whatever it is you think you know about me, I'm quite sure it's incorrect," Elizabeth responded in a short clipped tone.

"Well, I don't blame you. A woman should always be pleasured. A man must be made to know his place after all," Whitney said with a smile as she continued to antagonize Elizabeth.

Elizabeth didn't know how to respond to Whitney. What did she mean by "a man must be made to know his place"? It made no sense to her. She didn't have a good feeling about Bill's twin sister. She seemed just a little too nosey about such matters. It made her very nervous the way Whitney continue to look her over as if assessing her.

*****

Caroline looked at Richard with a mixture of concern and question. "Richard, what happened today? Who took Elizabeth?" her voice was soft yet demanding.

Sighing at the prospect of telling Caroline all the sordid details, Richard took a moment, and then started to tell the story. "After I left you, I called Darcy to tell him about Whitney. She was already at Bennet Industries, and she forced Elizabeth into a car. We chased that car down the highway, but after I crashed into the wall, we lost them." He opted for the short version of the story.

"You crashed into a wall! Richard, did you see a doctor?" her concern rising immediately for him. He could tell by her tone that she was getting a little too upset, and he didn't need a frantic woman fluttering about him. What he needed was to rescue Elizabeth! She was the one in trouble. God knows what Bill could be doing to her at this very moment.

"Fire and rescue were already at the scene dealing with another accident. They saw what happened and came to my aide. They helped to unpin my leg and check me over."

"Unpin your leg! Oh my gosh, Richard! That is not a small crash!"

"I'm fine. They checked me out – just some nasty scrapes and bruises. I'm a little sore, but that is to be expected," he explained, fatigue evident in his voice.

Darcy returned from the kitchen and began to explain what he had been up to, "I called out for food, and ... Elizabeth's father is on his way over."

"Seriously? Damn, he won't be happy," Richard interjected, glad for the change of subject.

"He is plenty mad; that's for sure. I should have called him earlier. We need to be better about keeping him informed about what is going on. He has every right to be mad. If she were my daughter, I would be. We need to respect his wishes; she would want us to do that for her. Once we have formed a plan, I think he will go along with whatever we decide. With Detective Lucus obviously not intending to keep us in the loop about whatever they find, we will need to do our own investigative work. Which reminds me – I should go check the computer for new Intel from the office," Darcy explained. He hoped that the helicopters from the crash scene were able to provide some information also.

"Here, let me do that. You wanted to talk to Caroline. No need to make her wait around here any longer than necessary." Richard quickly stood and walked down the hall.

Caroline watched him amble gingerly out of the room, not saying a word to her. She watched each little break in his stride due to his injuries. She couldn't help but want to take care of him. She could feel the sadness in her own eyes as he turned the corner. He didn't want her there. She could plainly see that his concern was for Elizabeth. It would do no good to try to recover what she had so heartlessly thrown away.

"You still love him, don't you?" Darcy quietly asked once Richard was out of earshot. He had been observing her and her reactions to Richard since Richard came into the room earlier.

Caroline peered down at her lap, pretending to straighten her dress. "Is it that obvious?" She lifted her chin to meet William's eyes.

*****

Bill walked into the room and took a seat on the couch. He glanced at both his sister and Elizabeth. One was confident and cocky; the other, on alert. "I hope my sister has been a good hostess while I checked on a few things. Can I get you something to drink perhaps?" he asked Elizabeth as if she had just dropped by for a visit.

202

"No thank you. Why have you done this, Bill? What purpose was there in taking me at gunpoint against my will? What do you plan to gain by this?" Elizabeth asked with a furrowed brow.

"My dear, I merely wish for you to see that I am the better man. I can't seem to get you away from those two hovering men for any amount of time to discuss matters regarding our relationship. Then of course there is that matter of the restraining order."

"Bill, those things have been done to protect me from you. There is no 'we' anymore. I told you months ago it was over. I have told you on several other occasions over these last few weeks that I am not interested in you any longer. I never had a wish to move in with you. It is no longer any of your business who I see or when I see them."

"Elizabeth, let me explain a few things to you. You are a young beautiful woman who will gain a lot of responsibility one day with the family business. I understand that perhaps I moved too fast and you weren't ready to commit to moving in with me. It had only been nine months. Or perhaps you needed to stretch your wings and explore other options. But you will see – I am what is best for you. I am what is best for the company."

"What is best for me? Do you really think kidnapping me will make me see you as the better man here Bill? You have lost your mind. As for what is best for the company – that is no longer your concern either." Elizabeth's voice was one of disbelief.

"Why are you with William Darcy, Elizabeth?" Bill asked frankly.

"What?" Elizabeth couldn't believe her ears. What was Bill's problem – was he deaf?

"Do you find him attractive? Or is it that he has all that money? Perhaps a business like your own father has – one that could merge the two into an even bigger one should you fall in love and marry?"

"Honestly Bill, where do you come up with this stuff? I have no idea where this is going with William, but I am pretty damn sure it is none of your concern."

"Come now Elizabeth, what about Richard Fitzwilliam? Does having two men at once get you hot?" Bill continued to pry, his tone becoming more and more condescending. He moved from the couch and slowly walked towards Elizabeth, keeping his eyes on her the entire time.

Elizabeth started to become very uncomfortable with how this line of questioning was going. She could see Bill wasn't going to let it go, and she could feel Whitney's eyes all over her. "Bill, I am not going to give you the satisfaction of an answer. I don't know what you are talking about."

"I think you do Elizabeth," Whitney said from her chair. She was smiling and enjoying Bill's line of questioning. If she didn't know better, Elizabeth thought, Whitney was anticipating something about to happen between her and Bill and wanted a front row seat. Elizabeth glanced back at Bill as he stopped before her.

*****

Richard returned to the living room to find Darcy showing Caroline out the door. He was thankful she was going. He couldn't stand to see the pain in her eyes, the concern on her face. It made him weak, and right now, he needed to be strong – strong for Elizabeth.

"I have some new information. The inquiries you ran discovered that Bill has a place just outside of town. It was a good call on your part, to use those TV choppers earlier to track Bill's destination. "

Darcy turned to face his cousin. "Good, then we can ride once we eat, and Mr. Bennet arrives. He should be here any minute. I don't want Elizabeth at the mercy of that man any longer than necessary. She has to be terrified after that car chase."

"Did you get any useful information out of Caroline?" he asked as he walked towards the couch.

"Some, she didn't have much to say. I think that the death of Whitney's husband could hold some interesting facts. I might have to pass that bit of information along to Detective Lucus. He may not want our help, but I want Bill Collins behind bars. If he had anything to do with that man's death, it would make it very difficult to allow him to roam freely."

"True." Richard leaned his head back with his arm over his eyes. He was tired and stressed. He ached all over and wanted nothing more than to soak in a hot tub then crash for hours. He wanted to hold Elizabeth, and tell her how sorry he was; he wanted to see her home safe.

"Richard, since we have a few minutes, how did your meeting with Caroline go this morning?" Darcy quietly inquired. He moved to the chair and reclaimed his tumbler.

Still leaning back with his eyes covered, Richard explained "Nothing of importance beyond what you know about Whitney. She apologized for going to Paris so quickly and for her rushed marriage. Why?"

Taking a moment to observe Richard, Darcy could tell he was still affected by Caroline. He seemed to be battling what was in his heart. He didn't like seeing his cousin in such a state. It had taken so long for him to even get to the point of going out again.

"It shows some character and strength on her part to ask for the meeting so she could apologize. She isn't in town long; she didn't have to bother calling you at all." Darcy tried to compliment Caroline's obvious inherent goodness.
"And your point is?" Richard said as he lifted his head from the couch.

"My point is, that I think you both still have strong feelings for each other. There is no need to be ashamed of them. She is only around a few more days. Perhaps you should take the opportunity to go out with each other."

"I really don't need this right now. Elizabeth is in the hands of Bill Collins and his lunatic twin sister, whom we know nothing about. Who knows what could happen to her? She is my priority right now," Richard almost growled.

"Elizabeth is understandably our focus at this moment. I am worried sick over her, but I am also worried about you."

"Then drop it. We need to get her back. Jesus, Darcy, we are going to take her home with us this weekend." Richard stood up and paced around to the back of the couch. He ran his hand through his hair before turning back to his cousin.

"I have feelings for Elizabeth. Feelings I haven't felt in a long time." Richard spoke with heart felt conviction.

"Feelings you haven't felt since Caroline," Darcy murmured.

Richard looked Darcy squarely in the eyes. "Yes, since Caroline crushed my heart," he spoke under his breath, but loud enough for Darcy to hear.

"Richard, let me say this without your jumping to defend yourself. When the entire incident happened in college with Sarah and Amy we made a pact. We decided to go down this unusual path in regards to our relationships with women. It has served us well, and I believe we have grown closer in our own relationship and become better men because of it. I believe it has also made us understand what we desire out of our love interests and our futures. We have talked about this revelation many times. I cared for Caroline; I can't deny that. Being in a relationship with her made me look at what I wanted for myself and helped me to understand the type of woman I ultimately wanted. I was already attracted to Elizabeth at that time, I didn't know if she could ever love me, however, and I needed to explore my options. I loved Caroline, but not in the same way you did. I would do anything for her – you know that, but I could not have remained a couple once I determined that I wanted to give my heart what it desired, and that was Elizabeth. But just like I love Elizabeth now in a way different from the way you love her, I'm not totally sure you could remain committed in this relationship with us. I can't make your mind up for you, nor do I know what your heart demands of you. But if you love someone, you should do all you can to secure that love. Don't settle, and don't force yourself into a lifetime of regret."

Richard listened to Darcy. He understood what he was saying, but didn't know if he was willing to trust or strong enough to fight. What if he loved both women? Elizabeth was so much more than he ever anticipated her being. What they shared was new and blossoming, and he didn't know if he could give up what she and Darcy offered for the potential of more heartache.

A knock sounded at the door, and Darcy rose to answer it.

Chapter 22

After having driven around town in circles for the past hour, Caroline pulled into Charles's driveway. Everyone was still at work, a fact she was thankful for since her mood was subdued and she didn't think she would be capable of holding an intelligent conversation at the moment. Jane would definitely fall to pieces when she found out about Elizabeth; she was already on the verge of a breakdown from the stress of all the wedding planning. She figured she would definitely need to be out of the house this evening before everyone came home.

Continuing to sit in her car, she again flashed back to the condo. Richard had seemed so distraught and confused. His eyes reflected the turmoil that roiled within him. She wished he had spoken more openly with her about what was going on in his head. She had felt compelled to hold him and make things better for him. But then again, she may have been the source of some of his discontent. It didn't help matters that Elizabeth could be in danger. Perhaps it would have been best if she had never returned from Paris.

Staring at the front door from her seat, Caroline grew tired and had the beginnings of a major headache. She thought she could excuse herself from visiting with Charles for the afternoon since she had been out most of the morning. He worked from home in the afternoons and would be home shortly. She just wanted to go lie down for a bit and think.

Having decided to head inside to rest, Caroline was just about to open the front door when Jane pulled into the driveway. Sighing at the prospect of having to be sociable and explain her dark mood, Caroline watched as Jane approached. The closer she got, however, the more Caroline could tell that something appeared to be wrong with Jane. She looked as if she was crying. Alarm set in. "She must have heard about Elizabeth already," she thought. She immediately went to her future sister-in-law to offer her comfort and support.

*****

Bill and Whitney had finally brought Elizabeth something to eat and drink after an hour of talking in circles. She had refused to speak to either of them on the topics they were choosing. Both had finally gotten fed up and left her in the living room, threatening her if she left it. They took her purse and phone with a promise to return them later. Bill informed her that he wasn't finished speaking with her about their relationship and that she needed to take some time to think about her future.

Elizabeth had kept an eye on her watch; she had been left alone for close to an hour already. She was tired from the after effects of the adrenaline rush she had experienced earlier. Her mind and heart were filled with worry for Richard after the gunshots and crash she had witnessed. She hoped and prayed that William had reached him in time to give any aide he needed. Then her thoughts drifted to her family; Jane was already in distress, and this would do nothing but add to her anxiety level. Yawning, she stood up once again and walked around the room. She glanced at pictures, books, magazines and the like scattered about the area. There was nothing that suggested Whitney had anything to hide. Everything in her home seemed normal to her; however, talking with her in person made Elizabeth think otherwise. There was something about that woman that wasn't right, but she couldn't quite put her finger on it. Maybe there were too many things amiss for her to focus on just one thing.

Then there was Bill. How could she not ever have noticed his interest or appetite for sexual adventure? Sex was good between them but nothing to write home about. Bill was never overly passionate or adventurous with her. It was just plain vanilla sex, but with the line of questioning he pursued with her, she began to wonder if perhaps he thought she craved more. It was just a feeling she got; especially after the questions he had asked and his reaction to some of her answers – they didn't seem to deter him. He also continued to believe in the delusion that he was the better man for her. Did he think that her current relationship with William and Richard had caused her to leave him? Could he believe that some sexual fantasy she desired could sway her into leaving a man if she really loved him?

Looking at her watch for the hundredth time, Elizabeth noticed it was approaching three o'clock. Realizing that they might not come back for some time still, Elizabeth decided she needed to try to search out a phone so she could call the police and alert them as to her location. She quietly tiptoed out of the living room and down the hall. She didn't know where Bill or Whitney had gone, and there was not a single noise to be heard. Even with Bill's threats of punishment should she leave the room, taking action beat sitting for who knows how much longer, helpless and frightened.

*****

208

"Bill, honestly, what do you think toying with that girl is going to get you?" Whitney remarked as she watched Bill set up her playroom to his liking.

"If she thinks those boy toys will satisfy her every fantasy, then I want her to know that I can do more than that. I can provide her with a lifetime of sexual fulfillment, if she will only open her mind to what I have to offer her."

"I don't know about that. She may have a dominant streak way down deep in her that has yet to be tapped. You want a submissive, not a Dom. I would be more than willing to help her find that side of herself for you," Whitney offered with a wicked grin. "But I don't think it is something she truly desires. What you need, brother, isn't what she can give you. Why would you even go to this extreme? Why would you out yourself if you're trying to win her back along with that company of hers? I thought the wholesome American business woman with a great body was what you wanted from her."

"You just let me worry about Elizabeth. If you can promise to keep your hands to yourself, maybe I'll let you watch. I've seen you sizing her up like one of your new subs. Remember, she's mine," Bill reminded his sister matter-of-factly.

"No harm in a girl looking. Do you mind if I change my clothes? If I can't participate, at least let me enjoy the show appropriately." She grinned suggestively.

Whitney found she was excited at the prospect of watching. She had always enjoyed voyeurism to some extent. She would watch her subs play from time to time even. But the thought of watching Elizabeth's fresh doe face react to what Bill wanted her to experience was electrifying. As a practicing female dominatrix, seeing a new sub introduced into the life always made Whitney's sexual appetite boil.

"Do as you wish; just remember hands off. I don't care if you're a Dom or not, when it's my sub, it's my way."

"Of course." Whitney enthusiastically rose from her perch and headed for the large closet of apparel she kept in her playroom for her and her guests to dress in. "Do you want me to pick out something for Elizabeth to wear?" She smiled at the thought of dressing the brunette beauty in something that would titillate both her and Bill.

*****

Elizabeth wandered down the halls in search of a phone. There wasn't one in sight. "Who has a home with no phones anywhere?" she thought. She began to grow more nervous with each passing minute. If she couldn't find a phone before Bill or Whitney found she was missing, how would anyone find her?

She entered what looked to be a home office. She didn't see a phone anywhere; however, she did notice a file marked Bennet Industries on the cover. She picked it up, and underneath it was another file with the name Corbin Jennings written across it. Wondering what Bill was doing with a file on a competing business known for hostile takeovers, Elizabeth snatched it up and flipped it open. Inside there were two pictures, one of Corbin whom she had met on several occasions, and the other that of his well-known son Drew. Seeing Drew's face made Elizabeth mildly annoyed. He had asked her out several times, and Elizabeth had turned him down every time. Neither of the Jennings men owned a heart. They were known by many and feared by all. They destroyed peoples' lives with no compunction whatsoever. What was Bill up to with a file filled with newspaper clippings on those two, along with what looked to be several bank statements?

The sound of a door closing put Elizabeth on alert. She replaced the files quickly and then happened to glance out the window. The nearest home was quite a distance away. She didn't know if she would be able to make it over there before Bill caught up to her. And if she should make it, would anyone be home?

Panicking at the thought of being caught, Elizabeth left the office and cautiously worked her way farther down the hall. What she needed was her cell phone and a hiding place. This home seemed large enough to hide in; she just needed to be quick about it. As she passed by a few more rooms, she happened to spot her purse on a chair in a corner. She warily walked towards it, looking around to see if anyone was in the room. Once she reached her purse, she dug around and pulled out her phone.

She heard Whitney say to Bill, "Just give me 20 minutes, and I'll be ready." Whitney's voice was close. With her heart pounding in her chest, Elizabeth quickly crawled under the large four-poster bed and prayed she wouldn't be found.

*****

Richard hung up the phone. "Okay, I called in some favors with two of my contacts at the police station. They are prepared to offer us backup. They said they would meet us at the entrance to the subdivision in an unmarked car. They are off duty and will act only if needed. We will grab some walkie-talkies from them when we meet." Richard checked his gun and holstered it. He was ready to get Elizabeth back, no matter how much physical pain he felt; she needed him, and he needed her.

"Then let's get moving!" Darcy ordered. The more time that passed since Elizabeth's abduction, the more on edge he became. He hated all this waiting around. Even though it had been only about three hours since the chase had happened, it seemed far longer. They had explained everything to Mr. Bennet while calls were placed. They had directions to Whitney's house, and now all three were prepared to rescue her. They decided to use Bennet's vehicle since Richard's was totaled and Darcy's wouldn't hold them all. With his own mind swirling at how many things could go wrong and how crazy Bill was, he hoped that Elizabeth was safe, and that they would be at Whitney's house. If they weren't holding her there, he didn't know what he would do. He couldn't let his thoughts go there; his heart could not bear it.

*****

With her heart pounding in her ears, Elizabeth didn't move an inch; much less breathe. She could hear Whitney moving around in the bathroom, opening and closing drawers. After a few minutes, she even seemed to be cheerfully humming. Curious as to what she was up to, Elizabeth tried to lower her head to the floor and peer in the direction of the noise.

The first things she caught sight of were bright red leather stiletto boots. Her eyes widened as they traveled up Whitney's legs, noticing that the boots stopped just above her knees. A black micro-mini leather skirt topped with a bright red leather corset laced up the back completed her outfit.

Why she was dressed in such a way, Elizabeth couldn't begin to fathom. She continued to watch Whitney's back as she fixed her hair and make-up. Then she saw her slip on long elbow-length black gloves and place a black leather choker around her neck with a few chains dangling down on her chest.

"Whitney, get your ass to the living room NOW! We have a problem." The sharp sounds of Bill's angry bark caught Elizabeth off guard, she gasped at her own startled reaction to him. Squeezing her eyes shut for fear of having been heard, Elizabeth once again didn't move or breathe. She could hear the boots clack across the bathroom floor as Whitney left her room.

She knew that Bill had discovered she was missing. She quickly crawled out from under the bed and straight to the closet, closing the door silently. Where she placed a call to 911 without further delay.

*****

Mr. Bennet concentrated on his objective of reaching his beloved daughter as quickly as he possibly could while he navigated the highway. Richard sat in the back, not even blinking as he stared out the window, and Darcy rode shotgun, focusing on the road ahead. All the men were quiet and deep in their own thoughts; not even the radio was turned on.

They all had one mission: to save a woman they each cared for deeply. Three and a half hours had passed, and there had been no word from the police, no calls from Bill demanding anything, no reason given for taking Elizabeth against her will and they were all worried.

No one needed to say it; they were all thinking it – if they found one hair on Elizabeth's head harmed, Bill Collins would pay dearly.

*****

"Jane, what happened? Why are you crying? " Caroline walked up to her soon-to-be sister and took her by the hand. She wanted to know what Jane was so upset about, but she certainly didn't want to add to her misery if she wasn't yet aware of Elizabeth's abduction. She instantly wanted to comfort Jane and protect her. She was such a sweet soul. The instant she met Jane, Caroline knew that she and Charles were made for each other. Each was so giving, kind and caring. How could anyone ever think ill of either? Caroline had often wished she had more of her brother's goodness in her. He was humble but confidant, a man who cared for those around him and for his own family more than himself. She knew he wanted her to move back home and have a bigger role in his life, but he also wanted her to attain her dreams and goals, and so he never once made demands on her or guilted her for her choices. He had even welcomed that slime of a husband she had married into the family, no questions asked.

"It's Elizabeth. Something terrible has happened; I just know it. Oh Caroline, Elizabeth is my closet relation, my best friend," Jane cried quietly.

212

"Jane, come inside. I'll make you some chamomile tea while you calm down a bit. I may be able to help some. I have some information to share with you about Elizabeth."

"You know something about what has happened?" Jane furrowed her brow as she looked at Caroline. Tears still trickled down her cheeks as she wondered how Caroline could know anything about what had happened earlier.

"I just found out myself. I was just going into the house when you pulled up. Come on; we can share what we both know and help each other. It may be a long night."

Caroline wrapped an arm around Jane's shoulders and helped guide her into the house. They moved slowly, both taking comfort in the fact they had someone to share their fears and concerns with.

*****

Elizabeth had finished her call to 911, having been put in contact with a detective Lucas. He wanted her to sit tight and hide while he sent two squad cars to retrieve her. The detective said they would be there within twenty minutes. The next call was to William. She needed to tell him what was happening. Just hearing his voice would comfort her while she waited. She also needed to know how Richard was doing.

"Elizabeth!" came the concerned voice on the other end.

She whispered her return, "Yes, it's me"

"Thank God! Are you all right?" Darcy continued to question, his heart beating swiftly at the sound of her voice.

"For now. I just found my phone and called 911. I spoke to a detective Lucas, and he is sending two squad cars to get me," she quickly explained in a hushed tone. "He wants me to hide till they arrive."

"Elizabeth, listen to me; I'm five minutes away from you. Can you get outside?"

"I don't know. Bill has just realized I'm missing and doesn't sound happy. I'm hiding in Whitney's closet."

"I need for you to be brave for me Elizabeth; can you do that?" Darcy asked in a tone that was both supportive and strong. He wanted her out of that house now. If Bill was angry, there was no way to predict what he might do.

"I think so. They're up to something William. I found business files on a desk," Elizabeth tried to explain. She felt he needed to know in case something happened to her.

Interrupting her, Darcy said, "You can tell me all about it once you are safe with us. Find a window or a door and just run. I will meet you outside. We are pulling into the subdivision now. Just get out!" he passionately implored.

"Okay."

"Keep this line open so I can hear what's happening. Do you know what part of the house you are in – the front or the back?"

"Not really."

"Okay, just get out. Richard and I are coming. Go! Now!" he insisted urgently.

With her courage bolstered by his commanding voice, Elizabeth quietly moved from the closet and walked towards the door of the room.

She listened at the doorway for any sounds she might hear. They were faint but there. She knew going back towards the living room and out the front door wasn't an option, since they would be looking for her there first. She turned and moved down the hall, quickly checking behind her every few feet. She could see a door ajar at the end of the hall and headed for that.

Pushing open the partially closed door, she peered into the space. Elizabeth's eyes widened at what she saw before her. She couldn't move forward or backward as her eyes roamed around the room. Along one wall, there were floor to ceiling mirrors spanning the width of the room. The remaining three walls were a deep rich purple and sported no art at all. Several different types of *equipment*– since she couldn't find another word for it – were scattered around the large space. None of it looked comfortable in the least, and she wondered what you would do with them. There was also a large leather sofa off to one side, and all types of pillows and wedges were scattered around the polished hardwood floor. Her eyes stopped on one wall at what looked to be a large section of pegboard with assorted items hanging from it: whips, chains, and what appeared to be some sort of paddle and a stick with feathers. This room gave her the creeps, and she certainly didn't want to be trapped in here with Bill or Whitney.

"Elizabeth Bennet, you need to show yourself. This isn't a game. I want to speak with you. I'm not going to hurt you; I just want you to listen to what I have to tell you."

Jerking her head to look behind her, Elizabeth moved into the room and silently clicked the door closed. Bill's voice was stern, and she knew he was angry with her. She didn't want to know what punishment he might have in mind for her having left the living room. Thankfully, this door had a lock, and she used it.

Scanning the room, she noticed a closet and a wall lined in black satin fabric like curtains perhaps. She quickly traversed a few pillows and around a few of the bizarre contraptions to see if a window could be found behind the fabric wall. Finding just what she was looking for, she quickly unlatched the locks.

"Elizabeth, open this door right now!" came Bill's infuriated command.

Elizabeth could hear him as he tried to pick the lock. She hurriedly pushed up the window and kicked the screen out with her foot. She moved the phone up to her ear. "William, I'm coming out a window; Bill is about to storm into this room. Where are you?"

Elizabeth sat on the ledge and pulled one leg through the opening while she placed the phone in her pocket. She was swinging her other leg over the windowsill when the door whipped open and Bill instantly spotted her.

"Don't do it, Elizabeth!" he yelled across the room.

At that moment, Richard reached the window and took hold of Elizabeth's arm pulling her through to safety. Startled at the sudden unexpected move, Elizabeth let out a slight screech as she swiftly jerked her head around to meet Richard's chest. "GO! RUN!" he ordered in a gruff tone.

Elizabeth took off running in the direction Richard pointed, with him following close behind her.

*****

Bill ran to the window, just missing Elizabeth. He leaned through the opening to see the backside of Richard Fitzwilliam following Elizabeth as they both ran for the front of the house.

"Damn it!" he shouted. He turned and took off towards the hall, quickly pushing his sister aside. He reached the front door and jerked it open to find two men in plain clothes standing on his front step, one with his gun pointed right at him.

"Bill Collins?"

"Yes, who the hell are you? Get out of my way!" He tried to move around the men, ignoring them and the gun.

"You are under arrest for the abduction of Elizabeth Bennet. You have the right to remain silent. Anything you say or do can and will be held against you in the court of law. You have the right to speak to an attorney. If you cannot afford an attorney, one will be appointed for you. Do you understand these rights as they have been read to you?"

Bill nodded as the first officer cuffed him while the second went inside in search of Whitney. Bill watched as Elizabeth was helped into her father's car, Richard sliding in behind her. Darcy stood on the opposite side giving him a stone cold face before getting into the front seat and closing the door soundly behind him. They all drove off, leaving a handcuffed Bill standing at the police cruiser, looking extremely odd dressed in his tight black leather pants and a pure white tee shirt that clung to his muscular frame.

*****

As soon as they were moving, Richard leaned in towards Elizabeth, wrapping his arm around her shoulders to pull her into his chest. "Are you all right? Did they hurt you in any way?" he asked in a voice deeply strained and concerned.

"I'm fine, just tired," she answered with a slight tremble. Her adrenaline was really pumping; she could feel her heart racing.

Darcy turned around, reaching his arm between the seats to touch Elizabeth's leg. "Thank God! I – we, have all been so worried about you." The relief was thick in his reply.

Elizabeth looked into William's eyes and could have drowned in the flood of emotions she saw in them. She reached her hand to cover his, "Truly, I'm fine," she softly replied.

Just touching him melted her heart. They both connected in a wordless moment caught in each other's eyes. It happened in a flash, but they both felt it, and they both recognized it. They both sighed with relief.

"Elizabeth, you wouldn't lie to your father, now would you? This old man can handle whatever you need to say. It's been a long afternoon, and that dirt bag doesn't deserve your protection." His voice was strained, yet Elizabeth heard the relief in his tone. She loved her father, and as soon as they stopped, she wanted to wrap her arms around him.

"I wouldn't protect Bill, not after today. He is certifiable. I will tell you all about it later, but right now I just want to be with all of you and rest." She turned to Richard, noticing the bandages on his arm along with several scrapes and what looked like at least one deep bruise. Tenderly she reached across and glided her fingertips over the new marks. "You were hurt earlier, weren't you?" she asked as she lifted her eyes to his.

"It's nothing; I'm a bit banged up but fine." He tried to remove his arm from her view. Richard held her tighter as he whispered, "I can't tell you how sorry I am, Elizabeth," his voice soft as his chin came to rest on her head.

"What do you have to be sorry for? My god, Whitney had a gun. I tried to stop her, but then she fired at your car. I heard the tires screech." Elizabeth pressed her head closer to his chest, listening to his heart. The memory of that event was still so fresh in her mind, the sounds she would never forget, or the sharp burn of Whitney's hand meeting her cheek.

"I'm sorry I couldn't stop him from taking you away," he said in a low tone, squeezing her a bit tighter before placing a kiss to her head.

Elizabeth pulled back from his hold to look into Richard's eyes. There was pain and worry there. She leaned in, kissing him gently on the lips while cupping his cheek in her palm. "Listen to me. There is nothing to forgive, and I'm perfectly fine. Will you just take me home now? Your home," she said with sincerity in a loving gentle tone.

The only reply he gave was a slow nod and a kiss to her palm. He tucked her head back against his shoulder and glanced at Darcy who had watched the entire scene. "My place it is," he responded looking directly at Darcy.

William nodded his understanding and turned around to face the front. The rest of the ride was silent.

*****

They all arrived at Richard's condo, tired and quiet. No sooner had the door closed behind them than Darcy's cell phone began to ring. "This is Will Darcy."

"Mr. Darcy, this is detective Lucas. I am sending lieutenants Denny and Saunders over to speak with Miss Bennet and take her statement."

"I understand. She would appreciate it if you could do it quickly. She is quite tired after the events of the day," he said in a mild tone but hoping for understanding of Elizabeth's situation.

"They shouldn't be long. I also wanted to mention that I don't appreciate your meddling in official police matters. I came very close to having you and Mr. Fitzwilliam arrested for interfering in police business, but it seems you have friends in high places," the detective growled. Darcy could tell he was not happy with the turn of events but didn't give one iota since that same man would not listen to him earlier while he was at the station.

"We just happened to get a lead and needed to check it out before reporting it to you. Miss Bennet called us herself, and we were only five minutes away. There was no time to inform you of the events taking place. We did, however, have two of your off duty agents with us. I'm sure you are well aware of that," Darcy politely informed the irate man.

"I'm quite aware of who was with you and who made the arrests. As I said before, the officers should be there shortly to speak to Miss Bennet," he repeated. Darcy knew he had said his peace and was ready to end the call.

"Thank you for calling. I'll let Miss Bennet know." Darcy hung up the phone and turned to see three faces staring at him.

*****

"Thank Goodness! Can I speak with her?" Jane's relief was instantaneous. Charles had come home and spent the last hour soothing his future wife's fears and anxieties. "Okay, I understand. Give her my love, and I'll talk with her in the morning. Thank you for calling me. I have been so worried."

"Elizabeth is home?" Caroline asked with sincere hope.

"Yes. That was my father. They got her back to Richard's about half an hour ago. She is giving a statement to the police and then going to bed," Jane explained. She couldn't see the pain that crossed Caroline's eyes at the news of Elizabeth's being at the condo.

Checking her own emotions, Caroline stood up and moved to Jane, hugging her. "That is wonderful news. I'm so happy she has been found. Is she all right?" Caroline asked in a genuinely caring voice.

"Thank you, that means a lot, Caroline. She is fine. Father said she would call me in the morning." Jane smiled, tears welling up in her eyes.

Jane turned to Charles who enfolded her into his arms, kissing her and whispering in her ear. Caroline watched the emotions of both for just a moment. Love was such a special and fragile thing. She was happy for her brother. What he and Jane shared was real and lasting.

Then her heart began to ache, and she could feel the sadness begin to overtake her. Quietly she slipped out of the room so as not to disturb them. She needed to be alone. Standing in her bedroom, Caroline brushed her long auburn tresses. The entire day had been such a roller coaster of emotions. First, there had been breakfast at the café with Richard, so reminiscent of how they used to spend their Saturday mornings. He was still everything she remembered and dreamed of, but there was something in his eyes now, something akin to loss.

This afternoon when she had been asked by Darcy to go to the condo, it had brought back so many memories for her. She almost declined the invitation, knowing how hard it would be to go, but Darcy sounded like he needed her. Once there, the place was the same as she remembered. It had been her home for several months. When Richard had appeared, fresh from the shower, she thought her heart had stopped beating.

It was just as if she had never left. So many times she had seen him in that very spot in those very jeans, holding a white towel. It was surreal to witness it again. She both cursed the opportunity to be there and was thankful to have been asked. The brief glimpses into the past, a time of happiness for her, brought her some measure of comfort.

When she had heard that Elizabeth was abducted and Richard had been injured in a bad accident chasing after them, she knew another had replaced her in Richard's heart. It wasn't as if she didn't expect it. But to be faced with it, to see his agony for another woman, made her insides churn in sorrow.

She could never ever be forgiven for what she had done to him; she could see that. Now Elizabeth was at his place – sleeping in his bed – and she just ached with the thought of it. She liked Elizabeth very much. She was in some small way happy he had found someone like her, and she hoped they would be happy. Richard deserved to be happy.

Falling on her bed, Caroline silently sobbed into her pillow. Her life seemed so hopeless. To love a man and not know how to make amends for her horrid mistakes had to be the worst feeling in the world. She wished she had never come back. There were too many memories causing her more pain than she felt she was able to bear.

*****

Richard leaned up against the doorjamb watching Elizabeth sleep, her hair spread across the sheets while she took short even breaths. She seemed so at peace to him. Darcy was standing just behind him. "She will be fine, Richard. She is so much stronger than we give her credit for," he softly said, his eyes watching her as well.

"I know, but I just can't shake the feeling I have. We could have lost her today. I could have lost her," Richard replied in a hushed tone. He couldn't get enough of looking at her.

"Come back to the living room. I have an idea, and I want you to hear it when I talk with Mr. Bennet about it."

Darcy turned and walked away after patting Richard on the shoulder. Taking a final glance at the woman quietly sleeping in the middle of his bed, Richard looked up to the heavens and said a prayer of thanks before leaving her to join the others.

*****

It had been a long, tiring day. William was exhausted. Earlier he had made sure that Elizabeth ate something and then helped her to shower and settle into bed. He would like to have held her longer, to have made love with her, but she had others needing assurances as well. He had spoken to her father not an hour ago about taking her away to see his family earlier than originally planned. He wanted to leave in the morning. He thought it was best for her to get away from all the media hype that might befall her should her abduction and rescue make the news.

He still needed to talk with Elizabeth; she had wanted to say something earlier about files at Whitney's place, implying there could be other motives playing into this situation, other than just a man desperately clinging to the possibility of regaining her favor – though from the looks of Bill's outfit this afternoon, he had other things in mind. He didn't get a good look at Whitney, but he felt sure that Elizabeth knew something about what was going on, and he meant to get to the bottom of it.

In the morning, Darcy and Richard would accompany Elizabeth to Jane's so the sisters could reconnect. He knew Jane was extremely upset at the events of the day and needed to see her sister to reassure herself that Elizabeth was all right. Once the reunion was over, he and Richard would take her to his parents' house. Darcy had a small cottage out in the back by the pond for his use when he went to visit. He and Richard had selected the plans and built it together on the spot they had chosen. Neither of them wanted to impose their lifestyle on their families even though both families were very open and accepting of it. Their families would welcome Elizabeth, and she could use the extra few days to just relax and rest.

Darcy was anxious for Georgiana to meet Elizabeth. Her own home was also built on the family property. It seemed everyone had his or her slice of the land. There was plenty of it. The Fitzwilliam clan was not far away. When Darcy's mother and Richard's father had inherited the Fitzwilliam land, the siblings had split it down the middle. Richard's older brother still lived in his parents' house, rarely leaving unless he came to town and stayed with Richard. Darcy wanted Elizabeth to meet the entire family. He knew she would love the land, the horses, and his sister, not to mention his old Aunt Catherine, a funny old bird.

Darcy quietly slipped into the bed, kissing Elizabeth on the cheek before curling up next to her and placing his arm around her waist. She hardly moved. He was so fortunate to have her back in his arms. He had missed her so much, even if it was only for a night. She belonged with him, and after the weekend away together, he hoped she would think so as well. He fully intended to lavish lots of attention on her.

Chapter 23

Waking before dawn, Elizabeth rose up on one elbow to glance over William's broad shoulders at the clock on the bedside table, it was only four thirty in the morning. Since she had gone to bed so early after yesterday's harrowing experience, her body's internal clock was a bit off. Both William and Richard were still soundly asleep. They had been through so much yesterday themselves that she hated to disturb them, so tried to go back to sleep.

It was a futile attempt, however. No matter which direction she turned, she found herself face to face with one of the guys, a *distraction* for her indeed. First she faced Richard, his tousled hair, broad shoulders and bare chest were almost more than she could resist. Even in his sleep, he was a handsome man. She watched him sleep for a few moments, his peaceful state touching her heart. She drew invisible lines with her mind using her fingertips along his cheek and jaw. She wanted to kiss him, to hold him close and take away the torment he had imposed on himself yesterday. He had needed her securely in his arms from the minute she had climbed into her father's car until they had arrived at his condo. It had been with a great deal of reluctance that he had released her then, she thought.

If the time had been right and had they been alone, she knew that they would have made love as soon as the door closed behind them. Richard's emotions had him tied in knots; she could see it in his face, his eyes and how he held her. He was conflicted, and she couldn't help but want to ease his discomfort. She could also tell by the tone of his voice that they both needed the reassurance of the connection.

Closing her eyes to the rising desire to be with him, Elizabeth turned over, hoping to give him the rest he so desperately needed. The accident had caused him a fair amount of physical pain that he had refused to allow himself to feel until she was finally safe at home last night. She certainly didn't want to make matters worse for him.

Flipping to her other side, Elizabeth almost rolled into William's back. It was covered in a soft light gray tee shirt. Thankfully he was still asleep. Lying there staring at his muscular form and dark hair only sparked more of her imagination. She itched to use her fingers to caress his shoulders, feel the muscles in his strong arms, and then run them through his dark silky hair. Her lips wanted to seek out the warm flesh along his neck, stopping to nibble on his earlobes.

Becoming frustrated at her own thoughts, Elizabeth rolled to her back. Maybe if she stared at the ceiling long enough, she would grow tired and fall back asleep. The only thing that seemed to be happening, however, was that her mind was growing more intent on thoughts of the guys' bodies and what they could do to hers. Not to mention what she wanted to do to them as well.

Biting her lower lip, Elizabeth criss-crossed her forearms over her face trying to fight the rising desires growing stronger inside her. Her breasts were starting to tingle, her peaks hardening, making her more aware of what she really wanted. With her eyes closed, her mind began to play out her heart's desire on the big movie screen in her head. Her vision started with William on one side, Richard on the other, both men pleasuring her at the same time.

Becoming restless at her inability to quiet her forbidden thoughts, Elizabeth decided it would be best if she put distance between herself and the source of her sexual frustration. Quietly, she peeled herself out from under the covers, gingerly crawling to the foot of the bed. If she hadn't thought that it would wake the guys, she would have taken a cold shower.

At the end of the bed, she turned and peered first at William, then Richard. Smiling at herself for not waking them, she tiptoed away.

*****

Darcy could sense Elizabeth's restlessness. She kept turning and flopping about until he almost pulled her to him to quiet her. It was 4:45 in the morning. How could she be awake at such an unearthly hour? Not one to enjoy waking so early, he remained still, hoping she would doze back off. He felt the bed dip slightly, and then heard her dainty footsteps as she left the room. He wondered if she had been having a nightmare. He rolled over to face the opposite direction when he caught a whiff of her pillow. It smelled so good... lavender, the fragrance she always wore, and it wafted right to his nose. Groaning at his own inability to stop thinking of her now, he decided he should go check on Elizabeth and make sure she was okay.

William walked into the living room to find Elizabeth curled up on the couch. Her head was closest to him so she couldn't see him standing in the doorway. She kept moving around trying to get comfortable and was having no luck. Her frustrated grunts made him smile; even with the early hour, he couldn't help but be captivated by her. He gradually walked towards the couch, hoping not to startle her. When he reached her, she suddenly shot up and looked at him. If he wasn't mistaken, she had a look in her eyes he knew well. She wasn't having a nightmare; that much was for sure.

"Why are you in here; it's so early. I got out of bed so I wouldn't wake either of you," she whispered.

"You were restless; I thought perhaps you had a bad dream," he said while moving to sit next to her on the couch.

Elizabeth pulled her legs out of his way to give him some space. "I guess with going to bed so early yesterday, my body clock just went off earlier than normal. I'm sorry I woke you up," she said, trying to adjust the blanket on her lap. She was a little flustered, Darcy could tell, making her all the more kissable.

William moved in while she wasn't looking and captured her lips with his own. It was an inviting kiss, one she happily enjoyed and repaid. "What was that for?" she blushed.

"You seemed to need a kiss. Perhaps there is more I can do for you. We are both awake; seems a shame to waist this opportunity or mood you seem to be in." He grinned slightly with his brow raised.

Embarrassed that he knew she was in just such a state, Elizabeth glanced down at the blanket then back up to William. From her lowered lashes, she grinned slightly and placed her hand on William's chest. She ran it down the length of his torso then up again. Though he still had on the gray tee shirt, she still could feel each rippled muscle along his abdomen. She craved him, wanted him, and if he were a willing man at this hour, she would take advantage of it.

"I don't know what has come over me, but I can't get this image out of my mind," she breathily explained.

Intrigued, he ran a fingertip down her cheek, along her neck and down between her breasts. "What image is that? How can I make it come to life for you?" he whispered as he approached her lips once again. He so enjoyed speaking in low tones to her. She reacted to each word with a shiver or a slight parting of her lips. She was everything he had always hoped she would be, a treasure for him to unlock.

Sighing at his gentle kiss, her heart began to thump louder in her ears. He was asking her what she wanted, what her fantasy was at this moment. Should she tell him or just let things go the way they were headed? He seemed willing to pleasure her, but what she wanted was both men. She returned his kiss and deepened it, her desire rising swiftly. Her hand traveled down his broad shoulder and towards his forearm before taking his hand in hers. She placed it on her breast and pulled back to speak, "What I want is to be pleasured by both of you together. My feelings for you are so strong, William. We have such a connection, you and I." Darcy stopped her speech by kissing her again.

This time his kiss was more impassioned. He probed her mouth with his tongue, savoring the taste of her. Elizabeth could feel herself slipping into the moment. Both arms wrapped around William's neck, pulling herself closer to his body. His own hand moved to her upper thigh and began to caress it all the way up her backside, pulling her to him. They broke the kiss, and Elizabeth found she was on William's lap. His hands ran down her sides finding the ends of her gown and lifting it over her head. Elizabeth watched his face. His nostrils flared at the sight of her unveiled flesh, while his eyes caressed her body. She loved how that made her feel. It would seem her words had inflamed him, making her want to do more to entice him.

"Tell me, what we were doing to you Elizabeth?" William asked as he focused on her chest. Swallowing before she spoke, she watched him closely. He moved his hands to cup her breasts and began to roll her semi-hard nipples between his fingers. Still not looking her in the eyes, he again posed a question, "Did we fondle your breasts, suckle them at the same time perhaps?" His raspy voice sent chills up her spine. She loved how he made her feel. They had such a passionate connection. She continued to observe his movements as he leaned in and began to do just as he said, suckling her nipple to a hard peak before moving to the next. She couldn't control her body's instantaneous reaction. He was so skilled at what he did to her.

"Yes..." she sighed. "Yes, you were both on either side of me." She leaned her head back, her hair floating towards her lower back as she enjoyed the sensations. He massaged one breast while he suckled on the other, and then switched; it was all so good.

He stopped and ran a finger from between her breasts down to her belly, creating circles around her navel. "Then maybe we should wake Richard," he offered, finally glancing up at her from his own lowered lashes.

"No, please don't wake him; it's only a dream. I couldn't. I'm not so bold, and it is so early; please don't." Elizabeth became a little panicked. Richard needed his rest; it was not worth it to wake a man for her own fulfillment. William was doing a fine job on her. "It's only a dream," she repeated taking his face in her hands and leaning in to kiss him. She moved down along his cheek to his earlobe, rimming his entire ear with her tongue before stopping to lick and nibble at the lobe. "You are doing a fine job all on your own," she seductively whispered into his ear.

Darcy was growing harder by the moment. She didn't just have a dream; she was in a world of sexual need. He could tell by how wet her crotch was on his lap, how responsive she was to his kisses, and that breathy groan she let out as he suckled at her breasts, it was definitely more than just a vision. She was horny, and he was going to take pleasure in listening to her scream in ecstasy this morning. He smiled at his earlier thought of rolling over and going to sleep now. He was more than thankful that he had decided to get up and check on her. But her declarations and pleading were not going to work on him. Richard would want to be part of this.

Placing his hands along her buttocks, Darcy got a firm grip on her as he leaned in for a deep kiss. He pulled her up with him as he stood. "William what are you doing?" she asked, wrapping her arms and legs around him so as not to fall.

"That bed is much more comfortable than this little couch. More rolling around room," he explained in a hushed tone, grinning before kissing the tip of her nose.

"William, please, I said not to wake Richard," she again pleaded quietly.

A deep scratchy voice came from the bedroom. "Not to worry, I'm awake," came Richard's reply.

Elizabeth shot a glance toward the bedroom to see Richard, his eyes half-opened, standing there with only his boxer shorts on, but definitely prepared to play.

"Seems Elizabeth is having dreams that are keeping her awake. I think you would be interested to hear about them," William said in a sexy voice as he walked her into the room. Elizabeth had buried her face in his shoulder. He found her so very enchanting when she blushed.

Elizabeth could feel her body come alive. Every nerve seemed to be on alert. Were they going to make her dream come true? Where they going to make love to her together, not one, then the other or one starts and the other joins, but together, from start to finish? She was excited and nervous at the same time.

As William passed by Richard, he stopped for a moment. Richard leaned towards Elizabeth to the ear facing out and whispered into it. "A dream, is it? I can't wait for you to tell me all about it. I've been dreaming of you as well." Then he kissed her cheek and ran his palm down her back as William walked to the bed. Again, Elizabeth swallowed at the sound of Richard's dark scratchy voice. He made her toes curl as his breath washed across her ear. She thought she might orgasm before they ever touched her, her anticipation growing by the minute, not to mention the wetness between her thighs.

William moved to his side of the bed and gently placed Elizabeth down. "Slide to the middle and close your eyes Elizabeth," he softly commanded her. She complied and scooted to the center of the large comfortable bed. The bedroom was still dark due to the early hour of the morning. A noise caught Elizabeth's attention. She turned to see Richard lighting a candle on his side of the bed. The bright flames illuminating the space while shadows flickered across the wall.

Before climbing onto the mattress, William quickly removed his shirt and boxers while Elizabeth was looking at Richard. He to did the same, speedily slipping out of his shorts to join them. With two extremely handsome men surrounding her, Elizabeth's hormones intensified into an erotic swirl of anticipation and desire. So much so that she couldn't determine where to look first. Her eyes wanted to feast on their bodies; her hands wanted to glide across their forms and map each of their hard surfaces.

"I'm not sure—" Elizabeth started to say. William quieted her with a gentle finger to her lips. His deep dark eyes caught her attention instantly, then as his eyes burned a path to her soul, he spoke, "There is nothing for you to think of or do. I want you to lie back and just concentrate on the sensations that you feel. I'm going to place a blindfold over your eyes to enhance your experience." He leaned over her lap to kiss her cheek then her lips.

"I don't want you to cover my eyes. I want to see you, both of you," she implored just a bit. Secretly she thought it was bold, and she wondered how it would be to be blindfolded—to have no control.

Richard engaged Elizabeth from her other side, running a finger down her cheek and neck, all the way to her chest, stopping to fondle her puckered pink flesh. "It will help to enhance the pleasure we want to give you, Elizabeth. We won't harm you; we just want you to enjoy this moment to the fullest." She had turned to catch a glimpse of Richard's face as he spoke to her. He was enthralled, and his eyes darkened while he spoke, his desire to please her evident in the language his body could not conceal.

Elizabeth's mind was whirling into mush at their suggestions. She wanted to relinquish her trepidation and give them the control to make her dream come true, to have them bring her to the heights of passion she had yet to experience, and she trusted that they were capable of creating that for her. The thought was heady indeed.

William took a soft scarf from a bedside drawer and tied it securely around Elizabeth's head. "This is for the pleasure that I want to give to you, my beautiful Lizzy," he whispered into her ear once he had finished. He helped to ease her back down on the bed, moving the covers to the foot, out of the way of all three of them.

While Darcy moved the sheets, Richard took her hands and placed them over her head. "Leave them here for now, my angel," he softly spoke. He couldn't resist trailing his palms down those arms, over her breasts, to her tight abdomen where he placed a feather-light kiss at her navel.

With her heart beating wildly, her nipples taut, and her core weeping in anticipation, Elizabeth listened more intently to what was going on around her. Two sets of hands touched her hands. Slowly they moved down from her wrists, past her elbows, trailing down the sides of her torso, skimming past the outer edges of her breasts until they reached her hips. Once there, they continued on their sensuous journey, palms alternately running down her outer and inner thighs. No one touched her where she craved it the most, but waves of desire continued to rise within her. Both sets of hands stopped at her feet and began to massage them. It was so relaxing to her. She could feel some of her anxiety start to ebb as they worked on her toes, insteps, heels and calves.

Since she had the blindfold on, Elizabeth allowed herself to just be in the moment—the comfort of Richard's bed, the wonderful scent of the candle he had lit, the massage. It all helped to ease her breathing and pounding heart. One set of hands lifted away, the other working on both feet simultaneously. She thought William was still at her feet, but where was Richard?

Then she heard him next to her ear, his husky timbre raising the hairs on her neck in a devilishly erotic way, "You are so beautiful in the candlelight, Elizabeth. If you could only see how sensual your body appears and how it affects me... your natural curves... how your skin glistens in the light. I'm going to make you understand just how desirable you are, how much we adore you. I need you to keep your arms above your head and trust that I will not harm you. I only wish to pleasure you." He moved to place a gentle kiss on her lips, lingering to taste her for a moment. When he released her lips, she felt a fiery sensation along each breast.

Inhaling instantly at the unexpected heat, Elizabeth listened to Richard praise her in a comforting tone, "You are so very beautiful, my angel. The wax will cool in a moment; just relax."

William's hands started to slip lovingly up her calves to her thighs and back down again, his movements helping to distract her from the warmth at her chest. He repeated the pattern, his hands inching closer to her center each time.

The warmth against Elizabeth's chest began to subside as Richard's skilled hands began to massage the liquid wax around each round mound, his palms and fingers working in unison, caressing every inch of her breasts, leaving Elizabeth breathless with this new incredible feeling. For a moment she thought she might even be drooling. With the stimulation of her chest, legs and feet, she couldn't remember ever being so relaxed yet turned on at the same time.

William's voice broke her tranquil musings, "Tell us, Elizabeth, what did we do in your dream? How can we fulfill your desires?" His voice always affected her insides, creating instant butterflies in her stomach. She didn't know what to say as they continued to stimulate her flesh. She could only feel the need rising for them to do more.

William released her feet while Richard continued his attentions to her chest. Then all at once their hands vanished.

*****

William let his eyes roam over Elizabeth's naked flesh, her stunning body displayed for his appreciation. Her skin shimmered in the dim light of dawn mixed with the candlelight. The thought that she trusted them this much warmed his heart. Watching the rise and fall of her chest as she breathed, her arms held still above her head, her chestnut locks splayed across the pillow, he wanted nothing more than to make love to her; he wanted to consume her and be consumed. He decided to speak his thoughts aloud. "Have I told you Elizabeth, how much you mean to me? How extraordinary you are? That I find you both mentally strong and physically beautiful at the same time? Even though we have only been together for a short time, you have taken hold of me body and soul. There is nothing I wouldn't grant you that was within my power," he whispered, his heart brimming with love and devotion for the woman before him.

*****

William's heartfelt confession swept through Elizabeth's mind. She felt his lips press against hers with affection and passion. His palm cupped her cheek delicately in a tender bond that fused them together. With her senses totally aware of each sound made and the atmosphere that surrounded her, it all suddenly seemed to fade away in a flash. There was only him. She knew she loved him just as much, even with their relationship's being so new, so unconventional, it felt so right to her. She felt so loved, so connected both in a physical way and an emotional way. How it could have happened so fast she didn't know, but William Darcy completed her. Both men fulfilled her.

*****

Richard watched Elizabeth react to Darcy's words. Her chest rose higher, and her body arched slightly in response to his kisses. She was so gorgeous, so innocent, and so compassionate. He could feel his own heart begin to ache at the chance to feel cherished once again. He knew he could love Elizabeth for a lifetime. She was so easy to love. But could he forget about those same feeling he had felt for Caroline at one time, that he might yet still harbor for her?

While kneeling at Elizabeth's side, he watched Darcy kiss her. He noticed Elizabeth's hand fluttered down to search him out. He offered her his own, entwining their fingers tightly together and squeezing her gently in acknowledgement. He lifted her hand to his lips to kiss her knuckles. That she even thought of him at a time like this filled him with awe. She had so much love to give to them both. He wanted to pull her into his arms and make love to her. He loved how genuine her heart was. She was too good by far, and he felt so undeserving of her affections. He was falling in love with her, and his heart still loved another at the same time. How could he ever explain these feelings to Elizabeth?

*****

Sitting up, William glanced towards Richard, catching his attention, and then he looked to Elizabeth's chest. Both nodded in understanding, they each placed a hand at her wrists, running their palm down her arms to her chest, where each man caressed a mound in his hand simultaneously.

The sensation of the two different hands on her skin at the same time was difficult for Elizabeth to process. They moved in unison, however she could almost tell which man was which by their touch alone. The blindfold had enhanced her senses, and she thrilled at the way they were making her feel.

It was Darcy who lowered his head first to run his tongue around Elizabeth's pert pink flesh. She arched sweetly higher, offering him more. With a slight groan escaping her lips, Richard glanced at her face noting her parted lips and rosy cheeks. He wanted her to react to him in the same manner.

Richard's hand continued to knead the plump flesh between his fingers, the glistening skin calling to him. While William suckled at her, he rolled the exposed nipple gently around in his hand, the stiffening peak drawing more moans from her throat. Not wanting to waste time, Richard decided to travel farther south. He extended his tongue out to glide along her ribcage and belly. She flinched slightly; most likely from the tickling sensation he created. It brought a smile to his lips to see her react so. He took his palm and started at her knee, working his way up the inside of her thigh to her center. She spread her legs farther apart granting him access to play and move about more easily.

*****

Elizabeth tried to concentrate on the actions of both men. She was consumed in a sensual haze knowing this was the best sexual experience of her life so far. These men left no stone unturned in the pursuit of pleasuring her. They touched and licked, bit and nibbled every square inch of her flesh. The need to be penetrated was fierce, yet she didn't want them to stop. She didn't want these feelings to end.

With Richard between her legs and William kissing her breasts, she felt that her constant groans were starting to sound like an engine revving up.

It was all so unfair; she wanted to touch them, to feel their skin beneath her fingers. Gathering her courage, she decided to take what she wanted. Rising up, she pulled the blindfold off. The men stopped their ministrations to stare at her quizzically. "I want you both to lie down. One of you put your head here on the pillow, the other at the foot of the bed," she ordered.

"Elizabeth…" William tried to interject.

"No talking. My turn to play," she said in a low sultry voice, her eyes dark and filled with sexual desire.

*****

Richard took a spot at the foot of the bed, lying on his side. He was not going to argue with a woman who knew what she wanted. It turned him on that she was being bold enough to making demands of them. He was more than eager to see where this was going.

William, on the other hand, sat staring at Elizabeth. She was being bold, and that really set him on fire. It was hard not to just scoop her into his arms and make love to her right then and there. He could feel his own raging desires pulsing through his system. The electricity that surrounded Elizabeth had his cock stiff to the point that it was beginning to ache. Yet, he sat there, still staring at Elizabeth's naked body, hungry to feast on her flesh.

*****

Elizabeth could sense William's reluctance to do as she wished. She decided to punish him a wee bit and turned towards Richard, who quickly had done her bidding. He was on his side watching her carefully with a wickedly handsome grin and incredibly seductive eyes. The way that he made her swoon with that face was just incredible. Not to mention that body of his— he just set her own to buzz every time she looked at him. Wishing to show her appreciation at his obedience, she ran her palm down his lengthy shaft all the way to his balls, rolling them gently against her fingers. Ever so slowly, she lifted her chin to glance at his eyes from lowered lashes, and then lowered her head until she could place her lips at the tip of his swollen member to lave at him slowly.

*****

"Oh God!" Richard growled as he watched every move Elizabeth made. Her touch coursed through his body, giving rise to his already hardened state. When her mouth suddenly started to suckle him, the warmth and motion had him flat on his back instantly. Richard could feel Elizabeth extend her tongue and swirl it around the tip of his shaft while her fingers grazed along his sack. Suddenly, without warning, she went down on him, taking him all the way to the back of her throat. The constricting action of her mouth almost drove him insane. His hands flew to her head, taking hold of her long brunette tresses.

"Elizabeth, please," he breathlessly cried out in rapture, "you are going to kill me if you keep this up."

He loved how her mouth felt on his cock. He had to fight the urge to pump in and out of it. He was getting so close.

*****

Elizabeth released some pressure as she slowly withdrew, only to dive back down and repeat the maneuver. She felt empowered to have such control over his release. If she wanted him to come, she knew she could do it. Hearing Richards's groans, his hips rising slightly off the bed, and the tight grip he had on her hair pleased her. It only encouraged her to do more.

The bed moved, and Elizabeth could see out of the corner of her eye that William had finally complied with her wish. She knew he wanted to experience what Richard was enjoying. It was only natural to crave such pleasure. They had both given her so much. She wanted to do this for them.

Smiling at her victory, Elizabeth released Richard's stiff member, kissing his shaft all the way down to his sack before rising and turning to William. She leaned down to his ear and whispered breathlessly into it, "Trust me, I won't hurt you." She took his lobe into her mouth and sucked it for a moment before releasing it to nibble her way down his neck.

It didn't take long for her to reach his chest, her body invigorated by the feel of his muscular frame against her fingers. She kissed from one shoulder to the other while pressing her own breasts against his skin. She lingered at his nipples, rimming each with her tongue. She was pleased that one of his hands seemed to be holding her hair out of the way so he could watch every move she made. It excited her to know how much he appreciated her efforts, his groans of pleasure music to her ears.

*****

Richard lay on his back fighting to control his urge to release the ache in his balls once Elizabeth had removed herself from his engorged member. Opening his eyes he glanced over his left shoulder to spy Elizabeth on her knees. She made a stunning scene, her backside curving out at her hips then back in at her slender waist. He didn't think he could just lie there while such an alluring picture was within his reach. When such an opportunity stared him in the face, a man had to react. Licking his lips, he made his move.

He pulled up to his own knees and placed himself directly behind Elizabeth. She was immersed in Darcy at the moment, so he took it upon himself to pleasure the little vixen. He placed both hands at the small of her back, gliding them up along either side of her spine and back down to her hips, caressing them before slipping down each luscious cheek to place a kiss to them both.

*****

Elizabeth had felt the bed move but ignored Richard as she continued to enjoy Williams's body. When she felt Richard's hands on her lower back, she only wished to enjoy whatever he had in mind. They were all so consumed with need, each wanting to touch and be touched. She was part of the game now, and that was what was important to her. How things continued to their mutual climax was all part of the experience.

*****

William and Elizabeth had been the first out of bed. Together they made some strong coffee and something to eat while Richard showered. They all enjoyed a relaxing morning, chatting contentedly together. They talked about the game plan for the day and finished packing for their trip. Elizabeth was so excited to be going away with the guys. She also couldn't wait to see Jane. She knew Jane had worried about her most of the day yesterday. Her father had called her as soon as they had returned to relieve her anxiety, but she knew seeing her in person would do the most good. It was a busy morning that seemed to fly by. Elizabeth often flashed back to how her day started, leaving her with a smile and happy heart.

*****

Elizabeth woke up to the sound of Richard's voice. "Elizabeth, angel, wake up; we are almost there," he soothingly cajoled.

With her eyes fluttering open, Elizabeth sat up straight and stretched her arms a bit. The ride had been long. The first hour had been taken up with chitchat, but as the afternoon had worn on, she had grown sleepy and had crashed for the last several hours. The intense and lengthy early morning love session having caught up with her. Now that the four-hour trip was at an end, she was looking forward to stretching her legs and seeing what all the talk had been about. The boys had spent some time regaling her with tales of their youth. They were so cute when they reminisced, she thought.

She glanced out the window at the passing trees and hills. It was quite nice she thought, a wonderful change of pace from the city. She loved her home and the family business, but it had been too long since she had seen open spaces filled with trees and grass.
"What is that smile all about?" Richard asked from the front seat.

She turned to answer him. "I'm happy; no crime in that, is there? I am having a great time so far," she cheerfully answered.

Richard chuckled at the statement, as did William. "And to think we have not even arrived at the house yet. Darcy, I think our job here is done. She is very easy to please; now we can kick back and enjoy our triumph."

Elizabeth snorted at them just a tad before turning back to stare once again out her window.

"Here we are" William said, as he turned a corner and drove through a large opening in a stone fence.

Elizabeth's heart started to flutter as the excitement of meeting the families of these two fine men would be realized in just mere minutes. She was glad they had stopped to talk with Jane before heading out. Poor Jane... Charles and Caroline had seemed to have everything under control, however, so Jane had urged her to come. Though she would have stayed with her sister if she had felt she really needed to, she was happy that it wasn't necessary.

While visiting, both Caroline and Richard had been quiet. Elizabeth couldn't help but notice the two of them; she sensed unresolved emotions between them. Though she had had good intentions the other night when she had left to return to her own apartment so the guys could sort things out, she didn't think much had been accomplished. This morning had been wonderful with both the men, and Elizabeth felt a growing attachment to both of them, though she knew in her heart that Richard was still conflicted on some level.

Detective Lucas had also called Darcy this morning wanting numbers where they could be reached while out of town. He explained that if the Collins twins made bail by Friday, they would be out on bond until a court date was set and more of the investigation had taken place. Pressing charges against two upstanding individuals in society was difficult. Since Elizabeth was only taken for a few hours and no harm had come to her, it was hard to make a case to hold them without bail at this time.

The new information that Elizabeth had given the men on Corbin Jennings, along with information on the files she found at Whitney's, were noted by William and Richard. They were going to look into it all once they returned to the office Monday. If there was anything funny to be found, Richard vowed he would get to the bottom of it. It could be a lead, or it could just be business dealings. So much talk about Bill and the awful things he could have done gave Elizabeth the heebie-jeebies. She just wanted to forget that yesterday ever happened.

She had been eager to get away. Now she was even more excited to see where these two men had grown up. They pulled into a circular driveway to the waves of an older couple standing at the top of the steps. Elizabeth thought it must be William's parents. She straightened out her sundress as she stood, hoping she looked presentable. William placed a kiss to her cheek and reassured her, "You look lovely, Elizabeth. My parents will adore you, just as I do."

She smiled up at his compliment, flashing her wonderful smile and lifting her bright eyes to his. He placed his hand at the small of her back and guided her towards the couple.

"William, it's so good to finally have you home." The woman hugged Darcy tightly as he wrapped her up in his embrace.

"Son, always a pleasure to have you," the gentleman said with a handshake and a quick hug.

"George and Victoria Darcy, I want you to meet Elizabeth Bennet," William proudly introduced her.

"I'm so happy you could come to visit us, Elizabeth. I have heard so much about you." Victoria gave Elizabeth a quick squeeze and smile.

"Thank you, I'm pleased to be here. William has told me so much about his family it's great to finally meet you both."

"I just bet he does. Young lady, any daughter of Thomas Bennet is welcome here. Come on in; I'm sure that long drive has left you parched. Richard, it is good to see you, son. Your parents will be here in a few hours for dinner. I suggest you boys get the bags down to the cottage so you can rest before we eat. Oh, and your Aunt Catherine is out on the back patio. She has taken up water painting."

"Water painting? What happened to her fascination with cross-stitch?" William asked.

"Son, that was a month ago. You know your aunt; she is always in want of new entertainments. The old bird even took up bonnet making a few weeks ago. I'm sure she would love to show you her creations." George Darcy chuckled.

Richard leaned over to whisper in Elizabeth's ear, "Once, she took up whittling. That cane she has is her pride and joy, but she uses it to get attention most of the time. Don't let her fool you; she can hear perfectly. She is tricky that way. Always wants to be part of the conversation, and will even have you believe she hasn't heard you, just to have you repeat yourself directly to her."

Elizabeth glanced over at Richard, and he gave her a wink and a smile. He was such a playful man. She found him so refreshing when he acted like this. It warmed her heart to see him happy. They all entered the living room to enjoy some ice-cold tea and to get to know each other better. After half an hour the men excused themselves and took Elizabeth off to show her the grounds and the cottage where they would stay. They had strict orders from Mrs. Darcy that dinner was to be served in three hours. William kissed his mother, promising not to be late as the three of them departed.

Chapter 24

Elizabeth had enjoyed a quick tour of the gardens nearest the house and a brief glimpse of the horse stables, when the boys had suggested they needed to return to the cottage. William promised Elizabeth a ride to the top of a bluff to get a better view of the entire estate before she left. Then Richard told her he would like to take her over to his childhood home and show her around. He had a collection of cars and motorcycles he wanted her to see that he was quite proud of.

With new exciting things to look forward to, they all got into William's car and drove over to the cottage. William pointed out his sister's house on the way. Elizabeth thought it was so quaint and hoped she would be able to see it before she departed. William explained that his parents had installed a small stone driveway to both homes so everyone could get around more easily. The ride took only five minutes as Elizabeth glanced from side to side, taking in the views from the car windows.

The car pulled up into a secluded area surrounded by several large oak trees; over to one side there was a natural pond that seemed inviting. The house itself was impressive but not overly large, certainly not ostentatious. The exterior seemed to fit both the men perfectly, she thought. Smiling at the appearance of the house as it emerged from their view of the trees, Richard turned around "Well, here we are. Home sweet home. Are you smiling again?" he teased. "William, this girl has the most enchanting smile I have ever seen."

"That she does. Elizabeth, don't mind him, I love your smile, and I hope to see you do it often. I'm glad that you are able to relax. So, what do you think?" Darcy asked while sitting behind the wheel. He glanced around at the spread he shared with Richard, wondering what Elizabeth was thinking.
"It's just beautiful, so many gorgeous trees. I have always loved the outdoors, and the grass is so lush and green here; that pond just sparkles in the afternoon sun, and the house, it suits you both from what I can see," she enthusiastically informed them. He could see from the rear view mirror that her face was all lit up. Darcy thought she looked just amazing.

"That sounds like very high praise to me. I'll grab the bags." Richard grinned as he opened the door to retrieve the luggage.

William got out and helped Elizabeth. He opened her door and offered her his hand. She graced him with a beautiful heartwarming grin. "William, it truly is wonderful. I don't understand how you can bear to not live here all the time. "

He pulled her into his arms and kissed her gently. "I grew up here. I suppose the more involved in the family business I got; the more exciting it was to be in the city. It really is a great place to raise kids. We had so much fun growing up here. When we go out riding, I'll show you some of the spots where we used to hang out and some of the trees we would climb. There is so much to see here, not to mention evening strolls in the gardens up at the main house. Now come inside; I want to show you the rest." He took her hand and held it tightly as they walked towards the front door, both enjoying each other's company.

*****

Richard had beaten them to the front door and was standing just inside, holding the door open for them. "Welcome, I hope you find these accommodations to your liking." Richard loved this house. He and Darcy had designed this place together after they had graduated college. It had been their first step in committing to the lifestyle they were starting together. The place was not overly huge like what they had grown up in, but roomy enough. There were two separate wings, one for each of them to inhabit. Each wing had two bedrooms and bathrooms, and they each had their own offices for any work that needed to be tended to while they were here. It had common areas to be shared — the living room more to Darcy's liking, the kitchen very much Richard's domain. There was a game room for shared entertainment with a bar and custom-made pool table, since they both really enjoyed playing, when given the opportunity.

They built the property to be used as a family home by one or both of them. The deed, however, was in William's name since it was built on his family's property. Both had equally invested in it, so should Richard move out, Darcy would repay his half. It had been agreed on and legal papers had been draw accordingly. Richard had actually given thought to building a home on his own property at the time Caroline had been introduced to the family. She had seen a patch of land when he gave her a tour of his family's property, and she had fallen in love with it instantly. Richard was quite fond of it himself. There was a stream that flowed between the two family properties. As children, both he and Darcy had spent countless hours playing in that stream. There was one particular spot where the stream was wide and shallow. It was surrounded by a grove of huge Spanish oaks.

Every spring the pasture just beyond the grove filled with wildflowers. It was just a perfect spot for a home to be built on.

"Richard…" Elizabeth softly called to him. He blinked and focused on the brunette before him. "Are you coming?" she asked sweetly as she smiled up at him.

"Yes. Right behind you." He closed the door and followed the others into the house. He pushed away his daydreaming to better focus on Elizabeth and what she was thinking.

*****

Elizabeth glanced around the living room, admiring everything she saw. The colors were definitely William's taste. They both enjoyed leather couches and this place was no different. This particular one was in rust toned suede leather and there were two matching chairs. Each chair was extra wide and very comfortable looking. The hardwood floors where in a dark Brazilian cherry. On the focal wall was a cobble stone hearth that ran up the entire wall to the ceiling, with a large wooden beam mantel stained in a rich walnut. The light and earthy tones were warm and inviting. The rug on the floor was in short shag in a medium creamy color, setting off the entire room. Here and there accents were spread around; it wasn't a country décor but there were definitely hints of a more relaxed and homey atmosphere. She walked around a bit before heading to the kitchen. She just had a feeling that Richard's style would be the most prevalent in that room.

This was his great joy, the kitchen. Richard took immense pride in his ability to cook and when they had built this house, he made sure that all his needs would be met. He walked up next to Elizabeth and placed his hand at the small of her back. She turned and smiled up at him "I can see you had a hand in creating this space. I love the amount of windows and natural light you have in here," she raved.

"Thanks, I like it too. I wanted the space to be more of an open concept where you could be in the kitchen and still interact with company and family in the living room or dining room. The bar is great for entertaining. I have used it countless times, and it works great as a serving area."

Elizabeth roamed the space; the center island had a three-inch thick chopping block counter top and underneath some shelving on one side and drawers on the other. The sink overlooked the covered patio with its fireplace, waterfall and eating area. She turned to Richard "What a wonderful idea, a pass through window."

"I can't tell you how much we have used that, even when it's just us. We can get stuff from the fridge or wash something and just set it out on the ledge. I think everyone should have one." Richard remarked in an animated tone.

"I can see I won't ever get either of you out of the kitchen," Darcy joked.

"Two peas in a pod you both are." Darcy chuckled.

"Well, you can always lend a hand," Elizabeth teased in return.

"Oh, I'll give you a hand; it just might not be the kind of help you were wanting," Darcy winked.

Feeling the playfulness in the room, Richard picked up on Darcy's tone and added to it. "Now Darcy, I don't think we have ever given this island a proper test. It is seven feet long and very sturdy," he commented as he walked over to the butcher block, placing his hands on it as if testing it for how sturdy it would be.

Elizabeth raised her brow at them both, "I would be more than happy to watch you both test out that island. I can see quite well from those bar stools over there. I'll even pop my own popcorn," she quipped back at them.

Both men stared at her. "I don't think so Miss Bennet. We are not those kind of men," William remarked as he strode over to Elizabeth and pulled her into his arms. He kissed her hard and possessively. "I like women way too much, particularly beautiful brunettes by the name of Elizabeth. Come on; let's go see the rest of the house. I want to give you time to freshen up before we go back for dinner."

"But I thought you boys wanted to test the island?" she said in an overly innocent voice that oozed sweetness.

"Yes, well maybe later," William replied placing a quick kiss to her nose before turning her to head out of the room. She chuckled at them as they walked ahead of her.

*****

242

The first stop was Richard's wing. They passed by his office to enter the game room. Elizabeth was greeted with the mild scent of wood and leather. The room was obviously male in both appearance and smell, with a billiard table off to one side and a beautiful mahogany bar on the other. She noticed an extra large flat screen television graced one end of the room, while at the other, a dartboard could be seen. "So, do you boys often play pool?" Elizabeth asked from her vantage point at the doorway.

"As often as we can when we're here. Mostly in the evenings," Richard replied while looking around the room.

The next stop brought the threesome to Richard's master bedroom. It was a simple, yet elegant, room. Elizabeth thought the colors were cozy with the blend of blues giving it a feeling of calm. The walls were painted in a bluish slate gray; all the moldings were in a pure white; even the windows were adorned in white plantation shutters. The bed itself displayed a navy comforter with assorted pillows in a patterned gray and white. The wood furniture was all in a dark walnut with pewter accessories scattered about the room. A large light gray shag carpet accented the hardwood floor and extended halfway under the bed. Off to the side, there was a comfortable lounge chair in medium gray leather with overstuffed white and navy pillows on it. A short white book shelf next to it also served as an end table with a lamp for reading. It was a welcoming room.

The second bedroom in Richard's wing was smaller with white walls, Brazilian cherry hardwood floor, and white plantation shutters. The only furniture was a futon dressed in navy and an armoire made out of walnut. A couple of pictures were on the wall but nothing notable or Richards's style. "I haven't gotten around to decorating this space yet. Frankly I'm not up here enough, and I can't see spending the money on something no one sees or uses," Richard tried to explain.

"I think you have done a great job. I love the mix of blues, whites and pewter's you have chosen. Your tastes are very well suited to you." Elizabeth smiled up to him.

"Thanks. I wanted something different from the condo. Blue is calming to me. It's a little more plain, but when I'm here it is usually a vacation, so I didn't want anything too fussy."

Richard decided to excuse himself to change and freshen up while William took Elizabeth across to the other side of the house to show off his wing.

*****

"This is where I work when I'm here," Darcy announced while opening the door to his office.

Elizabeth was impressed with what she saw. It was stately but comfortable. On one wall there were floor to ceiling bookshelves in walnut. The floor, still the same Brazilian cherry, was adorned with a large rug in wine, beige and brown tones. The walls were aged in a tan with brown glaze. Next to the window were two large wingback chairs that made an inviting place to read. He had a large wooden executive desk with a tall brown leather that chair rested behind it. There were a few scattered pictures and nick knacks on the selves. When she turned, a large family portrait captured her attention. It was William's family. She recognized George and Victoria and thought the young blond had to be his sister Georgiana, whom she had yet to be introduced to.

"That is a wonderful family portrait, William"

"Thank you. We had that made about four years ago. It has always been difficult to get all four of us together to have one of these made. Perhaps it's time we had another. Georgiana has changed, as we all have since this was made." He looked up at his family then over to Elizabeth. He glanced down at his watch and made a face. "Come on; we need to get changed. We should be leaving in the next half hour."

He escorted her down the hall to his second bedroom for a quick glance then to his master suite. He gave her a fast tour so they could both set about refreshing themselves for dinner.

*****

"William, come give me a squeeze, young man," the elderly voice cooed from the couch. Quickly striding over to the woman who rose in greeting, William smiled broadly at her.

"How is my favorite aunt this evening?" he asked with a grin as he embraced the woman, kissing her cheek.

"I would be much better if you came to see me more often. That goes for you too, Richard." She turned to the other man offering up her arms to him.
"Now Aunt Catherine, you know that we are very busy with the family business," Richard defended in an apologetic tone.

"Business is business, and family is family and you should always make time for family. One day you boys are going to find your lives have passed you by. Now don't be rude, introduce me to this lovely lady." She smiled and pushed past the men to approach Elizabeth.

"Aunt Catherine, I would like you to meet Miss Elizabeth Bennet," Darcy spoke up.

"Come here and give me a hug. Family is family, and if these two have brought you here, you must be something special to them. I don't see many lady friends of theirs around often. The last one was that redhead, Candice... uh... Colleen... no... Caroline it was." Richard winced a little at the recollection of his aunt. Then she continued, "It is nice to make your acquaintance. You are a very beautiful woman, if you don't mind my saying so. These boys need someone to keep them on their toes you know." She gave Elizabeth a hug and smile before turning back to the family.

"Well, where is that brother of mine. He is always running late. Come have a seat, Miss Bennet; it seems we have some time to get to know you while we wait for Richard's parents. OH! And Georgiana, is she coming tonight, George?"

"Yes, she said she would be running a bit late. She had gone out for a late ride today and was still in the barn when I last spoke with her," he explained.

"That child always has her head in the clouds. It if isn't her art, it is her horses; anyway, tell me, Miss Bennet, what do you do for a living?" Aunt Catherine began. She looked directly into Elizabeth's eyes and placed her hand on her leg.

William and Richard knew they had no hope of sitting next to Elizabeth so both took up seats on the couch opposite her. William's parents were in the two chairs to his left.

"I work with my family in the city. I coordinate all of our corporate fundraisers along with any marketing and advertising needs for the company. I met your nephews through the work that I do. Our families have done business for years, I believe." Elizabeth enjoyed speaking with the older lady; she seemed quite interested in what she had to say.

"Catherine, you remember Thomas Bennet, don't you?" George Darcy inquired.

"Thomas Bennet? The name is familiar, but I can't picture him."

"He and I have been dear friends since college. This is one of his daughters. Miss Bennet is quite good at her job, and both our family businesses have benefited from her diligence and extensive work with charities. I have watched Miss Bennet grow into quite a formidable young woman over the years. Her father gives her very high praise for her hard work."

Elizabeth blushed as he spoke. "Well, that so many have such good things to say speaks highly of your talents, Miss Bennet. You must bear a great deal of responsibility. I hope you find time for yourself, my dear. It would be quite a shame for a woman so young to be wrapped up in nothing but work."

"Aunt Catherine," Darcy started.

"Tut-tut, now William, I may be old, but I am wise. Youth passes very quickly, and then one day you realize that life has passed you by. All of you could benefit from that advice, I would say." Just as she had finished her sentence, the door was heard closing, and a familiar voice echoed through the entry.

"Hello, where is everyone?" a strong male voice called out.

"Ah, sounds like my brother has finally decided to avail us of his company. Herald, we are in here!" she called back.

Richard rose to greet his mother and father. "Mother, how good to see you." He hugged her and kissed her cheek. "Father, always a pleasure," he said, shaking the man's hand.

"Alex, been a while." He shook hands with his older brother who nodded his head and then moved towards the chair off in the corner, his laptop in hand .

"Good evening, everyone. Sister, how good to see you again," the older man claimed as he moved around to give his beloved sister a squeeze.
"Yes, well, you are late again. We have a guest among us. If I may, I'd like to introduce Miss Elizabeth Bennet." She smiled in Elizabeth's direction.

"Well, what a lovely lady. I take it Miss Bennet that you have arrived with my son and nephew? I have heard a few good things about you from my sister. " The elderly man smiled.

"Yes, sir," Elizabeth shyly answered.

William moved closer to Elizabeth and placed his hand at the small of her back. He could tell she was a little nervous, but her smile was soft and delicate, and she looked wonderful. She remained calm, he thought, for a woman who had just met most of his family. He was so glad she had agreed to come meet everyone. "Miss Bennet has had a harrowing experience over the last few weeks. Richard and I hope to show her around some and give her some much needed peace and relaxation. We came a little earlier than expected, but we are glad to be here."

"Harrowing experience?" Aunt Catherine repeated in a questioning tone. "My dear girl, what has happened to you?"

"Aunt, I think Miss Bennet would rather not discuss that with the entire family. It is a personal matter, you understand. I would suggest, however, that we all go to the dining room and investigate the source of that wonderful aroma that I have been sniffing for the last half hour. I am rather hungry," Richard confessed. His change in the conversation gave Elizabeth some peace of mind. She didn't really wish to discuss Bill with all these people. She just wanted to put him out of her mind and make him part of her past.

"Yes, let's do go eat before the cook is embarrassed by a ruined meal." Victoria smiled. She and her husband lead the way, followed by Aunt Catherine.

William leaned down and whispered into Elizabeth's ear, "Are you alright, Elizabeth?"

She turned and smiled at him. "I'm quite well, thank you."

"Don't let Aunt Catherine force you into speaking on any subject you don't wish to. She has a habit of forcing conversations people don't mean to have. Somehow my mother shares that same investigative gene. A crime really, no one in this family has a chance of keeping any secrets around here." William winked and gave her a quick hug.

"Come on you two, I'm starving," Richard said as he placed his arms around both of their shoulders from behind them. "Last one in the dining room will have to sit next to her." He moved through the two and made a beeline towards the dining room.

"Well, he does have a point there," William agreed and grabbed Elizabeth's hand to walk more swiftly.

*****

Elizabeth enjoyed the meal and the company. The food was delicious; she hadn't realized just how hungry she really was. The conversation was mostly about politics, work related items with William and Richard, and an upcoming trip the Fitzwilliam's were planning. Aunt Catherine had groused about not ever getting to go anywhere with them since her arthritis had become disabling in the last few years. Elizabeth noticed how she enjoyed all of the conversations to revolve around her or have her take part in them. But she liked William's aunt. When they were saying their farewells for the night, Aunt Catherine had invited Elizabeth to have tea with her the next afternoon.

Once the threesome arrived back at the cottage, they all three went to the living room and sat. It wasn't terribly late, but they were all a little tired. A knock at the front door had them all turning their heads. Richard got up first to answer it.

"Georgie, how good to see you. Come in," he happily invited.

William rose from his chair and walked to his sister. Elizabeth noticed that she was young; she had a creamy complexion, and her hair was long, blond and curled. She seemed so delicate to her. William hugged his sister and spun her around. "Georgie, it is so good to see you. It has been way too long. How are you? We missed you at dinner tonight." He was so animated with her— it warmed Elizabeth's heart. He obviously loved his sister.

"I'm sorry; after my ride, I worked in the stables and then started chatting with workers and before I knew it, I had missed dinner. I smelled dreadful and needed to shower, so I just ate something at my place; but I did want to come say hello to you and meet Elizabeth."

"Of course, come in. Elizabeth Bennet, this is my sister Georgiana Darcy. Georgie, this is Elizabeth."

Elizabeth smiled and stood extending her hand. "It's wonderful to meet you. I have heard so much about you," Elizabeth greeted her warmly.

Georgiana moved in closer for a hug. "I'm more of a hugger if you don't mind. My brother has had his eye on you for some time," she whispered in her ear. Pulling out of the hug she continued, "I'm so pleased you are here. He is just wonderful, don't you think? I couldn't ask for a better older brother," she beamed as she looked up at Will, her eyes revealing her love for him.

Clearing his throat, Richard interjected, "And what am, I chopped liver?" He made a show of acting insulted at being left out of the praise, his arms crossed over his chest.

Georgiana turned and smiled at her cousin. "Of course not, you are the world's best cousin. How could I ever forget? Elizabeth, there is no sweeter man on this planet than Richard Fitzwilliam. He has rescued me more than once from a local guy or two, and he is one of my best clients. He has several of my paintings in his office and at the condo in town." Georgiana beamed. It was very obvious that all three had a close-knit relationship.

Elizabeth couldn't help but smile at the three of them as they chatted together. The warm, respectful relationship they all had with each other was great to see. The only people that evoked that feeling in Elizabeth were Jane and her father. They were both very important to her.

"That's more like it. Good to see you too, cousin," Richard added then reached over and planted a kiss on her cheek.

All four took a seat in the living room, William got everyone a glass of wine, and they chatted for close to two hours, catching up on all the news in their lives. They made plans to meet for brunch at Georgiana's on Friday morning since she would be working at home tomorrow. Elizabeth didn't have much to contribute to the conversation but enjoyed listening to the animated stories they each told. It was clear to her that they all knew a great deal about each other's lives. Georgiana seemed like a wonderful woman and someone she would really like to get to know better. By the time Georgiana left, Elizabeth was exhausted. It had been a really long day, and she could hardly keep her eyes open.

William walked his sister to the door to kiss her goodnight. She noticed Georgiana talk in a low tone to him as he glanced back towards Richard who was picking up the wine glasses and taking them to the kitchen. She wondered what they were speaking about.

"Come on Angel, let's get you to bed," Richard offered. He reached his hand out to help Elizabeth up from her spot on the couch. William had locked the door and moved towards his bedroom, turning on the hall light for everyone. When they got to his room, William went to the bathroom and started the shower while Richard began to undress Elizabeth. "I can do that you know," she softly claimed.

"I know, but you are sleepy, and I don't mind. I like to undress you." He half grinned. He sat her on the edge of the bed and got down on the floor. Slowly he slipped her shoes off her dainty feet, kissing each big toe. Coming up on his knees, he leaned in and kissed her neck softly as he slid each strap of her sundress off her shoulders. Rising, he helped her to stand and finished removing the dress, letting it billow down around her feet. Then he ran his hands down her sides to her hips and tucked his thumbs under the lacy panties she had on to inch them down her legs.

Elizabeth remained quiet as he worked, studying Richard's face. He seemed to be taking a picture of her body, a mental video of sorts. In his eyes, she saw several emotions come and go. She placed her hands on his shoulders as he finished his task. William returned naked, calling to her from the doorway.

"Come on, let's get you nice and clean. The hot water will relax you and help you sleep so much better. Then you will sleep like a baby, hopefully until mid morning," he half joked with her.

Elizabeth took a little jab at his side. "I can't help that I am an early riser, Mr. Darcy. If you have issues with that, I'm sure Richard wouldn't mind if I slept in his bed," she teased as she toyed with him.

"You can sleep in which ever bed you wish, Elizabeth; I will find you. Now, let me get you all washed up." William opened the shower door for Elizabeth so she could go in.

As Elizabeth stepped into the warm running water, she thought about William's suite. Both the master bedroom and bathroom were spacious, comfortable spaces. His room, like the one at his apartment was in earthy tones. He had a California king with a solid chocolate comforter and a mix of burnt orange and brown pillows on top. The walls were painted in a terra cotta color; the Brazilian cherry hardwood floor covered by a rug with a mix of the rooms colors, adding both texture and pattern to the design. A fireplace that opened to both the bedroom and bathroom had a creamy colored Austin stone hearth that reached all the way to the ceiling. A love seat was positioned before the fire with one large chair and ottoman off to its side. She hoped she would be able to come back in the winter and curl up in that chair to read, right next to the hearth. Just how relaxing would that be?

William started to wash her hair, his fingers massaging all the day's excitement from her head. She hadn't realized how tense she had been. Her groans of contentment went unmentioned as William continued to work. Finished, he rinsed out her hair and started on her body. He carefully soaped her with his bare hands. The feel of his fingers against her flesh created warmth in her belly. The man had magic hands and knew how to use them. He moved quickly but made sure he touched every spot.

Elizabeth had kept her eyes closed almost the entire time. The feel of the hot water pelting her back as he soaped the front of her body was simply amazing. She never had known that taking a shower with another person could be so enjoyable. Now that she had showered with these men several times, she could not imagine not wanting them in here with her. Finished, William leaned down to speak into her ear. "I hope that relaxed you. Next time, I won't go so quickly. Miss Bennet, you tempt me so with your silky skin and long hair; if it were not so late I would ravage you this instant." He leaned against her body with his hardened rod slipping between the cheeks of her backside. "This is what you do to me." His hands ran down her sides as he sucked in her earlobe, his nibbles and breath raising the hairs on her body instantly. Now she was extremely turned on.

"Who is stopping you?" she softly replied.

"I am; tomorrow is another day. We enjoyed a wonderful morning together, so don't think I won't dream of that tonight. You need your rest, and it's late. Now go with Richard, and he will dry you off." He kissed her deeply and hugged her from behind before opening the glass door for her to exit.
Looking out, she stepped right into a large warm towel. Still a bit damp himself, Richard was only wearing boxers, and he had a raging hard on by the looks of it. He patted her dry and then dropped the towel. Elizabeth could hear him exhale deeply, almost in a sigh. She turned to face him; her own body now alive and humming from William's words and tender ministrations. She slowly moved her big darkened eyes up to meet Richard's. He leaned in and pulled her into his embrace to kiss her. With his hardened shaft pressed against her belly, he kept his hands tightly

wrapped around her. "Come on before I lose my self control. We all need to sleep."

He quickly turned, taking her hand and walking her into the bedroom. There, a lamp was turned on next to the bed and the covers had been pulled back. The cream sheets looked terribly inviting. With the dark brown comforter pulled down to the end of the bed, only a light blanket was left with the sheet to snuggle under. But with the weather so warm out and Elizabeth's current state of mind, she figured that was all she needed. Richard slipped a short black gown with spaghetti straps over her head and then some matching black string bikini panties. "Those are not mine," Elizabeth said as she looked at herself in the dresser mirror.

"No, but I wanted you to have them. I purchased it a week ago but never got the opportunity to give it to you. I had planned on your wearing it the night you went back to your apartment," he said softly.

"I like it very much, thank you," she replied, glancing into his eyes and making a connection. She was sorry she had left, and he felt bad for her believing she needed to go. He cleared his throat and stepped back a bit.

Taking in her body in the sexy attire, he complimented her, "You look great. I can't wait to peel you out of it in the morning. Now crawl on up there; we all need to try to get some sleep." Richard patted her butt gently but playfully.

William walked out of the shower and to his side of the bed, shutting off the lamp. They were all clean and relaxed now. Richard hugged and kissed Elizabeth good night placing and arm over her waist. William said his good night, also kissing Elizabeth. He snuggled up against Elizabeth wrapping a leg around her, his hand grasping hers, entwining their fingers together. Elizabeth could feel a grin spread across her face in the darkness. She was purely content and looked forward to what tomorrow would bring. "Good night, boys. Thank you, I had a wonderful day. Both your families are great, and I'm glad you introduced me to them." She sighed and closed her eyes, loving the feel of both men on either side of her.

*****

It was early when Elizabeth's eyes fluttered opened. Both the boys were still sleeping so she quietly sneaked out of the room. She hummed while she made some breakfast for her and the guys. They had awakened her during the night in a most pleasurable manner. There had been no holding back on anyone's part as they feasted on each other, well mostly on her she thought, though she had enjoyed a little feasting on them as well. It had been an amazingly satisfying experience, and the very thought of it brought a smile to her face as she remembered each man's touch.

Looking forward to what the day had in store for her, Elizabeth thought some quiet time would be a wonderful way to start her morning. While her breakfast casserole baked in the oven, she fixed herself a cup of coffee and went outside. Closing the front door, she inhaled deeply, enjoying the early morning smells of the countryside. It was so different from how her days started in the city. Descending the front steps, she strolled towards the pond she had spotted yesterday upon her arrival. She glanced around taking in the lush landscape. The green grass, tall trees, and colorful wildflowers – it was so invigorating. She couldn't help feeling calm and relaxed in such surroundings.

She spotted a wooden bench underneath a large oak and headed towards it. Taking a seat, she sipped at the warm coffee in her cup as she listened to the birds that chatted high up in the trees. This was such a tranquil area with the sun glistening off the water, bunnies hopping into the nearby brush, and the sounds of horses neighing in the distance. She braced her hands on the bench and leaned back and crossed her legs, smiling to herself. She continued to enjoy the secluded space while she finished her coffee and mulled the daydreams floating around in her head.

*****

William watched Elizabeth from his office window. To see her so comfortable in his home gave him great joy. His family had loved her. Georgiana had said she couldn't wait to get to know her better, and even Aunt Catherine was taken with her. His chest filled with pride to know that his own family had liked her instantly. He continued to watch her as she sipped away at her coffee, occasionally glancing at the pond in a dreamy state.

"Have you smelled the kitchen?" Richard announced walking into Darcy's office.

"Yes, it actually woke me. My stomach is rumbling something fierce."

"What are you staring at?"

"Elizabeth. She is outside sitting by the pond having her coffee," he replied, all the while not moving his eyes from the lovely vision.

"Let me see." Richard strode up next to William to peer out the window as well. "She looks so angelic," he quietly said.

"Yes, she does. She is beautiful," he wistfully agreed.
"Why don't we take her breakfast? We can sit out by the pond. It's a relatively cool morning. She went to all the trouble of cooking for us after we woke her last night, the least we can do is take her something to eat."

"That is a great idea. I'll get the blanket and the plates; you grab the food," William said looking at his cousin. It was a grand idea, and one he wished he had thought of first.

Both men collected their assigned items and headed out to greet Elizabeth. William had thought to grab a rose from the dining room table to surprise her with. He couldn't wait to take her horse back riding later. The day was looking very bright, very bright indeed.

Chapter 26

Richard worked swiftly, preparing the items he needed to cook and grill his special meal. Thoughtfully he set the dining table, carefully placing several candles in a variety of heights in the center. He wanted this meal to be something Elizabeth would always remember from her first visit to the cottage. He loved having her with him in the kitchen but was happy that he could actually make her a meal to come home to. Without much deliberation, Richard placed Elizabeth's plate at the head of the table so both he and Darcy could sit on either side of her.

He had decided on a meal that was both simple and elegant. There was a fresh cucumber salad made with minced red onion, fresh dill and a touch of sour cream and cracked pepper. He had thought that during the heat of the summer, it would be a refreshing change of pace. For their main course, he had marinated pork tenderloin in a spicy brown mustard and white wine sauce and then added some finely chopped garlic before grilling it. As a side dish, he had prepared sautéed baby portabellas with leeks in balsamic vinegar and olive oil adding a touch of cracked black pepper and salt. He had even cooked the fresh green beans he found in the fridge. He had placed them in the wok with minced rosemary and garlic, salt and pepper and a splash of olive oil. For dessert, he had soaked thin slices of fresh strawberries in amaretto. He intended to serve them over scoops of vanilla ice cream. It wasn't the fanciest meal he could make, but for a quick one, he thought it would be sufficient to impress her.

Looking everything over, Richard was pleased with the outcome. Turning, he headed to the living room to straighten it up a bit and light a few more candles before dimming the main can lights. Knowing that William and Elizabeth would be returning shortly, he hurried to his room to change into a fresh shirt.

Checking his appearance in the mirror, Richard hoped that tonight would be the beginning of what promised to be a great twenty-four hours with Elizabeth. Tomorrow they would have brunch with Georgiana, and then he would take Elizabeth to his home, show her around, and have lunch with his family. Hearing the front door open and close followed by the soft sounds of Elizabeth's laughter echoing down the hall, Richard smoothed out his shirt and left for the living room with a smile. He loved to hear her voice and was eager to greet them.

*****

"Richard, what is that heavenly smell?" Elizabeth inquired as she walked up to give him a quick hug before drifting towards the kitchen.

"That is your dinner, and it is ready and waiting for you," he cheerfully replied. He nodded to Darcy and both men followed her lead toward the kitchen.

Gasping a bit, Elizabeth turned around and stopped. "We're not late are we?" she asked, her face displaying concern at the possibility.

"Not at all, come into the kitchen; I have some wine chilling for us. How was your ride?" Richard asked as he poured out the glasses for them.

"It was wonderful. William showed me some of the spots where you both played as young boys, and the views from the bluff were spectacular." She accepted the glass of wine from Richard, her face radiant, her eyes bright with a warm smile. Richard just wanted to sweep her into his arms.

"I'd say riding suits you then." Richard grinned as he watched her animated retelling.

"Yes, I would have to agree with you. She rode Buttercup as if she were born and raised in the saddle. I was surprised it was her first time on a horse," Darcy praised her.

Each man couldn't keep his eyes off of her. Elizabeth was just stunning, her hair slightly messy from the wind, her cheeks bright and rosy from the exercise. She was a vision of loveliness, capturing the hearts of both men as they listened to her.

Before he eschewed dinner for an all out love making session on the dining room table, Richard told Elizabeth and Darcy to head into the dining room and take a seat so he could serve dinner while it was still warm enough to enjoy.

William pulled out the chair to seat Elizabeth. He had really enjoyed his ride with her and hoped that tomorrow afternoon, once she and Richard had returned, he might find some time to show her around his parents' house. He wanted Elizabeth to see everything while she was here, and that was a request she herself had made earlier in the day.

They all sat enjoying the tasty meal, conversation coming easily among the three of them. Elizabeth told the men about her afternoon with Aunt Catherine and their mothers. Darcy couldn't believe how much his aunt interfered in his business. He would have to have a talk with his parents about her meddling.

"Elizabeth, you did the right thing. Aunt Catherine can be overbearing at times. She means well. Don't misunderstand me, I love her; I'm just sorry if she made you feel uncomfortable," Darcy apologized for his family.

"Like I said earlier, I thought it went well, and I handled it. Richard, before I forget, your mother wanted me to tell you lunch will be served at one o'clock tomorrow," Elizabeth passed on her news.

"Hopefully, we will be hungry by that time; don't forget that Georgiana is having us for brunch at ten tomorrow morning. I can't wait to show you around the Fitzwilliam compound." Richard chuckled. The word *"compound"* always conjured up a mighty fortress in his mind. The Darcy family's spread was larger, but he never liked the sound of the phrase, *"country estate."*

"Well, if we are all finished, I'll clear away these dishes," Darcy offered, scooting his chair back.

"I'll help you. Thank you so much for that wonderful meal Richard. I really enjoyed it." Elizabeth smiled. She started to collect the dishes when Richard stopped her.

"Why don't you go take a nice hot bath? Since today was your first time on horseback, you're going to be sore," Richard suggested taking the dishes from her.

"I hate to see you do the clean up, too. You worked so hard on our meal; it's the least I can do."

"Really, I want you to. You'll be glad you did," he encouraged.

"Richard's right; go soak in the tub. We can handle this," Darcy agreed.

"Ok, thanks, you talked me into it." She kissed both men on the cheek and headed towards William's bedroom.

"Did she really ride well?" Richard asked in a hushed tone.

"She did. I was very impressed with her. She has a way with the animals; even Santiago let her pet him without flinching," Darcy related, his pride in her reflected on his face.

"That is impressive. Good for her. Since we both enjoy riding so much, it's great that she can share in the activity. Perhaps she would enjoy horse racing as well. Tomorrow, I'm going to show her my collection of bikes. I had hoped to take her out on one of my motorcycles," Richard thought aloud as he rinsed off the plates.

"She might be pretty sore you know." Darcy added, thinking of Elizabeth's well being.

Richard paused for a moment, hearing the concern in Darcy's reply. "Don't you think I would take into consideration how she feels before taking her out?" Richard asked. He was a little miffed that Darcy would even question him about such a thing. He would never deliberately cause Elizabeth any pain or discomfort.

"I," Darcy paused to think, "I'm sorry, of course you would consider her well being. I didn't mean to imply that you wouldn't. I'm sure she would love riding on your bike Richard." Darcy regretted even saying such a thing. He had never questioned Richard's care of any woman they had formed a relationship with in the past. He supposed after riding with her tonight, he was just a little tired and was being over protective.

Finishing up the last of the dishes, Richard commented, "It's been a long day. I think we should check on our girl. She should be good and relaxed by now. Perhaps she needs a little TLC in spots." He dried his hands and placed the towel next to the sink before heading to Darcy's bedroom.

William followed, thinking the same thing. He had wanted to hold Elizabeth all night long; hopefully, they would find her still awake.

*****

Elizabeth hadn't realized how sore she had become during dinner. With her body starting to stiffen, she gingerly stepped into the tub. Sinking into the warm water, she sighed in bliss at how wonderful it felt. She was ever so glad the men had talked her into this. Closing her eyes, she inhaled deeply, letting her body completely relax.

While soaking, Elizabeth thought back on how much she had enjoyed her first full day with the men. So many things had transpired. Their enchanting morning breakfast out at the pond, followed by swimming and lunch by the pool, the tea with the ladies, and a wonderful sunset horse ride with William, followed by the fabulous dinner Richard had made for them. Elizabeth couldn't help but smile. William and Richard had made her first day so memorable.

She opened her eyes to grab a nearby washcloth and soap it up. Once cleaned, she glanced around at her surroundings. The room had a cozy feeling, and she could only imagine how wonderful the fireplace would be in the winter or lit for a romantic evening. She felt at peace, and just like in the city, Elizabeth felt right at home as if this was where she belonged. Yawning, she stretched, deciding it would be better to get out before falling asleep.

Just as she stepped out of the water, William walked in. "It seems I have impeccable timing." His sultry voice lifted the corners of her mouth.

"It would seem so. Would you mind?" Elizabeth asked handing William the towel.

"It would be my pleasure." He gently wiped the water droplets from her body, his eyes drinking in her bare form. "How was your bath? I'm sorry I missed an opportunity to bathe you," he said.

Elizabeth's stomach fluttered at William's words. Glancing down at the top of his head while he dried each leg, she quietly replied, "There is always tomorrow."

"Yes, there is," he agreed, turning his darkened eyes up to hers before rising. He placed the towel on the edge of the tub. "How do you feel?" he asked, his care for her expressed in his look and tone.

"The hot bath was a wonderful suggestion. I'm a bit stiff, but I'll be fine. I really enjoyed our ride. If time permits, could we go on another before we leave?"

"I am quite sure that can be arranged," William offered, stepping closer to touch her cheek with a gentle stroke of his thumb. Their eyes locking on each other as they drew closer together to seal the moment with a tender kiss.

"Let me help you to the bedroom; we have something to help those sore muscles." Darcy placed his hand at the small of Elizabeth's back, guiding her towards the bedroom. Walking through the door, Elizabeth spied Richard sitting on the edge of the bed, his naked flesh catching her eyes in the dim candlelight. No words where exchanged as she approached the bed. All the covers had been moved to the foot and the pillows were on the floor. A large towel had been draped in the center.

"We're going to give you a full body massage, Elizabeth. Help work out the stiff muscles that come from riding. Just come lie on the towel, face down, if you please," Richard directed her in a low voice.

Not moving her eyes from his, she crawled slowly up to the center of the bed, her sultry eyes soaking in Richard's curves and muscles. Doing as he directed, she placed herself face down and waited in anticipation of their touches, her mind beginning to fantasize about just what type of massage they had in mind.

William had already begun to undress while he watched Elizabeth slink along the mattress. Her creamy skin begged to be touched as she situated herself on his bed. Licking his lips, William took a long deep breath to control his intense urges. Quickly, he glanced at Richard who held a bottle of oil in his hand while staring at Elizabeth, hunger filling his eyes. Moving his own eyes to visually drink in Elizabeth's beauty, William started at her shoulders and slowly moved his gaze down her back and on down to her shapely legs and small feet. He reached for the oil bottle on his nightstand and placed a small amount in his palm before working it into both hands. He was going to start at Elizabeth's legs while Richard took her shoulders, working everything from the waist up. They wanted to ensure Elizabeth was cared for, her tension and stiffness relieved.

Concentrating on his part, William placed his hands at the small of Elizabeth's back and began working his way back and forth with even strokes, caressing her hips with light pressure before moving around to her backside. He traveled slowly down the backs of her legs, his eyes running the long length appreciatively. She felt so smooth against his skin. Just the simple act of touch connected him to her instantly. He took one foot between his hands, his fingers pressing into her instep and running up to her toes. He tuned out everything else going on around him, his sole focus on the effect he had on Elizabeth as he watched and waited for her body's reaction.

Placing more oil in his hands, William gradually worked his way up each individual calf, making sure he covered the entire area. With each stroke he made, he could feel her muscles release a bit more. Knowing her thighs and butt would have taken the brunt of their excursion, William moved over top of Elizabeth to straddle both legs below the knees. He closed his eyes, using all his senses to work the tight muscles along the back of her thighs up towards her hips. With each moment that passed, however, he could feel his own eagerness for her rise.

Taking the oil bottle from the side table, William squeezed it directly across her buttocks. The glistening fluid mesmerizing him as it shimmered in the candlelight. His hands kneaded the slick gel into her skin, his eyes transfixed on her shapely orbs. With his own body so affected, he leaned over to place feather soft kisses across each cheek, savoring the warm flesh that made contact with his lips. He couldn't resist the temptation any longer. Inhaling her scent, he let his hand travel across her left cheek, around the hip, wrapping under her leg and moving it apart from the right. He placed his body to her right side, his cheek resting against the soft skin on her right hip.

Elizabeth moved willingly, encouraging him on. He could feel the tilt of her pelvis in a slight upward motion, her right hand becoming entangled in his hair, tugging erotically. The intoxicating mixture of the fragrant oil and Elizabeth's natural scent had William closing his eyes while he inhaled slowly, his fingers running up her now accessible inner thigh.

He could feel the warmth of her core grow stronger as he approached her eager womanhood. Splaying his hand flat against her skin, William moved slowly from the underside of her bottom up to the top, drawing a circle with his palm around one fleshy orb as he kissed the other. He draped his leg around her right one, needing more contact with her body. Taking a fingertip he placed it at the small of her back and watched as he traced it right down the center grazing at each cheek on his way down. Meeting the damp outer lips of her desire, he softly slipped down past her entrance searching for her secret bundle of nerves. With his treasure found, he slowly worked in slow soft circles, changing his pattern to please Elizabeth. She sweetly lifted herself to him enjoying the sensations he provoked in her.

His own needs growing, he again drew his fingertips up to meet the juncture of her being. Carefully he eased one finger into her depths, relishing the warmth that enveloped it. He could hear her soft moans as she grabbed more of his hair, tugging and clawing at him, as her need grew stronger to possess him.

261

Feeling both of their desires rising, he slipped in a second digit, moving them slowly in and out of the slick space. She continued to arch into his hand with each stroke he gave.

Not able to think of anything more than being with the woman he loved, William peered up above him. Richard acknowledged him with a nod. Both men removed their hands and bodies from her. William leaned down to Elizabeth's ear, "I have struggled in vain; you have bewitched me, Elizabeth." His palm came down on her shoulder delicately trailing a path down her back. "I need to make love to you, my dearest, loveliest Elizabeth."

*****

Having fought her own desires for some time as the men massaged her body, Elizabeth could no longer contain her cravings. Her body reacted to each touch William bestowed on her. Richard's fingers melted her tension away, his nibbles along her neck and shoulders complimenting each move William made. Together, these men brought her to heights of pleasure like a symphony she could never have imagined. Each held a special place in her heart and with each passing day, she found they filled the beating place in her chest more and more. When they withdrew their touches, she felt the loss keenly.

William leaned in to whisper into her ear, igniting more flutters. She listened to the words he expressed as his hand traveled seductively down her body. The bed moved on the other side while he spoke, and she instinctively knew what was next. She could hear the sounds of tearing paper that only made her move faster. She turned towards William, her eyes filled with dark passion. They focused on her lover, his own expressions of lust and desire matching hers. Carefully, William ran a finger across her cheek and down her neck before the others joined in, creating a fiery trail towards her breasts.

Elizabeth watched William's eyes drink in her body. He made her feel as if she were the most beautiful creature ever placed on the earth. To him, she was perfection and likewise, she found him the same. Slowly, Elizabeth rose, William's eyes connecting back to hers. He didn't speak, his face so filled with carnal desire, he only waited to see what she would do.

She sat up on her knees, her palm reaching for his chest. The instant she made contact, William's eyes closed. She watched his body rise and fall with each deep breath; he appeared to savor their bond, his face a washed with emotion. She moved her sights to his torso, her fingers grazing through the scattered hairs on his chest, along each rib, all the way down to his hip before she lifted her eyes back to his face.

William's eyes burned into hers; the intense look he had, setting her on fire. With her heart pounding in her ears, William reached out to take hold of her head and pull her to him, his lips searing hers in a deep ravenous kiss. The bed dipped again. Elizabeth felt two hands slowly glide up her back. Then warm lips pressed against her shoulder. The flood of emotions swirled in her head. They had never taken her at the same time, but she wanted it. She wanted them to both love her at the same time.

William pulled back and peered deeply into Elizabeth's eyes. "I want to make love to you now. I have wanted you since sunset at the bluff. I can contain myself no more." With that he guided her down sideways to the mattress. Instinctively Elizabeth reached out to wrap her arms around him. Richard had to have followed, for his hands caressed the entire side of her body, his fingers roving down her rib cage to her hips where he placed feather light kisses.

Elizabeth watched as William retrieved the oil bottle from the side table. Richard rose up to her ear, "We both want you Elizabeth. We want you to relax, and if at anytime you want us to stop, all you have to do is tell us. I can't just sit and watch, angel; I have to have you now myself. Your body is so damn beautiful; you just don't know how much you drive me insane." Richard's sultry soft words caused her to sigh; she turned her head to meet Richard's eyes.

"I want you both to make love to me. I want it more than I have wanted anything," she explained.

Richard placed his lips to hers; he could have kissed her all night long, but he wanted more. His hands wrapped around her waist as he molded his body against her back. His hand cupped her jaw holding it up while he assaulted her mouth.

Elizabeth grew more impatient; she needed them, and she needed them now. Taking his hand from her face, she moved it over her breast down to her mound. "Take me, please," she panted.

William leaned back down and handed Richard the bottle. He took it while Elizabeth watched. She didn't want to know how she just wanted to feel.

William drew her back to his face by taking her chin in his palm. "Elizabeth, Richard is going to carefully and slowly work your back entrance to accommodate him so that we can both penetrate you at the same time. Are you okay with this?" he asked. She nodded her affirmation. "If you change your mind, we will not be disappointed, and it in no way reflects on you to tell us no. We want to love you and to show you all the pleasure we can. It may be more than you can take, and if we think things are not going in a direction where you will enjoy it, we will stop as well. Neither of us would ever harm you Elizabeth."

There was so much love and affection in William's face that Elizabeth could hardly believe she could be so lucky. That these two men placed her needs, her emotions, her well being above their own desires was more than she could fathom. She reached up her hand to meet Darcy's cheek. Staring into his eyes with everything she felt, she replied, "I love you, William Darcy, and I know that neither you or Richard would harm me. I want to try this. I want to make love to you both at the same time." She turned to look at Richard who peered over her shoulder, his eyes so loving and tender. She moved her hand to cup his cheek as well, then spoke to him, "I want this as much as you do."

The men could only look down at Elizabeth; there was so much trust in her eyes. They each kissed her body, before they began. William scooted down next to Elizabeth; facing the woman he cared so much about. Elizabeth could no longer wait and pulled his face to hers. She kissed him hard and deep. He returned it while taking her leg and lifting it up and over his hip. He massaged her bottom, caressing the globe and her upper thigh.

Richard placed his body flat against Elizabeth's again and began to kiss her shoulders, his hand cupping her breast as he rolled her taut peak between his fingers. Both men were rigid and hard. They knew they needed to take their time, but time was not what they wanted to take. Richard used the oil to work slowly at Elizabeth's back entrance. She arched so sweetly towards his hand that he wanted to infiltrate her and hear her cry out in pleasure as he moved within her.

William was no better. He played with her bundle of nerves, slowly drawing circles around them. Elizabeth would try to maneuver closer to his finger, but he would only smile to himself and try something new. She was so wet, her body hot and ready. He knew it would take time for Richard to work on her, but he wanted to slip into her core and make mad passionate love to her. He wanted to feel her pressed against his chest, her lips against his own. Without warning, Elizabeth's tiny fingers circled around his erection. Her grip was firm, and it took the edge off of him a bit. Then she slowly stroked her fingertips down, grazing over his sac and up again. She repeated the action two more times before he took her hand and moved it over her head. "You, my dear, are a vixen. You drive me wild," He panted in a husky voice.

"Take me William, now; I can't hold out any longer," Elizabeth begged.

"Richard," he stated firmly.

"We can start," were the only words he needed to hear from Richard. He pulled Elizabeth quickly over his body, her legs straddling his midsection, while his tip sat at her core's entrance, the wet lips teasing his manhood. William peered into Elizabeth's eyes. "I love so much about you. If you need me to stop or Richard to pull back, just say so." His controlled tone belied his fiery need. Elizabeth didn't wait; she came down on him in an instant, plunging his shaft deep into her body. The feeling was mutual, when they both began to move at a steady pace.

"You are going to have to be still, Elizabeth," Richard admonished her. "I want to take this slow." He moved up behind her to stare at the woman below him. She was everything he had always wanted. He spread her apart and slowly moved into position. He knew he would have to take it slow. William would distract her as much as he could, and with luck, they would all three experience love at its most carnal, most pleasurable. Both men had only done this one other time. It was with Caroline, and the night they had taken her together was the night of his undoing.

"I don't know if I can be still," Elizabeth gasped, trying not to move while William was buried deep within her.

"You can," William said. He kissed Elizabeth hard, one hand snaking between their bodies to take hold of her breast. He moved her slightly to the side so he could roll her tight peak between his fingers. Elizabeth couldn't think. The pressure Richard was creating behind her and the need to be taken was fierce. She couldn't wait; once Richard started his assault, she arched up into him.

"Elizabeth stop, you will hurt yourself," Richard chided her. Her tight canal was going to be his undoing. He slipped in further, fighting Elizabeth's body. She began to pant harder, her groans and mews growing in intensity. He couldn't see her face, but he could feel her need. She was wanton, and her own lust would destroy her if they didn't move things along. He used the oil to ease in quicker. William was holding still, trying to calm and distract Elizabeth.

"Now!" she screamed at them both as her body started to shake within their grasp. Both men started to work slowly in unison, taking turns moving in and out of her body.

Elizabeth was trapped between the most important men in her life. She trusted them down to her soul. They moved slowly, carefully, so not to injure her. She knew they only wanted her to feel the pleasure, but her body was on fire. Her bottom ached like never before, the pressure so strong, but she didn't want it to stop. It drove her on. William's hands caressed her face as his lips sought out each patch of flesh within his reach. He moved gently in and out, Elizabeth ached to have him plunge in deeper, faster. She tried to set the rhythm herself. Soon enough the men complied plunging into her quicker. She felt like she was floating when her orgasm began to take hold. It built up slowly with the shift of each impaling she received. The men's own moans and gasps registered in her head. The two of them trying hard to control themselves for her she knew. Finally she relaxed and went limp in William's arms, and her body was washed over by a euphoric title wave of bliss. It was something she had never experienced in her life. She felt completely sated when they were done. And if she had been asked, she could not have moved.

*****

"Victoria, what did you think of Elizabeth today?" George Darcy asked while sitting in his favorite chair reading the newspaper.

"I believe she is the one for our son. She is everything he could possibly ever need. I won't say that life will be easy should the three of them remain together, but they are happy. He is happy, happier than I have ever seen him. Would you not agree?"

"I would. He is definitely protective of her. He can't take his eyes off her either. Though what man with a mind could?" he jested as he peered over at his wife.

"I suppose. Do you think Thomas would agree to the match?"

"I think he would. He has always favored Elizabeth above his other daughters. She is very much like him in many ways, from what I understand. It would present our boy with a challenge for sure. She is a

266

willful woman who usually gets what she wants, though I do not believe she has shown that to those boys yet. The relationship is still too new. Don't get your hopes up just yet, my dear."

"I think I might have a private chat with her tomorrow," Victoria announced while leaving the living room on her way to her private study. There she pulled a box down from the highest shelf. It was dusty and covered in cobwebs. She brushed it off to open it up. Inside were letters. She opened one up and smiled as she read the contents.

My Dear Victoria,

Do you know how much I love you? I know that George has always been first and foremost in your mind; he too has loved you far longer than I can remember. We have all been together now for some 8 month's and though we have so much love to give each other, I find that at times I want you for myself. This isn't easy to tell you but I have met a woman. She possesses the same spirit that you d and I have known her for two months now. I would like to introduce you to her because I believe you would get along so well together, but feel that would not be wise, as she knows nothing of our particular relationship. I know for your part that you show no bias in how you treat George or myself. You love us with equal measure. I also know that we both hold a different part of your heart. I hate to think of your being sad or downcast ever, but I want you to know that even if I decide to move on in life, I will always hold you in great esteem and love. I can never replace you, only add to the wonderful things you have done and mean to me. My dearest Victoria, I love you; never forget that. Should you ever in your life need me for any reason, I will be there for you always. George is a good man and will take care of you forever. We are such great friends, he and I, that I cannot imagine never seeing you again, so I want to wish you a great life but not goodbye

This is hard for me, and as I take this step into a new relationship, please know that you are forever in my heart. I have spoken at length to George about this. He wishes me to stay with you both, but he understands my need to make sure that this new relationship is not more than it appears. He has pledged his support, and I hope you can as well. There is nothing more I can say but that I will not be home tonight. I will have removed all my belongings by the time you see this. I thought it better to just go; I am not always as strong as I should be where you are concerned. Many hugs and kisses to you, my darling.

Forever
Thomas

Chapter 27

"I hope everything was to your liking," Georgiana softly said to Elizabeth while they cleared the table.

"It was wonderful. You are a great cook; must run in the family." Elizabeth grinned, glancing towards Richard who was in the adjoining room. "Thank you so much for having me. I have to say, your place is just beautiful. You have a wonderful eye for design; the décor is fantastic," Elizabeth complimented her kindly.

"Thank you." Georgiana blushed. "I find I do some of my best work when I'm here. Could be why I don't go into the city as often as I should, but nothing inspires me more than home," Georgiana wistfully replied.

"You are a very talented artist. I have seen your work in Richard's condo and your brother's place. I wouldn't dare attempt what you have so wonderfully accomplished. Your family must be so proud of you," Elizabeth continued to praise the young girl while washing dishes.

"I believe they are, though Aunt Catherine, if she had her way, would have me married with several children by now. I think she forgets I'm only 23 years old."

"She means well, I'm sure," Elizabeth counseled, while drying the dish in her hand.

"So what are my most favorite girls up to? Telling secrets, or do I dare ask?" William grinned walking into the kitchen, Richard on his heels.

Gazing at both men, a grin lifting her lips, Elizabeth coyly teased, "Perhaps we are, but I'll never tell."

"Darcy, I believe I'm going to whisk Elizabeth off before her good opinion of us is changed from too much female gossip," Richard joked.

"Oh, I couldn't leave just yet; I'm helping Georgiana clear things away," she protested.

"Don't worry, I'll help her. It's been some time since my sister and I have had time to sit and chat. You two go on; I'll stay until everything is done," Darcy insisted.

Richard gave Georgiana a bear hug, kissing her cheek. "Thank you for brunch; as always it was done to perfection," he approved readily.

"Coming from a man who cooks as well as you do, I'll take that compliment. You know you are always welcome." She winked in return.

William took the towel from Elizabeth's hands and gave her a quick squeeze. "Enjoy your tour and tell my aunt and uncle hello for me." He kissed Elizabeth tenderly and patted her bottom, before scooting her along towards Richard.

"We'll see you at the cottage later." Richard nodded towards Darcy.

Elizabeth glanced at Georgiana. "I had a wonderful time. Thank you again."

"It was my pleasure. I'm sure I'll see you again before you leave." Georgiana said as she waved goodbye.

"Definitely." Elizabeth smiled. "Well shall we go? I'm ready to be dazzled." She beamed up at Richard's face.

*****

"Oh, Richard, this is amazing!" Elizabeth expressed in astonishment as she took in the breath-taking scene before her.

"This is my most favorite spot in the compound. Growing up, William and I had many adventures in this clearing. It has always meant something special to me," Richard quietly explained.

"I can well imagine," Elizabeth replied as she strolled slowly around, soaking in her surroundings. She bent down and dipped her fingers into the cool shallow stream, letting the refreshing water flow across her palm.

Richard watched as she moved about his beloved spot. He had always hoped to someday share it with someone special in his life. Caroline had been equally taken. She had even expressed a desire to build a home on it. Richard watched closely as Elizabeth moved to the edge of the forested area. Just beyond it, she would see the most beautiful view of the pasture beyond.

He wondered what her thoughts would be and so began to walk towards her so he wouldn't miss it.

He moved up behind her just as she reached the edge and heard her gasp when she discovered the prospect. "Do you like it?" he nearly whispered in her ear.

Elizabeth turned to confront him, her face was so expressive, he instantly knew she was taken. He leaned down to kiss her parted pink lips, then spoke, "I'm taking a stab in the dark here, but I think you like it." He smiled.

"It's just. ...It's perfect. I can hardly believe you do not have your own home right here. This entire area, the stream, the tree covered alcove, this bright and beautiful pasture filled with flowers, it seems to fit you so perfectly Richard." She returned her eyes to the view as Richard wrapped his arms around her body and pulled her against him.

"I have thought about it many times. The cottage is great— don't get me wrong. I love it there; it is something William and I worked on together, and it reflects both our tastes and personalities. However, it is on his land, and if I were ever inclined to leave, it would only be for this place." He rested his chin on the top of her head, looking out over the field before him. With the sun high in the sky, he began to feel that perhaps the time had come to do just that. Maybe he did need to build his own home. This place had always felt so right to him.

They both stood staring out at the sun-splashed fields for several minutes, Richard's arms holding Elizabeth securely to him. He didn't want to break the moment, but there where more things he wanted to share with her before they had to meet his parents for lunch.

"I have something else to show you if you're ready to go," he softly offered.

"I would love to see more." She smiled, her eyes turned up to him, bright and expectant.

*****

Arriving outside of his own private garage at the back of the family home, Richard held his hand over the latch so he could speak to Elizabeth before they entered. "My most prized possessions are inside of this building. Not many have had the opportunity to see them. I hope you don't mind

270

indulging me for just a while. It's been sometime since I have been in here myself."

Fascinated by what could be inside, Elizabeth asked, "Is this not just a double garage?"

"It is, but I had it specifically built so it is, I guess you could say, very original. It is not what it appears to be on the outside," he explained with a straight face.

Richard opened the door and as Elizabeth stepped through to the inside, her eyes grew wide with what she saw. "Richard, I hardly know what to say."

Standing behind her, Richard glanced appreciatively around. He was quite proud of his collection. He moved around the shell-shocked Elizabeth, to get a better look at his pride and joy. Half way across the room, he turned towards her and held out his hand, "Come on, they won't break," he said as he smiled.

Still amazed at what was before her, Elizabeth moved forward. "I hope you have a good security system."

"I do. Now come look," he chuckled at her.

*****

Elizabeth couldn't believe here eyes. All this had to have cost a small fortune. Richard was right; this building was not what it appeared from the outside. She was staring at a state of the art facility with no less than two dozen antique cars and motorcycles housed inside. His black SUV paled in comparison to what she saw now.

"Why have you never mentioned any of this?" she asked, still blankly staring around.

"Not many woman, from of my experience, would care to hear about such a thing. I also have only brought two ladies home to meet my family, so there has never been a reason to admit to my expensive fetish for antique vehicles."

"You showed all this to Caroline as well, I take it? Did she approve?" Elizabeth asked wearily. She didn't want to upset Richard but she was very curious as to why he never pursued her if he loved her so much.

271

"Like you, I brought her to see the garage. She picked out a car she instantly fell in love with, but she was not really into them once we returned to the city. Even my own mother doesn't come in here often. I only come when I'm here visiting, which is next to never." Richard remarked as he took her hand in his. They started to walk around checking out the shiny polished cars; they were all lined up to perfection. He explained what each make and model was as they passed and answered any questions she had before he stopped and turned to her. "Would you like to take a motorcycle ride?" he asked in an upbeat tone. "I have one bike in particular that I take out every chance I get."

Thinking he really wanted her to join him, she cautiously replied, "I will get a helmet, right? And do you promise not to go to fast? I really am not so sure about motorcycles. They seem so dangerous," she replied in an unsure voice.

"I can assure you safety is always something I take seriously, no matter where I am, and as for speed, not to worry, we won't be going terribly fast."

"Ok, I trust you. So which motorcycle are we taking?" Elizabeth asked, peering around at the available choices in her sights.

"None of these, actually. Why don't you wait here and look around some more while I go get it?" he cheerfully offered.

"Oh sure, do you need any help?"

"No, I'll just be a few minutes," Richard said. He vanished around a corner at the end of the garage leaving Elizabeth to walk around and look at his collection. She drifted past several vehicles, admiring the fine collection Richard had. Soon she heard a door open and then close shortly after. Thinking Richard had left her alone in the building, Elizabeth started to walk quickly in the direction she had seen Richard go. She was just about to turn the corner when the garage door behind her opened wide.

"Elizabeth, are you ready for your ride?" he smiled, his excitement evident in his body language and tone.

Smiling as she examined what Richard stood next to, Elizabeth nodded and met him just outside of the garage. "Now you see why we won't be going terribly fast." Richard grinned.

"No, I suppose we won't," she happily replied.

"And here is your requested helmet." He handed her a sturdy modern version.

"What are you going to wear, Mr. Safety First?" she asked with a raised brow.

"I'm going with traditional gear," he said with flair. He pulled out an old leather biker's helmet with long ear covers and a black strap, along with a pair of goggles.

Elizabeth giggled as she watched him put it all on, then straddle the bike. With two kick-starts, he had it purring. "When you're ready, your chariot awaits."

She placed her helmet on and then boarded the leather-seated sidecar. "This should be fun!" Elizabeth loudly announced. Richard leaned over and checked her helmet to make sure it was securely on; then nodded his head in affirmation. He revved the motor a few times, signaled the thumbs up and they were off.

*****

The pair was laughing heartily when they entered the cottage several hours later. William was sitting at his desk checking on a few items on the computer, when he heard them. By the time he had shut down everything, he found Richard and Elizabeth in the kitchen. They looked dreadful.

"What happened to the both of you?" he asked puzzled by their appearance.

They shot a silent look of quilt in William's direction, as if they had been caught with their hands in the cookie jar. When they saw his face, both broke into fresh peals of laughter.

William hadn't seen Richard laugh so much in years, and it filled his heart with gladness to be a witness to it once again. Richard was beet red, holding his side and gasping for breath, while Elizabeth wiped tears from her eyes. They definitely made a sight to see. They were filthy from head to toe.

"Oh William, you should have seen us!" Elizabeth tried to squeak out between breaths.

"I wish I had. From the looks of it, it must be a great story, and I am looking forward to hearing it," he claimed. He took up a seat at the bar and sat smiling at them in anticipation.

"Well, I took Elizabeth over to see my collection, and she agreed, hesitantly at first, to a ride on my motorbike— so long as she had a helmet and I drove carefully." He looked to Elizabeth who nodded her agreement before they both glanced back at William, grins from ear to ear as they tried to suppress their laughter.

"So off we went. I took the back road behind my garage; you know the one," he told Darcy.

"Yes, I know the one," he agreed.

"So you know, it's lined with trees and offers the best views. Being so picturesque, I figured Elizabeth would enjoy it. So here we are riding along when Elizabeth pointed out something to the side. I glanced quickly and didn't notice a fallen branch, just as we came out of the third turn. I swerved to miss it, and we ended up off the road, down the small embankment and landed in the stream. We were both fine, and the bike was not damaged, so I tried to back it out. That didn't work, so I went with plan B. I had Elizabeth get onto the driver's seat so she could start the engine while I pushed it backwards out of the water. Mind you, it is shallow water, but the banks are muddy."

"Yes. Keep going," Darcy insisted. He had a feeling he knew where this was going but had to hear it from Richard's mouth.

I stood in front of the bike and began to push. It was then that Elizabeth let go of the clutch, and it popped; the bike moved forward instantly, pushing me into the stream."

Elizabeth jumped into the conversation to add, "I quickly jumped off the bike to check on him, when I slipped in mud and fell in myself." Elizabeth chuckled. Her eyes danced in merriment as they recounted their tale.

"I, being the gentlemen that I am," Richard started, "crawled over to aid her. We both got up and tried to push the bike out, dripping wet and full of mud. We had almost made it back up to the road, when I lost my footing and went face down into the mud again. Elizabeth wasn't able to hold the bike at that angle on her own, though she tried hard. She ended up loosing her footing and went down on her knees. The bike began to slip then, so I jumped up to help hold it, and it ended up taking me along with it towards the water again. The bike turned and hit a small boulder, the jolt of which threw me back into the stream."

Elizabeth giggled, "I sat watching it all from the mud laughing. It was like an old black and white movie. You know the ones with Laurel and Hardy," she said, looking back and forth between the men. "I swear it was like watching a slow motion train wreck."

"I am sure it was one of those moments where I wish I had been there to video such an escapade for all prosperity. Did all this take place after lunch with your family?" Darcy asked, a ready smile on his face from the telling.

"Well, not so much." Richard winced. "Once we finally had gotten the bike out of the stream and back on the road, we drove it to the garage. We were both so wet and caked in dirt, that I called up to the house and made our apologies to my mother. I could hear my father laughing in the background. I'm sure I won't want to eat there for some time. I'll never live this down, you know," he said to William and Elizabeth.

"No, I can't imagine you ever will." Darcy chuckled. "I think you two best get cleaned up. Elizabeth, are you up to having a later dinner with my family?" He asked.

"Once I have rested and had a little something to eat; I'm starved," she admitted.

"Then I'll fix us all a plate of cheese and crackers while you both shower and change. That should hold you over until dinner. Perhaps after we eat, I can show you those rooms you requested of me yesterday," William offered.

"Sounds wonderful. I'll be just a bit." She turned and headed to William's room, leaving the men in the kitchen.

"Seems you two had a wonderful adventure this afternoon. It's good to hear you laugh. It's been far too long," Darcy commented.

"It feels good to laugh. We had a great time. I'm going to get all cleaned up. I'll see you in a few."

*****

The Darcy family enjoyed a hearty meal out on the patio, the steaks grilled to perfection by Mr. Darcy himself. Georgiana had helped to prepare the vegetables and Aunt Catherine was holding court out near the pool, where mojito's were being served. "So my dear, you must be tired after your adventure today. Perhaps you would like to sleep here tonight," the old lady offered.

"Aunt, I don't think that will be necessary. The cottage has all her things, and it is just a short drive down the road," William quietly replied.

"Thank you Aunt Catherine, but William is right. I'm quite comfortable in the cottage, but thank you for the offer," she politely declined.

"Sister," George Darcy said from the grill, "leave that young lady alone. She is William's guest, not yours," he joked. But he was also trying to defuse the old lady's need to meddle.

"Fine, I was just asking. You know my dear; William's room is still kept ready for company. You should go up and look around upstairs. You never know. These boys may snore way too much one night, and you may find you can't sleep well," she added.

"Thank you, I believe William plans to show me around later." Elizabeth smiled before taking William's hand in hers for support.

*****

Eating out by the pool was very enjoyable. The slight breeze brought the scent of flowers wafting over all those gathered outside. Elizabeth was seated next to Georgiana and Mrs. Darcy. They all chatted very easily, and she felt right at home. She noticed that the men were gathered at the other end of the table, Aunt Catherine next to William. Elizabeth smiled to herself knowing how frustrated William would be later from deflecting his aunt's conversation all night.

Once the meal was complete, Victoria asked Elizabeth if she wouldn't mind helping her inside with dessert. Standing in the kitchen waiting for her instructions, Elizabeth watched Mrs. Darcy elegantly move about. She admired the woman who had such poise and had had a large hand in raising one of the men she was falling in love with. If things continued on their current path, this woman would someday become her mother-in-law, a fact Elizabeth found very exciting.

"Elizabeth, how much has your father told you about the relationship he has with my husband?" Victoria calmly asked as she went about her business.

"They have been dear friends since college. I know they collaborate as often as possible on work related ventures and fundraising events. They play golf occasionally, chat regularly, and ever so often, when I was young, I remember he would come for dinner."

Victoria continued to prepare dessert plates along with coffee and tea. She didn't look at Elizabeth but listened to her carefully. "I have a little more insight into their relationship if you would like to hear it?" She lifted her eyes up to meet Elizabeth's before she continued to place the finished items on the two trays.

"I would love to hear more; my father can be a bit vague at times. I have learned not to ask too much," she said as she smiled at William's mother.

"Then, come have a seat, and we will talk for a few moments. I'm sure my sister is entertaining everyone, so we won't be missed." Victoria pulled out two barstools from under the island, patting the one beside her. "Here— we might as well enjoy our dessert while we chat." She placed a plate before each of them.

"Mrs. Darcy, how long have you known Mr. Darcy? I mean, where did you meet, if you don't mind my asking."

"Your manners are impeccable, Elizabeth, but please call me Victoria." She kindly smiled, taking a bite of her pie.

"Of course, thank you," Elizabeth shyly replied.

"I have known both your father and George since we were in college together," she began.

"I had no idea you have known each other so long."

"Did you know I actually came to both yours and your sister Jane's christenings?" she asked, her brow arched in question.

Elizabeth shook her head, placing a bite of pie in her mouth. The topic of conversation had her captivated. She wanted to hear more.

"We were all very good friends back then. As time passed, we grew a little more distant, but that is to be expected I suppose, when you get married and start families. The men have stayed in touch, and that is what is most important. I would never wish to come between them. They have a very close bond you know." Victoria didn't look at Elizabeth; she just stared down at her plate, pushing the food around. She missed those times but did not regret how things had worked out in her life.

"It sounds similar to the relationship that Richard and William share," Elizabeth added.

"Some, those boys have grown up together. They have been close since birth. Their particular choices in relationships of late only came about while in college. Whoever marries them will have to be the sort of woman who can allow them their space and time together. If it came down to it, I think they would rather remain friends and stay close, then to have a woman who would drive a wedge between them," she said the last part softly.

Elizabeth swallowed her bite and felt just a bit awkward; she believed that Mrs. Darcy was trying to hint about what might be in her future. The fact that she also knew about the three of them made her blush a bit, but they were accepting and didn't really make comments on the whole situation. She also felt an urge to ask about Caroline. She wanted to know more about her and what she thought of the breakup.

"Do you mind if I ask you something personal about the boys?"

"I don't mind, but I may not have the answers you seek."

"I have been told very little of what actually happened to the guys in college that caused them to choose their current dating practices. I also know from William, that he has wanted to ask me out for many years and only recently did due to circumstances of my choosing. I also understand there is only one other woman who has been to meet all of you."

"Yes, Caroline Bingley or whatever name she goes by now."

"Yes, I have met her, she is a really great person, and someone I can see even being friends with. It is her brother who is going to marry my sister Jane."

"That is fascinating. You like Caroline do you? I can see how that would be; you are both very similar in some regards," Mrs. Darcy said after thinking a few moments.

"If we are so similar, why did Richard, or William for that matter, not fight to keep her once she left for Paris?"

Victoria just stared at Elizabeth for a second. She was letting the information roll around in her head so she might find a reply that would help Elizabeth. "I think, and this is just my opinion, Madeline and I do not talk about this often, but Richard was so in love with Caroline that when she suddenly left, he didn't quite know what to do. He waited, thinking she would return home. Work had become demanding and time slipped away. He emailed her and called her a few times, from what William told me. Then one day, they got an invitation in the mail to attend her wedding. Richard just seemed to shut down. He had no desire to do anything any more. William, or rather all of us, were worried for him during that time. You have been the first person to really bring him back to life Elizabeth."

It was a power she didn't know that she deserved. She loved William, no doubt, and thought Richard was the best man she had ever known; it was as if they had been friends forever, the three of them. Things were so comfortable, no awkwardness or rivalry amongst themselves. Richard was like the brother she never had, a lover she had always wanted, and yet, as their relationship continued to blossom, she felt like a sliver of his heart still called out for Caroline to be by his side. She didn't want that to always be the case; she didn't want to be second best woman for any man. She would rather that he have closure than to fool himself into entering a relationship he might not be ready to fully commit to. She thought the more time they spent alone together, the more he might come around to loving her fully, but even today when Richard showed off his collection of cars, she knew that Caroline had been there as well. She couldn't help but feel he had wanted her reactions to everything he showed her to compare to how Caroline had reacted when she had come to meet the families.

"As for William, he really cared for Caroline I believe. There was affection for her in his eyes. But years ago, when he met you at a fundraising event— I think you were just starting college, maybe 19 or so— he came home from that evening and said that he was going to ask you out one day. He made sure he went to anything he could that you were involved in. When you returned from college a few years later, he came home one day and was a little withdrawn. I found out from my husband that you had started to date a man who worked for your family's business. I believe he felt he had waited too long and that you were lost to him. Just know that even though Caroline is a great person, and we all liked her, it was Richard who was really in love with her. William, I believe, had his heart set on you. I, for one, am pleased with his choice." She smiled brightly at Elizabeth, who was rolling crumbs along the plate with her fork.

"Thank you. It means a lot to me that you approve of me. I do love your son."

"Now let me ask you a question, Elizabeth. This is none of my business, and you can tell me so. But, can you see yourself living with both men for the rest of your life? Is the connection you have already made with them strong enough to last, or would just one man complete your dreams if it came down to it?"

Chapter 28

Bill and Whitney arrived at the house Friday afternoon in silence. Having been locked up the last several days had made both testy and on edge. "Bill, just forget about Elizabeth Bennet. You will get your revenge on father; I know you will."

"Whitney, not now. I need time to think about what to do next. I'm getting my things and going back to my place," he snapped.

"Fine." Whitney shook her head and headed for her room. She needed a long hot soaking bath and a good night's sleep.

Bill couldn't believe he had been so close to having the girl who would have been the model wife, giving him the family business and revenge on his father. Now the possibilities for any of those things were looking slim. If the detective did any true digging around, he might discover his little dark secret. He couldn't afford any more delays in his plan, and jail would be a definite delay. What he needed was for his sister to get off his payroll so he could use the money to have more leveraging power against his father.

Having picked up his files from the office, he headed to his room. He could hear the sounds of water running in his sister's bathroom down the hall. An evil, horrible thought suddenly came to his mind. There were enough toys in her house and in the playroom, that should something befall her accidentally, perhaps by one of her many subs, his prayers might be answered. If a sub were to be the cause, all the better. There were certainly a few who might even be willing to take her off his hands.

He walked into his room and sat on the edge of his bed. Could he do something so horrid to his own sister? What good was she really? She had never been productive in her life and she was never around to care for their mother like he was. She had been a drain on him all his life. He had sent her to Paris, to hide her thirst for sexual dominance and desires from his world. It would not do to have a sister who behaved in such a way in public for the position of business that he held. He was at least able to keep his more moderate needs a secret. She had no compulsion to do the same. Then there was the ordeal of having to handle her high-powered husband.

The more he sat there and thought about it, the more his idea had merit. Who knows? If the good detective found out about her time in Paris and questioned her, she could very well crack under the pressure and threats. He certainly couldn't have that, not when he was so close to his revenge.

Quietly Bill walked across the hall to Whitney's room and rummaged through her handbag to find her cell phone. He pulled up her contact list and scrolled through it looking for the names of her favorite subs. She was even stupid enough to actually mark them.

He recognized a few of the names and decided to enter them into his own phone. He would call them from his place and see who would bite. Perhaps there would be other ways to make this happen. He could arrange for a party to be held here with drugs and alcohol. He could do the deed himself and make it look like an overdose. One of the guests could find her. There were many possibilities. He figured he would think on it more later.

Bill reckoned he needed to get out of Whitney's room before she returned, so he slipped out, taking his things from his own room, and quickly getting into his car to leave. The last thing he had done was leave a note on his sister's bed telling her he would be in touch and to stay put in the house until she heard from him.

*****

Elizabeth woke Saturday morning with the rising sun. She quietly inched out of bed, the guys left still asleep as usual. She made coffee for everyone and then set out for the pond. She really did love that spot in the mornings. It looked to be the start of a wonderful day— the sky was crystal clear, and the air cool against her skin, while the sound of birds and small animals could be heard about the area. She took up her seat and sipped at the warm drink in her hands. She hadn't slept well, the conversation she had had with Victoria last night, still playing in her head. She hadn't been able to respond to her last question, since William had walked in to help carry out the trays.

She couldn't believe her father had never mentioned Mrs. Darcy in any of his college stories. If they had all been such great friends, why had he not spoken of her? She would have to ask him once they returned home Monday. She sipped more from her cup, holding it close for warmth, as she continued to sit and ponder the question Mrs. Darcy had posed. Could she live with only one of the guys? She really didn't want to lose either of them; they both meant quite a bit to her at this point. The thought of saying goodbye to one or both just made her heart ache. What they all shared was special, and she felt they thought so as well.

With Caroline scheduled to go back to Paris tomorrow, it had to just be a matter of time until Richard stopped thinking of her. Caroline was just fresh on his mind— the gala, the calls, the restaurant, had given them so many opportunities to run into each other and talk; it was no wonder his mind was consumed by his old feelings. Elizabeth knew that Richard felt something for her; he showed her daily how much he cared. Even Victoria had said she had brought life back into him.

Needing to walk a bit, Elizabeth rose and began to move around the pond. It was a difficult question; each man meant something different to her. Could she love just one? William brought so much passion to their relationship. Though he was the younger of the two men by a few years, he seemed the older. He was like an old soul; he would watch from afar, and hold himself in perfect decorum while out in public. He never did anything that would embarrass himself, his family or his business. He was a perfect gentleman in every way, and knew how to treat a lady. That he expressed so much more of himself when they were alone or in a small group of familiar family and friends, made him all the more loveable, for that was when he expressed his affection the most for all to see.

Richard was the older of the two, but he had a youthful exuberance about him. He was a joy to be around; he had this great spirit about him. They enjoyed so many of the same things. He made her laugh, he made her cry, and he made her belly flip-flop around with each sizzling gaze he passed her way. The man had appeal and a little cockiness to go with it. He was forward but never in an outlandish way. He too, was a perfect gentleman, and she loved him for who he was.

Elizabeth thought she complimented each man. With William, she was the sparkle and wit he didn't show in public; together they were like fire and ice. With Richard she was more the timid one, the girl who he could coax out of her shell and make her behave in ways she didn't think she could. Elizabeth continued to walk around; she strolled down the path that went beyond the cottage leading to the barns.

She walked up to the corral to see Buttercup eating grass. Stopping to pet the horse, Elizabeth spoke softly to the animal, "And how are you today?" She smiled, patting the side of her neck. "You and I are going to have to go out for another ride soon."

"I think that would be a wonderful idea." Georgiana's voice caught her off guard, and she jumped a bit, turning to find William's sister walking in her direction.

"Hi, I didn't think anyone was around so early."

"I come up most mornings to help out. I have always loved horses. Ever since I can remember, I have been around them." Georgiana smiled. "I understand you and Buttercup got along very well the other day."

"I think we did. I really enjoyed riding her. William said we might be able to ride again before I leave."

"Would you like to go out now? We could go together."

"I'm not dressed to ride." Elizabeth replied glancing down at her appearance.

"I'm sure I have something you can wear up at the barn. I always keep spare cloths there just in case I need them." Georgiana offered.

"I suppose that would be okay. William doesn't even know I'm up here. I was just having some coffee and decided to take a stroll. Would you have a way to tell him where I am? I don't want to worry him or Richard." Elizabeth said, not sure she should go with out either of them knowing.

"Of course, there is a phone up in the office. You can give William a quick call if he is even awake to answer it." She smiled as she turned to head back to the barn.

"True, he does like to sleep in late." Elizabeth chuckled, following the young girl up the path.

"That he does. Even as a child he was like that. I can't count the number of times I went into his room to wake him for breakfast only to be asked to get out. And not so politely, I might add," Georgiana said turning her head back to Elizabeth with a raised brow.

"Your brother hasn't always been the gentleman he is today then?" Elizabeth chuckled in response.

"Heavens, NO." Georgiana laughed out loud. "Come on, let's get you into some better riding cloths and give him a call."

The girls laughed and chatted all the way to the barn. It was nice to have someone to talk with. Elizabeth really liked Georgiana.   Though she was only 23, Elizabeth found they conversed easily, just like her and Jane. It was a comfort to know she got along so well with William's family.

*****

"Who was on the phone so early?" Richard grumbled as he turned to snuggle back into his pillow on the other side of the large bed.

"Georgiana, she is taking Elizabeth out for a ride it seems."

Richard lifted his head off the pillow eyeing Darcy. "Out for a ride?" His tone was questioning and intrigued at the same time.

"Yes, that is what I said," Darcy muttered placing his back to Richard so he could get back to sleep. He was not concerned for Elizabeth's safety so long as Georgiana was with her. Now he could sleep in another hour at least, he thought.

Richard got out of bed and headed to the bathroom.

"What are you doing?" Darcy groused. Why anyone in the house couldn't sleep past 8 AM was beyond him.

"Dressing," Richard shouted from the other room. "If Elizabeth is going to be out for an hour or so then I'm going to try and get some work in," he explained.

Staring up at the ceiling, Darcy knew that would be the wise thing to do. With his hands over his eyes, he grumbled under his breath, "Why is it that everyone is always up so early? I just want a few more hours. Is that so much to ask?"

"Come on, sunshine, get out of bed. Collins was released yesterday. We need to check in on what he has been up to," Richard said passing through the bedroom on his way to the kitchen for a cup of the coffee he knew Elizabeth had waiting for them.

Knowing Richard was right, Darcy threw his arms down to his side in a huff and rolled out of bed. "You don't have to be so perky about it!" He yelled out in a cranky tone.

*****

"How was your ride?" William asked when Elizabeth returned. She looked fantastic to him; she was in jeans and a flannel shirt he knew belonged to Georgiana. Her hair was tossed up in a ponytail, and the fresh air had made her cheeks all rosy. While sitting in his desk chair looking up at her, all he could think about was how much he adored her.

"I had a wonderful time. Georgiana took me down to the shallow river and around to a wooden bridge where we threw rocks and made wishes. It was really quite fun. What have you been up to all morning?" She smiled, leaning over to kiss him gently on the lips and then moved to sit in his lap.

"Richard and I have been catching up on a little work while you were out. We actually have to head up to see my father in just a bit. I wanted to make sure you returned before we went up there." He kissed her nose while his hand rested on her leg. Looking into each other's eyes, the connection humming between them was heart warming and joyous. He wanted to go out and show her more, spend time with her, but he knew it was important that they take care of the business at hand.

"Well then, while you both do that, I'm going to enjoy a nice hot bath. I may even catch a short nap. All that fresh air made me a little tired."

"Sounds like you have it all planned out." William smiled. "I believe dinner tonight is with Richard's family. Most likely because you both missed lunch yesterday." He winked.

"What time?"

"My aunt usually serves dinner at six sharp. That means we should arrive around four thirty to visit," he said playfully.

"How long do you think you and Richard will be up at the house?" Elizabeth inquired as she stood up from William's lap.

"A few hours at the most. We can do something together this afternoon, if you like," he offered, rising from his chair.

Richard walked in then. "Hello, Elizabeth, did you enjoy your ride? Find any mud puddles to trot through?" He smiled, thinking back on yesterday's ride with her.

"No, I did not," Elizabeth joked in return.

"Did Darcy tell you we're having dinner with my family tonight?" he said kissing Elizabeth on the cheek.

"He did. I'm looking forward to it. Though yesterday's unfortunate incident is bound to have everyone laughing at our expense," Elizabeth added with great mirth.

Sighing Richard replied, "I have no doubt our adventure will be a topic of great pleasure to everyone."

"I, for one, can't wait." Darcy grinned. His eyes glistened in anticipation of Richard's impending embarrassment.

"Ok, ok, you don't have to gloat you know. Are you ready to get this over with?" Richard suddenly became all business as he started to leave the room. Both Elizabeth and William knew he would catch lots of ribbing tonight and was more than likely not looking forward to the experience. They both smiled at Richard's back, glancing towards each other with suppressed laughter.

"Yes, let's get our business taken care of so we can all enjoy the afternoon."

The men grabbed all the files and computers they needed, kissed Elizabeth goodbye and left her in peace to soak in the tub to her heart's content.

Chapter 29

Having enjoyed a nice hot soak in the tub, Elizabeth dressed and headed to the kitchen for a snack. She had just plated some fresh fruit and yogurt when her cell phone chimed with a text. She found it on the coffee table in the living room and glanced at the screen to see who the message was from. To her surprise, it was from Jane. She had just spoken with her yesterday, so she hoped all was well and that Jane was just checking in with her. Elizabeth clicked on the message and scrunched her eyebrows together as she began to read it.

Caroline left suddenly last night. She was very distraught and now Charles is flying to Paris. He expects to be gone a week to make sure she is well and convince her to move back home. I wanted you to know with so much going on here, can't wait to see you Monday.

"Elizabeth, what's the matter?" Richard said as he approached her.

With her mind still taking in the information from Jane, she didn't here the door open and close. Startled a bit by the deep voice, she glanced up. "Richard, where is William? Are you finished?"

Stopping before her, Richard peered into Elizabeth's eyes, then down at the phone in her hand. "Is something wrong? You seem upset," he repeated.

"I...I got a text from Jane; that's all. She will be happy to have me home on Monday. You know my sister Lydia leaves tomorrow for L.A. It is difficult on my family; that's all." She lied a bit; she didn't want to tell him, not yet, not like this. She needed to think. Maybe Caroline wouldn't come back; perhaps Charles wouldn't be able to convince her. She just needed to wait and speak with her sister Monday. See what news she had.

"Do you need to go home early? Would you like to be with your family and say goodbye to your sister?"

"No, it's fine. I made sure I told Lydia farewell before I left."

"It was wrong for William and I to keep you away from your family at a time like this. I'm sorry Elizabeth." Richard was being so sincere and thoughtful as he spoke.

Elizabeth began to feel guilty about having told Richard a little white lie. What was wrong with her? She glanced down at her phone, sighing before placing it back on the table. "Truly, I will be fine, and there is no need to be concerned. I would much rather be here with you and William riding horses, taking scenic drives on motorcycles and meeting your families. Lydia is old enough to make her own choices in life and to deal with the consequences from them. I'll see her again."

Richard wasn't sure, but though he felt that wasn't all she had on her mind, he decided to let it drop for now. "Well then I'll just have to find a way to distract you from thinking about your sisters." He smiled pulling her into his arms for a quick hug and kiss.

"Yes you will." Elizabeth smiled up at him, returning the playful gesture.

"Then I better get what I need so we can finish up our meeting." He kissed her nose with a soft peck as he slid his hands down her hips, then around to hold her backend in his palms.

"How much longer are you going to be?"

"No more than half an hour or so, I would think. Once I return with the information that is in a file here, it should go relatively quick." He released Elizabeth and started to move towards his office.

"Ok. I just made myself a snack, and I have a book I have yet to start, so take your time," she told him as he walked down the hall.

Richard grabbed what he needed and promised Elizabeth he would return shortly. He closed the door behind him, leaving her on the couch curled up with a book.

*****

Victoria was enjoying the late afternoon weather while tending to her prized roses, when she felt two hands snake around her waist. The gentle kiss to her neck that followed brought a smile to her lips. How she loved it when he did that to her. "You still know how to make my heart melt, George Darcy," she softly said as she turned in her husband's arms to look into his eyes.

"Then I am the luckiest of men, my love, for you melt my heart everyday when I wake to see your beautiful face next to me."

"You are such a flatterer." She smiled placing her arms around his neck and kissing him lovingly.

"My dear, you seem lost in your thoughts lately. Is it Elizabeth and William? Or is it her father that makes you so reflective?" he kindly inquired.

Victoria glanced down at George's chest before she answered him. They had always spoken openly of Thomas; it was not unusual, especially after the men had enjoyed each other's company on the golf course, at lunch or at a business function. What they had all shared seemed like a lifetime ago; but, there were times, like now, when it seemed like only yesterday to her.

Laying her head on her husband's chest, she listened to the rhythm held within to soothe her. Taking a calming breath, Victoria spoke from her heart, "Oh George, Elizabeth has grown into such a beautiful woman, and it pleases me that our son has chosen her. All these years we have heard stories of her and seen pictures of her, but now, now I look at her and think she is the most ideal woman for our son. Of all the daughters Thomas had been blessed with, I believe she is the most worthy of his heart."

"But?" George inserted, knowing his wife's mind had been working overtime since William had brought Elizabeth home.

"There is no but, their hearts are equally affected. Richard's is another story. He is conflicted like Thomas was. I don't want to see our nephew go through what we have or what Thomas has. I don't think Thomas is in a happy marriage. He would never admit such a thing, but I know, I can feel it every time I have the opportunity to be around him. He was too unsure of his place in our hearts to come back to us when Abigail left him. He only married Francis because she would have him. We have watched Thomas be only half the man he could have been all these years. Don't you see that?"

"It was his choice Victoria; he could have come and spoken to me, to us." George replied in a gentle tone. He knew his friend suffered, but it was out of his hands.

"Could he? Would you have invited him back after so many months away? We were engaged and happy, we didn't stop to think how miserable he was at the time. It is our fault for not confronting him. He is your best friend, and I loved him, still love him. I hate to see him so." She peered up to her husband, her eyes filled with guilt, heartbreak and love. It was hard for George to see her when she got like this. Over time, it had dwindled, but at times it was still very difficult for her. He wished he could take away her pain, her hurt over losing Thomas. That they were married and had enjoyed a joyous life, had children they loved and adored above all else, and had the luck to live next to such close relations and all get along, made him always count his blessings. His friend however was not as fortunate.

"I know, my love. I miss him just as much as you. Though I see him from time to time and we chat often, our relationship is not the same as it once was. I believe he misses you just as much, if it is any consolation." He stroked his wife's back and held her close. He kissed her crown and thanked God he had her in his life. He loved her with all his heart, and she him. Theirs was a strong passionate love, and it amazed him everyday how much love she had to give.

While still holding her, he thought a bit. He knew that if their son married Elizabeth, there was a strong possibility that Francis might find out one day just who Victoria was and what she meant to Thomas. He had talked with Thomas enough to know he missed her, and they all missed what they had once shared. They had all meant so much to one another. Though George had offered for Thomas to leave Francis and come live with him and Victoria several times over the years, Thomas had a family and he would do right by them. He could not let his own happiness cause the heartache of not one, but six women. George had never told Victoria of these conversations. He didn't see the point in getting her hopes up when there was little chance of reconciliation. They had a good life, and he still had his best friend, but he knew his wife suffered the loss of her other half significantly.

They held each other a bit longer; the later afternoon breeze cooled the air and scented it with the smell of sweet roses. Releasing his wife, he offered her his arm to escort her back to the house for dinner. With heavy hearts, they slowly wondered along the path, words left unspoken but acknowledge by their touch.

*****

The men had returned later than they had hoped, only to find Elizabeth asleep on the couch with her book on her chest. William thought she looked so beautiful when she slept. Richard thought she was an angel with her face so peaceful and calm. They agreed to freshen up quickly before waking her for dinner. Once William had gone to his room, Richard did something he knew he shouldn't. He took Elizabeth's phone and checked her messages. He hoped that Bill had not tried to get in contact with her.

He didn't see any messages other than one from Jane. So he crunched his brows together and replaced the phone. Not having read the message, he assumed she had told him what it had contained earlier. But something was not right. She had been a little upset by what she had read; he could have sworn it. He pushed it aside to get ready; he figured dinner was going to be an experience he wouldn't soon forget.

*****

Richard opened the front door and marched into the living room in a huff. Laughter could be heard filling the room behind him by William and Elizabeth. "Richard, don't be like that." Elizabeth chuckled half heartily.

"I'm so happy to have been able to entertain you this evening, Miss Bennet. I think I will retire to my room now. Good evening," he brashly replied. He turned to face the others to do a curt bow and then headed for his room. His door slammed behind him.

"Richard, it was all in fun. Don't go to bed angry," Darcy called after him.

Elizabeth started to follow Richard when William took hold of her arm, "Let him go sulk. He drank too much tonight; just let him sleep it off. He will be fine in the morning," Darcy tried to reassure her.

"I hate to see him go to bed like that. I could go talk with him for just a minute," she tried to convince William.

"No, come on let's get some sleep. You will see — tomorrow he will be a different man. Perhaps you could make him something special for breakfast. He would enjoy that," he tried to encourage her. William knew Elizabeth hated to see either of them upset, but in Richard's present mood, nothing good would come of going after him. He knew from past experiences it would do no good.

"Okay," Elizabeth reluctantly agreed.

*****

292

It wasn't even dawn when Elizabeth slinked out of William's bed and tip-toed across the house to Richard's room. She hadn't slept well all night worrying about Richard. She hated that he had gone to bed in such a bad mood. They had all enjoyed a wonderful evening, she thought. The food had been great, the stories of Richard and William's escapades as children poured from his family's mouths. She felt so welcomed and relaxed that all the talk of Richard's mishaps had her laughing so much her sides ached. He had indulged in several glasses of wine with dinner and a few of brandy, while they enjoyed dessert. She never meant for his feelings to be hurt by her. She felt bad and wanted him to know how sorry she was.

When she opened the door, she allowed her eyes to adjust to the darkness of the room. Once they had, she found that Richard's bed looked more like a war zone than that of a man who had sleep soundly. The need to hold him close and comfort him over powered her. She moved slowly towards the edge of the bed, taking care not to make a noise and wake him.

Having reached the bed she stared at his sleeping form for a moment. He was on his stomach, his arms wrapped around his pillow, holding it close. His upper body was bare, leaving his back on display for her to caress with her eyes. He had such a gorgeous body. Those broad shoulders, so strong and muscular, flowed down to a tapered waist. She couldn't see lower than the sheets tangled up around his waist, to know if he was totally nude or not.

Elizabeth slipped her gown off and let it slither to the floor, pooling around her feet. Her panties soon followed. She ever so gently moved onto the bed. Richard didn't move, so she snuggled on the unused pillow and watched him sleep. She hated to wake him but wanted to be there when he opened his eyes. She wanted him to know she was there for him. It didn't take long for her to drift off to sleep, comforted by the fact that she was there for him.

*****

Sunday morning Darcy woke well rested and content. He looked over to find Elizabeth had awakened earlier and knew she was probably either with Richard or making breakfast for them all. Since he didn't smell coffee or food, he figured she had gone to Richard's room. She had been rather restless all night. He smiled at himself knowing she just couldn't resist the urge to comfort Richard; but then, that was what he loved about her — the way she cared for them both and wanted them to be happy. He rolled over and burrowed into the covers, thankful that for once, he would get to sleep in late.

Chapter 30

Waking after a restless night, Richard stretched and rolled to his back. Something unusual caught his attention, and he turned his head to the left, to spy Elizabeth curled up on his spare pillow. He studied her for a few moments before turning on his side to face her. He knew he had gone to bed alone last night so had no idea when she had come to his room. He vaguely remembered the previous evening at his parents and the surly mood he had found himself in.

The longer he gazed at her, the more he thought back on last night, and the more his actions towards William and Elizabeth began to plague him, causing him to wince at the sight of the beauty beside him. What had started out as a retelling of fun childhood memories being shared, shortly turned into a litany of what he felt were his shortcomings with his adolescent mishaps and blunders along life's journey thus far. He remembered drinking more and more to mask his pain as the night wore on. By the time they had all decided to head back to the cottage, he was in a down right nasty mood if his memory served him correctly.

Mesmerized by Elizabeth's calm peaceful face and her slow shallow breathing, Richard couldn't help but feel badly about his ungentlemanly behavior. Continuing to drink in her appearance, he became transfixed on how her long lush hair fell across her exposed shoulder and down in front of her chest. He just needed her to know how sorry he was; it wasn't her fault, and she shouldn't feel guilty in any way. Slowly he moved his hand along the sheet towards her, touching the silky dark strands that met his fingertips. Twirling the curls between his fingers, his thoughts again wondered to the woman beside him. How could he have treated her like he had once they had gotten home last night? She didn't mean to harm him; just being here in his bed was testament to that. She had come willingly during the night to him, to his room, into his bed, and from the looks of it, naked.

Elizabeth's eyes fluttered open and their gazes locked. She was about to speak when Richard placed his finger next to her lips, "Please, let me say something first," he whispered quietly. She could tell by the look on his face that he seemed unsettled. She hoped he wasn't angry with her for coming to him uninvited.

"I'm not proud of my behavior towards you at the end of the night last night. I had no business taking out my insecurities and frustration on you or William. I drank more than I should have, but that does not excuse my actions in the least. I'm very sorry." His eyes were so expressive at that moment, filled with regret for what he had said and done. Elizabeth wanted nothing more than to soothe his sorrows away.

In the silence that fell between them as they gazed into each other's eyes, Elizabeth made the first gesture of forgiveness. Lifting her hand, she extended it slowly towards Richard's face, cupping his cheek. He leaned into her palm, closing his eyes tightly, while holding his breath. Elizabeth moved her face to his, capturing his hips with her own in a tender display of compassion and caring. Instinctively, Richard pulled her body to him, hugging her tightly.

"I'm so sorry, Elizabeth, forgive me please," he breathlessly asked.

"Of course, I will. We all have those moments. I'm sorry you felt we were laughing at you instead of at the moments we all can relate to. I didn't mean to make things worse for you or to make you think I thought any less of you for what happened so many years ago. Nothing could be farther from the truth you know. I find that through your own life's ups and downs, you have become a better man, and I am completely swept away every day by how much caring and support you show me. You're a wonderful man, and I'm so lucky to have you in my life."

Richard didn't know how to reply; he was so thankful she had such a forgiving nature. With his eyes still tightly closed, he gave her a quick squeeze of affirmation. Elizabeth nestled against Richard's neck, her hands gently roving across his back to soothe him. It was a moment they both needed to reconnect.

*****

It had been a long 24 hours, but Charles was determined to get to his sister's apartment. He had landed and found a rental car, and now with his map in hand, he was off in search of her. He couldn't shake the feeling that Caroline might never come home again, and he couldn't bare that. He knew her life had been rough since her divorce; she had lost some of her sparkle. He had supported her every move since they were young, and he wasn't about to let her slink away from his life. It had seemed she was happy when she first had arrived, but as the week had progressed she had become more withdrawn. He wondered if running into Richard Fitzwilliam had had anything to do with that. He was going to convince her to come home with him for good if it was the last thing he did. If she still refused, then he would strongly consider moving to Paris.

Charles and Caroline had always been close. Their older sister Louisa had married years ago and was living a modest life in Vermont with her three children. He only saw her every other year at Thanksgiving. That was the only time of year her husband would consider having extended family stay for a longer stretch of time, but airfare wasn't cheap, so every other year was his compromise. With their parents having died ten years ago in an automobile accident, all three siblings had been left in shock. Louisa, as the oldest sibling, had taken charge of everything. Three years later, she had found a man who would take care of her for a change and married him.

Charles thought he was a good man, but there where times he missed his sister, and the distance between them made it harder. Then it became just Caroline and him. They had spent all their time together, growing closer than ever before. They had rented an apartment together and enjoyed many good times. She had dated some, and then met Richard Fitzwilliam. Charles had thought for sure that Richard was the one for Caroline, but then one day she had suddenly left for Paris and within a few months, she was married to her manager. Life had taken strange turns, he thought, but she had been happy. He had been introduced to Jane just before Caroline left, and they had been inseparable since. Now that he was going to marry the girl of his dreams, he wanted his sister to be happy and back in the United States at least. He wanted her to be apart of his life, as much as he wanted to be apart of hers.

Finally after a forty-five minute test of his patience with a map, Charles found his sister's place. She had only been home a day or two herself. He hoped she was home since he had not bothered calling or warning her in any way he was coming. He hadn't wanted her to talk him out of the visit or to run off. He knocked at her door, tired, hungry and in need of a hot shower. It was just after eight in the evening, so he hoped she wasn't out for dinner.

Charles had knocked a second time, when he heard chains rattling against the door. Prepared for his sister's surprised reaction, he stood ready when the door opened a fraction and he could hear her voice, "Hello, what can I do for you?"

"Caroline," was all he said.

She opened the door a bit wider, confusion registering on her face. "Charles, is that you?"

"Yes."

Fully opening the door, she stood staring at him, "Charles, what are you doing here? When did you get in town? Why didn't you tell me you were coming?"

He thought the questions would not stop, so he interrupted her with one of his charming boyish smiles. "Are you not even going to ask your own brother in? Though I'm sure your neighbors would love to hear my answers."

"Oh yea…. sorry, come in," she stuttered, stepping aside to grant him entry.

"Thanks." He grinned wider and picked up his duffle bag. Once inside, he glanced around, stunned to find her place in disarray. There were tissues lying on almost every surface, empty ice cream containers and spoons, a pizza box on the floor, and— low and behold— a sappy romantic chick flick was on the television. "So what have you been up to since your return?" he asked sarcastically with a raised brow.

Caroline ignored him and started to scoop up the tissues and place them in the empty ice cream containers. "Not much; just relaxing really." She couldn't even look him in the eye. He might be male, but he wasn't stupid; he knew a pity party when he saw it.

He shook his head at how low she had apparently fallen and began to help her pick the place up, both of them silent. He knew his sister well enough to know that the silence would bother her eventually. If he just waited long enough, she would start to talk.

"Charles, why are you here?" Caroline asked in defeat as she took a seat on the edge of her couch, her voice clearly prepared for the battle she figured she would have to face.

Charles stopped what he was doing and joined his sister. She seemed tired, and her eyes were pink, no doubt from crying. They had much to talk about, but for now, for tonight, he just wanted to comfort her and let her know he was there for her.

He placed an arm around her shoulder and looked into her eyes. "We can talk about that tomorrow. Right now, I just want to hang out with you, perhaps get some real food. Why don't we both get a shower first; we both could use it."

"I'm not hungry, and you must be exhausted. You just got into town."

"True, but we could both use the down time. I need a shower, and I'm starved, so get yourself presentable to go out, and you can watch me eat, if that is what you want." He smiled reassuringly, giving her a slight squeeze.

Sighing, she agreed. "Good, now which way to the bathroom?" Charles asked eager to get changed.

*****

Darcy woke well rested, starting his day later than any since he had arrived. It was close to ten in the morning, and the most wonderful smells were wafting into his bedroom from the kitchen. He took a quick shower and threw on a pair of jeans and a white tee shirt. They would be heading back to the city later today. He hoped Richard was in a much better frame of mind this morning than he had been last night.

"Good morning," William greeted everyone. He went over to kiss Elizabeth on the cheek as she smiled up at him.

"Good morning, yourself. Would you like for me to fix you a plate?" she offered.

"I can get one for myself. Richard, I take it you are in a better mood this morning?"

"Yes, I am; sorry about my behavior last night. I shouldn't have let things get to me so much," he said in a low tone, taking a bite of his eggs.

"Not a problem; we all have those moments. So what are we all up to doing today? I think it would be best if we left around 4ish if that's okay with you both," William said as he fixed a cup of coffee and a plate for himself. The food looked wonderful, and he was starved.

"Well, aren't you perky this morning. Is this what comes from your sleeping in late?" Elizabeth teased with a raised brow and grin.

"Oh, I don't know Elizabeth, I'm sure he might be just as happy if he woke in the manner I did, regardless of the time." Richard didn't look up, but kept his face directed at his plate.

Elizabeth shot Richard a wide-eyed glare. She didn't want a squabble to ensue. Not to mention, she didn't care to have either of them play kiss and tell.

Darcy pulled out a chair and sat next to Richard and across from Elizabeth. He noticed the look on Elizabeth's face, and being in such a good mood, decided to taunt her playfully for a bit. He knew Richard had started the game and would be willing to play along.

"Richard's right, Elizabeth, there are some things that can bring a smile to a man's lips at all sorts of hours. Like… let's say…a great dream with a sexy siren." William glanced to Richard as he spoke. Richard in turn nodded his head in agreement.

"Or how about this?" Richard started to reply, "You're sleeping soundly when a pair of hands run down your body starting at your chest. They slowly go lower until you find yourself waking with an erection and a woman's lips…. well you know," he smiled, peering up at Darcy's face.

"I have to admit, I do love being awakened in that manner myself," William agreed with a knowing nod and grin.

Elizabeth sat there stunned at both men. It was like she wasn't in the room, much less at the same table across from them. She snapped her mouth shut when she realized she had dropped her jaw, and then leaned back to see just how far they would take this conversation while ignoring her presence.

Continuing in what William figured was a suggestively sensual tone, he offered more, "But, you know, that doesn't compare to when a woman comes up behind you while you're asleep naked, pressing her warm full breasts up against your back, her silky smooth legs rubbing up and down your thighs." He could feel Elizabeth's eyes boring into him, and it took some effort to keep his smile and laughter in check.

"Damn, you're right, and I couldn't agree more. I'm not sure I can top that one," Richard replied with a nod and high five to William.

Elizabeth figured it was her turn to play at this game, so jumped right in. "Well, you may not be able to top that, but I'm sure I can," she started off in a raspy tone that would catch their attention. When they both turned their gazes to her, she began.

"The ultimate way for a woman to be awakened in my opinion, is to have a pair of skilled hands caress her face while using their fingertips to gently flow from her jaw, circle her ear, then glide down her neck. " She used her own hands while explaining this concept to the guys with her eyes closed and her voice soft and sensual. Opening her eyes with a bit of a glazed and dreamy look, she continued, "At the same time, a second set of hands massages her foot, tenderly tracing each digit up her calves, enticing the woman to slowly wake in a hazy state of budding arousal and relaxation."

Proud of how well she had done so far, she took a moment to glance in the face of each of the guys. She had them hooked if their eyes were any indication of their enjoyment of her sexual rendition. Keeping her own features in check, she continued.

"These skilled hands would work in tandem, keeping the woman in a dreamy state, knowing she would be putty in their hands should they maintain her current state of bliss. Each stroke of their light touch would electrify the woman in question, and she would arch into their hands, still in that fuzzy dream state. While one would work at her chest, the other would caress or kiss her in other areas. Together, they would bring her to a point where making love to her would be nothing short of amazing."

Elizabeth was almost breathless from her story telling. Placing her hands back on the table after running them across her breasts and down her belly, she stopped suddenly and changed her tone, "Well, at least that is what I think. I'm going to take a shower now and dress. You boys can handle the clean up, right?" She backed away from the table and stood up. Smiling with bright eyes, she left the men gawking at her as she bounced out of the room. Chuckling to herself when she got to the bathroom, she locked the door behind her so she could shower alone. She figured a little agony would do them good for teasing her so.

*****

The guys watched as Elizabeth left the kitchen. Turning to each other almost speechless, William spoke first, "I think she's played this game before."

"Damn, that was hot; I'm ready for another go with her. Should we follow her?" Richard said.

One Good Man or Two

"I have a feeling she is on to us. You can go check, but I bet you have been locked out, man. She is a pistol, isn't she?" he smiled. He began to sip his coffee that had grown cold from the wait. Wincing at the awful taste, he got up and refreshed his cup. "I have to hand it to her, she has one sexy voice, and she knows how to use it." He grinned.

Richard stood and cleared his voice. "You got that right. I'm going to have wet dreams for weeks."

The men cleaned up the dishes and discussed what they would do for the day. The first order of business was to inform Elizabeth of the plans they had for Bill Collins. That also meant that William was going to ask her if she would mind staying with him a little longer at his place. He wasn't sure how well that would go over, since Richard seemed to think she would want to be with her family. Tonight would be out of the question due to the fact that they wouldn't get home until late. He also knew she would be ready to get back to work tomorrow. Both men hoped the Collins mess would be cleared up soon. They all needed to see Detective Lucas in the next few days. Hopefully with the work they had done over the last few days, all would be in hand shortly.

Chapter 31

Sitting in her office, staring blankly at the computer screen, Elizabeth was trying to formulate a way to speak with her father about Mr. and Mrs. Darcy. She was curious and had several questions for him about William's parents. They had all returned last night, and with the lateness of the hour, had decided to stay at William's apartment.

During the four-hour drive home, Elizabeth had voiced her readiness to return to her own apartment Monday evening. Though both men had disagreed strongly, she had stood firm with her decision. After she left work today, she would go over to William's place, collect her things, and go back to her place.

"I didn't expect to see you so early this morning. What a pleasant surprise." Mr. Bennet smiled from Elizabeth's office door. He strolled into her office, ready to greet his most beloved daughter.

Caught off guard, Elizabeth covered her startled look quickly "Well, I have been gone for several days. I thought I would get a jump on the pile of work I was sure sat waiting for me." She smiled in return, motioning at a tall stack of files next to her inbox.

They met in the middle of the room for a hug and kiss. "So how was your trip? Did those boys treat you well?" he asked jokingly, getting a good look at his daughter.

"I had a marvelous time. William and Richard were perfect gentlemen and showed me all around their childhood homes. I was also able to meet both families and had an adventure I can't wait to tell you about. Have you ever been to either house yourself?" Elizabeth asked.

"No, I met George in college, and it seems that over the years, we never went to each other's homes."

"Well, don't you think that is odd since you two are such close friends?"

"I suppose when you think about it, yes, it is; but, we have always met at other places and functions, it seems," he said as if it was no big deal.

Believing it was now or never, while they were on the subject, Elizabeth decided to just jump in with both feet. "Why don't we sit on the couch and catch up?" she offered.

No sooner had they both sat down than Elizabeth quickly threw out her first question. "Dad, how long have you known Victoria Darcy?"

He seemed a bit surprised at the question, and then glanced down while he thought on how best to answer her. "I got the impression from Mr. Darcy it has been a long time since you have seen each other". As soon as she finished getting that off her chest, Elizabeth inhaled deeply and let it out slowly. She had let him know she wasn't totally in the dark about her and hoped he would confide more than he might have without her having given him that knowledge.

Thomas Bennet leaned back into the couch. He never had intended to discuss his relationship with Victoria Darcy with his wife, much less his favorite daughter. He did not want her opinion of him altered, or to see the disappointment, sadness, pity— or worse anger— from her for his decisions years ago.

"I won't judge you dad; I'm only curious. Victoria told me she came to both Jane's christening and mine when we were babies. Why have you never spoken of her to me, especially once I became involved with William?" she asked softly. From the look on his face, he was a bit perplexed.

"Elizabeth, even your own mother knows nothing about my past relationship with Victoria. She believes that Victoria is the wife of my best and dearest friend and that is it," he replied softly with a bit of pain in his eyes.

"She didn't tell me anything about the past, but I thought there was a sadness in how she spoke to me. Just before we were interrupted after dinner the other night, she had asked me a question while we were alone. I was never able to give her an answer, but have thought on the matter for the last few days."

There was silence after Elizabeth finished. She wanted to give her father a chance to formulate some sort of a response. To give him some time, Elizabeth got up and walked to her credenza to pour her dad a glass of water. Handing it to him, she kissed his cheek and sat a bit closer to him.

Mr. Bennet took a sip of the water and placed the cup down on the end table. He looked at his daughter. He saw no judgment or expectation in her eyes, just love and affection as always. He knew he should tell her more. Having given his blessing to her current relationship, it would help her understand why he did so without questioning her. He only hoped that once he explained himself that she would forgive him.

"It was our freshman year in college. George and I were assigned as dorm mates and hit it off well. We had several of the same classes and found we spent lots of time together both in and out of school. We both dated, he more than I. He was what you might call good looking and outgoing." He chucked to himself at the remembrance. "One night we were at this club where lots of college kids hung out. We both spotted this amazing woman at a table with a few friends. We both danced with her, and we both made arrangements to see her again, though we didn't know it at the time. When we got back to our dorm that night we found out what each had done. We swore a pack at that moment to not let this woman cause any rift between us. We went about our days over the next few weeks. We both went out on our dates with the woman and both enjoyed our time." He paused to take a sip of the water. Elizabeth sat patiently; she didn't want to interrupt his retelling.

"We decided we would try to arrange second dates and see who she would say yes to, since we both liked her after the first date. Needless to say, she accepted both our dates. We figured she needed more time to get to know us better before she could pick one of us. After our fourth dates, we had decided we would question her more the next time we met with her. She didn't know we were roommates, and we didn't want her to play us off each other." Thomas grabbed his water glass to take a few more sips. Then he stood and walked towards Elizabeth's desk. He turned and leaned against it to continue his story.

"George and I had each been on four dates with Victoria at this point and spoken to her on the phone for hours in the month we had been seeing her. We were not kiss and tell men so not every aspect of our dates were disclosed, so you can well imagine our surprise when we both showed up at the same place one night for our date with her. It was at her apartment. There was a note on the door that told us to come in and sit on the couch to wait for her. George had arrived at 7 pm and I followed at 7:30 pm. The note also specified she had gone to the store and to make ourselves comfortable until she returned. She had left out some snacks and two glasses of wine."

Elizabeth couldn't believe what she was hearing. The direction this story was going in wasn't exactly what she would have guessed had happened. It was very interesting though, and she was eager to hear more.

"When I arrived and found George on the couch, we both looked at each other for a moment. At first, we accused the other of trying to ruin our date night. Then as time passed we began to wonder why we had both been invited on the same night half an hour apart and without her anywhere to be found. At 8 o'clock the front door opened and Victoria walked in. We didn't say anything, just waited for her to explain what was going on. She came over to sit in a chair in front of us. Explaining how much she really liked each of us and had enjoyed all of our dates, I just knew she was going to break it off with one or both of us. Naturally, I figured she wanted George for his good looks and personality over me."

"She didn't though, did she?" Elizabeth said softly in response. He father shook his head back and forth in reply.

"No. Once she finished talking, George and I were both surprised at what she said. She asked us to go home and think about what she was offering. She didn't want us to make a rash decision since it would affect each of us, and it was not an offer she made lightly. She explained how long and hard she had thought about this and wanted us to take that same time for ourselves. Neither of us said anything, we just left and headed back to campus. When we arrived back at the dorm, we just called it a night to lay in our beds in the dark and think. The next morning, we got up and went about our day. Then that night, George called me after his last class and asked if I would meet him at a local pub down the street to talk. I agreed to meet him; we couldn't avoid the topic forever."

"What did you decide after talking? That couldn't have been an easy discussion," Elizabeth said with understanding.

"We had a really deep conversation about what we both wanted in a relationship with a woman in general and what we wanted out of the relationship with Victoria specifically. What she offered us was something neither of us had any experience with. George was more taken with her at the time than I was, but I had formed an attachment to her and wanted to see where it might go. I figured if she got to know me better, or even both of us better, she would eventually be able to choose between us."

"That is understandable and a reasonable assumption," Elizabeth agreed with her father's thinking at the time.

"Well, you're old enough to hear this and considering your current relationship, you know there are definite advantages to having such an arrangement. Don't get me wrong— it was a lot of work for both George and me. There was a huge learning curve, but we were determined to try once we decided to agree to Victoria's offer."

Elizabeth blushed slightly and smiled. She and her father had had many delicate talks over the years. She was grateful that their relationship was such that they could talk comfortably about many topics and trusted that their thoughts and opinions would not be altered when they spoke openly. She never had enjoyed that type of a bond with her mother. She didn't regret it, though; between Jane and her father she had all she needed.

"What happened? Why did you leave?" Elizabeth couldn't help but be curious.

Mr. Bennet walked back to his spot on the couch and sat next to his daughter. With his elbows on his knees, he leaned forward, hands clasped together in thought. "We decided at the end of the semester to all move in together. Things were going well with us. One night, I had been at the library on campus and started to talk with a woman. Over the course of a few weeks, we decided to meet for lunch; then I started to call her, and we would meet for coffee. Finally, I talked with George and told him I wanted to go out on a date with this girl. I wanted to see if there was anything between us."

"But didn't you love Victoria?" Elizabeth said with her brows scrunched together in question.

"I did, but the relationship we all had was just that, three of us. It didn't seem like she was going to change her mind and decide on just one of us. I couldn't wrap my brain around the fact that there wouldn't be just one of us in her life, but both of us always. I cared for Victoria; she is the most generous woman— loving, caring, funny— and we always had a great time all together or even if it was just the two of us alone. I needed to see if someone else might possibly be the one for me. It would be a one on one relationship." He stared at the carpet and seemed so sad suddenly.

"What happened with the other girl?" Elizabeth softly asked.

"We dated for a long time. I actually moved out of the home I shared with George and Victoria once I started to date Abigail. I left her a note; I couldn't face her to tell her just to watch her heart break. But I felt I made the right decision. George knew I was leaving, and I knew he would take care of her. He loved her, perhaps more than I did even. I moved in with Abigail, and we were happy for many months. During that time, George and Victoria really became close and after talking with me and with my blessing, he proposed to Victoria. I was so happy for them. I missed them, but it was the right thing for them. A few months later, what I thought was a strong relationship of my own crumbled, and Abigail left me. I was devastated. George asked me to come back, but I couldn't. I withdrew and watched as my two best friends got married and lived happily ever after. I met your mother several months later. I never told her about my relationship with George and Victoria. She accepted me, and thinking that there was no one else who would, I asked her to marry me. I don't regret my choice. I have five beautiful daughters and a great life."

Elizabeth was so sad for her father. All these years he had secretly loved Victoria still; she could tell. "Oh father, why haven't you ever gone back to them, or kept in touch with Victoria?"

"Truthfully, it was too painful for me. At first we all hung out, and like she told you, both she and George came to both yours and Jane's christenings. But the more they were involved in my life and I in theirs, the harder it was for me to be happy with your mother. I had to cut the ties with Victoria. George and I have remained very close. He has even offered for me to come live with them over the years. But this is my place; it was my choice, and I have to live with that."

"Father, why? If you still love her, go to them, she misses you. I believe she would welcome you with open arms. You never forget someone like that, and you have to make yourself happy too." She tried to reason with him.

"Elizabeth, this is not to go any farther. I have spoken to you about my past and why things are the way they are. Now I don't want to hear any more on the subject," he said in a firm but soft voice. He kissed his daughter on the forehead and rose from his place. "I'm glad you have returned. There will be a meeting in half an hour in the conference room." Then he turned and left her office.

*****

William sat in his office, thinking back on the last several days. He had loved having Elizabeth at his family home. The cottage would never again seem the same without her. As he sat daydreaming, Richard walked in. "So have you called Detective Lucas yet?"

Straightening in his chair, he shook his head negatively. "No, I figured I would try to call him after a while. Elizabeth is coming over later to collect her things from my apartment. Are you coming over tonight?"

"No, I hadn't thought to. Should I?"

"I suppose not. If she left anything at your place, you can always take it to her."

Richard agreed. "She won't be gone long; you know that," Richard offered as he watched his cousin's face reflect his somber mood at the thought of Elizabeth's leaving.

"Perhaps, maybe tomorrow we can all meet for dinner. I think we should talk about the relationship," William said.

"If you think we need to. I don't see any problems though, do you?"

"Now is not the time or the place to talk about it. I'm going to call the good detective if you want to wait in here."

"No, I'm about to get a report from my security team and see what Bill has been up to for the last two days. With the information my father and yours has come up with, I'm ready to put our plan into action today. We can get together at lunch and share notes." Richard offered as he left William's office.

William waved him away as he dialed the phone. "Yes, Detective Lucas, please."

*****

Elizabeth finished her work and shut down her computer. It had been a long day but a productive one. She had gotten through most of the files on her desk and all of her emails. Jane had stopped by in the afternoon once she had returned from her meeting and invited her to have dinner with her since Charles was still out of town.

"I just can't tonight Jane. I need to run to William's and get my things; I'm going back to my apartment tonight."

308

"Why? Bill was released from jail on Friday. I don't like the idea of you staying alone at your place," Jane said with concern for her sister.

"Jane, it's time I go back there. I will be perfectly safe. If I know William and Richard, they already have a detail assigned to me to watch my every move. I just need some space. I have a few things I need to think about. Don't get me wrong; I really am happy with how things are going with them, but it's moving so fast."

"I understand your need for space; just promise me you will be careful."

"I will."

The two sisters chatted a bit longer and then parted ways. Elizabeth arrived at William's place, and they gathered what few things were left together. William loaded them into her car and asked if they could have lunch together tomorrow. She agreed and kissed him good night. She was tired from the long day and was ready to just relax and enjoy some quiet time.

Once she arrived back at her place, she walked around, looking at all her possessions. It was odd to be there actually. She missed the guys. Curling up on her couch, she turned on the television and watched a movie that was already playing. Her phone rang about fifteen minutes later.

"So were you ever going to call me?" came the female voice on the other end.

"Lacey, I'm so sorry. I have been out of town and just got home."

"Sure you did. I know when I'm being ignored," she joked.

"You know better than that. You're my best friend. So what's new with you?"

"Not much. Have you heard— my stupid brother and your sister are in LA now. I can't tell you how sorry I am at how he handled everything. I swear I don't know what goes through his head."

"Hey, don't worry about it. Lydia is fully capable of making her own mistakes. I think they will be good for each other. Each one is just vain enough not to see the problems their relationship will hold. Don't get me wrong, I love my sister, but this time she was warned and ignored us all."

"True. Hey, I wanted to ask if you would like to go out Friday night with Charlotte and me. We haven't been out to the club in forever. Come on— say you will come with us," Lacey begged.

"Let me think about it. I'll give you an answer on Wednesday. Okay?"

"You just want to see if those hunky studs will ask you out first. I see how it is," Lacey accused her with a chuckle.

"No— well, maybe. I'll let you know. Okay?" Elizabeth replied with a smile on her face.

"Alright, but if they don't ask you out, I'm dragging your butt out with us. Deal?"

"Deal. Nice to talk with you as always." Elizabeth chuckled at her friend's way with words.

"Yea, you too. Talk with you later."

Ready to call it a night, Elizabeth turned out the lights and headed to her bedroom. The sheets on her full side bed were cold and she longed to be between her two men. What she needed was to talk with Jane and see what was going on in Paris with Charles and Caroline. Tomorrow, she would try to find out. She needed to know who Richard's heart belonged to, she feared having hers broken if she continued to fall more in love with him.

Chapter 32

"Thanks for meeting me. I wanted an opportunity to speak with you before you joined us at the police station." William gave Elizabeth a hug and kiss before opening the door for her to a local café they were going to eat at.

"I thought Richard was going to join us?"

"He had a few more items that needed his attention back at the office. We're just going to meet up at the station in a bit. He was sorry he couldn't be here. He said he owes you a meal out."

"Oh, okay. I'll have to give him a little grief for that later." She smiled. "Is there anything in particular you wanted to tell me?" Darcy pulled out a chair for Elizabeth before taking the chair across from her. He had missed having her around last night; even Richard had gone to his own condo. He had slept poorly worrying about Elizabeth and knowing full well his capable security detail stood watch at her place hadn't eased his mind. Just to see her and hear her voice brought him relief and peace.

"Why are you staring at me like that?" Elizabeth softly asked while looking around at the tables near her. William cleared his throat and blinked. He noticed Elizabeth was blushing ever so slightly from his attentions.

"Forgive me. I missed you last night. I'm afraid I didn't sleep well as a result. I'm just happy you agreed to meet for lunch. It puts my mind at ease," he willingly admitted.

Elizabeth glanced down at her lap, nipping at her lower lip, "I must confess, I didn't sleep well either, Elizabeth said, glancing up at him from lowered lashes.

William reached for one of Elizabeth's hands and placed his on top of hers. "Come back to my place, even if it's just for the night," he asked in a low voice.

"I don't know. I need some time to myself. Things have moved so fast. I'm going to meet Jane for dinner later tonight. Perhaps tomorrow," she said with a question in her eyes.

"I'll take your company whenever I can get it. Tomorrow will be wonderful." He squeezed her hand lightly and smiled happily at her. "I suppose we should talk about Detective Lucas though, as much as I would much rather talk about us," he said withdrawing his hand from hers.

They ordered lunch and talked about what questions the detective might ask Elizabeth. After an hour, they parted ways. Darcy headed to the police station where he was going to meet Richard. It would be a few more hours before Elizabeth's appointment would take place. William promised to remain with Richard at the station until Elizabeth was finished with her interview. They wanted to compare notes on what was asked of each of them. With both Richard and William's fathers helping out with the investigation on the connection between Jennings and Collins, they wanted to make sure Lucas didn't mess things up and scare Collins away from any illegal activities that he might otherwise engage in. They wanted to catch him red handed. They figured it was just a matter of time before he revealed his true character.

*****

Richard sat in the station lobby waiting for Darcy. He was on his blackberry reading some messages when Whitney Collins came out of the back offices. She didn't notice him, but he noticed her. Her face was strained, and she went directly into the ladies' room. William came in just at the same moment. Richard waved him over. "How did it go with Elizabeth?" he asked quickly.

"She should do fine. Lunch went well, and I believe she plans to come over tomorrow night. You should plan to come over as well," William offered.

"Perhaps. Whitney Collins is here. She just came out of the back and slipped into the ladies' room."

"Did she see you?"

"No. She seemed a bit distracted. Bill could be lurking about. It wouldn't surprise me if he were here to either be questioned or to find out what his sister said. That man likes total control. Did you get those emails I sent you half an hour ago?"

"Yea, I read them after lunch. I'll call my father later and speak with him," William acknowledged.

"I should have a more in-depth report by the end of the day. The team reported nothing out of the ordinary from Collin's place. He didn't really go out Saturday or Sunday, just made a trip to a diner. While he was out, we got his phone tapped. Nothing on that yet," Richard explained in a hushed voice.

"Let me know if anything important happens. I don't want any of this to get back to Elizabeth. I want her out of it."

"I know. I don't want that either, and you know it. We all agreed to keep her safe. Don't worry. It's all going well so far. I haven't got the reputation that I have for failing in my duties. Leave it to me; we will get Collins."

"I know. Thanks. I'm a bit out of it today. I didn't sleep well last night. How about you?" Darcy asked Richard. He figured Richard would be in the same boat.

"I didn't sleep much either. Spent most of the night doing research. I slept on and off on the couch."

Both men sat in silence when Whitney came out of the restroom. They watched as she sat in a far corner and used her cell to place a call. She seemed unhappy and flustered. Both wished they knew whom she was speaking with and what was being said. Just then Lieutenant Denny came out, and he called to Richard to join him. William continued to watch Whitney. It didn't appear that she noticed Richard heading back. Perhaps he could tail her for a bit before he was called back himself.

*****

"Hi Jane, I hope you haven't been waiting too long."

"About fifteen minutes, but this kind man made me a very tasty drink." Jane smiled at the cute bartender, and then asked, "Could you make one of these for my sister, please?"

"Sure thing" he grinned.

"Jane, what is that?"

Taking a quick sip, Jane enthusiastically announced, "A black cherry mojito, and you're going to love it!"

The bartender returned, placing the beverage before Elizabeth, "There you go— one black cherry mojito. Will there be anything else, ladies?" he asked glancing between the two sisters.

"I think that's it for now. Oh wait! Could we get two menus?"

He quickly provided those with a promise to return in a few minutes to take their orders.

Elizabeth took a sip and sighed in delight. "Wow! That is good. I definitely needed this after my day."

Jane listened while Elizabeth informed her about the interview with detective Lucas and then her lunch with William earlier in the afternoon. After about twenty minutes, she had explained everything to Jane's satisfaction.

"So Jane, enough about me. How is Charles? Have you heard from him since he arrived in Paris?" she asked, interested to know what information Jane could provide.

"I talked with him last night actually. I think he is close to convincing Caroline to move back to the states. He said she is really miserable in Paris. I don't blame her; she is all alone there. Ever since her divorce, she has still had to work around that man."

Elizabeth listened as Jane spoke, and she started to feel guilty. "Miserable— that's terrible Jane. No one should be alone and miserable in another country. Did he say or give any reasons for her unhappiness, besides the obvious of running into her ex?" Elizabeth was concerned for Caroline. She didn't wish her to be unhappy. She also felt that some of her current misery could come from the fact that Richard must have appeared to have moved on with his life.

"He didn't want to tell me over the phone since she was nearby. For now though, he said she would move in with us. Charles has wanted her back home for sometime. I really like her, don't you? I mean, we all seemed to get along so well. I'm very excited that she will be my sister-in-law." Jane smiled.

"I know what you're trying to say, and yes, I think the three of us got along quite well. I think it's wonderful that she will be returning home soon. She will have a chance to be involved in all the wedding plans, and I'm sure she and I will conspire to throw you one heck of a bachelorette party." Elizabeth smiled as she sipped on the last of her drink.

It seemed she would need to do some soul searching and come up with a plan to bring the topic of Caroline up with Richard. In light of what she had discovered about her own father and Victoria's relationship, she didn't want the same for herself, Richard or Caroline. She even thought about discussing all this with William, since it would affect him as well, and perhaps together they could find a solution for everyone involved.

Elizabeth enjoyed talking with her sister for a bit longer before she headed back to her apartment.

*****

Elizabeth arrived home and found a note under her door. She picked it up and then locked herself in for the night. She had noticed her security detail outside and felt comfortable with the fact that she was being watched. She had told William she would go to his place tomorrow night— a fact she was excited about, since she hadn't slept well last night and figured after her day today, she wouldn't fare any better tonight.

Setting all her things down on the kitchen counter, she hit the flashing button on her message machine.

"Good evening, Elizabeth. Thank you for lunch; I really enjoyed your company. I can't wait to see you later and then tomorrow evening here at my place. Let's plan on going out to eat; there is no reason any of us should cook. Did I tell you Richard is going to come over also? I plan on its being a nice relaxing evening. I hope you sleep better tonight. You have definitely been on my mind. Miss you already. Good night."

Elizabeth smiled as she listened to William's message. He could be so charming. The beep sounded and the next message came on.

"Elizabeth, let's meet at 7 pm, okay? I'm running a bit behind at the office. Thanks; see you there."

Since Jane also texted the same message, she just deleted it and listened for the last message she had waiting for her.

"Elizabeth, I'll make this quick. Please look at the note I left you. It's very important."

Elizabeth's eyes widened at the sound of Whitney's voice. She shuffled the things around on the counter and found the note she had picked up at her front door. Concerned for what she might find within the envelope she just stared at it for a bit. Still unsure, she decided to give William a call.

"Elizabeth, listen to me— don't open it. I'll come right over. We may need that as evidence, and I don't want your fingerprints all over it. I'll get a kit from Richard's so we can dust it for prints and use gloves to protect the paper. You did the right thing by calling me."

"Okay, then I'll see you soon. Thanks, I feel better knowing you are coming over." Elizabeth explained.

Relieved William was on his way, Elizabeth poured herself a glass of wine and went to her room to change into something more comfortable. It had been a really long day, and she just wanted it to end at this point. So much had transpired throughout the day, her head was on overload. She took some Tylenol to combat the start of a headache before she walked back to the living room. Curling up on the couch, she flipped on the television finding a movie to watch until William arrived.

*****

"I'm going with you Darcy. I can use the kit to gather the prints since I'm better at it than you are. I also want to talk with who ever is on duty there. I have questions for them about who left the note and why we were not informed," Richard said. His tone was rather forceful, and William was in no mood to argue with him. If Richard tagged along, then he could spend time with Elizabeth and read over the note with her while Richard dealt with the paper work.

"Fine, I'll be at your place in ten minutes, so be ready. I don't want her alone, not if either of the Collins twins might possibly be lurking about."

"I'll be ready. I don't want that any more than you do. We should have insisted that she stay with us a bit longer; perhaps we can open that discussion back up. I'll see you soon. Bye."

Darcy hung up the phone, grabbed his overnight bag and headed out the door. He would convince Elizabeth to stay for more than one night this time. If she refused his place or Richard's, then he was prepared to stay with her.

It was a quarter to ten when the guys arrived at Elizabeth's apartment. Darcy hugged her first, and then Richard embraced her. It was good to see them both, and she could always use a hug, she thought.

"Have you noticed anything else out of place, any other notes or phone messages?" Richard asked as he sat next to Elizabeth on the couch.

"No, nothing. The phone message is still there if you want to hear it, but she only told me to read the note. She said there was important information in it," Elizabeth explained calmly.

William was in the kitchen pouring Elizabeth another glass of wine along with two others for him and Richard, so he hit the message button to hear the call.

"Elizabeth, was the security detail outside your apartment when you arrived home tonight?" Richard questioned.

"Yes, they were there. I actually felt reassured seeing them. When I first got home, I picked up the note not thinking anything about it, since my landlord leaves things there from time to time. It wasn't until I heard the message from Whitney that I rummaged through my mail to find it. That's when I called William."

Darcy walked toward the pair holding the wine glasses, "You did the right thing, Elizabeth. Let us handle this. There is no reason you have to deal with this alone. I left the letter on the counter Richard, whenever you're ready to dust it." William nodded towards the kitchen.

"Thanks, both of you. It's been a really long day, and I honestly got a little shaken up when I heard Whitney's voice. I certainly didn't want to read that note by myself. It means a lot to me to have you both here." Elizabeth placed her hand on Richard's leg and squeezed gently looking him in the eyes, then glanced up to William with a thankful smile.

Richard placed his hand on Elizabeth's and held it firmly; "You couldn't have kept me away!" He leaned in and kissed Elizabeth on the lips reassuringly before rising. "I'm going to go dust that note and then pull out the letter. Darcy, you coming?"

"Yea, give me just a second. Here, drink this, and we'll let you know what we find out. No reason for you to stand around in there. This may take a few minutes," William said as he placed the drink down on the coffee table. He leaned in to kiss Elizabeth gently on the lips and stroked her face with his hand before turning back to the kitchen.

Elizabeth nodded and stayed on the couch. She watched William walk away relieved they were there. She tried to just relax and watch the movie she already had playing. Having had a glass of wine already and a few drinks with Jane earlier in the evening, Elizabeth grew tired, and as she sat there, her eyes grew heavy.

*****

"There are three sets of prints on this. One set, we know is Elizabeth's; the other two, I'll have to run. I'll put the envelope in this bag and mark it. Now let's see what was so important that she left this for Elizabeth," Richard said in a hushed tone.

He carefully pulled the letter out of the envelope using a pair of tweezers. He and Darcy both leaned in closer to the counter to read the missive together once he got it opened up.

Elizabeth,

I wish to apologize to you for the distress my brother and I have caused you. I didn't mean any harm, but was coerced into helping my brother for reasons I don't have time to explain. He believes himself in love with you, but let me just say, stay away from him! He wants you for the sole purpose of gaining power and money. He sees you as a means to an end. He wanted access to your families business through a marriage to you. You must know that he has a secret side of himself that very few are aware of; he was even able to hide it from you for some time. Between your assumed innocence and All-American good looks, along with the power and wealth your family would provide him, he would achieve his life long goal of revenge against our father who abandoned us as young children. I can't say more for fear of his killing me by divulging such information. I also warn you that if he invites you to a party tonight, do not go. This is my only warning to you. I'll not contact you farther. I wish you well.

-W

Both of the guys read the letter again. Speechless for a moment, Richard looked down at his watch. It was ten thirty. If there was a party at Whitney's tonight, he needed to know what was going on there, who was invited, and if Elizabeth was in more danger.

"Darcy, I'm going to send the security detail to Whitney's as back up. Something is up. Why would Collins throw a party now after just getting out of jail and with the detective breathing down his neck?"

"I agree. Elizabeth will have to come with us. Are you thinking what I am about this letter? That Jennings could be Collins's father?" Darcy whispered.

"I think that is a strong possibility. I'll call my father now and let him know this new piece of information. I'll finish dusting for prints on this letter, pack it up, and then we can leave. I'll talk to the detail on the way out," Richard informed him.

"Ok, sounds good. I'll see that Elizabeth packs her things and is ready to go in just a few minutes. Are you going to head to Whitney's once we get her to my place?" William asked.

"I'm not sure yet. I want to know what's going on there and need to call the team. If it's just a sex party, Ill stay with you both; however, if there are business people there— including Jennings— then yes, I will head over."

Both men went to carry out their objectives before heading out.

Chapter 33

Whitney sat with Bill in her home office, listening to his rant about her earlier interview with Detective Lucas; he blamed her for being unable to keep her mouth shut. He also explained how they would both end up in jail again, if she didn't think before speaking. The strain of dealing with everything that was going on currently in her life caused Whitney to finally lash out at Bill, "When did you become such a complete ass? I was scared; we stayed in jail for several days – and you're going to lecture me? What has come over you? The last time I checked, it was you who killed my husband in Paris; it was you who demanded I get Elizabeth out of her office and into the car; and it was you, not me, who revealed to her your deep dark sexual preferences. Why did you move me here? Why did you demand I get remarried to some rich businessman, if you are so sick of me? I've had it with you Bill! After this party, I'm packing my things and leaving. Jennings hasn't been at the top of my revenge list like he has yours, so count me out of any more of your schemes." Tears streamed down Whitney's face as she yelled at her brother. She was hurt by the disgust she saw in his eyes. They had been very close most of their lives. Now as he grew angrier and more bitter about what life had handed him, she no longer recognized the man he once was.

Upon further reflection, she was pleased she had given Elizabeth the note earlier. She didn't want her hurt by him anymore. Bill had become a hateful man bent on revenge and determined to hurt anyone who got in his way.

"Don't be stupid Whitney – you have nowhere to go. You have no choice but to stay here, and here you will stay." Bill walked up to Whitney, towering over her. His eyes were steely cold, and a shiver of fear ran down Whitney's back at his appearance.

"You can't make me stay Bill. I'm going to go get ready for the party. Remember, these are my subs, and this is my house. I run the game room." In an attempt to be tough, she gave him a stern look, but inside, she just wanted to get away, far away from him.

"How could I forget?" he replied in a sarcastic tone, full of calculated calm.

320

Whitney turned and left the office; she headed straight to her room. The party wouldn't start for a few hours yet. She figured she would take the time to pack her things. Something was not right with Bill. It made her uneasy to be around him. Having reached her room, she locked the door behind her and sank down in a chair to cry, the flood of emotions and adrenaline getting the best of her. Suddenly, she felt trapped.

*****

Bill used what little time he had to check around both the inside and outside of the house. He didn't want anything to go wrong tonight. Whitney was on edge; she had divulged too much information to detective Lucas earlier. Time was of the essence if he was going to turn the focus of the investigation off himself and onto his sister. He hadn't worked so hard for so long to fail now.

With the house cleared, he prepared himself for the guests who would start to arrive in the next half hour. The two subs he had spoken with yesterday would come later. Whitney always arrived at the game room half an hour after the start of her parties. Her subs were expected to welcome her or be punished. Little did his sister know that he was the Dom in charge tonight. He had even gone to great pains to make sure Drew would be here. Finally things were going to go his way.

*****

Richard and William didn't keep anything from Elizabeth. They explained what they believed Whitney's intensions were in leaving the note. Stunned that Bill had hidden so many things from her, her father, and so many others for so long, only infuriated her. Bill obviously was unstable. She had known after he had abducted her that he was not who he had portrayed himself to be.

"I don't want either of you taking chances. Bill is so set on revenge; he could do something terrible to one or both of you just to hurt me. Please, stay here with me tonight," Elizabeth requested in an almost a pleading tone looking at both men. Since they had arrived at William's apartment, she had worried that both of them would leave her there alone while they tracked down Bill. They had been on their cell phones non-stop for the last half hour or so.

Richard finished his call and headed towards the bedroom. In the back of William's closet, he kept an emergency bag packed. He was going to change clothes and set out for Whitney's. With four men there and several dozen cars already arriving, warning bells were going off in the pit of his stomach. He knew Bill was up to something, and he needed to be there. If possible, he wanted to get inside.

The two men he had assigned to watch Whitney's house had befriended a few of her subs out at local bars, during the week, so they had an outstanding invitation to come anytime there was a party. They were to tell the person at the door who they were with and that they were gifts for Miss Whitney. When Richard returned to the living room, Elizabeth was talking with William. She seemed pale and distressed; he knew she wasn't happy with what was happening. He did some quick thinking and came up with a compromise he hoped Darcy would go along with.

"William, with the four agents already there, why don't I go alone and get a handle on the situation. I'll call you with any new intel. If the situation is under control, there is no need for you to come out there. It's after 11pm now, and the party started at 10," Richard explained hoping his idea would work.

William narrowed his eyes for a moment, then realized that Richard was trying to keep Elizabeth calm. He looked down into her upturned face; her eyes were misty, and the distress on her face was evident by her pale appearance. For her sake, he decided to hang back. "I'll only stay on the condition that you promise to tell me if there is a problem. Bill is unstable, and I don't want to lose any more of our security detail, much less you." He was serious, and Richard knew it bothered him to stay behind. They had already discussed earlier in the day that neither would go alone, that they would always have each other's backs no matter the circumstances.

"I'll call." With that Richard walked over to Elizabeth. She turned and leaned into him, holding him tightly around the waist. Her voice cracked as she spoke, but she needed him to hear what she had to say. "Please don't do anything foolish. I need you to come back to me. Do you hear me, Richard Fitzwilliam?" She glanced up into his face, searching for his promise.

Without answering her, he leaned down and kissed her possessively. Pulling her even closer to his body, he enveloped her in his arms, making a tight cocoon. He knew that by keeping Darcy here, she would be safe. Had they both left, there was a chance that she could have followed them and caused more tension in a situation that was already risky. He couldn't handle anything happening to her again, he care for her to much at this point.

322

Richard peered up to William's face when he broke the kiss and rested his chin on Elizabeth's crown for a moment. It was an unspoken language that both men understood; in that moment he told William to keep her safe and watch his own back.

"I expect to hear from you within the hour," William said breaking the silence in the room.

"An hour," he agreed. Elizabeth stepped back as Richard released her. William was there immediately at her side his arm stretched across her shoulders to give his support. Both men cared so much for her that she was their main concern. William hoped all would go well; he hated not being able to be with Richard, but he also knew he needed to be with the woman he loved.

"Please be careful," Elizabeth whispered as Richard picked up his black bag and headed out the door.

*****

It was 10:15 and all the guests had arrived, when Bill answered the front door. There in the doorway stood Drew Jennings. At the age of 25, Drew was everything Bill should have been, and it made him angry just to see him standing in his doorway. The privileges Drew had been granted, rightfully belonged to him. He was the firstborn son; it should be him to inherit control of the family business.

"Welcome. We will be meeting in my office. I'm sorry, but my sister is entertaining tonight. I hope to conclude our business quickly so that I don't detain you for too long."

"It's no problem. I have been busy myself. Both my father and I are interested to know why you have called a meeting," the young self-confident man replied.

"You will understand why I have called you here shortly. Again, I'm sorry for the lateness of the hour, but I'm sure we can work out something that will benefit us both. I understand your father will join us in a bit by conference call. I wish to make this worth all our time."

Having dressed in his business suit, Bill showed Drew to the office and offered him a drink. Taking his seat behind the desk, Bill immediately got down to business making his offer. He had a schedule to keep to tonight.

"Mr. Jennings, I'm prepared to offer you and your father a hefty sum for your business," he announced.

"Our business is not for sale. Why would you think we would even consider such an offer?" Drew asked, already annoyed at the audacity of the man before him. He sipped at his drink while waiting for Bill to explain himself or make the next move.

Bill pushed a file across the desk pausing a moment for Drew to look it over. Sitting calmly he sipped at his tumbler of scotch, watching Drew's face grow more incensed as he read. He figured this would happen and relished the feeling.

"I can see that you have no grasp of reality with an outlandish offer like this. Mr. Collins you have presented my father me and with something laughable. He will never agree to this. I can see you have wasted my time in coming here tonight. ," the man said in a cool tone.

"Oh, I think he might actually take me up on this. I have something else that might sweeten the deal so to speak. Before we call your father however, I think you should take a look at this." Bill slid a second file across to Drew. "Now, if you will excuse me just a moment, I need to check on my other guests while you look that over. Feel free to make yourself comfortable." Bill rose from his chair and left Drew alone in the office. He locked the door behind him as he checked his watch and headed upstairs.

*****

The time had come, though she didn't feel up to it tonight, Whitney was prepared to head down to her awaiting guests. When she opened the door to her room, two men she recognized greeted her; they were new subs from the party last month. "I believe you have lost your way gentlemen. The private quarters are off limits to all party guests," she said in a low authoritative tone.

As soon as the words left her lips, she noticed one sub grin slightly. Then movement in the hall caught her eyes. It was her brother who was walking towards them, wearing a business suit. Whitney was surprised "What is the meaning of this Bill?" she asked, trying to stay in character.

"These gentlemen are here to escort you down to the playroom at my request," he said, matter-of-factly.

"I don't think so," she replied in a stern tone, gripping her whip tighter. Bill was up to something, and Whitney wasn't about to play along. She knew how to use the fine piece of leather in her hand, and if her brother tried anything, she would let him feel the sting of it.

Suddenly each of the men took one of Whitney's arms, as she tried to wiggle out of their grasp, Bill approached her. He took his hand and took hold of his sister's chin. "You should not have been such a bad girl today, sister." His cold icy tone sent chills up her spine again. Bill released her so the men could take her back into her room. She tried to scream but her mouth was covered. Bill took possession of her whip and smiled. "Tonight I'm in charge. Now be a good girl, and this might go easier for you. I have some business to take care of downstairs and these men have their instructions already, so I wouldn't try to talk them out of it. They know the price of disobeying me." Bill nodded to the men and turned to leave the room. As he closed the door behind him, he smiled as Whitney cursed his name.

*****

Richard arrived, parking where the extra guards where camped out. He was immediately briefed about what was going on inside. He was then informed that Drew Jennings had arrived a little over an hour ago. Richard knew he needed to get into that house himself. He had a gut feeling Bill was up to something. For Drew that could only mean one thing. Retrieving the black bag from his car, he told one of the men to call Mr. Darcy and pass along all the information they had just relayed. The other was left with explicit directions to call detective Lucas if they didn't hear from him in half an hour. He wanted the house raided and information passed along to the police quickly.

Richard quickly approached the back of the house where he hoped to gain entry unnoticed. Turning a corner, he jumped behind a nearby bush when he spotted someone standing at the window. Taking a better look at the man, he recognized him as none other than Drew Jennings.

*****

William received the call from the detail and instantly went to his office. Elizabeth knew something was wrong and panicked. "Is it Richard? What happened? Please tell me what's going on."

"I need you to be strong for me, Elizabeth. I have to go and I need you to stay here. I'll call you when I know something. I have to be with Richard right now. I should never have let him go without me and I can't go help him if you're with me. You are too much of a distraction for us Elizabeth and should Bill catch you there, you could be in great danger. Please just stay here. Do you understand me? I promise to call once I get there.," he said in a firm but understanding way.

"But what has happened? Let me go with you" she pleaded.

"No I'm sorry, that isn't possible."

"Please don't go. I have a bad feeling about this. You both can't leave me," she begged as he grabbed things from his office. Finished William only kissed her and quickly departed. Placing his gun in its holster under his arm as he walked out of the room.

Elizabeth was left standing in the open doorway the evening breeze chilling her bare arms.. She couldn't believe that Bill Collins was behind all this misery in her life. How had she ever thought he was a man worth her love? She closed the door and paced for a few moments. She felt she had to do something. Finally deciding, she picked up the phone and called detective Lucas. After a short explanation from her, and an order to remain where she was, she hung up. Still needing to ensure the safety of the men she loved, she called her father. He of all people would understand her need to keep them safe and get them the help they needed.

"Elizabeth, stay there. There are things in play here you know nothing of, and that was by design. Richard and William's fathers are helping conduct an investigation. We have gathered more facts and are building a case against Bill. What I need for you to do is to remain calm. They are both grown men. Don't forget Richard is highly trained in defense and covert operations. Trust that they can handle themselves my dear. Would you like for me to have Jane come over?" he asked.

"No, I'll be fine. Are you going to go out there?" she asked worried for her father.

"I will contact both Mr. Fitzwilliam and Mr. Darcy and speak with them. The distance for them to travel is too great at this hour to help. I'm sure Richard has seen to the amount of security he feels he needs, and William is on his way out there; if more needs to be done, I'm sure he can handle it."

"I called Detective Lucas," Elizabeth blurted out.

"When did you talk with him? You shouldn't have interfered, Elizabeth. I hope that the police don't go there with lights and sirens blazing. The sudden attention could panic Bill into doing something he might not have. I will come over myself. Sit there and wait for me." He ordered.

"Hurry father," was her only reply then she hung up. She had no intention of sitting around. She went to the bedroom to change into some clothes better suited for where she was going and waited impatiently for her father to arrive. She would get him to take her to Whitney's, or she would go alone.

*****

Bill opened the office door to find Drew standing at the window. "I don't take kindly to being locked up in your office, Collins. What you have in that file means nothing to me. I have spoken with my father, and there is no deal," he angrily bit out. He moved towards the door and was going to leave when Bill stood before him blocking his path.

"You can't leave just yet. I have another option for you to consider." Bill noticed that the drink he had given Drew was empty. Good thing too, since the angry man would put up a bit of a fight when he tied him up.

"You can go to hell Collins, I'm leaving." He tried to go around Bill but was stopped when Bill grabbed his arm.

"I don't think you are, brother," he replied in a sinister voice.

Drew stared at him. "Don't call me that! You might have the same father as I do, but your mother is a whore, and I will never treat you or your sister as any relation of mine. Now get your hands off of me," Drew threatened.

"It just so happens that I put a little something in your drink. You won't feel up to doing much in about another 15 minutes. So perhaps you would like to reconsider your options since you're not going anywhere. My other option is on the table, and it seems the only one that is going to work.

Shame. I had hoped on doing business with you in a civil manner. But it was your call to make." Bill was so absorbed in his revenge that he didn't see Richard pass by the window.

*****

Clad in the tight black leather, Whitney was tied up to her bed. The two men standing guard over her sat across the room leering at her body.. Bill had given the instructions not to do anything other than tie her up. He had something else planned for her. They were to only act as guards and keep her in the room.

Shortly, there was a knock on the door. Bill asked the two men to step outside a moment. They brought in Drew Jennings and placed him on the bed next to Whitney. "What the hell have you done Bill? Have you lost your mind?" Whitney blurted out seeing who the man was.

"No, I have a plan, and since you did not want in on any more of my schemes, then sadly, you will have to be part of one unknowingly," Bill said with a wild look in his eyes as he tied Drew's unconscious body around his sister's. Whitney squirmed, but there was nowhere to go; all her protests went unheard. Bill placed Drew against her breasts after pulling her top down exposing them. "Now, that is much better," he said as he peeled some of Drew's clothing off. "I can't do anything so terrible as to harm my own kin, so these kind gentlemen have offered to do it for me. I'm sorry you found my demands so horrible, sister. Things could have been different if you had only listened to me."

"Bill, what are you going to do? Bill, answer me!" Whitney's voice became high and the inflection was that of a woman scared. Bill turned to leave, nodding once again to the men. They knew what he wanted, and they had 5 minutes to make it happen. He wasn't a total beast. Whitney wouldn't feel any pain; he had made sure of that.

He walked across the hall and changed his clothes while listening to his sister scream in terror. Since his father refused to deal with him, he had plans to blackmail him. He would have his money before word of Drew's death got out. The pictures of the two siblings in compromising positions would be spread all over the internet, should his father not comply. His father would either pay him or watch as his business crumbled around him from the family scandal that would ensue.

328

Bill figured on being paid, and he would be halfway around the world when the bodies were found and identified. He had a plane to catch in 2 hours, and he would be leaving as soon as he took a few snap shots of his sister and Drew doing terribly inappropriate things. Smiling, Bill could no longer hear his sister. Changed and having packed beforehand, he went across to see his sister passed out and placed in a compromising position with Drew. No one would hesitate to believe that these two individuals with their eyes closed, were not doing exactly what the pictures showed. He snapped a shot and had the men reposition the bodies. He took another few shots once they were untied. Done, he left the men to start the fire, watching as they worked. With all the noise they made, it allowed him the opportunity to lock Whitney's door behind him. There could be no witnesses and these men were expendable as well. He moved quickly down to his office to call his father and if need be send the photos. The smoke alarms had been disabled earlier when he had checked the house over, and there was no video surveillance currently running. The party was in full swing with music and laughter filling the lower level.

*****

Richard had watched as Bill dragged Drew Jennings from the office. He moved around to the side of the house to see the window that he rescued Elizabeth from, now unfortunately covered. There were lots of people in there, however, since he could hear laughing and socializing going on. A loud sound had him turn and see smoke billowing out of a window on the second floor. Two men were there trying to catch their breath, coughing and arguing. Time was not on his side. Richard needed to find Drew and get him out of there, if it wasn't already too late. He reached into his bag and took out a tool. He used it to break the glass window. He then yelled inside, "Fire! Get out! Fire!" several times. The crowd grew quiet; then screams could be heard as they began to leave the room.

Richard looked around to see how best to get up to that second story window. In the distance, he thought he could hear sirens. Not a good sign. If Bill was in there still, he might panic at that sound and do something foolish. Deciding to climb the drain spout up to a lower roofline and work his way to a nearby window from that position, Richard moved swiftly. The two men were throwing a sheet out the window, the smoke growing black. Richard broke out a nearby window and climbed in. The room was warm but smokeless. He could feel his phone vibrating but ignored it. He had a job to do. The sirens grew louder, and he could hear the faint sounds of screams from outside as the partiers were departing.

Scrambling off the floor, Richard moved out into the hall, being careful to look around. The smoke was starting to grow thicker as it billowed from under the door a few feet away. He pulled out a gas mask from his bag and headed down the hall. He couldn't open the door, which didn't surprise him. He stepped away and kicked at it several times before it opened. The two men were nowhere to be seen, so he moved forewords bumping into the bed. He noticed two bodies but could barely see them. The flames were engulfing the bathroom and running along the wall. He could see Drew and a woman whom he didn't recognize immediately. Knowing only one could be saved; he took Drew and pulled him out into the hall. He couldn't tell if he was breathing or not, but moved as fast as he could with the dead weight over his shoulder. He found the stairs and noticed a few party stragglers running out the door, their arms loaded with furnishings from the home. Outside, his staff quickly moved people to safety.

Richard had just hit the lower floor when he heard a gun cock at his right side. "Richard Fitzwilliam, how odd to find you here. Unexpected to be sure," Bill said.

"Collins, this is your handy work. If you haven't heard, the police are here, and your home is on fire, no doubt by your own hands. Don't add murder to your list of charges," He growled. Drew was on his right shoulder, creating a blind spot to anything on that side of him.

William had just arrived and was coming up the walk asking if Richard had been seen when he noticed for himself the scene inside the foyer. He pulled his gun out and moved silently towards the front door. With his gun raised, he was prepared to shoot. The staff continued to get the partiers away from the house. The sounds of cracking wood and popping glass could be heard inside and out, as thick smoke rolled down the stairs and out the windows.

As Elizabeth and her father were pulling up to Whitney's, the sight of a fire on the roof had her gasping in terror. "Father, we are too late. Help me find them, please!" she cried out as she hopped out of the car before it fully stopped. Not a minute behind them, the sound of fire trucks could be heard. There were already two squad cars on site, and several vehicles were trying to leave the scene. The long stream of cars down the drive kept the emergency equipment and help from reaching the home faster.

*****

"I think you have interfered with my plans quite enough, Fitzwilliam. You and Darcy have taken what was mine. Elizabeth was to be my wife," he growled. The gun was now pointed at Drew's head. "There is no saving Jennings; I will blow his brains out. My father must pay for what he has done to me and my family."

Knowing Bill was irrational at this point, Richard tried to turn slowly so he could see Bill's face. Darcy watched the two men carefully while he slowly approached. He didn't want to draw any attention to himself.

"Bill, look around. There is no way you're going to walk away from here tonight. There are several police officers in your yard along with my own security detail. Let Jennings go. Show some compassion; it might make a difference," he tried to reason with Bill.

"NO! I'm done with compassion, compromise, waiting. NO MORE!" he yelled. "I will have what I am due. He pulled back the trigger and just before he could shoot, Richard moved Drew out of the way and took the bullet himself. He fell back, dropping Jennings.

With an open shot, Darcy took it and shot Bill in the chest. Bill fell down next to the other two men instantly. William yelled out behind him to get a medic and ran to his cousin. "Richard, Richard, are you with me!" He pulled off his jacket and placed it on the wound against Richard's chest.

"God, that hurts," Richard weakly grumbled.

"Serves you right, coming in here alone. I should have been here," Darcy reprimanded him mildly.

"You were to watch Elizabeth. Where is she?" he asked.

"I left her at home with instructions to stay put," he replied.

"And you think she listened to you? You know she won't. Why didn't you stay there? She loves you. What if we had both been hurt or killed? She would be lost. " Richard rebutted.

"You can yell at me later. Right now we need to get you out of here. The fire is at the top of the step, and I think the floor just fell in down the hall. Can you move?"

"Yea, but what about Jennings? I don't know if he is alive or not, but I figured we needed to get him out of here. There was a woman with him, and two men climbed out the window of the room I found Drew in."

Richard winced and coughed. He was in serious pain and wasn't sure he could actually get up alone.

"Stay still," Darcy commanded. He was concerned for how pale Richard was looking and the amount of blood he had lost. He turned to yell behind him, "Where the hell is the medic?"

When he turned, he noticed the gurney coming up the front steps. He turned back to Richard. "Help is here; hang in there, Richard. Elizabeth will kick your ass and so will I if you don't fight."

"I'd like to see her try." Richard coughed again, wincing at the pain. The medics moved Darcy out of the way and quickly lifted Richard to the gurney to get him out of harm's way.

As they were coming out of the burning home, Elizabeth spotted William. She broke free from her father's grasp and ran toward him. "William, William!" she called out. Then she watched as Darcy stood close to the medics wheeling someone out of the home. She knew in her gut it was Richard. With her heart sinking, she moved towards them faster.

When she reached the group William barked at her, "I told you to stay put! Elizabeth this is no place for you to be."

Ignoring him, Elizabeth looked at a medic and asked how Richard was doing. She noticed the amount of red blood all over him. His face was pale and his eyes were opening and closing. "Richard! Oh Richard. God, what happened?" she worried aloud.

Richard could only turn his head slightly to look at William. "Take her home Darcy..." he faintly whispered.

Not wanting to leave Richard's side he knew he must. He stopped and moved to the other side to grab hold of Elizabeth. "Let them do their job. We will follow them to the hospital in my car," he told her. He was not happy with her, and once Richard was stable, he would give her a piece of his mind.

Mr. Bennet arrived at that moment. He saw how angry William was. "She wouldn't stay in the apartment. It was either I bring her or she was coming alone."

All three walked quickly to the cars. Elizabeth was placed in Darcy's while Mr. Bennet boarded his own vehicle. They took off behind the ambulance, leaving the security detail to speak with Detective Lucas. William had no doubt he would find him at the hospital shortly to question him further.

Chapter 34

"What were you thinking?" Darcy tersely asked Elizabeth as they followed behind the ambulance.

"I just knew something was going to happen. I can't explain it. You both should have stayed home and let the police handle this," she retorted with an angry snap.

"I needed to be with Richard. Had I not let him talk me into staying at home to keep you safe, then perhaps he wouldn't be lying in that ambulance shot and bleeding right this moment."

"It might have been both of you. Did you think of that?" she hissed back at him.

"It didn't do any good for me to let him go alone; you still followed us the moment I left. What is it with you? I have been trying to protect you from Bill Collins almost since the first day I met you." Darcy all but yelled. His patience's were thin and his emotions over Richard were getting the better of him.

All conversation in the car stopped. Hurt and upset over William's harsh words, Elizabeth turned and looked straight out in front of her at the taillights of the ambulance. She knew if she opened her mouth she would say something she was sure to regret later. She knew there was some truth in his words, since it appeared that she did need protection since she started to see him. Yes she had allowed William and Richard to take care of a few things, but she was still in control of her life. If she wanted to sleep in her own apartment that was her right, she still paid rent, and if she wanted to go to work, no one was going to stop her. If William regretted helping her then perhaps she needed to think about returning to her apartment permanently or possibly finding a new place of her own closer to Jane.

William knew he was taking out his grief and frustrations on Elizabeth, but he had honestly been angered that she could not follow his suggestion or Richard's and remain safe at the apartment. He knew he had no right to demand anything from her, and he had made no such demands of her, but every time she had decided to go to work, go to her own apartment, or

334

anywhere else that he couldn't be by her side to protect her, something had gone wrong.

He sat contemplating the reasons behind Elizabeth's continued silence and worrying about Richard's condition when Elizabeth's cell phone rang. "Hello" she said.

"I'm fine, father shouldn't have called you. I'm with William. Richard has been shot and we are following the ambulance to the hospital."

Elizabeth listened to her sister continue to talk before she answered. "No, William is driving, if he can't take me home I'll call a cab. Really Jane, don't worry about me. We are pulling up to the hospital now, I have to go. Okay, I'll call you tomorrow." She hung up and watched the ambulance doors open. The technician climbed out along with the driver, to pull Richard out.

Quickly, Elizabeth got out of the car and made her way towards the emergency entrance Richard had just passed through.

"Excuse me miss, can I help you?" The nurse at the desk asked.

"Yes, my boyfriend was just wheeled in with a gun shot wound and I need to see him," she informed the woman.

"I'm sorry – only family is allowed back there and right now he is being worked on. If you will just take a seat, I'll have someone update you on his status as soon as possible." She told Elizabeth.

"But I need to see him now, please. He was hurt really bad." Elizabeth replied in a pleading voice as she stared down the hall, her eyes starting to mist up.

"I'm sorry, but those are the hospital rules. Please take a seat someone will contact you when there is news." The nurse turned to leave when a male voice could be heard behind Elizabeth.

"The man just brought in with a gun shot wound to his chest- I'm his cousin. May I see him?" William's voice was deep and authoritative.

The nurse turned her head to glance up at William, noting his facial expression and body stance. "Fine, you may come-alone" she said glancing back to Elizabeth.

Elizabeth looked to William for support on her behalf, but he offered none. Instead he peered down at her and commented, "I'll check on him and let you know what's going on, ok?" He turned back to the nurse and followed her down the hall as Elizabeth stood watching.

Soon after they had disappeared into the room that Richard was in, a light came on in the hall. Several nurses went running in, followed by a man running as he pushed a cart. Elizabeth stood still, her feet frozen to the floor. A few more nurses ran past her, and tears started to silently flow down her cheeks. A sense of helplessness and dread began to descend on her. A man in a white doctors coat rushed past her and entered the same room. With so much activity happening in there, Elizabeth just knew Richard wouldn't make it. She had asked to see him and was denied what could have been her last opportunity to tell him how much she cared about him.

It seemed like an eternity until both doors opened and a rush of people entered the hall. They surrounded the bed Richard was on as they wheeled him out. They pushed him farther down the hall until they entered an elevator. He had to be alive, if only barely she thought. Her sobs grew louder and as the adrenaline began to leave her body, Elizabeth sank to her knees on the floor, her hands shielding her face from the world around her.

*****

William had watched as Richard crashed before him. He had just walked into the room where several nurses and a doctor were working on his cousin. They had his shirt off and blood was everywhere. The ambulance techs read off his stats and left. William felt helpless as he watched his cousin lying on the table. He was so pale, so lifeless in appearance. How would he ever face his family if the unthinkable happened? He should have been there; he should have been with Richard. He felt so much guilt, how had he let a woman stand between them. As he continued to stare at Richard more and more nurses began to flood the room. They used paddles on him and finally after four attempts they got a heartbeat. Things were happening so fast, when they just took him away. A nurse held on to William's arm talking to him in a calm voice.

"Sir, they need to get him up to surgery. I'll take you to a waiting room on the surgical floor and once I have any news, I'll personally bring it to you. Sir, we need to get moving." She was sympathetic and calm, and all William could think of was that he needed to call his uncle. They would want to be here.

"Can I call his family?" he quietly asked.

"Yes upstairs in the private waiting room there will be a phone for you to use," she replied.

Nodding his response William walked along side of the lady passing through the doors that she opened for them. He happened to turn and see a woman on her knees in the middle of the floor. His mind clicked and he asked the nurse to wait a moment. He moved slowly towards Elizabeth, hearing her sobs and beginning to feel terrible for what had transpired between them.

"Elizabeth…" he softly said as he knelt down next to her. He pulled her into his shoulder and held her gently as she cried. He stroked her hair and back with one hand. "Come with me, Elizabeth; we have to go upstairs now, ok?"

"Is he going to be okay?" she asked from behind her hands.

"I don't know. They have taken him to surgery. I have to go now; I have to call his parents. Would you please come with me?" he asked in a soft tone as he stood and released her. He held out his hand to help her up.

She rose slowly, and he placed his arm around her shoulders, and together they followed the nurse to the elevator.

*****

Mr. Bennet watched as his daughter and William entered into the hospital. He didn't need to be there with them at this time. He knew William would care for Elizabeth and he would just be in the way inside. What he should do is drive to George's place and get Richard's family. They would be in no shape to drive once they found out about his condition. Pulling out his cell phone, he dialed the familiar digits.

"Thomas?" came the familiar voice of Victoria.

"Yes it's me. Where is George? Victoria I need to speak with him, its urgent." He said in a tone that was gentle and one he hoped would not alarm her.

"George is not here. Is it William? Is he hurt?" she asked; panic laced her voice. She knew a little about what was in the works and just had a gut feeling something must have happened.

Thomas felt badly for her, but she would have to know the truth. "I'm on my way to your place now. Could you pack a few things in a bag for both you and George, and then get him back to the house. I need Richard's family packed as well. I'll drive you all to the hospital." He said.

"The hospital? Thomas please, tell me what's happened to my son. I can't wait while you drive here. Please Thomas." Her voice began to rise in pitch and he knew she was starting to panic.

"I don't have any news yet. I need to call the hospital for an update. Elizabeth and William are fine; they are with Richard. That is all I know. Please, Victoria remain calm - Richard has been shot. I'm not sure of his condition, however I don't think it is good. Get everyone packed and I'll be there as fast as I can. I need to hang up now."

"Ok, hurry please," she replied in a shaky voice then hung up her end of the line.

*****

The wait was horrible. It was an hour before the nurse returned to tell them that Richard was still critical and the outlook wasn't good at the moment. He had crashed on the table again and they managed to revive him. His internal injuries were great and he had lost a lot of blood. She promised to come back again when she had new information to pass along.

Elizabeth just sat still; staring at the hands in her lap wishing all of this would just go away. Her tears dripped down her face and fell upon her clenched fingers, as she thought back on all that had happened in the last several weeks. She couldn't believe that Richard might be gone from her life forever. He just couldn't. She knew that William would be devastated, and she looked over at him as he sat next to her thumbing through his cell phone and keeping to himself. How had everything gone so terribly wrong?

William rose from his chair and excused himself. Elizabeth watched as he walked away and out of the room. There was only one other person left in the room with her, and they must have also been waiting on someone in surgery. Elizabeth knew William had to be hurting. He and Richard were so close. He had to be feeling so much guilt over not being with him, and should Richard not pull through, Elizabeth didn't know if William would ever be the same man she had began to fall in love with. She had to do something to reach out to him, but right now he seemed to need space. Elizabeth's phone rang; she pulled it out of her pocket and glanced at the caller ID. It was William.

"Why are you calling me?" she asked quietly.

"I am down in the lobby of the hospital. Detective Lucas is about to arrive. I need for you to stay where you are for once and wait for the nurse to come and give you any information there is on Richard. Can you do that for me?" He was being a little surly with her but Elizabeth wasn't going to call him out on his behavior.

"Yes I will stay here. Can I do anything for you William?" she asked softly.

"Just what I asked of you. I'll be back up as soon as I can." Then he hung up.

Tired, Elizabeth leaned over in her chair to rest her head a bit. It was close to two in the morning and after all that had transpired she was exhausted. She must have fallen asleep for the next thing she knew the nurse was shaking her shoulder.

"Miss, Miss I have news for you," she offered.

Stretching and sitting up in her chair, Elizabeth blinked a few times. "Yes how is Richard? When can I see him?"

"He has survived the surgery. He is a tough man. It's 3:30 am; you won't be able to see him tonight. You should go home, get some rest and food."

"No, I'm not leaving. What else can you tell me?" She looked up into the eyes of the nurse and could see the regretful look from the woman. It wasn't good news Elizabeth figured but she wanted to hear it anyway.

"He is in ICU and will be for several days. Should he make it through the next several hours there is a chance for a full recovery. He has been through quite a bit, and his body suffered much internal damage and blood loss. The doctors will speak with Mr. Darcy shortly in more detail. I also understand his family is on their way in. Prayer would be good right now, Miss Bennet.

I'm sorry." She gently touched Elizabeth's shoulder and then turned to leave.

Elizabeth couldn't believe it. Fresh tears burned in her eyes as she sat there. Where was William? What was taking so long? And when did Richard's family find out what was happening? Elizabeth rose from her spot to walk off her stiffness and grab a cup of coffee around the corner. As she left the room, she saw William coming down the hall. He had his family with him and her father. Thankful that her dad was there to hold and comfort her Elizabeth ran towards him. He opened his arms, embracing his weary daughter.

*****

William had been speaking with Detective Lucas for half an hour when an ambulance brought in two more victims from the Collin's residence. The detective wanted Darcy to ID the bodies. The first was burned terribly. He winced at the site of what appeared to be a woman but he couldn't make an ID. An autopsy would need to be performed to correctly identify her. The second was Bill Collins. He had a gun shot to the head and a few slight burns. He was apparently taken from the home before his body was burned. William had to fill out a report on the death of Bill Collins. He had killed the man with his own gun and willingly gave all the information needed. William found out Drew Jennings had been brought in after Richard. In all the commotion, William hadn't even thought to find out anything on his condition. Drew had been drugged and was recovering in a room on the fourth floor after having his stomach pumped and tending to some nasty scratches he received from his rope burns. He had also suffered a slight concussion from the fall when Richard went down and needed treatment for smoke inhalation. The detective would be visiting him in the morning. He passed on his wishes for a quick recovery for Richard and departed. It had taken so long to deal with all the questions and paperwork that William had fallen asleep in a chair just inside the lobby.

His own mother woke him as she hugged his neck soundly. He then took the opportunity to tell them all what had happened over the course of the evening. He told them Elizabeth was on the surgical floor in the waiting room incase any information was forth coming about Richard. He imparted how grave it seemed from the last report, but he emphasized that Richard was young, strong and would put up a good fight. He watched as his aunt cried in his uncle's arms and prayed that Richard would pull through. His own nerves were shot, and he hadn't slept more than half an hour in that chair.

340

Together they all got on the elevator to head to the surgical waiting room.

*****

Once they all met upstairs. William along with his uncle and father decided they needed to go speak with the doctors and see about visiting Richard now that he was out of surgery. That left Thomas with the three women. They all decided it would be best to go down and walk around since it was close to 5:30 in the morning. Each had been sitting for hours at this point. There was one coffee vendor open, and they wanted fresh cups, and perhaps a little bite to eat. They were all tired. Thomas explained to his daughter that he had called Victoria shortly after leaving the hospital. Once Richard had arrived he knew he didn't need to come in and could better serve William by helping the family. After he had made the call to them, both William's and Richard's families had quickly packed and jumped into their own car to meet him along the way. This saved time, and the drive was not as long as it could have been. Elizabeth was pleased to see both families so soon. The ladies visited a little passing pleasantries to each other.

Even as tired as she was, Elizabeth noticed her father glancing from time to time towards Victoria. It had been many years since the two of them had seen each other. Elizabeth thought perhaps she could persuade Richard's mother to walk with her and find the men, while giving her father and Victoria time to catch up, besides she really wanted to see Richard and knew his mother did as well.

"Father, I'm going to take Mrs. Fitzwilliam back upstairs to find the men. We both want to see Richard. Would you both mind grabbing a few more cups of coffee once your done and bringing them with you?" she kindly asked.

"Sure, we can do that. Would you rather we all go upstairs though? I'm sure Victoria would like to know about her nephew's condition." He glanced at the woman next to him and watched for any sign she might give.

"I think letting them go ahead of us if fine. They won't let us all in to see him, so they should go first. We will bring the coffee up. You go on." She decided.

Elizabeth thanked them and with her arm around Richard's mother, they headed back towards the elevators.

Thomas and Victoria sat in silence for a few moments, sipping at their coffee. Victoria spoke first. "Elizabeth has turned out so beautifully Thomas; you must be so proud of her."

"Yes, I am. Though at times I think she is too smart for her own good."

Victoria chuckled a bit and took another sip of coffee. "It was great to visit with her these past few days. I think both she and William are perfect for one another."

"Do you? What about Richard? He is part of the equation from what I understand. What about that?" Thomas reminded her in a low tone as he glanced around.

"They are good all together, but Richard is not as committed I believe. His heart is good, but he was hurt a little while ago and has never really recovered from it. I'm not so sure he would stay. I'm not sure if Elizabeth has spoken with you, but I questioned her one night. I wanted her to really look into her heart and see if she could love my son. Should something happen and Richard walk away I wanted her to be prepared," she confided.

"She did mention something to that effect to me." He quietly responded. It all sounded so much like their own relationship to him that it brought back memories he would rather not deal with right now.

Victoria quietly glanced down at her wedding ring and whispered "I would hate to see her hurt by either of them. It is difficult when you open your heart up to a new experience. A larger view of what happiness could be like without the strictures of society's position on what normal should be, it can be freeing I believe." She moved her eyes to meet his. There she found a touch of sadness and then quickly grabbed her coffee cup again.

"Victoria, I know I've said it before, but I'm so sorry. I hate to think you have lived your life with regret, pain, or sadness of any kind due to choices that I made."

"I know what you have said in the past, but you can't change my feelings. No matter how much time passes Thomas, I will always love you. I'm only sorry you felt you had to cut me out of your life. I would have so enjoyed being apart of it in some small way."

Thomas moved his hand to touch the top of Victoria's. Both were trembling slightly when they looked up into the others eyes. "Come back Thomas.

You don't have to live like this, not with her. I know you are not happy. George has told me a few times that he has spoken with you on the subject. Come back. George would welcome you, as would I. The girls are all grown now."

"You know that is impossible. I made a commitment and I will abide by it. So many years have passed Victoria. I'm an old man now, my oldest daughter is going to get married soon, Elizabeth is finally in a good relationship, Mary and Catherine are doing well at their jobs, and Lydia, well she is hopeless, but not under my roof any longer. I can not leave my wife to fulfill my own selfish desires."

Knowing this was not really the time or place to discuss such things, Victoria rose from her chair. "Let's go find out how Richard is doing. We can discuss this later. I'm sure Elizabeth could use her father. William is preoccupied it seems and not being much comfort to her," she said switching gears suddenly.

Thomas watched her for a few moments. She was still so beautiful to him. He loved her still, but knew that he could not leave his wife. Victoria was well loved and cared for by his best friend. He knew she would be fine. Mrs. Bennet would not have that same luxury if he left her. Rising from his chair, Thomas nodded his head and threw his cup in the trash. They walked side by side in silence; both wishing things had been so different in their lives.

Chapter 35

Elizabeth sat snuggled up in a blanket reading on the couch. It seemed that most of her days were routinely spent fixing meals, running errands, or reading when the time presented itself. It had been six weeks since that fateful night Richard had been shot. They had almost lost him several times, not only that night, but a few days later while in ICU as well. He was a strong man, and beat all the odds to recover soon after. He was even put into his own room for a few weeks before being released. William, along with Mr. and Mrs. Fitzwilliam, had brought Richard here to his apartment just a week ago. He was still recovering, but in his own home where he could relax and rest better. Elizabeth had taken a leave of absence from her family business a week ago to help care for him. She drove him to his physical therapy twice a week and did what ever was needed around the house. She was so thankful to have Richard in her life; and wanted to help where she could.. William stayed every night, and after the first two days, Richard's parents returned home so Elizabeth came to stay and take over some of his care that his mother insisted needed to be done.

Detective Lucas had been by a few times to check on them all. The case against Bill and Whitney had been closed following their deaths. Only her dental records had identified Whitney, since she had been burned so badly. Elizabeth had felt sorry for her in the end and made sure she sent flowers to her funeral. Both Drew and his father were extremely thankful to Richard for helping get Drew to safety. They had shown their appreciation by donating to one of the foundations both William and Richard has started at the last fundraising event Elizabeth had organized. Mr. Jennings was not in the least bit apologetic of how he had treated his children from his first marriage and showed no remorse over their deaths. It was a sad situation brought into the limelight by the media once the entire story had been leaked to the newspapers. The death of Whitney's husband in Paris by Bill was also discovered with the help of both the Darcy and Fitzwilliam families. The Paris authorities where very thankful for the information they received so they to could close the old case.

So much had taken place in the last six weeks that the time seemed like a blur to Elizabeth. While the media attention had kept Elizabeth busy, she found out from Jane, that Caroline had moved back to the states. A stroke of luck had come Caroline's away, and a new modeling agency had signed her, paying her moving expenses back to the United States. Apparently

Caroline's work in Paris had been noticed by several American fashion houses, and when they heard she wanted to leave Europe, she had two ready offers within days. It took a few weeks to pack and her affairs handled, Charles had stayed with her to lend a hand. Caroline had come to see Richard while he was at the hospital, but only once. He had not been in the best shape then, but Elizabeth had understood Caroline's need to see him. Richard had seemed happy to see her; his eyes had lit up when she entered the room. They had chatted only for a bit so not to tire him, she left him a chaste kiss to his cheek and a small smile. Elizabeth and Caroline had been to lunch several times themselves, working on bridesmaid stuff and planning Jane's bachelorette party. They were becoming fast friends, and the strength Caroline had displayed in starting her life over was inspirational. She was doing quite well for herself now and asked after Richard occasionally.

Jane and Charles had made all the final arrangements for their wedding once he had returned from Paris. The big event was only twelve weeks away. Time had flown by so fast, and Elizabeth was genuinely happy for her sister. The wedding was going to be lovely. Even Lydia was going to try and make it back for the ceremony, though their father would not have her back under his roof, since George Wickham had gotten her pregnant. George had refused to marry Lydia once she had informed him of her condition. Elizabeth had known that their relationship was doomed from the start and rubbing it in Lydia's face would do no good now. She was, however, excited about having a niece or nephew in seven months. Lydia's job had not worked out, but she loved California so she had decided to stay, finding odd jobs here and there for the time being. Elizabeth had heard that George had found modeling work in California, and from what Lacey had told her, he was making good money— too bad he would be a shallow man all his life. Elizabeth couldn't believe she ever had thought that man was her knight in shining amour.

"Elizabeth, can I get you some hot tea? I'm putting the kettle on," William announced from the kitchen.

"I would love some— thanks," she replied.

After Richard had come through the worst of his injuries, William and Elizabeth had taken a few days and gone back to his cottage to reconnect. His parents had stayed back in town at his apartment while the Fitzwilliam's stayed at Richard's condo. They all had wanted to be near him for a while and visited daily. Both Elizabeth and William had needed to mend some of what had come between them since the fire, and the time alone together was good for both of them. They had done some honest talking about their relationship and the expectations about what their future might hold. They both had agreed that they wanted Richard to be a part of it. Elizabeth had brought up her concerns with William about Caroline and the lingering love she thought both she and Richard had for each other. He had agreed with her to some extent and thought that when the time was right, they should confront Richard about it. Neither of them wanted to see Richard or Caroline unhappy. Feelings had been hurt and egos bruised, but nothing was beyond repair if they really wanted to be together. After watching William's mother and Elizabeth's father over the last few weeks, it had been obvious that they still loved each other; life had thrown them a curve ball that neither dodged.

Elizabeth had tried to talk to her father about it but was turned away and told to never bring it up. She was saddened that her own father wouldn't at least confide in her, even hurt to some degree. But she respected him for staying with her mother. Mrs. Bennet didn't deserve a man as good as her father was and some small part of her hoped someday he would find his way back to the people who really mattered to him. She knew he loved her and her sisters beyond life itself, but he only had a small amount of affection for their mother. No one should ever have to feel obligated to make others' lives livable, Elizabeth concluded, and both she and William would work to make sure that history didn't repeat itself through them and their relationship.

"Here you go— a nice cup of Chai just like you like it," William said as he placed the steamy cup down on the coffee table and sat next to Elizabeth on the couch. He leaned in to kiss her cheek before grabbing the newspaper.

"Thank you. Have I ever told you how wonderful you are to me?" Elizabeth smiled as she placed her book down to savor the tea.

"Hmm, not since this morning I believe." He winked.

Elizabeth let her mind wander back to this morning and the wonderful time they had enjoyed together in the shower. *"What a way to start the day,"* she dreamily thought.

William grinned as he watched Elizabeth blush slightly and sigh. He had never been happier than he was right now. Richard was making great strides in his recovery; he and Elizabeth had made immense progress on their relationship, making it stronger than it had been before the fire. Life seemed to be going his way, for the first time in a long time.

"What are you thinking about over there?" Elizabeth asked in a soft voice. She always looked so cute curled up with her coffee mug in hand. He couldn't resist the temptation; so he put the paper down to answer her.

"I was just thinking how lucky I am to have you here with me," he replied in his most charming voice. He took hold of her mug and placed it back on the table so that he could kiss her without the danger of burning either of them. Leaning over her body, he wrapped his arms around her, and she immediately reciprocated in kind, the simple gesture he had made suddenly turned into a deeply passionate make-out session.

The sound of a throat clearing made both jump. "So is this the type of service I can expect? Getting my own lunch, while watching the two of you make out" Richard joked sarcastically from the bedroom door.

"Hey, how are you feeling?" Darcy asked. He pulled himself off Elizabeth to speak with his cousin.

"I can make you something, why don't you come sit down?" Elizabeth offered.

"No I want to do it. Time to take all this physical therapy I've been enduring, and put it to work," Richard commented in an odd tone.

Elizabeth and William watched as Richard slowly made his way to his own kitchen. It wasn't always easy to see him in his current state, but William knew he had to let Richard do things his way. He was a proud man and had always been strong and independent. Elizabeth fretted more about the possibility of a relapse, but William took hold of her hand and glanced in her direction with a look that said, *"Just have faith and trust him to do what he knows he can."*

"You two can go back to what you were doing. I'm just fine," Richard admonished them. He hated feeling that he needed to be cared for. He also wanted to show Elizabeth he could be the man he was before the fire. He had missed her terribly, and when he found out she had taken a leave of absence from work for him, he was humbled. She really did care for him. He knew he needed to just let go of the past and give her what he knew she needed, his full love and affection. He just didn't know how to go about forgetting Caroline completely so his heart would be free.

Elizabeth turned on the television for a little distraction; the silence was becoming to awkward. Richard would be seeing the doctor at the end of the week and hopefully cleared to do some part time work at home along with a few other things. He needed the mental stimulation. Staying cooped up in bed and unable to work all day was making Richard cranky. She could definitely understand his need to do things for himself in order to begin to get back into the swing of things.

Elizabeth tried to relax and just let Richard figure things out for himself. She picked up her tea, leaned back into the cushions, and attempted to read. William followed her lead by picking up his paper and flipping to the section he wished to review.

Wincing at the noises that were coming from the kitchen, Elizabeth found it hard to concentrate. After fifteen minutes, she couldn't take it any more and rose swiftly, placing her book on the couch. William only smiled and shook his head side to side, "I should be happy you gave him fifteen minutes," he whispered under his breath as he watched her leave the room.

"Yes, you should," she whispered in his ear from behind the couch. She kissed his cheek and went to check on Richard.

*****

Elizabeth stood at the entrance of the kitchen watching Richard strain to pick up a few things he had dropped on the floor. He was trying so hard, and the frustration on his face was evident. Elizabeth knew he was a proud man, and her heart ached that he felt he had to do too much so soon, just to prove a point. She quietly walked over and reached down to help him. His first instinct was to take from her hands what she had just picked up.

"I can do it," he snapped, glancing up to her face.

"I know. I just wanted to help. There is nothing wrong with accepting help Richard," she softly informed him with a small smile.

"It's been six weeks Elizabeth. When is it okay for me to do things for myself again?" his tone was clipped and Elizabeth knew something else had to be bothering him.

She rose from the floor and stepped back to allow Richard time to finish picking up the last few utensils. He did it quickly and turned away from Elizabeth without another word and went back to his cooking.

Trying to give him some space, Elizabeth moved towards the island and started to clean a few things up. From over his shoulder Richard again spoke, "I said I can handle it."

Stopping, Elizabeth turned and watched Richard's back. He kept moving, almost ignoring her. Trying to decide what was the best course of action to take, Elizabeth stood silently.

"Please leave. I don't need you staring at me." Richard turned to glare at her, his face filled with regret and pain. "I don't need your pity or your help," he repeated in a frustrated tone.

Elizabeth could feel the sting of tears threatening to fall, but she inhaled deeply instead and walked towards Richard. He watched her, his face unchanged.

Reaching up to place her palm against his cheek, Elizabeth just stared into his eyes. Her heart filled with care and affection for the man before her. "Tell me, what is really bothering you? Let me in, let me…"

Richard placed his fingers on top of Elizabeth's lips; he searched her eyes for several minutes, his own emotions naked for her to see. "I need you," he softly confided, his brows furrowed, hoping she understood his meaning.

Elizabeth removed his fingers gently, "I'm right here."

"No," he shook his head. "I need you to physically love me. I'm no fool Elizabeth. I'm not the same man— I'm altered, and I can't give you what you need. I know this, you have not even looked at me with the same passion in your eyes you once had. But I need you," he choked out, his face reflecting his longing and anguish.

"You see the doctor this week; we can talk with him, ask questions," she offered.

Richard turned away from her, attempting to continue cooking his meal. He was hurt. He knew that William and Elizabeth had been finding places to make love without him, and he felt left out, like a third wheel in a relationship that he had never given his complete heart to until he realized what he could be losing— again.

"Richard please, don't turn away. I love you. William and I have been so worried for you." She could feel the drip of her own tears on her cheeks.

"I don't want your pity, Elizabeth."

"God Richard, is that what you think? We both love you, and I want nothing more than to be with you. I want to feel your hands on my body again, to have your lips caress mine. I want to know you're alive and real and that this has all been a bad dream. Do you know how hard it has been for me to stay away from you? To give your body time to heal without interfering or making it worse?" her voice started to crack as her emotions started to get the better of her.

*****

William could hear the conversation in the kitchen. He knew something was going to happen one way or the other. Both Richard and Elizabeth's emotions had been running high, just like his. He had been blessed with the opportunity to talk with Elizabeth; to work through the emotions and to show her how much he loved her. Richard had been denied that, as had Elizabeth. He walked to the edge of the kitchen entrance and watched the two people who meant the most to him work out their feelings. He didn't agree with Elizabeth that Caroline still had a hold on Richard's heart. Caroline had hurt him, and there had never been closure between the two, but he knew Richard had strong feelings for Elizabeth. Their connection was just as strong as his was with Elizabeth— it was just different. Richard needed to take a stand now and make his feelings known. If he couldn't, then perhaps the three of them would not be able to make things work out for the long run.

He continued to listen as Elizabeth and Richard broke down the walls of their hearts, trying to find a way to connect once again. He would be there for them if he needed to step in, but for now, he watched as both cried and talked, the pain so evident in them both, that his own eyes misted at the words he heard.

*****

"All I know is that since I was shot, you and William have gone away to the cottage— yes, my mother told me where you both had gone. I had asked for you and you were nowhere to be found. Worried about you, my mother had just come in to visit and informed me of the getaway. Then while you both thought I was asleep or out of earshot, you secretly found ways to make love. How do you think that makes me feel, Elizabeth? I'll tell you— I feel like a third wheel, only half a man, and what there is of me repulses you.

350

You can't even kiss me longer than a peck." His words were harsh and filled with pain.

"Stop! Please stop!" Elizabeth said in utter horror as her tears streamed down her face. "Do you want to know what happened after the fire? I'll tell you— while you were in that ER room, William left me in the lobby out of spite. We had a fight while following the ambulance. I was unable to see you at all that night, to tell you I loved you, while you lay on that table dying slowly as they tried to revive you. He was there with you; he watched. I was left alone, scared and helpless to do anything but fall to the floor and cry. I have wanted to hold you in my arms for weeks. There is nothing I want more, but I'm afraid of hurting you. I'm afraid that you will relapse. I'm afraid of losing you forever Richard. How can you not know after what we shared before the fire, that I care for you? How could you think I would ever be repulsed by you?" Elizabeth almost yelled her reply. Overcome by her own rushing emotions, she stepped back to grab hold of the island for support.

Richard and William both watched as Elizabeth grew pale, the emotions and words breaking down what strength she had left. William wanted to go to her to hold her to him and soothe away her pain, but he restrained himself and waited for Richard to do what he knew he should. William silently prayed Richard would do the right thing.

Richard knew how much Elizabeth cared, but he had never heard about that night from anyone, not even William. He felt horribly guilty for having been such an ass just now. He had hurt her, and he had meant to. He had wanted her to realize how hurt he had felt, and now as he watched her heave and gasp as tears ran down her pale cheeks, all he wanted was to finally hold her in his arms. He moved slowly towards her, his own facial features blanched and tear stained. When he was before her, he placed both hands to her face and lifted her eyes to meet his. The pain and love mingled together, tangible in the space around them. Gently Richard leaned in and kissed Elizabeth. Neither moved from that spot, only their lips pressed together, healing the broken heart of the other.

William wanted to help, so he walked softly towards them. In Richard's ear, he whispered "Let's take this to the bedroom."

Richard knew his strength was vanishing, and he wanted to hold Elizabeth, to touch her and have her close. He knew William was going to help him through this and trusted them both implicitly. Pulling back from the kiss, Richard took up one of Elizabeth's hands and kissed her palm. "I'm a fool, a stubborn, headstrong jerk, and I said things that I should not have. Please, I need you to know that I love you Elizabeth Bennet. I can't ask for your forgiveness yet, but I want to make amends for jumping to conclusions. I want to earn your trust, and let you know that I do care deeply for you. Will you join me in our bedroom?" he asked just above a whisper. His eyes never left hers, as he tried to dry the tear stained cheeks of the woman he had hurt terribly.

*****

Elizabeth had gone before the men and fluffed the pillows for Richard. The entire episode had been draining on her and she could only imagine how much strength it had taken from Richard's already tortured body. She was fearful, grateful and apprehensive all rolled into one. It took several minutes for the guys to reach the bedroom. The determination on Richard's face helped to ease Elizabeth's anxiety. She stood next to Richard's side of the bed while William got him situated. Each wince on Richard's face only made Elizabeth ache to be next to him, to ease his pain and make him forget about it, if only for a bit. She watched as Richard whispered into William's ear and his nod of affirmation.

When William was finished, he turned to Elizabeth with an odd look on his face. He stepped behind Elizabeth to her puzzlement. Then he leaned down and whispered into her ear, and she understood. She glanced down at Richard, whose eyes were glued to them both. He was tired and weak, but he needed this moment as much as Elizabeth did. They wanted to connect and William was going to make that happen for them. She was glad he was there; she wasn't sure she could do this without him. She was unsure of what she should or should not do with Richard while in such a vulnerable state, but together they would all figure it out.

*****

William began to kiss Elizabeth's neck, trying to get her to relax. This would take lots of patience from both of them. The hurtful words still lingered, and the level of high emotions between Richard and Elizabeth had ebbed some, but forcing something at this point would be harmful. This was going to have to be a slow, methodical seduction, one that allowed Richard to participate when he felt he could and to feel connected to Elizabeth and vice versa. William knew this was not about taking what he wanted or placing any demands on either of the other participants, but rather in aiding them in connecting, in finding the love in their hearts and expressing that love in a soul touching manner.

With Richard's eyes focused on Elizabeth, William began to move his hands up and down the sides of Elizabeth's arms, caressing her while he continued to nibble on her neck. He knew Elizabeth was watching Richard. The slight tremble of her body signaled her unease. Wrapping his arms around Elizabeth's waist, William pressed his body against hers. He began to slowly breath in her ear; a move he knew would send chills up her spine and ignite her underlying passion. ,

Elizabeth leaned back relaxing some in his embrace. She tilted her head in a silent invitation for him to continue. Taking a hand, William ran his fingertips gently down from Elizabeth's ear, along her neck, over her shoulder; until they slid down to brush his palms over her breast. Closing his own eyes to concentrate better, William began to hear the fain mews that slipped past Elizabeth's lips.

Richard sat just a few feet away; he watched the scene before him, aching to participate. Elizabeth had closed her eyes when she tilted her head and he studied the rise and fall of her chest while William slowly began to unbutton her blouse.

*****

Elizabeth popping her eyes open, glanced at Richard, his eyes riveted to her body. They held a yearning, a need, and she knew what that felt like. She needed to touch him, to love him, and if this were going to help make that happen, she would gladly do it. He seemed mesmerized by William's action of unbuttoning her shirt. She was close enough to almost touch the bed, and as soon as she was free of her shirt, she had a plan of her own.

The sound of William breathing into her ear had helped promote the mood; she could feel her body start to respond to his touch, a touch she cherished. However tonight she wanted to feel Richard's hands on her body. Focused on the man before her Elizabeth bent down on her knees between his legs. Taking up Richard's hand she placed it at her neck and slowly moved it down towards her breast. Gazing into Richard's eyes the entire time, her brown orbs filled with love for him.

Richard was only too happy to move his line of site to the plump flesh in his hand. He took an active role and began to stroke at her pale pink circle, causing it to pucker. It had been so long since Richard had actually touched her, that Elizabeth moaned slightly as Richard worked. His hand was warm, and she closed her eyes to savor the feeling of his palm next to her skin. Wanting more, Elizabeth leaned down and ran her finger down the side of Richard's face. Her eyes found his and together they aligned, peering deep into each other's thoughts. Elizabeth moved closer and brushed her lips against his. The kiss was not demanding or hard, but full of love and tenderness. Their tongues explored each other's mouths as if they had never done so before. The exhilaration each felt transferred into their hands. Richard's hand moved to wrap around Elizabeth's back while hers held his cheek. The kiss lasted only a few moments, the connection speaking volumes. Elizabeth released Richard and softly spoke, "I have missed you."

"I have missed you to. I'm so sorry Elizabeth." His voice a mere whisper.

"I want to show you just how much you mean to me, Richard. How much this moment means to me," Elizabeth vowed.

She rose from the floor turning towards William. She whispered into his ear and with a nod he moved to the other side of the bed. Richard watched him closely, as he finished removing his clothes and just sat on the edge of the bed. Turning back to Elizabeth, Richard noticed she had removed what was left of her own clothing as well. Elizabeth motioned for Richard to scoot back fully on the bed. William helped to undress him while Elizabeth slowly inched down to the end of the bed and climbed on it. She moved between Richard's legs carefully, hoping not to cause him any more pain or discomfort. She stopped and sat back on her heels, using her now free hands to run down Richard's thighs.

*****

Her touch was pure pleasure to him. It had been so long since Richard had felt her hands caress him in any manner that the simple act affected him deeply. Just like his dreams, Elizabeth sat, naked and beautiful. He wanted to touch her in return but was exhausted. She continued to run her fingers gently down his inner thighs, past his knees to his feet. She used a delicate touch, which only drove him more to the edge of desire. His heart had begun to beat more swiftly and his cock twitched as it sprang to life. He wanted her to straddle him. He wanted to plunge into her depths and make love to her, but it would be foolhardy to try. He knew he had limits for now and was thankful that Elizabeth was being careful.

As he watched her move, she smiled seductively at him. "I have a gift for you," she winked. Her playfulness brought a smile to Richard's face as he watched her bend forward. She took him into her mouth, the warmth making him jump. Elizabeth stopped and waited a moment while he adjusted to the sensation before she continued.

*****

William had watched enough— he wanted Elizabeth. She was hungry, and though she was giving to Richard, he knew she needed release as well. He crawled behind Elizabeth as she worked on Richard. Neither bothered to look in his direction. William noticed Richard's hands were holding onto Elizabeth's arms, stroking them or tangling his fingers in her hair. William decided his course and placed his hands on Elizabeth's back to caress his way down. His lips massaged her flesh and nibbled in the spots she loved. Together the three of them would perform a lover's dance. Aligning himself behind Elizabeth, William eased into her. Her warm wet depths enveloped him, causing him to groan in satisfaction. Richard, who had closed his eyes, began to moan as well, both men enjoying the pleasure Elizabeth bestowed on them.

Holding onto Elizabeth's hips, William moved slowly in and out, savoring the feeling as he worked. Elizabeth continued to taunt and tease Richard, the gratification of each sound he made and how he arched achingly into her while his hands pulled on her hair, made the effort on her part sweeter. Her experience was only heightened more when William began to stroke her back before pushing his hard length into her. Together the three of them made love. They connected on a level they had not in some time, each doing what they could to ensure that the others were pleasured. It meant something special to each of them, and when they were finished, they all curled up in bed and held onto each other, stronger for what they had experienced and what they had been through in the last few months.

*****

Elizabeth was amazed at how fast time had passed. It had been two weeks since Richard had been cleared to work part time from home. She would return to work on Monday after taking a month leave, but today she was meeting with Caroline and Jane. The wedding was drawing closer and a final list had to be decided for the bridal luncheon. Some of Jane's closest friends were all going to get together to celebrate in a few weeks. Caroline had made a few connections since moving back to town and was able to book a great venue for the occasion. Today they were meeting with the restaurant's chef for final menu selections.

Elizabeth was almost finished getting ready when a knock came at the door. She yelled out to Richard to answer it. "Oh! Hi!" Caroline said, her surprise evident. She was looking wonderful. She had such a glow about her. Richard was awe struck. He hadn't seen her since she had come to visit him in the hospital. "You are looking so much better," Caroline said with a smile.

"Thank you. It's been a tough road, but I feel better. Sorry— where are my manners? Come in," he offered and stepped aside.

Caroline moved in and glanced around, "The place still looks the same," she quietly commented.

"Yea, you know me— I'm a creature of habit. Took a long time to get this place the way I like it."

Caroline walked over to the couch and took a seat. She always had like this place. There wasn't any sign that Elizabeth had changed anything, and there were no picture of her around either. She wondered how serious the relationship could be, but wasn't about to ask. Her life had finally gotten back on track. She loved her new job, her new apartment, and the life she was making with a soon-to-be new sister-in-law. Her love life was just something she hadn't had time to think about.

"I understand from Elizabeth that you are enjoying your new job. I'm glad that you decided to move back to the states. I'm sure your brother is pleased to have you here, especially now with the wedding so close," Richard remarked as he took a seat in a chair across from her.

"It's been really great to be back. I missed it more than I thought I did. I love the Bennet's. Elizabeth, Jane and I are really getting to know each other. I haven't had any girlfriends that I could count as close friends for I don't know how long," she admitted.

"I'm happy for you. You look great. It's been a long time since I've seen you look so well," Richard complimented.

They stopped and each glanced around the room trying to think of something to say. Breaking the awkwardness Richard asked, "Can I get you something to drink, a glass of wine perhaps, some water?" he offered kindly.

"No, I'm fine. Is Elizabeth about ready, I don't want to be late."

"She should be right out. Would you like me to check on her?"

"No."

Elizabeth stopped just outside the entrance to the living room. She watched as the two interacted; they seemed happy and at ease, both a little flushed. Elizabeth had to admit that Caroline looked really good these days. She had lost a little weight; her skin glowed with a newfound happiness and vitality. Her self-confidence had really rebounded over these last few weeks. Her life was finding meaning again, and Elizabeth was proud of her for making such strides. To look at both her and Richard, it would take a blind man not to see that there was chemistry between them.

Though the relationship with Richard and William gave her so much pleasure, and she loved both of them, Elizabeth couldn't shake Victoria's words. She figured she had to do her own investigation of sorts and either help these two get back what they had lost or get the answer she had hoped for, that Richard was finally over Caroline and could live his life with her and William. Deciding she would start today, she put a smile on her face and walked into the room

"Hey Caroline, sorry for the delay… just had to finish up my makeup. Did you want anything before we go?" she kindly offered.

"Oh no, I'm fine. Richard already offered anyway."

"Great, then let's get moving, I think Jane will chew my head off if we get there late." Elizabeth chuckled.

"True, we should go," Caroline agreed with a ready grin. She rose from the couch and looked at Richard. "It's great to see you doing so well, Richard."

Caroline was sincere, and Richard could see it in her eyes and hear it in her voice. She looked amazing to him, and he walked over to hug her. "Don't be a stranger. It's great to see you again, too. You are looking wonderful. Have fun, you two," he said. He walked over to Elizabeth and kissed her cheek. "Have a great afternoon, angel. I'll see you later."

Elizabeth kissed him in return and smiled. "I shouldn't be but a few hours. William wanted us to go over to his place tonight for dinner. Something about wanting to surprise us."

"Okay, I'll be ready when you get back then. I'll just leave you ladies to it. Caroline, we should do lunch sometime. Catch up. I would love to hear about your job," Richard commented.

"Oh… uh… sure…" she replied, confused at his request. The ladies left, and Richard returned to his work, his thoughts drifting to the fiery redhead that just left his apartment.

Chapter 36

It had been a few days since Richard had seen Caroline at the condo. His mind kept flashing back to her beautiful smile and the way her face glowed. Having resisted the urge for days, he directed his mouse towards a file on his laptop. Double clicking, his eyes waited in anticipation until his heart skipped a beat at the sight of the first photo that appeared. It was a familiar one, but it had been so long since he had seen it that he just stared for several long moments before moving on to the next.

Caroline had always been beautiful in his eyes. Her long auburn curls—that he had loved to run his fingers through, silky skin—that he had run his hands over, and a tall slender figure—that had melded perfectly next to his, had captured his heart almost from the first day he had first met her. He continued to scroll through pictures of some of the best memories he had made with her, but photos didn't compare to what he remembered of her the other day. He couldn't remember her ever looking so vibrant, so happy.

"Richard I'm home. How was your day?" came Elizabeth's voice from the front door. He quickly closed the file and went to greet her.

*****

"William, would you mind if we had a small dinner party for Jane next weekend?" Elizabeth asked between bites of her salad.

"I don't see why not. Did you have a place in mind?" he asked while motioning to the waiter for the check.

"I only thought to ask how the idea sounded; I haven't really given much thought to the details. How about the condo? It would be intimate, and we could have it catered so none of us would have to cook or clean," she suggested quickly.

"We would need to clear it with Richard. I think he's up to a quiet dinner party, but if not, we can do it at my place if you like. How many people do you anticipate will come?"

"Eight to ten, I believe, but no more than fourteen. Do you think Georgiana would like to come? I haven't seen her in a while, and it would be a great opportunity to introduce her to Jane and Charles."

"Sounds like the perfect opportunity to me. If she isn't busy, I'm sure she would love to. Did you want me to speak with her, or did you want to ask her yourself?"

"I'll call her. This way we can catch up a bit." She smiled.

Having enjoyed a nice workday lunch together, Elizabeth and William said their farewells and headed their separate ways after a hug and a kiss, knowing they would see each other after work. Elizabeth hurriedly made her way back to the office so she could send out an email to Jane informing her of William's acceptance of their idea. Since Caroline had come to the condo, Richard had seemed a little distracted so a plan was starting to form in Elizabeth's head. She hadn't felt neglected in the least by him, in fact, since they had had the misunderstanding in the kitchen a few weeks ago and had reconnected, things had been really great between all three of them. Elizabeth just needed confirmation one last time that Richard was finally committed solely to their relationship. She was fine with Richard and Caroline having a close relationship and would even encourage it, to some extent. She herself had really enjoyed the budding friendship she had begun with Caroline and wanted to make it stronger now that she was going to be part of her family.

*****

"Richard, I wanted to thank you again for hosting this dinner tonight, it means a lot to me." Elizabeth sweetly smiled as she hugged him around the waist while looking up at his face. "I know you're not quite up to entertaining yet, and I promise I will clean everything from top to bottom, and you will never know anything took place here tonight." The happiness on her face was so genuine that it matched the shimmering twinkle in her eyes.

Richard enjoyed the feeling of Elizabeth's body up against his, and her excitement for the evening was infectious. She was so adorable when she was this happy. He leaned down and kissed her forehead. "Well, if it's not, you will owe me... let's say... *favors*." He grinned mischievously at her.

"Oh, Richard," Elizabeth playfully swatted at his shoulder, "it's not as if you need to bargain for those."

Richard returned her swat with a pat to her rump as she squealed and peeled herself away from him.

"Are we ready?" William asked as he entered into the living room dressed for the evening's entertainment. He grinned at the playful interaction he caught sight of as he entered. He hoped that later, if Richard wasn't too tired, they might enjoy some time all together. They were all three in excellent spirits, which always translated into a great time all around.

"Yes we are. Richard was just laying out his plans for later this evening, once all our guests have departed," Elizabeth replied as she flashed a playfully raised eyebrow in Richard's direction.

He winked in reply, "That I was."

*****

The food had been superb, and everyone had complimented Elizabeth on her fine choice of caterers. A few of the guests had already said their goodbyes, when Elizabeth noticed Richard move to the chair near Caroline and Charles to join in their conversation. Elizabeth had been speaking with Jane and Georgiana, so she excused herself to go to the kitchen to check on something.

While passing behind Caroline, she noticed Richard's expression. He was captivated by whatever Caroline was saying. Elizabeth went to the kitchen to grab a cup of coffee and thought for a bit how the evening had been going. She had really enjoyed the evening. Jane was so happy, and all the girls had chatted about the upcoming luncheon and bachelorette parties. It was really nice to have a group of woman that she felt comfortable with. Her future was looking bright; she had the love of both the men in her life, a great job she enjoyed, and awesome friends. Though Richard talked some with Caroline, she didn't notice anything to worry over. Filled with renewed spirits, Elizabeth reentered the living room. Jane, Charles and Caroline were getting ready to leave.

"I will see you at work Monday. Jane and Caroline, we're still on for lunch Wednesday, right?" Elizabeth asked.

"Yes, definitely. Thank you for a wonderful evening. I had a great time," Caroline kindly admitted.

"We will have to do it again soon," Richard interjected.

Caroline looked at him and shyly smiled. "Sounds great." She glanced back to Elizabeth to hug her good night and turned to leave with the others.

Georgiana was saying her goodbyes to William before she approached the two at the door. "I'll see you two soon. Don't be a stranger, Elizabeth."

"Never. I'll call you later in the week," Elizabeth promised Georgiana.

Once the last of their guests were gone, all three fell to the couch with a collective sigh. "Richard, how are you doing?" Elizabeth asked with concern, turning her head to glance at the man on her right.

"I'm tired but good. It was a great evening Elizabeth; you make an excellent hostess." Richard smiled as he praised her.

"I agree. Great party Angel," William added.

"Thanks, guys. I think I'm going to go soak in a hot bath for a bit and relax if you don't mind. I'll clean up in the morning," she said rising from her spot.

William grabbed her wrist. "Just sit and relax with us a bit. No need to run off. That bath will be there later," he insisted.

Elizabeth glanced down at William's face. There in his brown eyes she saw the smoldering fire that she recognized so well, yearning to be set free. She quickly glanced to Richard, who though tired, had a face filled with promise. "If you wish," she softly replied to William. He released her hand as she reclaimed her spot between them.

"Would you care for a drink? You have entertained our company tirelessly all night," William smoothly spoke. His hand was on her upper thigh, the warmth and proximity to her other body parts capturing her notice instantly. She caught herself staring at William's hand, then Richard placed his on the same spot on her other leg. The electricity bolted up her spine, knowing both men were in such a mood and she would be the recipient of their erotic intentions.

"No thank you, I'm good," she whispered in William's direction. She didn't think that the guys would be in the mood for anything tonight, especially Richard, but apparently she was wrong.

*****

Jane and Charles dropped Caroline off at her apartment. It had been a fun evening, but it was late, and she had promised to have brunch with Charles tomorrow. Working her way to the bedroom, Caroline left a trail of shoes and accessories behind her so that by the time she reached her room, she had already started peeling her pants off, followed shortly by her blouse. She continued into the bathroom to brush her teeth and prepare for bed.

Brushing her hair, she stood before the mirror thinking how much she really enjoyed Jane and Elizabeth's company. It had been a lifesaver for her to have two great women become friends with her, and it couldn't have happened at a better time in her life.

For the first time in a long while, Caroline felt comfortable around everyone in her life. If only she could make her heart stop skipping a beat every time Richard looked at her, spoke to her, or if she were honest with herself, by simply being in the same room with her. She didn't think that she would ever forget Richard and what she had shared with him. But she respected Elizabeth and valued all her new friends too much to allow this to come between them.

Richard had obviously moved on. He had chosen Elizabeth, and she didn't blame him— she was a wonderful person. Finished with her nightly routine, Caroline moved back into her bedroom, glancing around the room slowly. Her eyes stopped on a picture she had up on a bookshelf. She unconsciously walked towards it and picked it up. It was a favorite picture of hers. She had packed it away for so long, and when she had moved back from Paris, she had decided to display it. The reflection of two happy people with wide smiles stared back at her. She loved this picture. It was of her and Richard the day he had taken her to meet his family. They had enjoyed a long horse ride and upon returning, she had slipped off the horse and into a bucket of water making her topple over into a mud puddle. She remembered laughing so hard, that when Richard had come to help her up, her mud-caked hands caused him to slip face-first down into the mud with her. Georgiana had been there to snap the picture, and it was one she loved and cherished. Caroline looked at the photo for several minutes before returning it to its home on the shelf. With a smile on her face, she turned to her bed and crawled in. Switching off the lamp on her nightstand, she glanced in the direction of the picture and sighed. If only she had never left to begin with… if only she had done things differently.

*****

Each man had chosen a different part of her anatomy and was sensually massaging away all her stress from the day. Elizabeth was going to fall asleep any minute if they continued much longer. She had placed her head in Richard's lap where he slowly rubbed her forehead and scalp, and every stroke felt so good. William had her feet in his lap, and was not only massaging away all her fatigue, but also kissing her ankles, causing electric chills to run up her spine. These men definitely knew how to butter a girl up. She was starting to feel like a warm and toasty marshmallow, all relaxed and limp, with gooey insides.

"Feeling better now Elizabeth?" Darcy's sensual voice broke through her hazy thoughts.

She answered slowly, "Yes," to his question, since she didn't think she possessed the strength to actually respond with a full sentence.

William's hands began to leisurely inch up her legs and under her dress, and Elizabeth didn't have any inclination to stop him.

Richard glanced towards the other end of the couch to speak, "I think she's purring."

The comment made Elizabeth grin while she stretched her arms over her head. "Can you blame me? You are both so skilled with your hands."

"I haven't begun to show you how skilled I am with these hands," William promised in his sultry masculine voice.

Just to hear his smoldering voice made Elizabeth shudder involuntarily. Richard took the opportunity to run both his palms down Elizabeth's outstretched arms, down towards her unprotected sides, till they met her hips. William had his hands wrapped around them already, so Richard took hold of the fabric of her dress and gradually peeled it off her body.

"You're so beautiful," Richard whispered as he stared at Elizabeth's closed eyes before leaning down to brush his lips against hers. He traced his fingers down her face, following the line of her neck, until he could circle the soft creamy mounds of flesh that made up her breasts. He watched as Elizabeth inhaled deeply, her nipples puckering tighter as she enjoyed the sensations he and William were rousing in her. He never tired of her perfect body, naked before him. He loved so much about her. While he gently caressed Elizabeth's flesh, his mind wondered at how similarly he had felt this attraction for Caroline as well so long ago. Two women who had so captured his heart and mind. Could he love two women the same? Could he give to each of them all that he was, or would the relationship with either suffer for his unwillingness to choose just one.

William's voice and Elizabeth's movements snapped him back into the moment. He was going to go back to the office full time tomorrow for the first time in weeks. But tonight, he wanted to love Elizabeth. To show her how much he cared and wanted her. Tomorrow was another day.

*****

Richard had left earlier than normal for work, since it was his first day back in the office in some time. Elizabeth supposed he was excited at the prospect of getting out of the house for a change. She decided to take advantage of the extra time and get some additional snuggling in with William. Last night had been amazing for all three of them. Life was finally getting back to normal for Richard, and she was happy. William took the best of care of all of them. Today she was going to see Jane for lunch. She nuzzled into William's side, his arm automatically wrapping around her. How she loved to lie in his arms. She always felt so safe and adored in his embrace.

"You're up early this morning, Angel. Did we not tire you out enough last night?" William's scratchy morning voice sounded above her head.

"You did just fine, Mr. Darcy. I just can't go back to sleep now that Richard is gone. I hope you don't mind some additional snuggle time with me."

"Never, as a matter of fact, I could enjoy a bit more than a snuggle this morning." William turned toward Elizabeth, pulling her to her side so that he could spoon up against her body. He was fully awake Elizabeth noticed, and she smiled to herself. This was going to be a great start to her morning.

*****

Richard sat at his desk, going through his emails. It was strange to be in the office, but he was glad to be there. He was distracted though, and turning his head, he stared at the phone. He didn't know if he should or shouldn't pick it up. Inhaling deeply, he just went for it. He entered the digits and waited as the phone rang. He started to get a bit nervous when the female voice came over the line.

"Hello."

"Hi, Caroline. This is Richard. How are you this morning?"

"Oh, hi, I'm good; how are you? I had a great time last night by the way. Elizabeth sure knows how to throw a party. Give her my congratulations again, won't you?"

"Sure. I was wondering if you would like to have lunch today— if your not too busy. I know it's last minute. I'm actually at the office today, so I'm in downtown," Richard explained.

"Wow, that is a big step for you. Umm... sure. I'm free around one if that works for you."

"One sounds fine with me. Where would you like to meet?"

"How about that cute bistro down on Fifth Street?" Caroline offered in a sweet tone.

"Sure, I'll see you there at one."

"You're on. 'Bye now," Caroline replied as she hung up the phone.

Richard replaced the headset and stared at his phone a few minutes with a big grin spread over his face. He could feel his heart skip a few beats. He was going to have lunch with Caroline today. It was exciting to think about. He hadn't been able to get her off his mind in weeks. Perhaps if he just had a nice lunch and some time to talk with her, he would be able to place her in more of a friendship status in his mind. He had really enjoyed Elizabeth last night and wanted very much to make her foremost in his heart. He just needed to decide.

With lunch plans made, he dove into his work, energized for his big day.

*****

It just so happened that William came into the office an hour late, much to the enjoyment of his cousin. Richard met William at his office door, his raised brow "Late today, I see. You feeling alright?" he sarcastically jested. He knew exactly what had transpired since he would have done the same thing given the chance.

"Good to see you back in the office. I'm not going to give you the satisfaction of an answer, though," William replied as he moved to sit behind his desk. He casually turned on his computer.

Richard finished getting a file out of a cabinet and took a seat in front of his cousin. "It's good to be back. I have to say I have missed this place. So what is on the agenda today?"

"Nothing much; been rather quiet. I was going to have lunch with Mr. Bennet today. Would you like to come?" William offered. It was a business lunch he had set up a few weeks ago to discuss an opportunity for another fundraising event. If Mr. Bennet approved it, then Elizabeth would be brought into the picture for the planning stage.

"I have lunch plans already. Let me know how it goes. I should get back to my office. " Richard smoothly replied as he rose from his chair and strode out of William's office.

*****

Mr. Bennet and William Darcy were enjoying a nice lunch on the patio of a local bistro when William noticed Richard going through the front door. He didn't think he had mentioned to Richard where he was dining, so he decided to go inside and track down his cousin. He excused himself from Mr. Bennet and went in search of his dear friend. When he got inside, he noticed Richard hugging none other than Caroline. Stunned to see them meeting for lunch, he didn't move from his spot and just watched as the pair was seated inside. He didn't wish to intrude, so he returned outside to finish his lunch with Elizabeth's father.

*****

"Thanks for agreeing to have lunch with me. How are you?" Richard asked as he pushed in Caroline's chair for her.

"I'm good, thanks. I had brunch not too long ago with my brother, so I'm not starved, but this place has an awesome pastry selection so I thought I would indulge while you eat lunch. I hope you don't mind," she said, her eyes filled with brilliance and joy.

"Not at all. Sorry, you should have said you were eating out already; we could have made this for another day," Richard explained, feeling bad to have asked her out so soon after another meal.

366

"No, I wanted to see you. I mean, it's not like we have lunch often. Since you were free, and I was downtown, it seemed like a logical time to meet." She sweetly smiled.

"Well, thanks. How are you enjoying your new job?" Richard asked, obviously interested in her answer.

"I really love it. I'm so glad to be back in the states. I probably never should have left in the first place," Caroline replied, moving her eyes down to her hands that were on the table. She was trying to be good and not give him any signals that she was still in love with him. If he wanted to be friends, then that is what she would be. Having Richard Fitzwilliam in her life even as a friend, was better than no Richard Fitzwilliam in her life.

Sighing at that remark, Richard too glanced down at the table. "I'm glad you have moved back. With your brother getting married, it couldn't be better timing. I know Elizabeth has enjoyed your company very much. You both seem to get along really well," he commented. He knew that the girls would make great friends. They had some similar qualities, which when he thought about it, must be why he was attracted to both.

"I've enjoyed getting to know her and her sister. Charles is thrilled I'm back. You know he stayed in Paris with me for several weeks and helped me pack and move home. I don't know what I would do without him." She smiled.

"Family is important."

They went on and discussed several topics, both falling into an easy rapport with each other. When William left, he noticed the couple still enjoying some coffee and laughing. He supposed he would hear all about it later. He walked Mr. Bennet out to his car and then headed back to the office.

*****

William didn't hear anything about Richard's lunch and wasn't sure if he wanted to bring it up. Elizabeth would only worry; she already had it in her head that Richard never had gotten over Caroline. When he walked in the door of Richard's condo, he found Elizabeth and Richard cooking together in the kitchen. It was a common thing for them to cook together lately. William enjoyed sitting at the bar having a glass of wine as they all chatted. Today however, he was more drawn into watching how the two of them interacted. He was not about to let Richard hurt Elizabeth. If he were, for some odd reason, still attached to Caroline, then he would have to own up to it and not lead Elizabeth on.

They seemed happy, and William didn't notice anything out of the ordinary. He even watched Richard kiss and nibble on Elizabeth a few times. He had all the signs of a man in love with a woman. Perhaps he was letting Elizabeth's notions get to him too much. He relaxed with his wine and enjoyed the rest of his evening.

*****

It was Wednesday, and Jane and Elizabeth were going to meet for lunch. Elizabeth was busy all morning working on a new proposal for another fundraising event with William's company. It was still four months off, so she had some time, but venues and caterers booked fast for such events, so she had spent the entire morning on the phone. She was so ready to just relax and talk with Jane over a nice hot meal.

When Elizabeth arrived at the restaurant, she noticed Jane and Caroline sitting together. She hadn't expected to see Caroline, but thought it would make for a fun lunch and take her mind off work for a bit. The girls all said their hellos with hugs and cheek kisses. The food came quickly thankfully, and they devoured everything. While they sat chatting, Caroline kept receiving texts to her cell phone. Elizabeth didn't think anything of it really; Caroline was discrete about answering them. She assumed Caroline had lots going on with her own job, so she didn't ask her about it.

At one point, while Jane was speaking, Elizabeth noticed how Caroline seemed a bit distant towards her, which was unlike Caroline. When they all decided to depart, Caroline hugged Jane and her, but something was off. Elizabeth couldn't put her finger on it, but it was different. She brushed it off thinking perhaps she was just tired and headed back to her office to finish her day.

*****

Two weeks had passed, and Richard sat at his desk at the office, humming away. He had enjoyed several lunches with Caroline, along with several emails, texts and phone conversations and had decided that perhaps he could be friends with her and, at the same time, give Elizabeth his full attention. Things seemed to be going well so far, and he was pretty happy. He loved Elizabeth, and he loved that he could still be friends with Caroline.

He heard a knock at his door and looked up to see William standing in his door way. "Hey, what are you doing out there? Come on in."

"Are you busy? I wanted to see if you could have lunch with me," William asked. He didn't seem to be in a particularly good mood, so Richard thought he better go with him and find out what was wrong. He hadn't noticed Elizabeth being upset, , so he thought it had to be some work related issue.

They walked down a few blocks in silence. "So what's up? Not like you to be this quiet," Richard asked with some concern.

"We are almost there, and then we can talk," he replied in a somber voice.

The men arrived at the bar and grill that they frequented a few days a week. They always had a beer with a burger and did some of their best talking here, Richard thought. William asked for a booth, which surprised Richard as they had always sat at the bar. Something was very wrong, he determined, and he was ready to hear what William had to say with some small amount of anxiety.

"A booth— must be important," Richard tried to joke.

William looked at the waitress and ordered two beers for them. "I need to talk with you."

"Okay, what's up?"

"It's about Elizabeth."

"Is she okay?" Richard asked, suddenly worried something had happened to her.

"She's fine for now. How long do you think that you can carry on the way you have and not have it affect her though?" William questioned him with a calm concerned voice.

"Carry on? I'm sorry, but I don't know what you are talking about. Could you explain to me what you think I have done and why it would affect Elizabeth?" Richard said, surprised at his cousin's comment and a bit defensive over it.

369

Ever since the night that Caroline came to the condo to meet Elizabeth, you have slowly been reconnecting with her. I have seen it for myself," William explained.

"Darcy, the only thing I have done is take the time to be a friend to Caroline. I love Elizabeth. I thought things had been going well with all three of us. Did Elizabeth ask you to talk to me? Is she concerned about something?"

"No, she has no idea about any of this. I am coming to you as a friend, a cousin, a man in love with a woman who doesn't want to see her heart shattered, when she finds out from anyone but you what you have been doing."

"Darcy, I'm not sure what you think is going on, but I have done nothing wrong. Just because I love Elizabeth doesn't preclude me from ever speaking to another woman or having friends that are of the female persuasion. How could you think that I would ever harm Elizabeth?" Richard was at a loss as to why William felt he was harming Elizabeth. He would have walked out if he hadn't wanted to get to the real root of this problem with William. Maybe William was having second thoughts about Elizabeth and wanted to use him as his way out.

"Are you happy Darcy? Do you still love Elizabeth? Are you wanting to rekindle the relationship with Caroline?"

"What in the hell would make you say that? I have always wanted to be with Elizabeth— even when we were with Caroline. I had great affection for Caroline, she is a beautiful woman, but I knew then that should you wish to marry her, I would have allowed you to be with her and stepped aside. I was more interested in seeing if there was any relationship to be created with Elizabeth. Even you said you wanted that, and at the time, Caroline was just a woman who turned into more for us both; but for you, it became a deeper love. A love I think you still harbor."

"I admit— I do love her. Caroline meant the world to me, and you know that. But she left me; she married that ass of a manager and moved away. She walked out on us," he angrily bit out in a mild tone so not to arouse suspicion of the other customers.

"And now she is back. She has become close friends with Elizabeth and her sister. She is a person that we will see often and have close contact with. I saw you a few weeks ago having lunch with her. I know you have seen her since, as well. Your secretary told me of two other lunch dates with her. I don't think you can have your cake and eat it too, Richard. You have to choose which woman you want in your life as a partner. I love Elizabeth, and I won't let her be torn apart by any of this uncertainty that you are dealing with. I want to marry her. I would love to have a unity ceremony with all three of us, committing to a life together. We always said if the right woman came around, one that we both fell in love with, that we would make that happen. You claim to love Elizabeth and not wish her harm but I just don't think Elizabeth is what you really want deep down in your heart. Listen, I'm not faulting you or blaming you. I just want you to really think about what it is you want. Elizabeth will eventually find out about all of this, and it will hurt her. She already believes that you are still hung up on Caroline. I have tried to convince her you're not. I suppose she has better intuitive vibes than I do, since she seems to be right on this one."

"What do you want me to do? You want Elizabeth all to yourself? You don't want me around anymore?"

"I didn't say that at all. I want you to be happy and make the decision that is best for you, be that with us or with Caroline, I will always be your cousin, your best friend in the world. "

"What do you want me to do?"

"I believe you need to take some time and think. Get away from both women and search deep within your soul and figure out what it is you want out of life. Can you see yourself happy with Caroline and marrying her, or being with Elizabeth and me in a life we create together, one where the rules of society have no place, and we love the same woman who loves us equally in return. Remember, I said *equally*. You can't give her half of yourself; that is unfair to all of us."

The men finished off their beers, and William stood. "I'm going to go for a drive. I'm not much in the mood to work. I wish you the best, but I don't want to see you in the office the rest of the week. I'll take Elizabeth and go to my apartment tonight. I'll tell her you had to go out of town on business. I hope you figure it all out. I'm here for you man you know that. Call me if you need to talk. My ear is always yours."

With that, William left the bar and walked several blocks realizing that something he had wanted for many years may well be falling apart. He walked for near an hour before returning to get his car. He couldn't have Elizabeth over at his place without first stocking up the fridge and airing the place out. It had been several months since they had been there. He went to the store and picked up some food and fresh flowers.

*****

It had been several days since Richard had arrived back home with his parents. They had been glad to have him. He had taken long strolls around the grounds, eaten lunch with Aunt Catherine the first day he was back, and today would entertain her for an early dinner since his Aunt and Uncle were going out. He had showered and was getting ready to walk next door when a knock came at the door.

He opened it to find a box that had been left on the porch. He didn't see anyone around, so he brought it inside. A note was taped to the outside. He pulled off the envelope and pulled out a note.

"Missing you terribly."

He didn't know whom the note was meant for, so he opened the small box. Inside was a framed picture. He pulled it out, and a smile spread across his face. It was a picture of both Caroline and him with huge smiles on their faces. He recognized it as the picture that Georgiana had taken when Caroline came to meet his family. She had fallen into a bucket and then to the ground, getting not only herself but also him covered in mud.

He quickly put the box down on a table and opened the front door. He walked out and looked around. Did she bring it herself? If not her, then who did, he wondered? He saw a female face peer around the trunk of a tree. "Caroline?" he asked in anticipation. It had to be her; who else would leave such a thing?

Caroline stepped out from behind the tree. "Yes, it's me. I hope you aren't angry with me. I was told that you were here. I...." She stumbled and hadn't mustered the courage to continue when he placed his hand under her chin and lifted her eyes to meet his.

"I'm glad you came. I love the picture; it was one of my favorites," he softly spoke. She looked great to him. He had been thinking about both women for days, but his mind always came back to Caroline. Seeing her here now only made him realize that perhaps Darcy was right. He loved this woman with *all* his heart and wanted to make *her* his life. "Can you stay for dinner?" he asked her.

"I didn't bring anything with me. I should get back. I didn't mean to intrude. I was just concerned when you left town unexpectedly. I hoped it wasn't due to a set back in your recovery. I saw Elizabeth, and she told me that she understood you were here. So I came to check for myself."

"I'm glad you did. I should have let you know I was going out of town for a while. It was a last minute decision."

"You don't owe me an explanation."

"Yes, I do. I came here to think. I came here to think about us," he confessed, looking into her eyes.

"Us?" she asked with some concern and confusion.

"Yes, I have never gotten over you, Caroline. When I saw you at the ball that night so many months ago, it was as if you had never left. I have never been able to get over you all these years."

"But Elizabeth, you have to know she loves you. I could never come between you. She is my friend. I shouldn't have moved back. I'm so sorry, Richard." Caroline was horrified that she was going to cause Elizabeth heartache. She never intended for that to happen, and she didn't think she could remain friends with her if something happened to end the relationship between Elizabeth and Richard.

"Whether you moved back or not, my heart has never forgotten you. She knows this. She is a wonderful woman, and I care so much for her. I love her. But I can't marry her."

"Marry her?" she asked, her eyes wide with emotion at the word.

"Caroline, let's go for a walk." Richard took hold of Caroline's hand and began to meander down to the spot he needed to have her see.

When they reached the area, Caroline was confused and turned to him. "What is this?"

"This is our future." He smiled. He turned his head to look at the ground with stakes in it.

"I don't understand," Caroline said.

I came here with Elizabeth and William a few months ago before I was shot. I brought Elizabeth out here to see this spot. Our spot. I thought that perhaps her reaction might be like yours had been, and though she loved it; she didn't love it as much as you had. This is our spot and these are the outlines of the home I'm going to build for us."

Richard turned to take hold of Caroline's other hand. He looked her in the eyes and smiled. He was an amazing vision to Caroline. He was so filled with emotion, his eyes glistened and his complexion was clear and glowing. He knew what he wanted, and he was not in the least bit conflicted. "Caroline, hear me out. I'm not going to ask you to marry me, not today, not tomorrow. What I do want is a chance to see if we can rekindle what we had once. I still love you, and I don't want you to leave me again. What I am going to ask is this: Are you willing to try and see if we can be *us* again? To take a chance on loving each other again? I'm going to build this house, and someday I want to bring you home to stay, but only if you want that too. I don't want you to feel pressured, and I am fine with your taking time to think about it. It has taken me a long time to actually think things through myself."

Caroline didn't know what to say. She just glanced around the area and released Richard's hands. She walked amongst the forms, stunned that any of this was happening. He actually wanted to give her another chance. He said he couldn't marry Elizabeth. It was more than she had ever hoped to wish for. She kept walking until she reached the end of the tree-lined area and looked out at the field before her. It was an amazing spot, and she had fallen in love with it when he had showed it to her several years ago.

Richard came up behind her and wrapped his arms around the redhead beauty. He inhaled her scent and wondered at how right it felt to have her in his arms in this place. "What do you say? Will you give us a chance?" he whispered into her ear.

*****

William had told Elizabeth that he had someplace to be Saturday morning. He knew what was about to happen and was going no farther than the parking lot, but Elizabeth didn't need to know that.

Not ten minutes after William had left, a knock came to the front door. Thinking William forgot something, Elizabeth put down the laundry she had been working on and walked to the door. When she opened it, she found Richard with a dozen red roses in his hand. She smiled instantly, having missed him all week. "Welcome home," she happily exclaimed as she almost leapt into his arms. Seeing him meant that things were going to be fine in her eyes.

Richard hugged her in return but did not kiss her. He wished he could, but it was no longer his right. "Hey there Angel, I missed you. These are for you." He offered her the flowers as he closed the door behind him. She looked great, and he didn't relish what was about to take place.

"I'll just go put them in some water," she happily replied. "Does William know you're home? We can all go out tonight. How was your trip?"

Richard knew this was going to be a difficult talk, but one that needed to happen. He hoped that everything would work out in the end; he didn't want to make Elizabeth an enemy. They would have a lifetime together, birthday parties, holidays, vacations, all the things that the three of them would have done, just now it would be the four of them and it wouldn't do for the ladies to not get along. He knew that William was waiting for his departure and would sweep back into the apartment to be with her and soothe her broken heart if that was what was going to actually happen.

"My trip was good." His voice was not as upbeat as it had been a minute ago, and Elizabeth could sense that something was on his mind.

She had known that Richard had spent the week at his parents' place. Georgiana had mentioned it while speaking with her one night. It was actually Elizabeth who had told Caroline where Richard was while they were having lunch one day. She didn't know if anything came of it, but somehow she thought it had. She suddenly began to move slowly while she cut the ends of the roses under water and put them into a vase.

Richard walked into Darcy's kitchen and leaned against the fridge. "I have something I want to discuss with you Elizabeth," he said in a somber tone.

Taking a deep breath and continuing to cut and place the flowers, she responded, "It must be important for you to bring me roses. Did you know that I talked with Georgiana this week?"

A rush of heat hit Richard's neck. He didn't know that but had a feeling Elizabeth might have an idea about what was coming. Her voice was a bit softer, and she was moving slowly. "No, I didn't," he responded meekly.

"Yea, I talked with her during the week, and she mentioned having brunch with you one day while you were with your parents. I happened to have lunch with Jane and Caroline and told her you were there since she was concerned about not hearing from you in several days. She thought you might have had a relapse."

Elizabeth finished and turned the water off. Again she inhaled and closed her eyes, not quite ready to turn and face Richard. She thought she could hear her heart break when Richard walked up behind her. "Elizabeth..." he whispered.

She turned to look him in the eyes. It would be hard, but she loved him enough to let him go. She had known he harbored strong feelings for Caroline and had been prepared to let him go in the event that they wanted to be together again. She liked Caroline so much and didn't want to harm that friendship or the one she had with Richard. He and William had given her the best experience of her life. She was grateful to him for the love he had given her and would continue to give her. They were all connected at some level, and the closeness their relationships represented would give them a wonderful bond for life.

Without speaking, Elizabeth took her palm and placed it on Richard's cheek. They both had so many emotions running through their eyes that neither spoke for what seemed like minutes. Each had tears rolling down their cheeks, the unspoken words of love between them searing into each other's heart. "I will be fine..." Elizabeth whispered from her trembling lips, as another tear rolled down her cheek.

"I never meant to hurt you. I love you," Richard choked out. He turned his face into her warm hand and kissed her palm, his eyes shut tight to the pain they were both experiencing. The burn of letting go so that both could live.

"I know. I will love you always too. Never forget, I'm here for you... forever," she softly whispered. She moved her hand from his face to see him look at her again. The pain in his eyes matched that in hers. It was difficult, but both knew it was for the best.

"Forever my angel, you will hold a place in my heart. It was you who gave me the wings to fly again. To love again," he said as two tears slid down his face.

He pulled her to him and squeezed hard one final time. Elizabeth felt his warmth— the love he had for her was real, and though he loved Caroline more and chose to have his life with her, he still cared immensely for her and always would. She knew that. It was a precious gift to have the love of two good men, men who would be forever in her life.

He released her and with a kiss to her crown he left the apartment. It was the most moving moment Elizabeth had experienced outside of the night that they had reconnected a few weeks ago. She was so thankful for that moment now. As she slid down to the floor of the kitchen and cried into her hands, two stronger ones lifted her from the floor, and within the embrace of her one true love, she found solace. She found peace, for he cried as much as she did in the silence that enveloped them.

Epilogue

The morning sun had not yet begun to peer through the bedroom window when Elizabeth carefully removed herself from her husbands hold. She rolled across the vast California king bed they shared, to slip unnoticed from the warm covers and start her day. She glanced back at the man she left sleeping soundly and smiled to herself. She felt so blessed to be married to him and be at this particular place in her life.

Elizabeth loved the calm tranquility of dawn, rising early offered her time to enjoy a cup of tea in her favorite spot. With a warm mug in hand, she quietly shut the front door behind her, walked down the steps, and along the well-worn path. In the last week she had noticed the air becoming crisper, which made for an invigorating stroll. Inhaling the fresh scent of the morning air around her, she came to stop at the small wooden bench and seated herself. Sipping at the warm liquid in her mug, she peered out over the pond to watch a few ducks swim in circles.

By the time the sun had risen above the tree line, Elizabeth was ready to return to the house. She had just stood when she heard footsteps approaching. "Good morning Elizabeth" the deep timbre of her husbands voice broke into the silence, which had surrounded her.

Smiling in his direction Elizabeth replied "Good morning to you to, what a nice surprise."

William walked up and wrapped his arms around his wife kissing her warm pink lips. "I have been nominated to retrieve you, so if you would kindly join me back at the house, there is a surprise awaiting you."

"Oh, then lead the way Mr. Darcy, I can't miss out on a surprise. " she coyly replied with a genuine smile on her lips. They took each other's hands and leisurely strolled back to the house.

When they entered the house Elizabeth heard the scuffling of little feet along with whispers to be quiet. She glanced up at her husband with her eyes twinkling and a smile on her face, her brow raised. William placed his hand at the small of her wife's back and escorted her right into the kitchen, there the table was set for breakfast and piping hot pancakes sat on a large platter with loads of bacon and a bowl of fruit salad. As soon as they

378

crossed the threshold of the room, two tiny voices shouted out in unison, "SURPRISE!"

Placing her hands over her mouth Elizabeth gasped and squealed in delight. "Oh my, what is all this?" she questioned in a spirited voice.

"Mommy we made you breakfast. Daddy helped us," Her proud four year old daughter stated.

"I set the table" came the small voice of their two-year-old son.

"It was all their idea" William graciously credited their offspring. Both parents smiled and gave hugs to their children, Katherine and Thomas. Today was a special day, and the entire family would be gathering later to celebrate a birthday day party up at William's parents.

They all sat cheerfully chatting at the table and devoured the entire table of food. Finished and full, they made their way to the living room to sit and enjoy the morning paper and a few cartoons. They had always loved their weekends here at the family estate. Most of the time, William would take off early on Thursdays and they would drive down so they could enjoy a nice long weekend. Here in this magical place, they were always carefree and relaxed. It also was the best time to socialize with the entire clan, which was something they truly cherished.

*****

For all the enjoyment they got from the cottage, Elizabeth and William had decided to live in the city and opted for a larger condo to accommodate their growing family and entertaining needs. Being CEO of the family business, William had to be on the road occasionally. He also needed to take late dinners in the city with clients, nothing that was not expected of a man in his position. Elizabeth still worked with her own family, but was able to do it from home most of the time. This gave her great satisfaction knowing she could continue what she loved doing and care for her children at the same time. Sometimes however, they would stay at the cottage for a week or two if work and time permitted. Elizabeth loved the cottage, and it had just enough rooms for the entire family. The kids had a wing all to themselves and Elizabeth and William each had an office of their own. With Elizabeth's being in the children's wing so she could work and keep a watchful eye on her beautiful blessings. The cottage also offered all the running and outdoor play space the city could not. William took the kids on hikes and had introduced Katherine to horses. Elizabeth had made a few changes to the interior decor here and there, but had loved the place since the first time she had been invited, and left it mainly untouched.

With the new condo in town and the birth of her children, the last five years had seen many changes in not only her life, but also that of both hers and William's extended families. Charles and Jane were married shortly after her relationship with Richard changed. It had been an experience that she would treasure always, being with both men, and as hard as it was at the time to deal with the breakup, she easily overcame it in short order, with Williams's love and support. She knew that Caroline was such a wonderful person, and with her sister's wedding approaching, it brought them all together while handling the preparations, so it hadn't taken long before the girls were back to feeling at ease around each other once again. The boys were just as close as before, making everything comfortable and easy for all of them.

There had been some awful events that had also taken place in the last five years as well, pulling all their families even closer together. A few months after Charles and Jane were married; Elizabeth's mother went to Los Angeles to help Lydia move into a new apartment for her and her baby. There had been a hit and run accident at an intersection near her new place, leaving their mother, Lydia and her unborn baby dead. It was a devastating time in all their lives. Kitty had been in fits of despair for months, Elizabeth and Jane leaned heavily on their significant others and each other. Mr. Bennet and Mary took solace in the bible.

It took a year before they were back to some semblance of normal. During that time Elizabeth and William had made plans for their own wedding. After the year anniversary of her mother's passing a date was set and within three months Elizabeth, on the arm of her father, walked down the isle taking Fitzwilliam George Darcy as her husband to love and cherish always. It was a wonderful event; Richard was the best man, Jane the maid of honor. Caroline was one of her bridesmaids and Charles a groomsman. It was a great party and it was just what everyone needed to spark life back into their lives. It was very soon afterwards that Katherine Victoria Darcy was born, much to both Elizabeth and William's great joy.

The joy was short lived however when Richard's father had a stroke not even a year later. The family rallied around him and he recovered for the most part. He was a bit slower in his walk and speech, but everyone was happy to still have him around. It prompted Richard to finish building his dream home. Since he and Caroline were still dating, she helped in small ways giving it a woman's touch. It took two years before those two decided to become engaged. Aunt Catherine of all people threw them a spectacular engagement party. Elizabeth had grown to really enjoy Aunt Catherine over the years. Her personality was a rare one and something she would always remember about the older Fitzwilliam sibling. She had great stories, most of which revolved around her four marriages and her daughter Anne. She was a recluse that no one ever saw, since she had moved to Vermont. She lived in a cabin in the woods with her dog, writing romance novels and appeared to be content with her life.

Elizabeth's father had slowly come out of his self-induced seclusion. Elizabeth and Jane had tried their best to get him to come over to their respective homes and have dinner, or to just go do anything, but he was fighting a battle in his head and no one was able to help. Not even his dearest friend George Darcy who called daily and drove to town every week to check on him. After just over a year, he finally began to enjoy life when his favored daughter wed. It was during the reception then that Elizabeth started to see the small flicker of light and hope in her dad's eyes. George Darcy had been by his side for months, but it was Victoria, and her ability to listen and offer advice that seemed to ease his heart and mind. She was very compassionate towards Thomas's loss and in those days shortly after reconnecting with Victoria, things started to change.

Slowly Elizabeth noticed her father began to take more of an interest in his business affairs, go on more client lunches, and even showed a desire to help in the planning of a new fundraising gala. Thrilled by the process her father was displaying, Elizabeth felt more comfortable leaving town for the cottage for an extended amount of time. She had even talked her father into coming with her to stay with them a few times. The first time he came he stayed around the house reading and wondering about the grounds. He did join them for dinner with the rest of the family at the main house, but he had been reserved and kept to himself. George would come down to the cottage and they would play chess or cards a few hours each day. It was a rejuvenating time and it allowed Elizabeth's father to find some inner peace and begin to feel comfortable with the new life that now lay before him.

*****

The late afternoon found the Darcy children rested from their nap, dressed and ready to depart for the party.

"Come on Dad, we have to go, Aunt Georgie promised me we could go visit the stables so I could pet Stardust." Little Katherine urged her father on by taking his hand and moving towards the front door.

381

"Did she now?" William asked.

"Yes she did, please hurry" she insisted with a stronger tug on her father's arm.

Chuckling at her daughter's impatience, Elizabeth finished combing the dark curls on her sons head, "Well seems we need to get moving then, can't keep Aunt Georgiana waiting." Elizabeth smiled at her husband.

"Mama when do I get to ride horses like Kat?" Thomas inquired with a small pout.

Elizabeth glanced up to William, her brow raised in question.

William scooped up Katherine and crossed the living room to go down on one knee before his son. "Thomas, I think that we might have to ask Aunt Georgie if she thinks you are old enough, she is after all the one who volunteered to teach Katherine. But I don't see any reason why you couldn't start once you turn three." He patted his son on the back.

"Did you hear that Kat, when I turn three" he smiled joyfully.

Katherine hoped out of her dad's arms and took her brother's hand "Let's go Thomas, Aunt Georgie will teach you I'm sure of it." The youngsters ran towards the front door.

"You have just made his year" Elizabeth smiled up to her husband as he rose from the floor.

"For the moment perhaps, but when my parents give him his first pony later, all his smiles will be for them." He jested. He wrapped one arm around his wife and kissed her lovingly.

"Come on we have to go" Katherine insisted as she opened the door.

"I think we are being summoned" William winked.

"Indeed" she smiled to her husband "then lead the way you two." She called out to her children.

William and Elizabeth walked hand in hand following the happy giggles of their offspring, up towards the main house.

*****

Everyone was gathered outside on the patio when William and his family arrived. As Thomas and his sister rounded the corner they stopped in their tracks when a loud "Happy Birthday" echoed in unison from those gathered.

The entire clan converged on the family of four and a round of hugging and kissing commenced.

It was not long after that little Thomas and Katherine had their Aunt Georgie marching towards the stables, with carrots in hand for Stardust. Richard and Caroline were seated on a sofa talking with Aunt Katherine when Elizabeth sat down next to Caroline. She rubbed Caroline's belly and asked how she was feeling.

"I'm fine. Not much longer thank goodness." She sighed.

Richard reached over as well and placed his hand on his wife's belly and remarked, "I can't wait. Though I will miss this bump." He smiled at Caroline and winked at Elizabeth.

Richard and Caroline already had a son. Little Adam Benjamin Fitzwilliam was the cutest little ball of fire. He had bright red hair and at the age of 14 months was already the apple of his parent's eye. He was off playing with his grandparents at the moment. William walked up and took a chair next to Richard.

"How is everything? I see you still haven't given birth yet." He glanced at the bulging belly Caroline sported.

"Not since you saw me yesterday no" she quipped back.

Richard glanced at William winked and then turned to his wife. "William and I could help things along" he playfully teased. Knowing full well his wife would roll her eyes.

It had never been an issue that all four had at some point been involved. They embraced the closeness and could joke and fool around comfortably with each other about it. Hugs and kisses amongst them were common, and so was Sunday brunch every week. Richard and Caroline worked from their home and a few days a week Richard would drive into the city to do a few things that William needed. They talked constantly and were involved in each other's lives fully. They were each other's godparents for their children, they attended functions together and the kids all got along well. Elizabeth was so pleased with how everything had turned out with William and Richard. Elizabeth and Richard still enjoyed cooking together and did it often. Caroline was not much in the way of a cook. The big joke was that they each married a person who cooked so no one would starve in either family. Elizabeth also realized that she could talk to both William and Richard about anything. Caroline had the same in the men; the ladies often spoke about how grateful they were to have such wonderful husbands. Ultimately, both men were part of her life and she didn't have to settle for just "One Good Man".

The End

www.ingramcontent.com/pod-product-compliance
Lightning Source LLC
Chambersburg PA
CBHW070359260626
47161CB00001B/199